Lady HELL

Praise for *Lady Hell*

"It's my first horror novel I've read, and I don't think any others can hold up to it. The politics and religion in it just make it that much better."

-Raeri

"This was my first horror (novel) and wow, was it a fantastic step into the world. So beautifully written, I couldn't wait to dive back in every chance I got."

-Mikayla

". . . it was captivating and absolutely a breath of fresh air. Very different from my usual choices. I think that's what I like most about it."

-Mareanglina

". . . a perfect blend of gothic horror, romance, and witchcraft."

-Ember Johnson,
Author of *Daughter of Shadows and Ash*

ALYSSA PAGE
Lady
HELL
PORTRAIT OF A DEAD GIRL
FIRST INSTALLMENT

Purple Fern Publishing
Copyright © 2025 by Alyssa Page

Hardcover: 978-1-7332480-7-5
Paperback: 978-1-7332480-6-8
eBook: ASIN B0D3M5CSGX

First Edition, January 2025
Cover art by Zoe Violett, *Lady Hell,* oil on canvas
Internal illustrations by Darcy Kelly-Laviolette
Title page illustration by Edward Ortego
Edited by Christine Page

BOOKS BY ALYSSA PAGE

Catatonic: Author's Cut
Switch: Bloodthirst (TBA)

<u>as Alyssa DiCarlo:</u>
Scarlet Sunday

there was a whisper within the walls

the faint rattle of rusted chains

a wide, wet grin, teeth stained red

the new Lady of Valen has arrived

*For the girls who dream of running through a
gothic mansion in nothing but a silken robe
while your lover warms your bed . . .*

this one is for you.

To Lauren Short.

You deserved to be a part of this one, too.

ELANTRY
EST. 1488
CASTLE NO
WESTCASTLE
THE SHORES
THE CAPI
HAVENSWORT
ABLER BLACK
THE CRAIK
HELLTHORNE
MANOR
THE OUT
MINNEHEL
VALEN
IMMORIUM
THE LONG ROAD
SARSIN
MYLO
GYLSEA

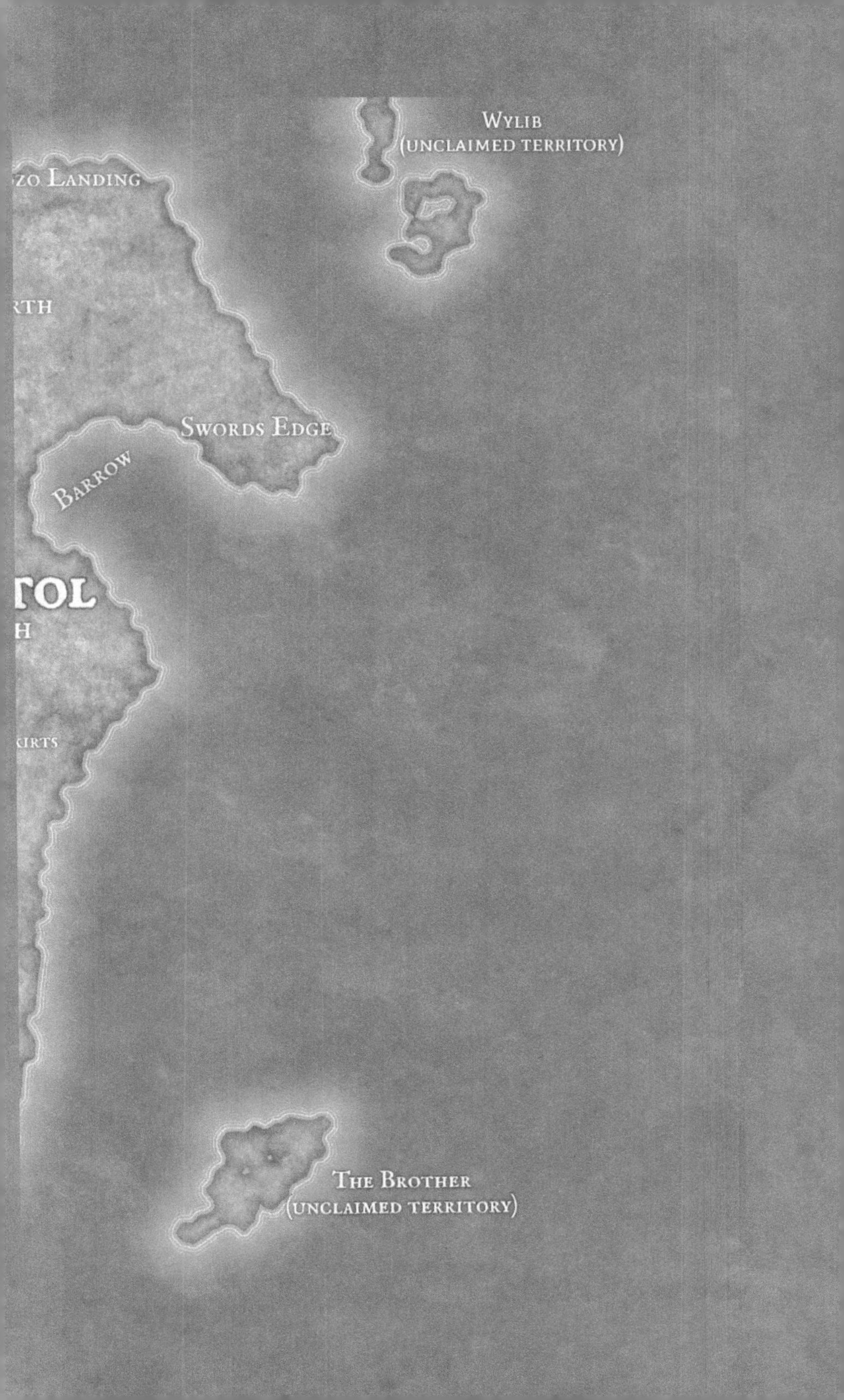

WYLIB
(UNCLAIMED TERRITORY)

...zo LANDING

...RTH

SWORDS EDGE

BARROW

...TOL
...H

...IRTS

THE BROTHER
(UNCLAIMED TERRITORY)

CONTENT WARNING

Lady Hell is a gothic
horror/fantasy/romance that features
mature themes such as:

Graphic sex, body horror, mentions of
suicide, demonic possession, self harm,
murder, blood and gore, disturbing
imagery, sexual assault, eating
disorders, mental illness, religious
abuse, child abuse and neglect, and
other potential themes that may not
be listed.

PRELUDE

Mother always said that one day the sky would spew blood.

The inky clouds would barely part—just enough to show off the bold, blinding red of the sun—and then, it would weep.

Bright, bulbous tears would slip from the cracks, drizzle down, soak through the soil. The rivers would run red, spilling over the banks, drowning the very land that once held life.

It would find the light, and snuff it right out.

TO WED

They found Belle by the water.

Right on the lip of the coast, bare feet swallowed up by a fizzling, ice cold spray. Their voices were drowned by roaring waves, spatters of sea water adorning the lower half of her union gown. She could sense their presence—they were bound to spot her at one point—but instead of acknowledging their arrival, she merely studied the endless stretch of blue laid out before her. She always wondered what laid beyond the waves. Past the horizon. On the opposite side of the rising sun.

A palm claimed her shoulder, fingers curling around the dense fabric of her deep ebony dress. She felt their fingers lightly tug, forcing Belle's gaze towards their bloodshot stare. Her name tumbled off of their tongue in a low plea.

It was her mother.

She was an aging woman with a head full of fiery red hair almost identical to Belle's, her cheeks littered with bronze freckles and wary wrinkles. Her final pregnancy took a terrible toll on both her health and appearance, and the woman called Gladys spent most of her days indoors, shielded from the roaring rays of the sun, which generated blinding headaches within the woman's skull.

She tightened her hold on Belle's collar, thin lips pulled into a frown as she said, "the entire town is waiting for you, Belle. *He* is waiting for you."

Belle Byron was the eldest of seven sisters, barely twenty and already auctioned off to the most eligible bachelor in all of Elantry. She'd met him once before on the eve of her sixteenth birthday when she'd followed her father to Valen for one of his customary trades. They'd barely spoken more than two words to one another, and Belle hadn't even bothered glancing over her shoulder to catch another look at him when they departed.

"This isn't right," Belle murmured, tugging out of her mother's hold. Gladys took a significant step backwards as another wave washed over Belle's toes, chilling her down to the bone. "I'm not ready to marry, I don't know him at all!"

"He's the Lord of Valen, Belle. Marrying Bramwell will make you a lady. It will do wonders for your future, and for the future of our family. He's promised to help us in exchange for your hand."

Belle caught a glimpse of her mother's shy smile after mentioning their financial situation. The Byron's weren't well off—not even close—and Belle spent her youth cramped in a tiny bedroom with three of her six sisters.

"Come back to the holy house, Belle," Gladys urged, reaching out to grab her daughter's hand. Her bony fingers slipped between Belle's, squeezing hard. A shiver slid down Belle's spine. "Please. Don't embarrass us like this. The entire town is in attendance. You're the first Byron girl to wed, and to a *lord*, nonetheless. This is the event of the season."

"Yes, mother," Belle murmured, taking one last look at the sea before accepting her fate. She tangled her hands within the dense material of her dress, laboriously hiking the outfit up and out of the water. The six-foot long train of her dress was soaked and sopping, collecting an abundance of sand and dirt within every crevice as she negligently towed it through the earth. She'd ruined the garment the second she'd stepped out of the holy house—that much she knew—and although her sister Evelin couldn't stop gawking at the soiled cloth, Belle couldn't help but laugh.

"It's a work of art, isn't it, Eve?" Belle beamed, a stray scarlet curl slipping out of her braid and falling across her eyes. The wind was picking up, and eighteen-year-old Evelin had to hold her strawberry blonde hair in place.

She'd always cared more about her appearance than her elder sister had.

"You're going to wed the Lord of Valen looking like *that?*" Evelin gasped, shuffling behind her sister in order to claim the base of her dress. "Let me at least get all of this rotten dirt out of it! The wetness, however, I can't really help. You'll stand before the Goddesses looking like you've just taken a dip."

"Don't even bother, Evelin," Belle said, sloppily tucking her fallen hair behind her ear. "If Lord Bramwell wants to wed me so badly, he'll wed me as I am. What else would he expect from the daughter of a fisherman?"

"Maybe an *inkling* of class," Evelin muttered, giving up on Belle's wasted dress. "You do look charming, sister. Black was always your color."

"Well, then it's a good thing it's standard practice to wear black as a bride," Belle sighed, taking Evelin's hand in hers as they followed close on their mother's heel. Father hadn't shown his face, for he was surely keeping the holy house busy as his wife searched for the runaway bride. It wasn't every day that a woman to wed had fled the ceremony mere moments before it was due to start.

Not the best way to begin a union.

"I know you don't believe in Plirity," Evelin whispered, nodding curtly towards their mother, who was several paces ahead and constantly glancing over her shoulder. She feared that at any given moment, Belle would take flight once more.

"It's a little difficult for me to believe that our every move is evidently predicted and planned by a trio of Goddesses," Belle countered, tightening her hold on Evelin's slightly smaller hand. "Enough of this talk, before Mother hears. She'll start quoting the Good Book and tossing rice over my head until I beg for mercy and forgiveness if she knew."

Belle's chest tightened when they approached the grandiose double doors of the holy house, the three Goddesses—Lottie, Lilen, and Liv—adorned the stained wood, their heads poking through a cautiously carved dahlia. No one quite knew what the women looked like, but the guesses were always amusing. In this particular adaptation, they were round-faced with bulbous eyes.

Belle paused right before the doorway, prickly blades of grass tickling the bare skin of her toes. It was then that she'd decided she would wed barefoot. Her mother offered her a forgotten pair of shoes, which she swiftly denied. Gladys tried to protest, but if Belle must marry, she would do it as she pleased.

Barefoot, a soaked dress, and a windswept, messy mane. Just the way it was meant to be.

"Open the doors, will you, Eve? It's time for me to wed." Belle said, drawing in a deep, steady breath. An additional gust of wild wind sent several strands of roaring red hair astray, the lengthy locks tickling Belle's blushing features.

Evelin nodded curtly, unable to stifle her wide smile as she and Gladys claimed the brass handles, gently pulling the doors open to reveal a multitude of widened eyes.

Showtime.

Belle's father—a tall man who was dreadfully thin for his height—stumbled into view, slender lips pulled downwards into a frown as he viewed Belle's soiled dress. His daughter didn't seem to mind, for she strut a large, cocky grin as if to mock the event as a whole.

Typical Belle.

"My bouquet, mother?" Belle requested, outstretching her hand. She could hear a chorus of low murmurs resonating through the chamber, but at the very end of a direct path stood her to-be husband, a man nearly as tall as her father, but with wider shoulders and rounder arms.

She wasn't entirely sure, but for a brief second, Belle could've sworn that she'd seen Lord Bramwell crack a smile. For just a second, and then it was gone.

The chapel on Immorium Hill only comfortably sat sixty, and as Belle slowly strolled down the path littered with daisies, she couldn't help but notice an abundance of guests stuffed up against the rear wall. Some of the attendees were uncomfortably cramped, but nevertheless, they craned their necks in a desperate attempt to catch even a single glance at the lady-to-be, who was dressed in a soaked black gown and practically tiptoeing barefoot along the silken rug.

The sweet scarlet satin beneath her toes felt heavenly, and she wondered just how much Lord Bramwell spent on such a luxury, for the people of Immorium usually recycled their homemade aisle runners, passing them down to their children and grandchildren to use.

A youthful girl—maybe twelve at most—openly sighed at the sight of the bride, pudgy palms cradling her cheeks as she delightfully grinned. Belle's gaze instantaneously settled upon the child, a sympathetic smile etched across her lips as she paused before the pew, earning a puzzled gasp from several onlookers.

No bride ever paused on their way to the groom.

"Don't rush it, sweet girl. Enjoy your youth," Belle purred, slipping the elegant bouquet of ruby roses into the girl's open arms. Her little eyes boggled at the kind gesture, but before she could thank Belle for offering up her stunning floral arrangement, the bride had resumed her course, delicately dancing along the aisle on the tips of her toes.

Once more, Lord Bramwell's lips upturned into a smirk, pearly white teeth peeking through his parted lips as Belle took her spot opposite him. The Holy Man—a man easily halfway into his sixties with a head full of paper white hair—glanced down at her feet, brows pulled together in distaste as he peeled open the crimson leather cover of the Good Book.

"Shall we begin?" the Holy Man questioned, emerald gaze bouncing between a grinning Belle and a clearly amused Lord Bramwell. The two nodded in unison, seamlessly joining hands as if they'd done it a million times before.

Lord Bramwell's coarse, calloused fingers eased between Belle's delicate digits, and she paused, for she'd never thought of a lord to have such rough hands. The elite hardly lifted much more than a finger in Valen, for their daily duties were done by a plentitude of servants. There were whispers among the penniless that the elite even had help with emptying their bowels, but Belle always found such a thing completely preposterous, and slightly comical.

The Holy Man without a name droned on, reciting common lines from the Good Book that usually made Belle yawn. She hardly paid any mind; it was nothing but nonsense to her anyways. Lord Bramwell refused to tear his stare from her upturned smirk, a smile mirroring her own plastered along his lips as he studied his bride. She was dainty—*teeny*—a defined jaw, protruding cheekbones, bug-like brown eyes. Her gown nearly swallowed her miniscule frame whole, and he wondered just how small she really was beneath all of that fabric.

"Is something the matter, Lord Bramwell?" Belle coyly whispered, studying his solid gray gaze. It was clear that he, too, found the entire event curiously humorous.

He was doing her family a favor. A grand one, at that. Taking Belle's hand in marriage guaranteed that each and every Byron child would be fed until their last breath. There was truly no higher honor than to marry a lord, especially one of Valen—such a warm, welcoming place full of light, love, and riches.

Polar opposite of Belle's hometown Immorium, which was barely a step above Minnehel, a village with barely enough food and even less money.

Lord Bramwell looked Belle up and down—drank her all in—before replying in a tone so hushed that the Holy Man could barely hear him over his own thunderous speech full of empty words.

"I thought I was marrying a woman, not a siren. I can still smell the sea on your skin," he said, slightly squeezing Belle's hands.

"The sea is a part of me," Belle muttered, mourning for her home. Valen was nowhere near the coast, and although it was decorated with a series of winding rivers and luscious lakes, they would never compare to the salty, sweet spray of the ocean.

The Holy Man pulled the pair from their hushed discussion, requesting that Belle's best bridesmaiden come forth with the stunning gold rings. Belle had never seen such beautiful jewelry, let alone owned any.

With this ring, I pledge my whole soul.

When the Holy Man insisted that Belle and Lord Bramwell kiss, her fresh husband slightly stunned her, avoiding her pouty lips entirely as he instead placed a stiff kiss to the flat of her forehead.

The crowd erupted in cheer as Belle's twelve-year-old sister, Lilla, danced her fingers along the loose keys of the aging piano. It was a tune Belle immediately recognized—one that she used to hum in the little girl's ear as an infant to get her to sleep—and she choked back tears at the sound, watery eyes glancing over her shoulder to view a cheery Lilla, lips pulled into a toothy grin.

Her young sister simply nodded, encouraging Belle onwards as the new Lady of Valen slipped her hand into Lord Bramwell's.

To the lord and lady of Valen.

The crowd tossed a profusion of bird seed over the aisle, welcoming the newlywed couple along the path as they marched towards the exit. Belle couldn't help but grin, clearly amused by the guests' reactions as they showered her with love. Lord Bramwell's expression slightly differed, lips strung into a straight line, empty eyes fixated forward as he politely pulled Belle along towards the double doors.

Before the doors stood Belle's parents, both red-eyed with emotion as they tugged the doors open, releasing the new couple from the confines of the holy house. Belle's mother placed a kiss atop her daughter's forehead, whereas her father clamped a sweaty palm over Lord Bramwell's shoulder, nodding curtly as if to approve of the arrangement. Only, he already approved of it months ago. Belle was certain that her father was ready to auction her off from the moment he heard that Lord Bramwell was to take a wife.

Twenty and nine was incredibly late for a lord to wed. Typically, they'd have upwards of three or four children by such an age, but Bramwell himself came from a nonconventional family. The late Hellthorne's only had a single child, and his presence was completely unheard of until after their untimely demise.

Belle told her mother that she loved her, and then she left—off to an awkward, intimate breakfast with her new husband before meeting the guests once more at the reception two hours following.

To the Lord and Lady of Valen—to many years, happy tears, and a bundle of beautiful children.

THE PRICE OF GOSSIP

Two women dropped dead at Belle and Bramwell's wedding reception.

It was halfway into afternoon tea, a chorus of chatter claiming the hall as the newlyweds wandered the room, thanking each and every guest individually for attending. It was more people than Belle had ever seen at once—the entire population of Immorium, which wasn't much, but still quite a bit—plus several travelers from Bramwell's homeland

Valen, some wealthy folk from the Capitol, and even a couple from the poorer section of Minnehel, who'd scraped up just enough funds to attend the wedding of the year.

Belle spent most of her time conversing with the couple from Minnehel, who barely survived above the poverty line and spent most of their money feeding their nine children. She held a lot of respect for the impoverished, for she'd grown up borderline broke, surviving on seafood from her father and sharing clothes with her abundance of sisters.

It was halfway through a pleasant conversation between Belle and the pair that the incident occurred. It started with spilled tea, a horrified gasp, and a noisy *thump*, immediately followed by an almost identical sound.

The crowd fell silent, widened eyes maneuvering along the room until they settled upon the limp ladies collapsed beside one another on the floor, both of their floral teacups untouched. They were both face down, bums raised to the sky, knees unceremoniously buckled. If they were simply unconscious, Belle might've stifled a laugh. But it was as if every guest automatically knew that something far worse had occurred—both women had been dead before they'd even met the floor.

People still spoke of the startling incident nearly a half year later, hushed whispers dancing along the differing towns of Elantry before regrettably meeting Valen, the very last place it was ever to meet.

The middle-aged women were known gossipers in the seaside town of Immorium. The blonde-haired pair knew anything and everything about each individual beside the coast, and they even had a friend at the Capitol who fed them word about the inner workings of Havensworth, a place the two had never even been. Only the wealthy resided in the head of Elantry, a population of pristine, attractive individuals with more money and jewels than smaller areas like Immorium and Minnehel had ever seen.

The women had plenty to say about Lord Bramwell and his deceased parents during the wedding reception, rushed mutters bouncing between their sinful lips as they quietly expressed their own individual doubts. The hateful venom sliding along their tongues ultimately turned to blood, and a mere hour after Lord Bramwell overheard their distasteful expressions, they were dead.

Onlookers recalled Lord Bramwell making direct contact with the duo, a soft palm laid along the larger one's shoulder, before boldly announcing, *"must not speak ill of the dead within the walls of the Goddesses."* He claimed that they were exchanging impolite stories of his parents, and how *evil* it was to hide their son from the masses.

Although they were right, Lord Bramwell did not take lightly to their chatter, and he had every right to correct them on their behavior. This, however, led to suspicion on Bramwell's behalf, and less than two days following the wedding, the dead women's families insisted on proper autopsies under suspicion of poisoning, although neither of them had even touched their tea.

To all of Elantry's delight, both autopsies proved Bramwell's innocence, and the Hellthorne name remained pure, much to the glee of Belle's family. Their savior—their knight in shining armor—could never bring harm upon another human being. According to Belle, he was even reluctant in exterminating vermin and bugs, and instead called upon the help to remove of them so he did not have to.

The deaths were ruled as sudden simultaneous apoplexy, and with Lord Bramwell's name cleared, the Hellthorne Manor remained sinless and moral.

For now, that is.

DARLING, FLORENCE

"Please eat something, Belle. You haven't had a bite of anything since yesterday at sunrise." Florence softly begged, nudging a tray of fresh-baked bread and jam in Belle's direction.

"I'm not hungry, Flo," Belle murmured, brushing her knuckles against the wooden tray. Much to Florence's dismay, Belle nudged the food away, refusing to look Bramwell's ward in the eye.

Typically, one of the housemaidens would bring breakfast up the steps for the lady of the house. There was an array of different personalities that worked within the manor—women who were grandmothers, women who were mothers, ladies too young to yet be a mother—but Belle was never fond of having help, and although she'd been the Lady of Valen for half a year, she still wasn't used to it. Domestic servants in Immorium were unheard of, mainly because no one could afford such a luxury.

"Lady Belle," Florence pressed, lips strung into a tight line. The woman was beautiful beyond recognition—lengthy, coal-black curls constantly pulled away from her face. Her lovely brown skin was soft, smooth, and mostly unblemished, all except for her fingernails, most of them bitten and cracked from years of worry.

Although Florence was free to leave the manor as she pleased—for she was closer to her thirtieth year than her twentieth—there was something that held her back. Grounded her. Kept her within the walls of Hellthorne Manor, even well after her eighteenth year, and well before Belle Byron's arrival. Bramwell had given her plenty of opportunities to leave—*you are free now, little one*—and yet, she never had.

She'd been an orphan since two weeks shy of her fifteenth year.

Her father had been long dead by the time her mother stopped breathing. Florence's mother—such a wonderful, selfless woman—the blood sister of the late Lady of Valen. The sister of Bramwell Hellthorne's mother.

By the time Florence's mother had perished, Bramwell's mother had been buried beneath the dirt, her lungs neglecting to intake air, her eyelids sewn shut. With no family, no guardians, and nowhere to go, a teenage Florence was ushered into a carriage bound for Valen, where she would join the company of one Bramwell Hellthorne, only in his eighteenth year, entirely new to his position, and on top of that, the new legal guardian of his own cousin.

"If you call me *lady* one more time, I'll pinch you." Belle said, unable to stifle her broad smirk. She was seated at the window, the glass panes extended outward as infrequent gusts of frigid wind wafted inward. The breeze sent the deep mahogany drapes afloat, framing Belle's thin frame like a cloak. Prickly goosebumps showered her exposed skin, cascading up the length of her arms and disappearing beneath the thick fabric of her dress. It was a cloudy day, the sun barely peeking beyond the clouds, casting a gray glow along the land.

Her pale blue dress nearly swallowed her whole, and Florence feared that she'd perhaps lost another pound overnight from malnourishment. The thought, however, dissipated from her mind when she pondered over Belle's statement once more.

With a smirk, Florence spoke. "Maybe I'd appreciate that pinch, *lady.*"

Belle glanced over her shoulder; a toothy grin etched across her lips as she met Florence's amused stare. It wasn't unusual for the older girl to have such a silver tongue in Belle's presence, but nevertheless, it always caught the frail lady off-guard.

She rose from her spot at the windowsill, frigid fingers yanking the wrinkled sleeves of her lengthy dress down to her wrists as she summoned Florence over towards the four-poster bed. The bread and jam lay forgotten and cold by the window as Florence obeyed, nearly skipping towards the mattress as Belle settled upon the inky black bedcover, neatly drawn and ready for her sleepy frame.

"Sit with me, Flo," Belle said, taking her spot on the foot of the bed. She beckoned Florence forward, tiny palm patting the silky surface of the bed as she reserved a spot just for her.

"As you wish, *lady.*" Florence playfully slurred, clearly amused by Belle's expression. The pale girl's cheeks reddened by the second, heart erratically thumping within her chest as Florence claimed her spot beside her, bottom lip drawn between her teeth. She was achingly close—barely a quarter of a meter between them—and Florence swore that she could hear Belle's pulse restlessly drumming against the sturdy cage that housed both her lungs and her heart.

"If I may, I'd appreciate that pinch right now." Florence whispered, the statement barely slipping over her pouty bottom lip. Her fingertips danced along the inky black duvet, creeping closer to Belle's stiff palm laid upon her own lap. She had a weak spot for Florence—she did since the moment they'd first met the night after Belle's wedding—and although the idea of food undoubtedly repulsed her and nearly turned her stomach inside out, she desired it, *craved* it, just so she could see Florence smile at the sight of her snacking.

"I suppose I'll take a bite," Belle whispered, flinching slightly when Florence's forefinger tickled the curve of her thumb. Instantaneously, Florence's features brightened, a gorgeous grin slithering along her lips as she tore her bottom from the bed and rushed towards the tray of food.

"Oh, *Belle!* I'm so glad you agreed to eat! Even if it's just a small bite, it'll make my night. I swear." Florence exclaimed, nearly tripping over her own two feet as she curled her fingers around the golden handles of the food tray.

Florence could hardly contain her excitement as Belle reached out towards the food, slender fingers curling around the corners of the bread. Florence smiled broadly as the lithe lady brought the jam-smeared toast to her mouth, lips parting slightly as she took a tiny bite.

"I've never seen someone eat so elegantly," Florence mused, setting the tray down atop the mattress. "You take the gentlest bites. You remind me of a sweet little bird, the way you pick at your food. I could watch you eat for an eternity."

Belle blushed, taking another small bite as the woman opposite her positively gleamed. Things were a bit peculiar between the pair—sentimental and sweet—and often, Belle wondered what her dreary husband would say if he'd caught a glimpse of their breathless kisses in the hallway.

As if he could even say a thing at all. He'd never laid a lustful hand on his wife. Nothing more than a peck—a sealed-lip kiss—and a small hug. He even requested they remain in separate rooms.

Belle was barely a flat mate with her husband, if that at all.

"Do you remember our first kiss?" Belle whispered; bare toes draped across the garish green rug at the foot of her bed. She was barely tall enough to touch the ground when seated upon the mattress—such a small, thin woman—but a slightly taller Florence always found this fact amusing, and she could hardly stifle a smile every time she saw Belle's tiny toes struggle to reach the floor.

Florence struggled to swallow a particularly large bite of bread, the homemade jam sticking to her teeth as she danced her free fingers along Belle's arm. "Of course I remember. It would be difficult to forget the fact that you wept for nearly an hour afterwards."

Belle's face fell at the memory—the way her reddened cheeks were drenched with tears, red-rimmed eyes swollen and puffy as she persistently brushed Florence away. It happened only a week after Belle's arrival to Hellthorne Manor—she and Florence instantaneously clicked, like old friends, old *lovers*—and things transgressed during a hearty meal on the evening of Belle's seventh night.

For the first time since Belle's arrival, Bramwell's ward, Florence, was in attendance during supper. Although the Lord of Valen had been her legal guardian while she was still underage, Florence held no royal title, and thus, she took it upon herself to sneak back and forth to the kitchen, consistently weaving in and out of the dining hall by the housemaidens sides. It was a garishly large room, one with a dazzling, golden chandelier that painted wonky shapes along the deep auburn walls.

The table could comfortably seat twenty, but the lord and lady sat on complete opposite ends, whereas Florence bounced between several seats. The other chairs remained absent, *invisible.* Belle felt oddly alone on her end of the table, Bramwell's features incredibly far from her reach as she poked and prodded at her food. Florence hadn't said much at all. When she wasn't mingling with the house-maidens, she was stuffing her face with an array of eats, marveling in their texture, their taste.

Bramwell took notice of Belle's abnormal eating habits, but he never asked about her finicky behavior during mealtime. He didn't ask, and she didn't tell. Instead, they made small talk—spoke of Belle's upbringing in Immorium, her life by the sea. They only spoke of Belle, never him.

It was as if he never had a thing to say.

Florence and Belle stole several alluring glances whilst frolicking between the dining hall and the kitchen, and the ward even stole several plates from a housemaiden, her knees folding into a playful bow, and she served the lady of the house her food, fingers casually brushing against Belle's cold hands as she replaced the lady of the house's barely touched starter plate with the main course.

A whisper of goosebumps pricked along Belle's forearms, creeping up towards the bend of her elbows as Florence simply smiled, an action so sweet, but nevertheless riddled with amatory intention. Belle could see it in Florence's eyes—the desire, the want—and she'd quickly brushed her palms against the raised surface of her skin, awkwardly attempting to rid her arms of the prickly bumps.

Bramwell barely noticed their lustful glances, for he seemed to be sheathed in complete unawareness. It was as plain as day—the coquetry, the playful teasing—but he was oblivious to it. Whether by pure ignorance or by choice, he simply paid no mind to his cousin—*his ward*—as she looked his new bride up and down the entire evening.

Immediately following dessert, Belle had risen from her seat, excusing herself from the table and Bramwell's boring stories about royalty in Valen.

At this point, the goosebumps had spread—coating Belle's arms and legs as she followed close on Florence's heels to the kitchen. A shy giggle tickled her tongue as she snuck around the corner, greedy, curious fingers outstretched towards her husband's ward as she captured her elbow.

It was impulsive—*gutsy*—completely out of character for a young Belle Byron, (now known as Belle Hellthorne, but the name just seemed too peculiar, too *new*), but none of that mattered in the moment, for she'd seen the glances, the smirks, the stares. She'd caught Florence red-handed, and if the woman had interpreted the woman's wishes correctly, this was where she was supposed to be.

Fingers threaded around the flimsy fleece of Florence's evening gown, her pulse quickening, wildly thumping against the bony cage like a savage bird. Hushed giggles, prying hands, dilated eyes. Belle had kissed the older woman before she could question her motives, desperate lips barely brushing against the smooth, supple skin of Florence's lower lip as if to tease, to test.

Florence bit down, drawing Belle closer, sealing the gap. It was rushed and wet, roaming hands, breathless whimpers, racing hearts. Belle hadn't kissed anyone so fiercely—so *ar-*

dently—not even her childhood love, the sweet boy called Dalbir, the one she thought she'd spend an eternity with.

Florence's lips roamed, dipping down to Belle's neck, nipping at the flesh. Belle was dizzy with desire and could barely stand up straight, but what she'd witnessed during that moment was enough to jolt her back into reality.

Someone had seen.

It was a housemaiden, a woman of sixty-and-something called Jeanne. She was a mute—sworn to silence, or so they said—and Belle could still picture the way her blue eyes widened at the sight of Florence's lips on her neck. It had all happened so fast. So sudden. The connection was there from the start, all it needed was a little spark to ignite the flame buried deep within.

Belle fled to her bed chamber almost immediately—she could barely look Bramwell in the eye, her *new husband*. She'd betrayed him less than eight days into their marriage, soiled the bond they had barely begun to share. Florence snuck into her room shortly after she'd disappeared, only to find the little lady curled up beneath the blankets, painful sobs wracking her chest.

She'd confessed to Florence that Bramwell refused to make love to her. A week into their marriage and all they'd shared was less than three kisses, all short, static, and with sealed lips. She'd asked him plenty—begged him, almost. *That's what married couples do.* But he seemed disinterested.

It broke her heart, shattered her. Made her feel unwelcome, unattractive.

Undesired.

She worried that perhaps he'd learned of her teenage affair with Dalbir, the same one she'd thought of while kissing Florence for the first time. She'd betrayed her future husband by fornicating with her adolescent love, an act that was usually looked down upon in their religion, but both her and Dalbir barely believed in the trio of Goddesses. It was nothing but nonsense anyways, and she knew what they had was special.

Belle was still convinced that she would've married Dalbir if it weren't for his strict lineage, for he was destined to marry a woman of his same heritage.

"Hey," Florence purred, thrusting Belle back into the present. She tucked a stray strand of hair behind the smaller woman's ear, a sympathetic smile etched along her mouth as she summoned her love back into reality. "There's no need to dwell on the past. It's been half a year and Bram has done nothing but hold your hand in public, peck your cheek, and treat you as if you're his sister. You deserve love, you deserve *affection*, Belle."

"Not like this," Belle sighed, brushing Florence's hand away. "Not behind closed doors. Not in secret. I'm married to the Lord of Valen, and I'm running around behind walls with a woman that he trusts. We've both betrayed him, Flo.

We continue to betray the man with every second we spend in each other's arms."

"So, we tell him," Florence simply said, capturing Belle's hands in hers. "If you feel that we should, we will."

Belle's big eyes widened; lips parting in protest as she swiftly shook her head. She had a soft spot for Bramwell—just as Florence did, he was a good man—and the thought of betraying him, of *hurting* him, was enough to make Belle's nearly empty belly roil.

"You'd be shunned," Belle pressed, blinking back tears. "You'd have nowhere to go. Nowhere to live. Your place is here, in the manor, in your own quarters yes, but most importantly, in my bed. In my arms. If keeping you a secret is selfish, then consider me so. There's no telling what Bramwell would do to me."

"He wouldn't lay a single hand on you," Florence countered, "and he wouldn't shun me, either. If he wanted you, he could have you. But it's been half a year, and you've never lain in his bed. He arranged for you to have your own chamber. Forgive me for saying so, Belle, but I don't believe that he loves you. If he did, he wouldn't be able to keep his hands off of you."

Florence was right. Belle's wedding night was still fresh in her mind—it was something she thought of often—the way Bramwell dismissively tore his hand out of hers as they sat side by side in the carriage. It was a three-hour trip back to Valen, and her new husband had barely spoken a single word to her, which prompted Belle to silently weep as she gazed out of the filthy window.

He'd rejected her erotic advances. She knew how the wedding night should go. Nearly as soon as they'd arrived upon Hellthorne Manor, she'd mounted his lap, peppered needy kisses along his jaw. Bramwell was impossibly stiff beneath her. Not even a sigh, a groan, a mewl. Instead, he was entirely neutral. *Detached.* When her hand traveled down to his slacks, settling upon the oddly unchanged region of his groin, he pushed her off, insisting that she simply *should not.*

It was clear to Belle that Bramwell was not attracted to her. For a split second he'd pressed his lips to hers—breathed a bit of life into her soul—before snatching it away in a hurry.

"Why would he marry me if he didn't intend to love me?" Belle murmured, nuzzling her nose into Florence's neck. Florence's steady pulse drummed against the tip of Belle's nose—wet, hot tears dipping down the length of her lover's brown skin.

"Let's go down to the sitting room, I'm sure we'll find him there. It's best if we speak with him, or if you prefer to speak to him alone, I will busy myself somewhere else."

"Browse the books in the sitting room," Belle insisted, claiming Florence's hand in hers. She drew her hand upwards, curled knuckles caressing the curve of Belle's parted lips as she pressed a series of sweet kisses along the surface. "I need you there. Even if you're not directly involved. Just busy yourself with looking through the shelves, find something small to do. Your presence will ease my worries. It'll make me strong."

"You're a lot stronger than you think, Belle." Florence purred, tearing her hand away from Belle's mouth. Her fingers brushed the lady's chin, her thumb gently etching circles into the flushed flesh of the tiny woman's cheek, as if to reassure her.

Just as Belle's lips parted in preparation to speak, the walls shifted and groaned—something she'd never quite heard before—and she shot Florence an anxious stare. It almost, *almost* sounded as if the house were alive, and the sound of both Belle and Florence's droning voices had begun to irritate it.

Belle's widened eyes met the soft, supple amber gaze of Florence—*her darling*—and she appeared calm; completely unphased by the peculiar noise.

She wanted to ask something along the lines of: *did you hear that, Florence? That very distinct groan that the walls made?*

Instead, she bit her tongue, head shaking from side to side as if to banish the event from her memory entirely.

It was just the wind. There must be a storm brewing.

"I get my strength from you," Belle countered, failing to mention the moaning walls as she placed her hand in Florence's. "Let's go ahead and go. The longer I take, the sicker I feel."

Florence nodded, and the pair fled the room, navigating the halls in search of the particularly passionless Lord of Valen.

THE BLUE-EYED BOY

Just as Belle and Florence had predicted, the Lord of Valen was in the sitting room, lounging against an old armchair that matched the color of his vest. A steadily burning cigar was pinched between two slender fingers, a trail of smoke easing up towards the vaulted ceilings before settling along the surface.

Only, he wasn't alone. In the sturdy armchair opposite him sat another man, one a lot less muscular and lacking the broad-shouldered build that Bramwell strut. Unlike the lord's dark-headed self, his guest was more silver than blond, with gentle waves that trailed down past his shoulders and crept down toward the center of his back. He looked youthful beside the hardened, expressionless lord—features soft, borderline feminine. His lips were pink, plump, and slightly pouty, but when they peeled back, they revealed a sweet, toothy grin. His canine teeth were unusually sharper than the rest—pointy, even—and often, it was the first thing people noticed about him, and the one thing he was perpetually teased about as a child.

Bramwell leaned forward in his seat, a leather-bound box balanced atop his fingers as he offered the guest a cigar. The man took one, but it remained unlit, mostly residing between his twirling fingers. At his back, a crackling fire roared in the fireplace, painting the surface of his ivory vest a lively orange.

Settling back into his seat, Bramwell loudly cleared his throat. "How's business been, Lyren? Busy, I presume?"

"We never seem to have a shortage of deaths, so I'd say that business is pretty consistent." Lyren replied, awkwardly eyeing his unlit cigar. Bramwell hadn't asked about the fact that it remained unlit and mostly forgotten, but if the lord had done so much as lightly press the subject, Lyren would cave and ask for a light.

Bramwell was excellent when it came to influencing others. It was almost as if it came naturally to him.

"Do you enjoy cutting people open? Is it enjoyable? I always shudder at the thought, even blood makes me queasy sometimes. You know me and my weak stomach," Bramwell said, unable to stifle the shiver that crept up his spine. He'd asked Lyren a similar version of the very same question several times before over the last ten years, but nevertheless, his friend entertained him with an identical answer.

"It's a job that I enjoy doing very much. I couldn't see myself in any other position."

It was true. Lyren was incredibly particular about his passions, that much was evident from the moment he'd crossed paths with Lord Bramwell a decade earlier, barely a year into the young lord's regime. He was still so fresh—so *new*—to it all. The entirety of Elantry had only learned of his existence immediately following the death of his parents.

He was their best kept secret.

For royalty standards, the sitting room was a dreadful mess. It was the one room that Bramwell requested to tidy himself, and the housemaidens usually complied—until the space became so unkempt that they couldn't stand to look at it for a second longer. Although peeved by their actions, the lord never protested, for it was known countrywide that he treated his housemaidens the best in all of Elantry. People lined up to work for him—*begged* even, when he ventured out into the public eye—but he kept a small team, a loyal one.

Although the sun had nestled itself beyond the horizon, the vermilion curtains remained drawn, exposing the men to the thriving garden just beyond the glass. The Lord of Valen took great pride in the appearance of his gothic manor, and kept the exterior decorated with a plethora of red. Blood-red chrysanthemums, rosy, ruffled marigolds, heaps of shiny, scarlet amaryllis, an occasional patch of romantic roses.

His favorite, by far, were the poppies. They dominated the garden, nearly overtaking each and every edge as they blossomed and bloomed, defying all odds and sticking around even when a pearly-white blanket of snow suffocated the soil.

For a flower that despises a wet environment, the poppies at Hellthorne Manor refused to die.

It was perhaps a mystery all in itself, but enigmas surrounding the macabre mansion only multiplied tenfold, and the people of Valen were starting to take notice. Nothing was ever quite . . . *right* . . . on the somewhat secluded peak of Valen, the very one that held the largest home in the land.

"I can't believe you finally took a wife," Lyren spoke, interrupting Bramwell's silent trance. He'd been pondering over the poppies, and how they'd light the snow up a bright, bloody red come the deep winter months.

"Is it that hard to believe, friend?" Bramwell teased, lips curling up into a toothy grin. "Am I that undesirable?"

"Of course not!" Lyren exclaimed, hooking his index finger behind the suddenly tight neck of his ruffled shirt collar. He was more eccentric with his attire, whereas Bramwell preferred to dress plainly, desperate to avoid unwanted attention. He admired his friend for being so bold and brave in his fashion choices, but as much as he felt so, he'd never voice it.

"The Capitol has been breathing down my neck for nearly a year about taking a wife. Evidently, it's customary to do so before the eve of one's thirtieth year. They threatened to revoke me of my status in Valen if I failed to do so." Bramwell dryly explained, beckoning a middle-aged housemaiden into the room, for she'd popped her head in to ask if he and his guest desired a beverage or a bite.

"Both will do," Bramwell said, his tone low and hushed as the woman rounded his chair, barely batting an eye in Lyren's direction. He'd seen her once before during a banquet Bramwell hosted the summer prior, but he never quite learned her name.

"Clare's prepared some tea and biscuits for us. She always makes the best," Bramwell informed his guest, excusing the housemaiden called Clare from the room with a small wave of his hand. She'd barely grazed the doorway before being called on once more.

"Bring out some of those ripened pears to complement the biscuits, will you, Clare?" He was kind. *Delight-*

ful. The housemaidens hardly complained when working for Bramwell Hellthorne.

Clare smiled, curtsied, and masked a blush as she narrowly avoided Lyren's stare. "At once, Lord Bramwell."

"She's a good woman," Bramwell said, bouncing his leg. "I'm lucky to have such kind housemaidens within these walls. I do my best to repay them well and treat them right. Anyway, where were we, Lyren?"

"Speaking of Havensworth," the silver-haired man replied, swallowing hard. "They have no jurisdiction over your ruling of Valen. They may run all of Elantry, but there is a very thin line between politics and royalty. The spoiled brats up in the Capitol wouldn't have a clue how to reign even if it slapped them upside the head. They can hardly handle the jobs they already have."

"As much as I wish that statement to be true, unfortunately—*thanks to my late parents, Bless them in Goddess Lilen's name*—Havensworth does have some say over my position as Lord of Valen. Without a wife by thirty, they would have had every opportunity to cast me out. So, I wed."

Clare returned with a stunning silver tray, two steaming mugs of tea politely placed between plates full of buttery biscuits and carefully cut pears. She handed each of the men their tea—adding three cubes of sugar to Lyren's, per his request—and ended her visit with another curtsy, unnecessary under Bramwell's eye, but nevertheless appreciated.

The sleepy-eyed lord thanked the woman once more, ensuring that she'd seen his broad, pearly smile before exiting the lounge, nearly tripping over a disorderly stack of miscellaneous books.

"Your wife is from Immorium, isn't she?" Lyren asked, slowly sipping his tea. It slightly singed the pretty pink curve of his upper lip, and he bit back a hiss before pulling the cup away. Bramwell, however, appeared unphased by the temperature of the drink, a rather large sip easing down his throat.

"Yes, she is. She's the daughter of Hemlock Byron, only the best fisherman in all of Elantry. You've met him, he's supplied the seafood to all of my events within the past five years. Wonderful man, even more lovely of a daughter." The lord couldn't help but smile. He'd taken quite the liking to Fisherman Byron, and taking Hemlock's daughter in marriage was the least he could do to assist the family in their finances.

There was simply no other woman in Elantry eligible enough for Bramwell. Belle just might have saved him from the Capitol's nasty wrath, for if she hadn't agreed to wed him, he would be counting down the days until his retirement from the throne.

Valen would be in shambles without him.

"It must've been odd to consummate the marriage when you'd only just formally met on the day of your wedding," Lyren said, running his fingers through the frilled fabric of his collar. "It had to have been lovely though, was it? I've heard that the night of the wedding is the most romantic, there's nothing that compares. To make love to the one that you'll have forever."

Bramwell's expression shifted—dark, bushy brows anchored together in discontent as he sipped his tea. To hear his dear friend ramble on about the magic of consummating a marriage nearly made his stomach churn, and even Clare's delicious biscuits instantly turned his gut sour.

"We haven't," he unintentionally spilled, interrupting Lyren's never-ending speech.

For a moment, the blue-eyed lad opposite him merely froze, expression unchanging as he barely blinked. Truthfully, he wasn't quite sure if he'd heard Bramwell correctly.

"I don't think I heard you properly," Lyren spoke, forehead creased in concern. "Could you repeat what you said?"

"I said *we haven't*," Bramwell clipped, tone riddled with impatience. He felt as if he were going to leap out of his skin.

Stop asking questions.

"Haven't . . . *what?*" Lyren pressed, as if begging Bramwell to say it. He had an idea, but it was absurd—*ridiculous*. There was just no way that the mature man beside him had yet to make love to the woman he'd wed half a year prior.

"Haven't *fucked*, Lyren!" Bramwell hissed, careful not to raise his voice. For all he knew, Clare was still stalking around the corner, and the last thing he wanted was for the housemaidens to have something new to gossip about, *especially* in reference to their employer.

To Bramwell's complete dismay, Lyren remained expressionless—*perfectly perplexed*. The lord knew of his friend's antics, how he'd taken a woman five years his senior when he was only fifteen, much to his mother's disapproval. How on another occasion, he'd defied their religion—cursed the names of the Goddesses aloud as he fucked a woman in the alley of the busiest nightspot in The Outskirts, the rounded balls of her pearl necklace leaving indents against his fingers as he claimed her neck. Once, he heard, Lyren had fallen into bed with two women and another man, rotating between the three until he was breathless and spent, sticky with sweat.

"I don't understand," Lyren eventually spoke, shaking his head from side to side. "Surely you have . . . surely she's wanted to?"

"She's begged me, actually. She *does* want to. It's me who doesn't." Bramwell said, sighing into his tea. He thought that perhaps his closest friend would understand him—*sympathize* with him—but just as he'd feared, the idea of denying sex was almost too much for Lyren to comprehend.

After all, what man would ever do such a thing?

"That's not entirely *normal*, Bram." Lyren breathed, setting down his tea. The biscuits and fruit still remained untouched. "Please tell me you've at least been with someone before Belle. I know it's not desired in the religion Elantry practices, but I have yet to meet someone of our age who hasn't done so."

"Well, now you have."

The men sat in a buzzing silence for several seconds too long before Lyren spoke once more, desperate to discover the true reason behind Bramwell's odd practices. After all, they considered themselves close friends, and friends frequently discussed such things. Hell, Lyren had admittedly *overshared* some of his escapades with Bramwell, and it dawned upon him now that his friend had never shared any stories of his own.

It was because he had none.

"I'm worried, friend. This just isn't normal." Lyren said, his soft tone slightly wavering as a shaken sea of blue swiftly connected with stone-cold gray eyes.

"What isn't normal, Lyren?" Bramwell pressed, the corner of his lip slightly upturned. He refused to break eye contact with the dainty man, whose lips had begun to part, lazy gaze glued to the swirling, dark rain clouds within Bramwell's stare.

"I–" Lyren began, stuttering over his words.

He had absolutely no recollection of their recent discussion.

"We were discussing Havensworth," Bramwell said, finishing off his tea before grabbing a biscuit. "How the Capitol forced me to wed. Surely you recall?"

"Yes," Lyren croaked, clearing his throat. He remembered their talk of Havensworth, the Capitol of Elantry, and how wretched of a place it truly was. About his new wife—a woman named Belle, the first-born daughter of Hemlock Byron, a fisherman from Immorium.

To Lyren, the discussion of Bramwell's unusual habits never even occurred.

"I'd love to meet her," Lyren said, leaning forward to snatch both a biscuit and a slice of pear from the dainty plate.

Just as the statement left Lyren's tongue, Belle eased into the room, Florence following close on her heel.

"Speak of the lady," Bramwell beamed, standing to his feet. He offered an arm to his wife, fingers playfully parted as he lightly wiggled them her way.

Perplexed by his unusual actions, Belle anxiously stepped into his embrace, nearly flinching when the man coiled his arm around her slim waist, drawing her impossibly close. The tip of her nose collided with his collarbone, a sweet scent of pine dancing along her nostrils as she inhaled Bramwell's unfamiliar scent.

It had been months since she'd been so close to him.

"Lyren, I'd like you to meet my wife. Belle, this is my closest friend, Lyren Deth." Bramwell purred, nodding in Lyren's direction. The blond was already on his feet, nearly knocking over another stack of dissimilar novels on his way to the pair, his half-full cup of tea almost spilling over the sides of the mug.

"M'lady," he said, slowly bowing in Belle's direction. It was comical to see—for he was clearly disoriented—but Belle said nothing, for she was still stunned by Bram's incredibly bizarre gesture.

He was unlike any man Belle had ever met before—*especially* in the poorer, seaside region of Immorium. From just a single glance, she could tell just how soft his hands were, free of any marks, scars, calluses. Entirely opposite of the hands of any working man. Even Bramwell's fingers were rough—*coarse*—and for the first few weeks of their union, Belle wondered how they'd feel on her skin, between her thighs, along her walls . . .

"It's a pleasure to meet you, Mr. Deth." Belle smiled, admiring Lyren's long silvery-blond hair. He was dainty and delicate, with full, nearly feminine lips that were the prettiest pink shade. She shied away from his curious stare, side-stepping out of Bram's bizarre hold.

"If you don't mind, Lyren, I'd like to speak to my husband in private. It'll only be a moment, I hope." Belle whispered, avoiding Bramwell's perplexed gaze.

"Leave us, Lyren," the lord ordered, dismissing his friend with a stiff wave of his hand. Lyren didn't protest, and instead, followed close on Florence's heel as she led the man from the sitting room, sealing the broad, double oak doors behind him.

"I apologize if I made you feel uncomfortable, Belle." Bramwell said, snatching another biscuit from his plate. "The sudden affection probably puzzled you. I'm not quite sure why I did that, perhaps I felt insecure about our lack of intimacy in front of my friend."

Bramwell's admission of insecurity slightly warmed Belle's heart, but almost as quickly as the heat rushed through her veins, it froze; turning her blood to ice.

"I've been wanting you to hold me like that for half a year, Bram," she hissed, features void of expression. Although she still craved his presence—*just a sliver of affection*—it was too late.

Belle blinked back tears. "You've made me feel unattractive, unwanted, and unloved. A woman can only feel so alone for so long–"

"You're right, Belle." Bramwell breathed, pausing to take a bite of his biscuit. "That's why I'm pleased that you have Florence to show you all of that, since I cannot."

A stiff, weighted silence filled the room, widened, feminine eyes meeting in a rushed embrace. Florence was still by the door, palms clasped behind her back as she held her breath. The warmth had completely drained from her face, leaving behind a sickly, pale expression. She looked *petrified*.

He knew.

Before Belle could pry, Bramwell explained. His demeanor was considerably cool—*calm*—and he appeared completely at ease as he slipped a sliced pear into the depths of his mouth. He took notice of Belle's rigid stance, the way she froze—still as a statue, a product of the of an angry Goddess. There was a flicker of fear behind her eyes, and the lord felt guilty for frightening her.

"I approve of it," he assured through a mouthful of fruit. "Both of you, *relax*. You look as if I'm going to commit arson."

Belle openly gaped at the man as he chuckled, vivid visuals of the room erupting in roaring, blue flames riddling her thoughts. The curtains would fry first, suffocating the room in smoke, painting it all a bitter black.

"You . . . *approve* . . . of this arrangement?" Belle stammered, barely able to spit the words out. She glanced over her shoulder to view an equally bewildered Florence, who was flattened against the doors, as if ready to run.

Bramwell shrugged, smoothing his palms along the silky, jet-black fabric of his slacks. He stepped forward towards the cluttered table, brushing the teacups aside before claiming his box of cigars, an ornate 'H' embroidered upon the aged leather. He offered both girls a cigar, and to his surprise, Florence crossed the room to claim one, easing it between her trembling lips before requesting a light.

The action amused Bramwell, and he couldn't help but grin as he struck a match, a diminutive flame dancing along Florence's face as he lit her cigar.

"It would be cruel of me to expect you to remain celibate," Bramwell said, avoiding Belle's widened eyes. "You are a young, beautiful woman who deserves intimacy, affection, and dare I say—*sex*. I would never shame you for your desires. All I ask of you is to remain my wife, to hold my arm in public, and to honor the Hellthorne name. The rest—frankly—is none of my business."

Florence's fingers danced along Belle's thin arm, knotting through the baggy fabric of her sleeve, as if out of reassurance. To Bramwell's delight, she smoked the cigar along with him, twirling the object between trembling fingers as she keenly avoided her cousin's curious stare.

"You may let Lyren back in, Florence. Unless there was something else you wanted to speak of, Belle? If so, I'm happy to converse." Bramwell said, offering both of the women a treat from his snack plate. Belle shook her head, but Florence claimed a sliver of pear, slowly chewing on the fruit, as if to test if it were poisoned.

"Why don't you want to be romantically involved with me?" Belle breathed, bony chest nearly concaving inwards on her heart and lungs. She hadn't intended on asking him so outwardly—so *directly*—but she wanted to know, she *needed* to know. After all, she was his wife, and the duties of a wife (especially in the eyes of the Goddesses) was to love her husband, to *cherish* her husband, to *fuck* her husband . . .

"It is just not something I desire, Belle," he replied, freckled cheeks reddening with shame. She'd never seen him so open—so *honest*—and for the first time in half a year, she felt as if she was finally seeing the *real* Bramwell. The man beneath the stone-cold, expressionless mask. He was always so lovely—so full of smiles and pleasantries, especially with his people and out in public—but the moment they were together—*alone*—he froze. The smile faded, lips downturned into a clear frown. Deep-set lines claimed his forehead, doubling his age. His breaths always thinned when Belle attempted to make a move, chest inordinately heaving when her hands wandered, mouth sealed in detest when her lips brushed the surface.

It is just not something I desire, Belle.

Belle blinked back tears, her bulging brown eyes brushed a sad scarlet. "Or do you just not desire *me*?"

Bramwell stiffened, but his expression remained unchanged. "You can ask Florence yourself how many women I've carried on my arm. How many women I've welcomed into the manor."

Belle defiantly shook her head, balmy tears dripping down the slope of her rosy cheeks. She suddenly felt hot in her daytime gown—*claustrophobic*—and although the garment

nearly swallowed her lithe frame up whole, she felt constrict-
ed by their bonds.

Bramwell's expression hardened. *"Ask* her, Belle. Ask her
how many."

"H-How many, Florence?" Belle choked over her own
words, biting back an ugly sob. She feared the answer—*too
many to count . . . you're the only one he's been repulsed by*—and
before her love could even answer, her knees had buckled,
sending her toppling to the floor.

"Belle!" Florence exclaimed, mirroring Bramwell's actions
as the pair both lowered to her aide, wandering hands wedged
beneath her arms.

"Look at me, Belle!" Bramwell called, a hint of worry un-
derlining his usually tame tone. His warm, wide palms cradled her flushed, wet cheeks, and she hesitantly glanced up to
see his dark gaze glued firmly to hers.

"You're the *only* one, Belle. The *only one.* I've never in my
life held another woman on my arm who wasn't my mother.
Your lips are the only ones I've ever tasted. There has been no
one else, and I don't want there to *be* anyone else. It's difficult
for me to explain because I never had to before—I never felt
the need to. Until I was forced to marry, threatened with
being stripped of my title if not. You were my first choice,
for I'd come to adore your father, and knew he would be
pleased to be a part of the royal family. I only hoped that
maybe—*maybe*—you'd enjoy my presence enough to not feel

unwelcome or unloved. But I see now the damage I've already done. The *hurt* I've caused."

A constant stream of sadness oozed from Belle's blurred gaze, dampening the surface of Bramwell's thumbs. He gently wiped the tears away, bottom lip quivering as he, too, felt himself slipping.

"I've grown to love you, Belle Byron. There is no other woman I'd want as my wife. But you need to understand me, you need to know that I do not show love the way you do. The way most people do. I don't need physical affection to be happy. I don't want it. I just want a partner. A wife. You're enough, just as you are. And, Belle, I understand if I am not enough. That is why I give you your own wing. Your own *space*. Whatever you choose to do with your free time—*whoever* you choose to do—is up to *you*. You have my full permission, always. That is something I will never take from you, and I ask that you do the same for me. Respect my wishes, and I will respect yours."

She'd never met someone so honest—so real, so *raw*. No man she'd ever met before Bramwell Hellthorne would ever openly admit that they do not desire physical touch. That they were not driven by sex and desire. He *did* desire her, but in ways she'd never known to even exist.

She was the only woman he'd ever desired.

"Thank you for being honest with me, Bram." Belle whispered, fingertips smoothing along his rough, calloused knuckles. "I promise to always respect your feelings towards intimacy, and I promise to always be the woman on your arm. Forever."

THE FROSTED WINDOW

Lyren came by frequently.

He seemed to spend an abundance of his time in the sitting room with Bramwell, but when he wasn't in the presence of his longtime friend, he wandered the manor, cheekily flirting with Bramwell's help. He even found himself in the garden, a toothy grin spread along his lips as he conversed with the gardener, a boy on the cusp of adulthood with sleek black hair and a line of sweat across his forehead.

"He's a handsome one, isn't he?" Florence purred, lacing her arms around Belle's bare chest. Her pointed chin settled on the pale woman's scrawny shoulder, eyes fluttering closed with content as the pair sat nude in the window nook.

Per Belle's request, Bramwell recently had the cushion replaced in the window seat, for it was her favorite place, and within just six months she'd managed to nearly flatten the cheap seat that remained untouched for many years up until her arrival. The new one was considerably comfortable, so much so that the lady found herself falling asleep in the cold crook of the window quite often.

Her room had the best view of Bramwell's garden, where Lyren stood beside the gardener called Henry.

"How long has he been friends with Bram?" Belle asked, threading her long, dainty fingers through Florence's shorter digits.

"For as long as I've been Bram's ward, easily over a decade, now. He became my guardian shortly after he assumed his position, and after both his parents and my own mother died. I never knew them, but I've heard they were decent people from the townsfolk. Although our mothers were sisters by blood, my mother hardly breathed a word of her sister. Bram rarely speaks of them, either. Only in passing, similar to how he mentioned his mother to you the other day. Never anything more. I don't blame him, they kept him a secret like he was some bastard boy that they were embarrassed of. Perhaps, he is one."

Belle raised a brow, curious stare still focused on Lyren's lengthy self. He was dressed to the nines in the most intriguing outfit she'd ever seen, handsome jewels littering his entire being. Only a single finger laid empty—his ring finger, naturally—and his earlobes even donned several sparkling earrings, nearly up to the hard cartilage.

"He *is* very handsome," Belle said, bare chest growing hot at the thought. "He's different from any man I've ever seen, especially in Immorium. Most of them would mock him for his appearance. Insult him for dressing so feminine. I find it alluring. *Charming.*"

"You like him, don't you?" Florence teased, playfully pinching Belle's side. A trio of faint purple bruises lined the curve of Belle's neck, courtesy of Florence's needy mouth. She reattached her mouth to the surface of Belle's skin, a tiny groan traveling up her lover's throat as she struggled to keep her eyes open.

She wanted to see him. To see *Lyren.*

"He's Bramwell's longest friend," Belle countered, but the words were meaningless. They both knew that Bramwell had given her full permission to seek comfort and intimacy in the arms of others—but just how *many* others? And what if those people were closely acquainted with him?

Florence was his ward, Lyren was his friend . . .

"Besides, I like *you*. I'm loyal to you, Flo. He's just . . . very handsome. Nothing more." Belle countered, craning her neck to meet Florence's bright eyes. She had the most gorgeous gaze, one Belle could get lost in. It reminded her of the sea. Of home.

"I'm not the jealous type," Florence whispered, nipping at Belle's earlobe. "It's okay, you can admit it. He's handsome—unbearably so. I've thought it from the moment I met him so long ago. He was younger then—*youthful*—barely over his boyhood. He's blossomed into an intelligent, stunning man."

Belle watched as Lyren threw his head back in laughter, a pearly-white grin snaked across his lips as Henry, too, shared a pleasant laugh. The young gardener was busy shaping the roses, and although the breeze was bitter and full of ice, he wore a short-sleeved tunic, one that displayed the curly black hair sprouting up between his pecks.

"He's grown immune to the cold, Henry has. He's from up north. Szo Landing. It's significantly colder up there and stays cold year-round. This probably feels like summer to him. Any day without snow is a warm day for him." Florence purred, nipping at Belle's neck. Her fingers trailed around to the smaller woman's front, a series of goosebumps gradually rising with every smooth stroke. Florence couldn't help but grin, she just loved the way Belle's body reacted to her—*needed* her.

Craved her.

Florence's lazy eyes suddenly snapped open when Belle violently flinched, a gasp cascading over her tongue as she peered down through the window. Curiously, Florence scanned the scene, a hearty smirk tugging at her mouth when she realized that Lyren's inquisitive glare had traveled upwards, eventually stopping at the sight of the two naked women in the window.

"It's okay," Florence said, tightening her hold on Belle's stiff frame. "Let him watch."

Henry failed to notice Lyren's instant shift in stance—the way his chest abruptly heaved, the quivering fingers laced around the weeping stem of a picked rose, his coal-black pupils steadily dilating. It was the gardener's worst trait, he could never pick up on body language, and most of the time, it landed him in some awkward situations, the other person just itching to get away.

Fortunately for Lyren, Henry's lack of attention allowed him to study the women in the window, and although the glass was gently frosted and foggy, he could make out the small lady's features enough to realize that it was Bramwell's wife, Lady Belle. He could tell by the dainty, honey-brown arms wrapped around her bust that the person behind her was *not* Bramwell, but instead, another woman.

His breaths thinned as he tightened his hold on the rose, Henry's ramblings about Szo Landing fading into oblivion as he made direct eye contact with a noticeably frazzled Belle. She was a stunning porcelain white, her skin the shade of freshly fallen snow, and it was a beautiful contrast against the inky exterior of the manor, the walls as black as old blood.

Her fiery red hair was an untamed mess, framing half of her face as the mystery woman threaded her dark fingers through the strands, brushing through the knots with care. Her breasts were petite and perky, with nipples so perfect and pink. He felt a curious heat blossom within his chest, cascading down towards his stomach as Belle refused to tear her glare from his. She hardly blinked, and it almost made him chuckle.

It was as if she was challenging him.

Keep watching.

Henry continued on with his fond memories of Szo Landing, the northernmost tip of Elantry that remained frozen over for ninety-nine percent of the year. He spoke of ice fishing and swimming in frozen ponds and all the talk of ice caused a chill to creep up Lyren's spine, only to be instantly warmed by the carnal heat swallowing him up whole.

Belle's ladylove seemed to find amusement in the situation, for Lyren noticed a sly smile as she trailed her fingers down Belle's navel, dipping lower and lower and *lower…*

The man nearly gasped when her hand found the in between of Belle's legs, parting them, opening them wide.

Showing him every bit of her.

"I'm planning to ask Lord Hellthorne for a leave of absence so I can visit my mum for the upcoming holiday, but Szo Landing is a far trip that not many carriages are willing to take often. The drivers that do agree usually charge three months salary for a one-way trip. Do you know of any cheaper carriages that travel that far up Elantry, Mister Deth?" Henry chattered, finally tearing his stare away from his work. He noticed Lyren's lack of attention, but he hadn't thought to follow the finely dressed man's stare. Instead, he tightened his hold on his shovel, and continued to dig a spot for some fresh black roses, per the lord's special request.

Unsurprisingly, Henry continued talking, mostly to himself as he tended to the manor's garden. Lyren laid entranced beside him, the stem of his rose pinched between reddened fingers as a devious smirk stretched along his lips. It wasn't every day that he received a free show, not to mention one from the Lady of Valen herself. He felt naughty—*awful*—for openly watching the wife of his longtime friend through her window, but something deep within his mind urged him to do so—*don't look away, they want you to stay*—and he bit the tip of his tongue when Belle's neck rolled—*tipped* back, eyelids fluttering closed, lips parted in pleasure as the other woman's fingers met her center.

He recognized her, then. It almost made him chuckle as he pieced the dots together. After all, he'd seen the two of them tumble into the sitting room only days prior, eagerly requesting a private conversation with Bram.

Belle was fucking the lord's *ward*. His own cousin. The woman he was once the legal guardian of.

Lyren wondered for a moment if his friend knew of Florence and Lady Belle's affair—*perhaps he watched, the sly dog*—but regardless of how incredibly inappropriate it was to witness such a thing, he kept watching. He wasn't even shy about it, either. He knew of Henry the gardener's presence, and he figured that he'd seen, too.

He just didn't have the heart to care.

Belle's lustful lids peeled open once more, chocolate brown eyes fixated on the man below as Florence rubbed circles against her, lovely lips peppering kisses down the slope of Belle's jaw. The moment their gazes reconnected, Lyren smiled; a broad, toothy grin, one which showed off the pointed curves of his canine teeth. He gradually brought the drooping rose to his nose, playfully concealing his expression behind the flower as Belle openly laughed beyond the glass. He couldn't hear it, but he could picture it—sweet and silky, a girlish giggle. It made his toes curl within the leather home of his boots.

He woefully averted his stare once Florence's mouth met Belle's, heart steadily racing beneath his ribcage as he watched Henry tend to the roses. Beside his feet were an abundance of new buds—black as the night, almost the same hue as the exterior of the home—and Lyren found himself snorting at the sight. If he ever needed anything black, Hellthorne Manor was the first place he'd look.

"It's been a pleasure, Henry. I wish you luck on finding a carriage that can take you to Szo Landing for less than three months wages." Lyren said, winking when the gardener shot him a warm smile.

He was listening after all.

"Pleasure meeting you, Mister Deth! Anytime you need to talk, you can find me in the garden. Unless I'm in Szo Landing, of course. But I don't think you'll travel all the way there for me. It's a long trip." Henry rambled, shaking his head when he realized how much unnecessary information he'd spilled.

"I may take you up on that, Henry. I've never been to Szo Landing," Lyren grinned, waving kindly in Henry's direction. "If you don't mind, I'll be taking this rose with me."

Henry smiled. "It's all yours."

Lord Bramwell was nowhere to be found when Lyren eased back into the warmth of the manor. A slight chill crept along his spine, and he shivered, the rose still pinched between his fingers.

He knew the home well enough to locate Belle's bedroom, and he paused for a moment when he realized that it was in an entirely separate wing from Bramwell's. It was possible that it was only a room where she and Florence escaped to, but it almost seemed too cozy—too *familiar*.

He passed by several housemaidens on his way to his desired spot, the discomfort in his trousers steadily rising as he denied a fruit plate from a lady called Clare, the same one who provided him and Bramwell with snacks several days prior. She seemed curious of Lyren's presence and Bramwell's absence, but she chose not to pry.

This particular wing of the mansion was exceptionally dark, walls stained a deep vermilion. Even the staircase was dyed a dark black, completely opposite of the wondrous white stairwells in the very front of the manor. A plethora of portraits lined the walls, none with faces that Lyren recognized. There were several of a teenage girl with hair as black as coal and eyes a pale green. She looked melancholy in most of them, but one in particular grabbed Lyren's attention so much that he found himself pausing in the middle of the hallway.

She was seated stiffly upon a lush brown chair, the ruffled sleeves of her gown concealing both her hands and arms fully. It appeared as if it were a considerably normal painted portrait, that was, until he found her eyes.

The forest-green hue was gone, and its place was a cold gray color. Empty. Extinct.

The more Lyren stared, the more he believed that the girl in the portrait might've actually been dead.

A shiver danced between his shoulders, and he moved on, a dreadful, sinking feeling enveloping his chest as he trekked towards his destination. Several feet forward, he abruptly paused; a brutal, chilling sensation entwining his legs as he froze in place. He wasn't sure why, but the urge to glance over his shoulder suddenly arose—*look back*—and with a gulp, he did just that, eyes settling upon the portrait of what he assumed was a deceased teenage girl.

Instead, he was met with an empty portrait, nothing but a boring brown chair painted against a dark green backdrop.

She was gone.

A bitter shiver cascaded down the length of his spine, a curious sigh slipping off of his lips as Lyren stared utterly perplexed at the painting. He was *certain* that someone had been drawn into the portrait, for why would an artist paint nothing but a boring chair, and why would Lord Bramwell hang such a meaningless object in his home?

Convinced that his eyes were simply playing tricks on him—*you're just jittery, Ly, it's the nerves from seeing the girls fondling one another in the window*—he snorted, voicing his inner thoughts aloud, as if to conquer the undeniable bubble of fear rolling about within his belly.

"It's just your eyes," Lyren muttered, a breathless chuckle rolling off of his tongue. He forced his thoughts back to those of Belle and the Florence, the way the women lustfully coiled around one another like slithering snakes, skin slick with desire, mouths watering with need. His stiffened cock twitched within his trousers, heart irregularly fluttering within his ribcage like a panicked hummingbird as he finally tore his gaze from the empty portrait, determined to locate Belle's room.

The moment his attention diverted to the hallway; he was achingly aware that he was—in fact—not alone. His heart abruptly ceased to beat, eyes rounded and bulging with fright as he choked down a scream, one which never had the chance to emerge.

Lifeless gray eyes met a shaken sea of blue, and with a black, rotting smile, the woman from the portrait let out a laugh, one which prompted each and every little hair on Lyren's skin to stand up tall. She raised an arm up to meet her mocking grin, black teeth crooked and chipped, and revealed what laid beneath the too-long sleeves of her blouse.

The fabric slowly slipped away, revealing her hand beneath. As soon as the sleeve rolled down, the smell hit Lyren like a blinding wall of rain—rank and rotting, sickeningly sweet, a scent he'd experienced countless times during his duties as a forensic pathologist. Typically, the smell didn't bother him, but this one did—so much so that he violently dry heaved, palm cradling the surface of his stomach as he desperately attempted to disappear.

The woman from the portrait only laughed—a strange, maniacal sound—before reaching out to meet the dizzy, trembling man. Lyren gasped when her frozen fingers met his throat, a bubbling, black smile stretched across her lips as she tightened her grip, squeezing and squeezing and *squeezing* until he saw nothing but stars.

He opened his mouth to scream, but the creature prevented the noise from escaping, her hold shifting to his windpipe to stifle the sound.

Instead, she spoke in his place—a fizzing blob of a black, syrupy substance dripping from her cracked lips, traveling down to the mahogany carpet.

"You're *mine*."

"You're *mine*."

NOTHING BUT DUST
AND PORTRAITS

"Right there," Belle purred, head tossed back in ecstasy as a pair of eager lips decorated her thighs with a series of ecchymoses. Her skin was sensitive—*pale*—and she often bruised like a ripe peach in the hands of a young toddler. The fact used to bother her, but now, she wore the marks with pride, for they were etched into the surface with love.

"Stop squeezing my head," Florence said, chuckling slightly at the sensation. Belle's legs were wrapped tight around her skull, unintentionally tightening with every passing second, as if to push the woman away. Only, she didn't want her to leave. With words unspoken, she consistently begged her to stay.

"Sorry," Belle breathlessly sighed, reaching down to capture Florence's soft curls. She tangled her fingers between the tendrils, manicured nails grazing the surface of her scalp as she gently massaged the skin.

Florence groaned in response, inching upwards to meet Belle's swollen lips, which had stretched into a smitten grin. She kept hold of her lover's hair, admiring it, caressing it.

"You're beautiful," Florence whispered, dipping down to place a kiss upon Belle's mouth. She pulled away a moment too soon, a grin snaked along her lips at the sight of Belle's obvious irritation. "How is it that you're mine?"

"Dumb luck, I suppose." Belle teased, earning a playful pinch from a buzzing Florence. Their lips met once more—a burning passion igniting deep within Belle's chest as she knotted her fingers through Florence's soft hair, pulling her closer—*more more more.* Florence's tall, stunning frame nearly dwarfed Belle's considerably tiny body, and within Florence's arms she felt safe. Held. *Home.*

A gleeful groan tickled Belle's tongue when Florence's knee gently grazed the pulsating warmth of her clit, a pressure so delightful and desired. The sensation made Belle's head swim, a dizzying dance of lust leaping about within her skull. Even as a teen, she'd never felt such passion with Dalbir—with him, it was mostly sloppy and rushed, and she'd shuffle back into her clothes with an aching, unfulfilled want that needed tending to later that night by her own hand.

Just as Florence's smooth knuckles skimmed the beating bud of Belle's center, a whisper of a knock came at the bedroom door.

Florence lightly giggled, eyeing the closed door in curiosity as she withdrew her touch, much to Belle's dismay.

"Looks like someone decided to come *play*," she purred, redirecting her lewd gaze back to a flustered Belle beneath her hips.

Belle's jaw dropped, realization pooling within her belly as she politely brushed Florence aside. She snatched a gray, silken sheet from the foot of the bed, a flurry of goosebumps prickling her skin as the cold material settled along her opposingly warm body.

"You really think it's him?" she whispered; wide, doe-like eyes rotating between the door and Florence. Her lover had crawled up to the pillows, golden brown skin shimmering within the gentle glow of the flickering oil lamps. Her skin was always stunning—so smooth and flawless—but it was exceptionally perfect beneath the warmth of the sun, for she'd glitter and gleam like a bundle of diamonds.

"You saw the look on his face when he watched us," Florence said, drawing her bottom lip between gnawing teeth. "Truthfully, I've been watching him for years. I've always been curious about him."

"Is he really bold enough to just come right in like that? He must know that Bram's home," Belle countered, jumping slightly when the knock returned. This time, it was louder. Forceful.

Open up. Let me play.

"Coming!" Belle exclaimed, her tone hoarse and hushed. She heard Florence chuckle over her shoulder, and she shot her a stiff stare, arms crossed over her chest as she tightened the sheet around her nude frame.

Her fingers met the frigid brass handle, and she drew in a shaky breath, preparing to come face to face with the man she'd just erotically teased. She pondered over how she'd welcome him in—how the wrinkled silk would flutter to her feet, the way his blue stare would widen at the sight of her small frame. There wasn't much to her—her skin was white, thin, pulled tight over her bones. When she bent a certain way, the bumpy ridges of her spine would protrude, a rugged road leading down her back. Often, her lower ribs would show their face, especially when she arched her back in pleasure, every last breath vacating her lungs.

To the best mistake she'll ever make.

She twisted the knob, prying the door open at an achingly slow pace to peek around the portal, heart irregularly thumping within her chest.

There was no one there.

"Hello?" Belle called, confusion riddling her features. She pulled the door open as wide as it would go, a single foot stepping out into the hallway as she craned her neck to either side.

Empty.

The bed creaked behind her, and Florence voiced her confusion. They'd both clearly heard the knocks—the second one, especially—but all that lay before Belle's widened eyes was a barren hallway, nothing but dust and dreary painted portraits within her sight.

"That's incredibly odd," Florence announced, shuffling into her day dress. "I could've sworn I'd see Lyren on the other side. I actually applaud him for resisting his urges, perhaps he felt guilty considering his relationship with Bramwell."

"Yeah," Belle murmured, disappointment riddled within her tone. "You're right. He *is* Bram's friend. A longtime one, too. It would be just as inappropriate as what you and I have."

"Your husband *did* say that what you do behind closed doors was none of his business," Florence pressed, tying her hair back with a baby blue bow. "If it bothered him, he would say so. He's an oddball, that one. I've never met a man who would so willingly deny sex."

With a final sigh, Belle sealed the door, the sheet dropping to her feet as her lengthy nails gently slid along her left breast. "I wouldn't consider him *odd*. I think it's fine to not want sex. As lovely as it is, I can see how some people may simply not desire it. It's awful that he feels embarrassed by it. He shouldn't feel such a way. He's a great man, Bram is. Although I was unhappy to marry him half a year ago, I find myself rather pleased with our arrangement."

"Well, why wouldn't you?" Florence teased, slipping into her shoes. "You get to live in a fancy mansion, wear anything you want, eat anything you'd like, and fuck anyone you desire. It's a dream, I'd say."

"Watch your tongue, Flo." Belle pressed, unable to conceal her grin. The woman was right, and Belle was certainly blessed beyond measure.

How was it that she managed to land such a perfect spouse, by an arranged marriage, no less?

Another knock tore the two from their banter, only this time, the sound made Belle freeze. Her expression paled considerably as she met Florence's wistful gaze, trembling fingers lowering to meet the discarded sheet once more.

"Open it," Florence whispered, taking a small step forward as Belle wrapped the sheet around her shaking self.

The lady obeyed, fingers knotting around the knob as she pried the door open once more, fully expecting an empty hallway. Instead, the sight of a human being sent a shiver down her spine, a startled cry bouncing off of the walls as one of her housemaidens—Ula was her name—stood on the opposite side.

Ula flinched at Belle's reaction, a palm flattening against her heart as she looked the frazzled woman up and down. "My dear lady, I apologize for frightening you!"

"She's just jumpy today," Florence cheekily slurred, meeting Belle's side as she greeted Ula with a nod. "To what does Lady Belle owe the pleasure, Ula?"

Ula was tiny—even smaller than Belle, which was slightly shocking, for the woman was incredibly small—standing barely over four feet. Her cheeks were rounded and pink, big brown eyes fixated on the pair as her eyelids pulled into small slits.

"Fancy meeting you here, Florence. I was just reporting up to inquire about supper. Jeanne's roasting a chicken, and we're considering dressing it with potatoes, snap peas, and honey rolls." Ula said, looking both of the women up and down. Florence's bedroom was in Bramwell's same wing, so for her to be on the opposite end of the manor—and in Lady Belle's *bedroom,* nonetheless—was enough to raise the woman's brows halfway up her forehead.

"My whereabouts are not up for questioning, Ula." Florence bit back, venom dripping from her tongue. The only housemaiden who plainly knew of Belle and Florence's relationship was Jeanne, for she'd stumbled in on their very first kiss. However, the middle-aged lady was a mute, and she had no way of spilling the secret to the others, not that she would even want to. She was never a fan of gossip like the younger ladies were.

The others had their suspicions, but Florence was discreet.

Deny deny deny.

Although Belle had begged the woman to sleep in her bed every night, Florence refused—she belonged in her own bedroom across the mansion, several doors down from the room the housed the Lord of Valen, himself.

"Are you going to tell the lady why you're here, or are you going to continue to waste her time?" Florence pressed; feet planted firmly beside Belle. The woman was suddenly very aware of the fact that she was naked beneath her thin sheet.

Ula cleared her throat, diverting her angry stare from Florence as her features immediately softened. She met Belle with a smile—a fake one, no doubt—hands crossed before her chest. "The lord has requested your presence in the sitting room. He wanted me to inform you that you've received a very special letter from your sister, Evelin."

Belle's lips tugged into a joyful smile. It had been weeks since she'd received a letter from Evelin. She was due to turn eighteen in eight days time, and Belle missed both her and the remainder of her siblings terribly.

"Thank you for informing me, Ula. Let him know I'll be down in a hurry." Belle said. The woman couldn't help but grin—for her sister had finally written her back.

The day was as lovely as they come.

PORTRAIT OF A DEAD GIRL

"Does the lord require a drink?" Ula purred; palms flattened against her chest.

She always admired Bramwell—all of the housemaidens did, he was just wonderful to them—and the thought of caring for him until her last breath was enough to make the woman's toes curl within her withered, aging shoes.

"No thank you, Ula. However, my guest could use another warm towel, his has gone cold." Bramwell requested, dismissing the housemaiden with a small wave of his hand. Ula disappeared beyond the parted doorway, her absence prompting a sigh to slip through Bramwell's parted lips.

"She's clingier than the others," Lyren spoke, his tone hoarse and thick. He never liked Ula—she always had this look about her that oddly pissed him off—and her temporary absence brought him comfort. He had a bad feeling that the damp rag she'd return with would singe the skin of his forehead right off the muscle.

"She does her best," Bramwell countered, slipping his hands into the loose pockets of his lounge briefs. "Are you feeling up to talking about what happened in the west wing?"

The west wing.

Belle's wing.

Lyren's stomach churned, visuals of his outlandish encounter with the dead, decaying woman riddling his mind. He didn't want to voice the fresh memory aloud—it seemed silly—but he had no other explanation for what had happened on his journey to Belle's room. He was only steps away from her door, and then, he woke up groggy and nauseous on the stiff sofa in Bramwell's sitting room.

"Ula found you unconscious during one of her rounds," Bramwell added, pacing back and forth. "Henry, my gardener, is on his way to town to fetch a physician, I sent him the second I received word of your condition. You gave us all a scare, Lyren. I wasn't sure if you would wake. You were clammy and pale, barely breathing, lips blue."

Lyren swallowed thickly. "I was?"

"Yes," Bramwell replied, biting down on his bottom lip. "It was frightening to see. I'm just thankful to see you awake, and the color back in your cheeks. Now, will you tell me what happened to you? I know I'm not the healer, they should be here within an hour, but I can at least talk you through it. It must've been traumatizing."

It was.

It wasn't until Ula had come and gone once again—this time with a damp rag, a bit too hot just as Lyren had suspected it would be—that he finally opened up to Bramwell. Just the thought alone of telling his friend was enough to make his stomach roll, and when the words torturously tumbled from his lips, he nearly bent over the side of the sofa to spill the contents of his stomach.

Bramwell brows moderately raised—nearly meeting his hairline as he claimed a cup of tea from a book-riddled table, a thin layer of dust coating the covers.

"Well, Lyren," Bramwell began, standing before the sofa with his tea. He avoided his friends' weary gaze, instead settling his sight upon the drowning slice of lemon in his steaming mug. "I hate to say this, but that portrait doesn't exist."

"What?" Lyren balked, swinging his legs to the side to pull himself into a sitting position. He nearly kicked Bramwell in the shin, and the moist rag tumbled needlessly to the carpet.

"I may be wrong here—Hellthorne Manor is massive—but I have no recollection of said painting, especially in Belle's wing, so close to her quarters. Why don't you show me? Do you feel well enough to walk? The physician will probably arrive just as we're nearing the sitting room on our way back. It'll be good to stretch your legs a little, they must feel stiff."

Bramwell was right, Lyren's legs were painfully sore and stiff, but it just seemed impossible for the painting to simply *not exist* . . . no . . . he'd seen it with his own eyes. He'd seen her—*felt* her—smelled the sweet rot of her decaying hands before they coiled around his throat . . .

"Yes," Lyren croaked, nodding curtly. "Let's go. I'll show it to you. She's difficult to miss, she literally looks dead. I'm completely convinced that she *was* dead when they painted her. I've heard rumors that the wealthy would do that when they lost a child so young, and she didn't look any older than twenty."

"Well, if there's a portrait of a dead girl in my home, I'd like to know about it." Bramwell said, index finger curving beneath the flap of his embroidered cigar box. He offered one to Lyren, but he refused. "Lead the way, friend."

The pair walked in a sore silence, the only evidence of Bramwell's presence being that of the floral scent of his cigar. He reminded Lyren of his father when he smoked like this—for the man always had one pinched between his teeth—and it made his stomach turn. He wasn't fond of the invasive thoughts of his father, and with a sharp shake of his head, he banished the memories away.

Lyren visibly flinched when they rounded the corner leading directly to Belle's bedchamber, for he'd unintentionally collided with a considerably small Belle, her fiery locks pulled back into an elegant braid.

The little lady cursed, palm flattening against the surface of the wall to steady herself. Lyren profusely apologized, wild eyes hesitantly colliding with Bramwell's amused stare.

"Just knock over my wife, why don't you, Lyren?" the lord teased, tone slightly muffled by his cigar. He tore the burning object from his lips before addressing Belle for the first time that day.

"Lovely to see you, Belle. Have you had a pleasant day?" Bramwell asked, a small smile snaking across his lips. She looked flustered and flushed, and he couldn't help but wonder what her and Florence had been up to mere moments before their arrival.

"I'm fine," Belle murmured, avoiding Bramwell's piercing stare. "What brings you both to this wing?"

Lyren noticeably stiffened, slender fingers creeping up to the collar of his tunic. He wedged his index finger between the suffocatingly tight cloth, restlessly tugging it away from the slick skin of his neck. There was no doubt that Bramwell had his suspicions about Lyren's whereabouts—after all, he was discovered unconscious by the help mere feet from Belle's bedroom—but there was no chance that he would let the admission slip.

Please don't say it.

"Ula found Lyren unconscious in this hallway," Bramwell revealed, studying the portraits that lined the walls. "He said there was a portrait of a dead girl somewhere along these walls. Can you show me where, friend?"

Lyren nodded, gently brushing past an equally stiff Belle as he skillfully navigated the corridor. The air felt significantly lighter than before—fluffy and free, like a cloud—and it made him feel weary.

Something wasn't right.

Lyren approached the very spot that he saw her less than an hour prior—*this was it, he could feel it*—and with a gasp, his quivering fingers danced along the bare wall.

Empty.

"Are you sure this is where it was?" Bramwell asked, brows pulling together. The cigar was back in his mouth—pinched between curled lips, circular puffs slipping from the dainty cracks on either side—and Lyren huffed, frustration riddling him to his very core.

"I *swear* on our Goddess Lottie that there was a portrait here. I can still see her face in my mind. It was haunting—*horrifying*. It makes me nauseous to even think about her." Lyren spilled, scaling the walls for a single sign of her.

She was gone.

"Bram, what's happening?" Belle breathed; arms apprehensively crossed. It was as if she, too, could feel the imbalance in the air.

"Lyren said he saw a portrait of a woman he believed to be dead before he lost consciousness," Bramwell dryly explained, touring the hall in search of said painting. "I've memorized almost every inch of the manor, portraits and all, and I couldn't recall hers. I just had to see for myself."

"I'm willing to pledge to the Good Book that it exists. Maybe it was moved. Perhaps your help—Ula, I think—moved it after she found me. Maybe–"

"Lyren," Bramwell sighed, resting a hand atop his friend's shaking shoulder. "I need you to take a deep breath. The physician will be here any moment, they'll be happy to look you over and calm your racing thoughts. I believe you, Ly. You saw something strange, and you're panicked. We'll get to the bottom of it."

Lyren shook his head, bitterly brushing Bramwell's hand away as he suctioned his palm to the very spot where her portrait once laid. "This can't be possible. I *know* what I saw. *It was real.*"

"I believe you," Bramwell pressed, nodding in Belle's direction as if to assure her that he did—in fact—believe his dear friend's mysterious sighting. "Let's get you back to the sitting room. Belle, it would be lovely if you could join us. I have a letter with your name on it from one *Evelin Byron.*"

Belle's flushed features instantaneously brightened, swollen lips peeling back to reveal a pearly-white grin. She outwardly cheered, unable to stifle her glee as she jumped up and down.

Bramwell couldn't help but smile at her reaction—she was so precious, that girl—whereas Lyren busied himself with pacing the premises, watery, boggled eyes studying each and every surface of the wall.

This just didn't make sense.

"Let's go, Lyren. There's a cup of lemon tea and a warm rag with your name on it." Bramwell purred, snaking his arm around Lyren's shoulders. His friend shakily sighed, taking one last look at the spot where he'd seen her—where he *felt* her—before accepting his defeat.

It wasn't real.

Bramwell extended his arm outward, offering for both Belle and Lyren to lead the way back to the sitting room as he claimed his spot at the very rear of the group. He paused as the two departed, the curve of his boot barely brushing the surface of the carpet as he held it suspended.

Shifting his foot slightly to the side, he glanced down at the small bubbly black puddle of spittle beneath his foot. A sharp breath hitched in his throat at the sight—for it looked angry, *alive*—and with a weighty exhale, he stepped over the sludge, leaving it unblemished and untouched.

Abandoning it as if it never existed at all.

Out of sight, out of mind.

LITTLE BYRON

A carriage carrying a bubbly Evelin Byron arrived at the cusp of dawn nine days following, a beaten-up trunk in tow as she stumbled and nearly fell face first out of the creaky wagon.

The middle-aged coachman stifled a smile as he darted forward in hopes of catching her, a deep shade of scarlet peppering along the young lady's cheeks as she thoroughly thanked him, only to be knocked onto her bottom immediately followed by an over enthusiastic Belle, tears rimming her eyes.

"Oh, *Evelin!*" Belle cheered, coiling her arms around her younger sister. She dotted playful, slobbery kisses along Evelin's blushing cheeks, eyes crinkled in amusement as she showered her sibling with love.

"Okay, *okay,* Belle. My Goddess, you're nearly suffocating me." Evelin said, crawling out of Belle's arms. She took in the mansion before her—a sight to behold—and a gasp graced her tongue. "Is *this* where you live?"

"It's beautiful, isn't it?" Belle purred, craning her neck to admire the gargantuan, gothic structure. Hellthorne Manor claimed the highest peak of Valen, a mountain nearly two-thousand feet above the incredibly flat sea level of Immorium, and the air was admittedly thinner up there, prompting Evelin to wheeze as she breathed.

"It's colder up here," she said, pulling her shawl tight over her chest. "Can you see all of Valen from up here?"

Belle grinned. "You can see the beginnings of Westcastle from up here. It's gorgeous, but also dangerous. Bramwell's very strict on how close I can venture towards the tip, it's a steep fall, and I value my life."

Evelin chuckled. "I'll trust him on that one. Goddess, this is all so *strange.* You're *wealthy,* sister. Your morning gown probably cost more than every article of clothing in my trunk, and even the trunk itself. It's Papaw's, you know. Hasn't seen a trip in decades, Mother had to search good and hard for it. She sends her love."

Belle blinked back tears. "I miss you all. Please, come inside. It's starting to get cold here. Winter is coming."

"Maybe I'll get lucky and see some snow while I'm here," Evelin purred, frozen fingers curling around the cracked leather handle of her trunk. The rusted metal clasps wheezed in discomfort, and she wobbled beside Belle, anxious to see the inside of the grand, gothic mansion. She'd never seen so much black and red in her existence.

Henry, the gardener, skipped along the pebbled walkway, a small pant cascading over his lips as he approached the duo. A series of apologies spilled over his tongue as he grasped at Evelin's trunk, insisting that he carry it inside for her. She was reluctant to offer it up, but after some reassurance from her sister, she handed it over—admittedly relieved to be rid of the hefty case.

"So, you're Lady Belle's sister?" Henry breathed, struggling to stifle his pants. He was surprised by the weight of the trunk, but he masked his discomfort well, carrying it up the walkway with ease. He took notice of Evelin's outfit—patched hand-me-downs—and it reminded him of his upbringing, a childhood filled with holey clothes. He was unaware of how poor Lady Belle actually was before her marriage, and it brought a smile to his face to know that his employer would wed someone of such low social status.

"That I am," Evelin gleamed, taking Belle's warm hand in hers. "And you're Henry, the gardener, who also carries trunks into the manor?"

Henry blushed, pulling the doors open to welcome the women inside. "I do some odd things around Hellthorne Manor, but gardening is my specialty. Every time you see a flower, you'll think of me, I hope."

Belle snickered. *Charming.*

"Perhaps," Evelin smiled, taking notice of Henry's raving blush. She found him quite handsome—lanky, yet muscular—patches of stubble raiding his chin.

"Henry, you can take her trunk up to my room. She'll be staying with me." Belle said, squeezing Evelin's hand.

Henry raised a single brow. "She's not staying in the guest quarters?"

"*No,*" Belle countered, a hint of annoyance present in her tone. "She and I shared a bed for years. I expect no different while she visits. Please, take the trunk to the west wing."

"Yes, Lady Belle." Henry said, avoiding Belle's stern gaze as he bid the Byron sisters farewell, disappearing up the marble staircase without another word, heavy trunk in tow.

"The guest of honor has arrived!" a voice emerged, startling Evelin and prompting her to flinch. She tore her hand from Belle's, widened gaze searching the foyer in search of the sound.

Belle's sister visibly froze when Lord Bramwell strut into view, dressed in his best Sunday suit and clutching a floral mug filled nearly to the brim with raspberry tea. He looked charming as ever—alluring and sophisticated—so much so that even Belle found herself intimidated by his stance.

He oozed royalty. Power. *Virility.*

Belle would undoubtedly let the man take her any which way in that moment, for her chest heaved and ached at the sight of him. After all, he *was* her husband, and whether or not the two ever acted upon their marriage, she wouldn't necessarily *deny* him if he chose to do so . . .

If only . . .

"Miss Evelin, it's a pleasure to have you here," Bramwell announced, a friendly smirk etched across his lips. He extended an arm, offering to shake her hand as if she were his equal.

With a trembling palm, Evelin took his hand, shaking it as tightly and confidently as she could. It had been half a year since she'd been in Bramwell's presence, the last time being his and Belle's wedding reception. He looked different, now. Happier. *Bolder.*

She wondered if Belle had made him that way.

"Thank you for welcoming me into your home, my lord." Evelin smiled, chest inordinately heaving. She wondered if he could feel her racing pulse against his incredibly warm palm.

"A Byron is always welcome at the manor," Bramwell revealed, sipping his tea. "Raspberry tea, anyone? Clare made it special, there was word that Miss Evelin favored raspberry."

"I love raspberry," Evelin beamed, a faint blush tickling her cheeks. "Thank you for making me feel so welcome, Lord Bramwell. I don't mean to be rude, but would it be possible for me to be shown somewhere that I wash up?"

"I can show–" Belle began, but her husband rudely interrupted her, something he seldom did. It was unusual for him to cut her off mid-sentence, and the action prompted a fury of unappreciative flutters to invade the woman's belly.

"Clare can show her to your wing," Bramwell said, handing his unfinished tea to a smiling Clare, who managed to seamlessly appear beside him. She was stealthy—*quick*—always making Belle jump out of her shoes in fright.

"But–" Belle began, only to be disrupted once more.

"Lyren requests your presence, Belle. It's urgent, he says." Her husband explained, appearing unbothered by the matter.

Belle audibly gulped.

Lyren Deth.

He'd been staying at the manor ever since his odd encounter with the fictitious portrait of a dead girl. When the healer had cleared him of any injuries or illnesses—*he must've eaten something sour, his mind played tricks on him*—he refused to leave, persistently visiting the west wing where he claimed the woman once was.

Although Bramwell insisted that his friend stay in one of the cozy guest rooms, Lyren refused—instead taking up space in the cluttered sitting room, his nose constantly glued into the center of a dusty book, an endless supply of lukewarm lemon tea at his side. He seemed restless—*anxious*—as if the thought of departing the manor was enough to send him spiraling.

As if he was waiting for a sign that maybe—*maybe*—he was right by what he saw.

"He's doing better," Bramwell assured her, sensing her worry. "He woke up this morning speaking of his work, excited to return. He just needed a few days to rest off whatever he experienced. Go ahead, there's some fresh lemon tea and biscuits in the sitting room with him. You must be starved."

Belle nodded, delivering a gentle pat to the in between of her younger sisters shoulder blades as Evelin took off, following close on Clare's heels. It was a relief to see her sister again, for they'd never been apart for so long, and the thought of her being on the other end of the manor was enough to make Belle's stomach churn.

She hadn't realized until that moment just how homesick she really was.

As expected, Lyren was lounged in the sitting room, droopy gaze glued to the printed word of his newest read. The pages were withered and old, a musty yellow, and Belle was curious if it had ever even been read by Bramwell. She'd never even seen him touch any of the books.

"You wanted to see me?" Belle chirped; hands crossed behind her back. Every time she saw Lyren, her pulse achingly raced, her mind trailing back several days to the window. The way he grinned at her behind his flower, watching the show her and Florence had put on. He'd seen every inch of her most private areas, and even though they were separated by the delicately fogged glass, she knew that he saw everything there was to see. Her entire body burned at the thought.

Lyren shifted his stare to meet an awkward, stiff Belle; beautiful brown eyes downcast to avoid his. It was a sweet sight, and he nearly matched her wild, scarlet blush as he snapped the book shut, instantly forgetting what page he was on. The thought was insignificant, for he had more important matters to address.

"I wasn't sure if you'd come, you've been avoiding me since I decided to stay." He stood to his feet. "Do you want a biscuit? They're still warm."

"No, I'm not hungry." Belle lied, her stomach immediately betraying her. It gurgled and groaned, painfully empty and desperate for a meal that it probably would not get. Admittedly, she hadn't eaten since the previous morning, and the mere thought of food made her nauseous.

Lyren raised a suspicious brow. "Your stomach says otherwise. Just a bite?"

His dainty fingers curled around a warm, flaky biscuit, lightly pinching the snack as he tore it from the floral dish. He took several confident steps in her direction, his lanky limbs adorned with a profusion of black. It looked charming on him—highlighted the smooth paleness of his features—and oddly, Belle wondered what his slender form would look like in one of her favorite evening gowns.

Lyren shyly approached the slightly smaller woman, clouded blue gaze fixated on her pouty pink lips. Although she barely knew the man, she felt considerably warm around him—*safe*—as if he'd never let her experience any harm. It was a juvenile thought—so childish, so *silly*—but Lyren Deth was unlike any man she'd ever encountered, such a stark opposite of her emotionally absent husband, and frankly, their friendship didn't make an inkling of sense to her.

Did they even have a single thing in common?

"Just one bite," he whispered, a pleading stare. He brought the pastry up to her mouth, hesitating when she refused to entertain him.

It wasn't that she didn't want it, she just couldn't bring her body to *take* it.

Belle frowned, shifting her head to the side to avoid the snack. For a moment, she felt like crying; hot tears brimming the corners of her eyes as she bitterly blinked them away.

Lyren noticed her reaction instantly, a sympathetic frown dancing along his lips as he tossed the pastry aside. "Food isn't your friend, is it?"

Belle didn't have to reply, he just knew. He'd seen what anorexia nervosa could do to a person. He'd performed autopsies on countless victims who had wasted away, and confirming it on record always made his chest slightly ache. He knew what it was like—a revulsion to food—for he'd suffered for most of his youth, only to recently learn ways around it.

He related heavily to Belle, and the fact almost made his heart swell.

"It's my enemy," she finally answered, rounding the sofa as she took a seat. She fell against the cushions with a sigh, a single tear dipping down her cheek as she hastily brushed it away. "It has been for as long as I can remember. I don't like to tell people. I'm afraid they'll lock me up for it. Label me as mental."

"You are *not* mental," Lyren exclaimed, collapsing beside the stiff woman. She flinched at the sudden dip in the cushion, red-rimmed eyes keenly avoiding his gentle glare. "I understand, Lady Belle. More than you know."

Belle wiped another stray tear away, pulse irregularly thumping within her ribcage as she took notice of her extremely close proximity to the man. She could almost smell him—a mixture of dry cedar and grapefruit—and she nearly swooned, entirely entranced by how sweet he smelled.

"What did you want to ask me, Lyren?" Belle said, brushing the intrusive thoughts away as she continually avoided his stare. She could see him through her peripheral vision—a sweet mess of silver hair and stunning blue eyes—and she couldn't quite bite back the blush that crept up her neck.

"Oh," Lyren mumbled, mindlessly toying with the rings circling his fingers. "Well, you know about the dinner tonight, right? Bram's throwing it in honor of your little sister's arrival. There'll be maybe twenty people in attendance. Most from here in Valen, some from the Capitol."

Belle raised a curious brow, a bitter tightness pulling at her chest. "No, I actually was not informed of this dinner. I wonder if Bram planned to even tell me until the moment of."

"It just slipped his mind, I'm sure. Bram's a busy man sometimes," Lyren dryly defended, although his tone gave his true feelings away. "Anyways, after the dinner, he planned to go to the opera with some of the men. I was invited, but the opera was never my place. I was wondering if perhaps you'd like to visit a nightspot with me just on the outskirts of Valen? It's not too far, a twenty-minute carriage ride at most, but I think you'll enjoy it. You can bring your sister–"

"–Evelin." Belle finished, studying the weighty drapes over the windows, just barely parted enough to allow in several slivers of sunlight. The remainder of the light in the room was supplied by a surplus of flickering oil lamps.

Lyren smiled. "Your parents had good taste in names."

"There's five more girls besides us," Belle snorted, pleasant memories flooding her mind. The Byron's never had much—a quaint cottage by the sea, three tiny bedrooms—and yet, they always made it work. Belle roomed with Evelin, Ema, and Lilla, whereas the three youngest—Dorothy, Loen, and Fayne—were cramped in the smallest room, often sharing a bed.

Lyren's eyes boggled. "There's *seven* of you? I couldn't imagine sharing with so many siblings. I only have the one, a sister called Lyudmilla. She's a stylist in the Capitol, spends her days pampering wealthy women for considerably good pay. Doesn't make her any less of a witch, though."

Belle let out a snort, absentmindedly picking at the dry skin around her fingers. She could never fathom calling her sisters such a foul term, but then again, they were all innocent little angels, every last one of them. Even Evelin, who was just freshly eighteen.

"I'll go with you tonight," the lady said, standing to her feet. "After the dinner, I'll go with you to this *nightspot*. I'll ask Evelin if she'll go as well, I can't see why she wouldn't."

"I asked Henry to go as well, so she'll have a friend and won't feel awkward being a third." Lyren explained, snatching his book up from the cushion. He shuffled through the pages in search of where he left off, brows pulling together in frustration.

A third.

As if they were a couple.

Belle stilled, her heart racing at the thought of going to the nightspot as Lyren's date. They were friends—acquaintances, actually. Nothing more. "Henry? The gardener?"

"He's much more than a *gardener*," Lyren smiled, settling on a certain page. His slender, ring-clad fingers curled around the hardcover, pulling it close to his wild grin as he disappeared beyond the pages. "We leave at midnight. Be sure to dress warm, it'll be at or just below freezing."

With that, Lyren resumed his reading, leaving Belle absolutely stunned as she struggled to collect her thoughts. Her name reverberated off of the manor's walls, a tone paired only with that of her sister Evelin.

After all, she'd promised to give her sister a tour of Hellthorne Manor.

She left the sitting room without so much as a goodbye, glancing over her shoulder one last time to view a cocky Lyren, his nose stuffed in his book, jeweled fingers dancing through his locks. Her stomach fluttered at the sight, and she slammed the doors shut behind her with a sigh.

Fucking hell.

TASTELESS TREATS

"Are you sure it fits properly?" Evelin wondered, spinning in slow circles in the center of Belle's bedroom. She was wearing one of her elder sister's favorite evening gowns—a deep vermilion dress made out of shiny satin, with a neckline so high that it completely cloaked her throat.

"It looks lovely on you and fits perfectly." Belle assured, smiling sweetly at the sight of her sister dressed so darling and fancy. Before her marriage to Bramwell Hellthorne, Belle had never once worn a gown as lavish as these, and now, she had a wardrobe full of them.

"Thank Lilen for that, you're even smaller in the waist than I am, I was afraid it would suffocate me." A bright-eyed Evelin announced, admiring the decorative cuffs around her wrists. "This gown is probably worth more than an entire years salary from Father."

Belle frowned, a sore twinge tugging at her chest. She knew that her husband was consistently sending money to her family since the day of their union, but Evelin was right—the gown she currently wore cost almost double the amount of funds their father would bring into the home in a single year.

"It looks absolutely darling on you, Evelin," a smiling Florence spoke, standing lax beside Belle's open wardrobe. It was achingly organized—courtesy of Florence's obsessive need to keep things tidy—and Belle couldn't help but grin at the sight of her sweet love. Every moment they were apart, she missed her. *Craved* her. Her touch, her voice, her smell.

Belle wanted nothing more than to skip across the room and take Florence into her arms—to pepper loving kisses down the slope of her jaw, to tangle her fingers in the sleek black braid that trailed down her back . . .

"I don't think I ever caught your name, actually," Evelin said, interrupting Belle's lurid thoughts. Her gaze was glued to Florence, who still had that sultry smirk slapped across her mouth.

"It's Florence," Belle said only moments before her love could speak, a slight blush creeping up the skin of her neck. She loved saying her name—*Florence Florence Florence*—and she wanted to shout it from the rooftops, spell it in the brush on the mountainside, just along the ledge, so it would be visible for all of Valen to see.

Florence, my love.

"Florence Smyth, actually." Florence added, stepping forward to properly button Evelin's gown up. "It's a pleasure to make your acquaintance, Evelin. Your sister and I are rather close."

Belle blushed once more.

Rather close indeed.

"I'm glad to hear that," Evelin said, inaudibly thanking Florence for buttoning up the back of her borrowed dress. "I was worried that Belle would be lonely all the way up here in Valen. It's good that she has someone to be close to, especially someone who lives in the manor. I have heard of you from my father, actually. How you are a cousin of the lord, how you came to be his ward shortly after he began his reign."

Suddenly, Lyren's request crossed Belle's mind—talks of a nightspot on the outskirts of Valen, midnight sharp—*dress warm, it'll be just at freezing.* She recalled the generous invite of her sister, along with Henry the Gardener, who according to Lyren, was much more than just the gardener.

"Evelin," Belle started, smiling sweetly when Florence stepped over to assist her with the buttons on her gown, along with the complicated ties of her corset.

It's the latest fashion in Havensworth, don't you know?

"Yes, sister?" Evelin replied, admiring her reflection in the mirror. Her pink lips were pulled upward into a smirk, widened eyes fixated on the pricey gown as she thoroughly admired it, pinching the fabric between curious fingers and holding on tight, as if it would vanish from her form with a simple blink.

Florence knotted her fingers around the laces of Belle's corset, pulling tightly as the lady let out a tiny, uncomfortable gasp. She caught wind of Florence's hushed apologies—*royalty must look the part, breathing properly is optional for a lady*—and Belle finally answered her sister, a small cough cascading up her throat.

"I have another friend—an acquaintance, more like—who invited us to a nightspot at the cusp of midnight. He's bringing Henry along, too—you met him outside upon your arrival, he brought in your trunk—and he said it'll be cold, but lovely nonetheless, I think we could have a fair time–"

"Oh, *Belle!*" Evelin cheered, skipping forward to throw her arms around her sister's neck. "I'd be delighted to! I've always heard stories of nightspots, but as you remember, Immorium doesn't have anything of the sort, but Telly Vaine—remember the Vaine's down by the hollow—she told me *loads* of stories of nightspots in Havensworth, and how people would drink and laugh and kiss and *fuck*–"

"Great *Lottie,* Evelin–"

"Don't be such a *prude,* Belle. I'm eighteen, and I'm no stranger to such acts. Don't act all innocent when you and Dalbir were sneaking off at obscene hours of the night–"

"Okay, *okay!*" Belle exclaimed, her pale cheeks glowing a bright red. She heard Florence snicker behind her, still working hard on the ties of her corset. She'd briefly told Florence of her adventures with Dalbir, but she'd never actually confirmed the fact with her sister, for she was terrified that she'd skip right down to the lip of the water and tell their father everything.

"Jeanne's cooking tonight. She's your favorite cook, isn't she, Belle? Anyway, she's prepared not one, but *two* different soups, and a delicious, dressed rosemary fish for the main course." Florence said, patting Belle simply on the shoulder to signal that she had finished tying her corset.

Belle blushed. "Will there be potatoes?"

"Always for the lady," Florence teased, a twinkle in her eye. Evelin was too busy admiring her gown to pick up on the gentle flirt that danced between the women. "Lady Belle, if you mind, I'd like a private word with you, perhaps in the bathroom, where I can help you freshen your makeup?"

"Certainly," Belle purred, glancing over her shoulder to view her younger sister. A curious smile stretched across her lips at the sight of sweet, young Evelin—the way her dainty, nimble fingers smoothed along the satin surface of her dress, gentle eyes widened to the size of saucers as she admired the garment, nearly too stunned to speak of such beauty, such elegance, such *luxury*. Before Belle's wedding day, Evelin had never even considered coming so close to wealth, and now it was draped around her shoulders, tightened around her hips, flat along her stomach.

"Evelin, I'll see you down at dinner?" Belle said, yearning to take Florence's hand as the woman shuffled towards the door, fingers looking rather empty and considerably lonely.

"Yes, sister," Evelin grinned, dancing her fingertips along the curve of her cheeks. "It'll be the most expensive supper I've eaten, besides your wedding feast, of course."

Belle only nodded before abandoning her sister in her bedroom, greedy fingers playfully pulling at Florence's braided hair, beckoning her backwards to meet her kiss.

Florence cheerfully opened her mouth the moment they filed into the washroom, a pearly-white smirk snaked along her lips as teeth clattered upon impact, a shy sigh from her darling Belle spilling onto her tongue.

"It was torture to feel your fingers fiddling with my corset," Belle whispered between warm, wet kisses. "All the while, I kept wishing you were taking it off of me, instead of pulling it tight. I can barely breathe, you know."

Florence chuckled, teeth cautiously grazing the swollen skin of Belle's bottom lip as she cradled her fair, pink cheeks in her hands. "You'll fit right in with the guests, then. It's always been a high fashion statement—the tighter, the better. But never mind that . . ." the woman paused when Belle's greedy mouth dipped down to meet her neck, eyelids fluttering lightly closed as she breathed a sigh of content.

"Did I interrupt your train of thought?" Belle teased, her dark tone vibrating along the center of Florence's throat. She placed confident pecks along the surface, decorating the sweet skin with lovely wet patches, places just aching to be marked—*bruised.*

"There were whispers of your private meeting with Lyren Deth among the housemaidens. I overheard while rummaging through the kitchen for some peaches," Florence finally spoke, kind eyes met with widened, worried orbs. Belle had pulled away from Florence's neck, lipstick sloppily smeared along her mouth as she felt her pulse quicken within her chest.

"Nothing happened, Flo–"

"I wasn't accusing you of such," Florence interrupted, taking Belle's hands in hers. She reassuringly squeezed, as if to inaudibly say, *it's okay, I trust you.* "Actually, I was rather curious of what he might've asked. You know, I've fancied the man for a few years, now. He's an interesting fellow, and I've found my heart racing on several occasions where he was present. And now with him evidently living at the manor, tucked away beneath a stack of books in the sitting room . . ."

Belle raised a brow. "What are you implying, Florence?"

For a split second, Belle was certain that she witnessed a blush creep up Florence's neck. She'd never seen such color blossom along the woman's skin, and it only made her more beautiful—more *desirable.* Belle wanted to fold the woman up and stuff her in her pocket, to carry her around with her everywhere she went.

"I'm just *saying,*" Florence began, tightening her hold on Belle's hands once more. Her pulse had quickened so drastically that she wondered if the redheaded girl could feel her racing heart just through the thin skin of her palms. "If Lyren expressed any interest, and you feel so inclined, you should do as you please."

Belle tore her hands from Florence's, a perplexed expression drawn along her crinkled brows as she fiddled with the material of her achingly tight corset.

"Flo, I don't know if I understand–"

"Goddess *alight,* Belle," Florence laughed, eyes rolling within her skull as she cupped Belle's face in her hands. "If Lyren Deth falls to his knees and kisses your feet and begs you to put your mouth to his—or maybe even somewhere other than his mouth—*I want you to.* Doing so wouldn't be a betrayal to me. *I want you to.*"

I want you to.

Before Belle could protest, Florence had drawn her in for a kiss. It was the perfect way to silence her, and as soon as their lips met, Belle's mind went blank—a groan easing up her throat as she wound the tail of Florence's braid around her finger.

They pulled away with a sigh, and the moment Belle's vision steadied once more on Florence's flawless features, she witnessed the drip.

The bulbous bead had landed directly onto Florence's left cheek, crimson in color and perfectly circular. The woman flinched when it met her skin, fingers mindlessly drawing upwards to meet the foreign liquid.

Just as her index finger swiped along the surface, another drop fell—decorating Florence's nail red, swallowing it up whole.

"Oh, my Goddess," Belle breathed. "Flo, that's *blood.*"

"What?" Florence's forehead crinkled; her soft stare glued to the liquid dipping down the slope of her finger. "Belle, it's just water. There's probably just a leak in the ceiling. I'll let one of the housemaidens know."

Belle's eyes widened to the size of saucers as Florence dismissively dried her finger against the pale pink fabric of her dress, smearing the surface with the mark of death.

"Flo, what are you talking about? That's *blood!* I can practically smell it!" the lithe lady began to panic, heart erratically thumping within her throat as she claimed a fistful of Florence's dress in her hold. Sure enough, the stain remained; bright, fat, *red.*

Someone was dead.

"What's above us?" Belle questioned, shifting her stare to the source of the blood. Directly above Florence's head was an oozing sphere of crisp blood—vivid and fresh—as if freshly harvested from a barely rotten corpse.

Her palm met her lips, mouth contorted into a dramatic o-shape, and she stumbled backwards, nearly toppling to the tile floor in fear. Her eyelids slipped tightly shut, eager to block out the sight—the expanding stain, the evidence of foul play.

Someone was dead.

"It's just the attic and Belle, it's *water.* Look at me." Florence pressed, her frigid fingers curling around Belle's dainty wrists. *"Look!* It's not blood, it was *never* blood. Are you ill? Tired, perhaps? Belle, *look.* It's *water."*

Reluctantly, Belle blinked back into reality, her somewhat blurred vision struggling to focus on Florence's dress.

The bloodstain was gone.

Her heart skipped a fearful beat, and she glanced upward, widened eyes desperately searching for the sight that she'd sworn to have seen, only to be met with nothing but a measly water bubble.

Leaky pipes.

"Flo, I–"

"It's the nerves," Florence said, pressing her lips to Belle's forehead. "Your sister is in town, Bramwell's acting odd, Lyren Deth is telling ghost stories about a portrait of a dead girl. You're allowing the anxieties to feast on your mind, Belle. You can't let the thoughts win."

"It looked so real, Flo," Belle gasped, blinking back tears. She wasn't crazy, she wasn't. It was *blood.*

"Lyren said the same thing about the portrait," Florence politely pressed, lacing her fingers between Belle's. "I won't deny that the manor is eerie. It's easy to see things that aren't really there. But that's just it, Belle. It's never really there."

Every big name in Elantry was in Belle's line of sight.

After nearly forty minutes of nauseating pleasantries, supper began—one too many varieties of soup, and a rosemary dressed fish dish that made Belle slightly homesick. Evelin, however, seemed uninterested in most of it, claiming that father's fresh catch was better than anything the Hellthorne kitchen could cook up.

Belle knew that her younger sister was merely being proud. The Hellthorne kitchen held more spices than the Byron family could even afford, and the main course was cooked so perfectly that the meat nearly melted upon their tongues.

Belle hadn't eaten much—mostly poked, prodded, and pushed things around her plate—but the chatter from the surrounding guests lined along the table made it seem as if she'd consumed every last piece.

There was a gentleman with a pointed top hat and a wiry red mustache named Topher Hardt, and according to a jittery Bramwell, (with a smile so large and fake that it made Belle cringe), Mister Hardt was a very important individual in Elantry's government, an esteemed member of the Capitol itself.

Belle knew next to nothing about politics, especially in all of Elantry, but she knew that members of such a high jurisdiction typically held some kind of authority, and although Bramwell was royalty, even he seemed rather tense around the man.

Hardt sat directly beside Bramwell during mealtime, with a considerably younger lady sat dangerously close to his right hip. Belle wondered why she even had her own chair, for the furniture was so close to Hardt's that the wood was practically smooching, and every time the jolly man shifted in his seat, the timber would groan and creak.

He introduced her as his *lady,* but the woman looked young enough to be his daughter. The thought made Belle's stomach churn, and she did her best to avoid glancing their way, instead making small talk with the other influential beings of Valen.

She'd never felt so much of an outcast until that evening, surrounded by people born and bred into wealth, into blessedness. They'd never known what it was like to struggle.

The thought almost made her sick. *Almost.*

"Lady Hellthorne," an aged, feminine tone cheered from across the table, almost four chairs down the row. The cheery greeting knocked Belle from her dazed trance, empty eyes settling upon a middle-aged woman with brassy blonde hair and foggy, wide-rimmed spectacles. Bramwell had briefly introduced Belle to the woman just before supper was served. Her name was Ithabell Throne, and she was second in line to become Elantry's Head.

"You called, Miss Throne?" Belle said, still her silverware anxiously poking and prodding at her fish.

"The Lord of Valen informed me that you were raised on the seaside in Immorium. I've only been to visit briefly, but I've heard nothing but pleasant things. There's been talk of a technological expansion in Immorium, a business that typically resides out east in The Shores. They're trying to expand along Elantry's coasts. It could be very good for Immorium, it could bring many jobs, more population." Ithabell explained, her spectacles slightly slipping down the oily curve of her nose. She dismissively jabbed them back against her face before shoveling a particularly large piece of fish into her mouth, which was *still* spewing an array of information that Belle didn't care to hear.

Before Belle could reply, her younger sister chirped up, evidently quite bothered by the announcement of Immorium's future.

"There's not enough open land or food for such an invasion in Immorium."

It was then that Ithabell's trap finally sealed shut. She seemed positively stunned to be so boldly interrupted, especially by someone so low-class such as Evelin.

Although Belle was of her blood, her title automatically granted her the honor of *high class*, whereas Evelin still sank below the line, barely bobbing above the penniless that resided in Minnehel.

"I'm sorry, I don't think we've been acquainted–" Ithabell loosely spoke, but Evelin was confident, *bold*. She countered the older woman's words with such a sureness that Belle found herself growing envious of her courage.

"I'm the sister of Lady Hellthorne," Evelin simply said, setting down her silverware. "I still reside in Immorium, and people there are starving. My parents barely make ends meet as it is. The holy houses are flooded every Friday with starving elderly and sickly children, all lining up for complimentary bread and soup. Most of the town survives on nothing but. Most are famished, many are malnourished. There's barely a physician, he bounces between Immorium and Minnehel. Most of the town is *dying,* there is no room for advancement. There's no room for the big, the wealthy, or the privileged. Unless Elantry's higher-ups plan on taking care of who already reside there, no more should impede."

The table fell silent. Even Bramwell, who was in an especially fine mood this evening, had succumbed to a sour frown, darkened eyes glued to a stiff Belle, as if to scold *her* for what her sibling had said.

He'd married into a family of vexing, loud-mouthed youngsters.

Lyren Deth, whose presence just became known to a now squirmy Belle, currently sat directly beside the lord, and could barely contain his glee. He was proud—openly so—and he even laced his fingers around the stem of his wine glass, bringing the liquid to his lips in order to conceal his smile. Sat directly beside him was an equally amused Florence, her own fingers laced around a silver fork as she pushed a piece of fish around her plate.

"Well, that was quite a statement." Topher Hardt suddenly said, wiping his mouth with a severely stained cloth napkin. "I'm sure your view of Immorium is a bit clouded, child. Elantry has always taken care of their people, that I can assure you. Even the penniless in Minnehel are taken good care of. You can count on that. Not a single child of Elantry goes hungry."

At that statement, Belle swallowed a sarcastic chuckle. Everyone in Elantry knew just how skewed the government's views were of their country—*everything was always perfect, nothing less*—and she knew that they fibbed frequently to other nations on the mainland. Elantry was its own continent—a secluded island surrounded completely by water—but word often traveled beyond the water to places nearby, whether it be by boat or by a simple note tied to the foot of an eager bird, it got places.

The heads of Elantry would never let any other country think that their land was anything less than perfect.

Belle's soft, brown stare studied her sister's strained expression, a shy, pink tint staining her cheeks as Topher Hardt's words dug deep. Evelin was young, but not even the slightest bit foolish. The Byron sisters were taught from a young age by their father of the toxicity and corruption within the walls of Elantry's Capitol—how the people of

Havensworth, even those not a part of the government, were so deeply propagandized. Even the lives of the severely poor in Minnehel were heavily fabricated—leaving the wealthy thoroughly convinced that the penniless were content, healthy, and heartily fed.

None of which were even remotely true.

Minnehel housed the largest criminal institution in all of Elantry—a frigid, stone-walled establishment that reeked of rot and decay. Black, bubbling mold crept up the walls, food was sparse, illness persistently present.

All of Elantry's criminals were sent to Minnehel to complete their sentences. None of which would ever finish, for they'd often succumb to starvation, disease, insanity, or cold-blooded murder by a fellow inmate.

"Elantry treats its people well," Bramwell suddenly spoke, his faux, cheery tone slicing through the silence like a rusted blade. "It's a privilege to have you in attendance, Mister Hardt. Your presence is always welcome in Valen, and especially so at Hellthorne Manor. The people of Valen think very highly of those in our government. We like to think that we're a family of sorts to those in Havensworth."

"And that you are, Lord Hellthorne," Topher Hardt said through a mouthful of potatoes. "If you weren't tied down to this ruddy estate, I'd have half a mind to appoint you a senate position up in Havensworth. Although, such a spot would strip you of your royalty, and your ties to Valen. For that, I could never do."

"The thought is well appreciated," Bramwell said, smiling softly at the statement. For a moment, Belle felt a bit of resentment bubble up within her chest, for her husband's pitiful, kiss-ass speech had certainly embarrassed her in front of her sister. She wasn't completely certain of Bram's views about Elantry's government—politics were not a topic discussed amongst the pair—but the idea of her betrothed being so blind, so *eager* to accept and support such a corrupt government almost made Belle see red.

Almost.

Topher Hardt spoke once more.

"You pump her pregnant yet, Bramwell?" the man asked between mouthfuls of food.

Evelin nearly choked on her food, and Belle's heart ceased to beat.

"Not quite yet," Bramwell lightly dismissed, stiff in his seat. "We're still so recently wed, you know."

"Your father gave all of us a right good scare hiding you away, you know," Topher said with a shake of his head. "When the news broke of both his and your mother's death, we were all certain that the Hellthorne reign had come to a close, with no heir to assume the title. Then some teenage boy none of us had ever even known crawls from the bowels of the manor, and thus, you were awarded the crown. Then, barely still a boy yourself, you take on a ward, your orphaned cousin. Still mostly a boy, and the guardian of a girl less than five years your own age. It was quite a time, then, Bramwell."

"Quite a time indeed." Bramwell muttered, meeting Florence's small stare. It was evident that Topher hadn't even recognized the woman, now that she was more woman than girl.

"That it was," Topher mutually agreed. "Don't follow in those footsteps of your father, Bramwell. The man was a ruddy liar, a thief, a killjoy. Nearly ruined the Hellthorne name and did worse by keeping his kin some strange secret. Take that girl to bed and fuck her nice and good. Put a baby in her soon, and do it well, Bramwell. Valen would be pleased to see a Hellthorne child, it's been far too long."

The remainder of supper was, for the most part, mostly pleasant to everyone but the Byron sisters. Ithabell Throne and Bram cracked corny jokes, most of which in regard to old money, subjects Belle barely understood.

Florence slowly shoveled food into her mouth, her bright eyes catching Belle's as often as possible. Every time their stares met, a batch of butterflies frolicked about within Belle's belly, a blush threatening to creep up her neck as she watched her darling girl silently eat. To others, Florence was nothing but Bramwell's ward. Another playing piece in the manor on top of the hill.

But, to Belle, Florence was like a bright, beaming, ball of pink light—her presence instantaneously brightening the room every time she entered.

She even caught Lyren's stare several times, and noticed that he, too, was fond of Florence's company, a dash of a peppered, red blush tickling his pale cheeks when their eyes briefly met.

Florence's voice echoed between Belle's ears.

I want you to.

Suddenly, a fantasy struck Belle's vision—a lovely sight. Two warm, welcoming bodies, a tiny Belle laid snug in between. Florence's thick curls sprawled across her bare chest. Lyren's thin, curious fingers dancing along Belle's bony hip.

Metal met glass as Bramwell tapped the tip of his fork against his half-drank glass of wine. The members of the table quickly quieted, and the lord clambered to his feet, a crooked grin slapped across handsome features.

"That concludes our supper," he began, raising his glass. "If you don't mind, I'd like to toast to my beautiful wife, if you'll all join me in raising a glass."

Belle's chest ached, widened eyes inquisitively focused on a confident Bramwell, his own gaze unfaltering.

"To Belle. This dinner—and all of the meals to come—is for you, and for your darling sister, our guest of honor. Welcome to Valen, Evelin. And Belle—my wife, the one who keeps me whole, keeps me *grounded*. Everything I do is for you."

"To Evelin and Belle." The table cheered, and everyone took a sip.

Everyone but Lyren Deth, who hadn't joined in on the chant, nor had he taken a sip of his wine. Instead, the rim of the glass just barely brushed his lips, a hint of melancholy hidden beyond his blank expression.

Evelin's fingers laced around Belle's knee, forming together to elicit a small squeeze. It was evident that she was overjoyed for her sister, beside herself with glee.

In Evelin's eyes, Belle was the luckiest girl alive.

"Now," Bramwell continued, finally tearing his stare away from his clearly confused bride. "If the men of the table would join me for a traditional night at the opera, where we will smoke cigars, drink brandy, and have our fancies tickled by sheer, raw talent until the wee hours of the morning. To the wonderful women in attendance, if you wish to stay the night, there are plenty of empty rooms at Hellthorne to house most of Immorium."

There was a soft chuckle amongst the crowd, the loudest laugh emerging from Hardt himself.

"My best ladies, Ula and Clare, will accompany each of you to your own rooms. Awaiting you will be a small stack of books, lavender tea, blackberry scones, and a warm, comfortable bed. It's been a pleasure hosting all of you on this fine night." Bramwell concluded, bowing slightly as the room erupted in applause.

Neither Lyren, nor Belle, contributed.

As the room emptied and both Ula and Clare began to guide the women towards Belle's wing, Bram requested the presence of his wife in private.

"Is that necessary, Bram?" Belle whispered, careful not to let any of the guests overhear. On the outside, the couple appeared content. *Happy.*

What none of them knew, was that they slept in separate beds on entirely opposite sides of the manor, and during the day in Belle's bed frequently laid a nude Florence, who to most, was nothing more than just the ward.

"Please cooperate with me, Belle," Bram lowly begged, his tone indistinguishable. He didn't ask much of the woman—hardly had any favors or requests at all—so she felt compelled to oblige, knowing that whatever it was, it must be of some importance to the man.

He led her to a nearby sitting room, one that was infrequently used due to its diminutive size. Thick layers of dust cloaked the furniture, masking the once lavish furnishings with a muddy, dark gray hue. Belle nearly felt a sneeze coming on just from being present in a room so dusty.

"Why do the housemaidens never clean this room–"

"I'm sorry, Belle." Bramwell said, avoiding her stare. His fingers barely brushed against hers—a tiny inkling of affection, and she took note of how visibly uncomfortable he was by just touching her hands.

"I overstepped. I made you uncomfortable. Certainly, I made Florence uncomfortable as well. I never want to overstep the bond between you two. I just—I need for us to appear *convincing*, Belle. Topher Hardt was the one who threatened to strip me of my title, he was counting down the days until my thirtieth year, taunting me, almost. I can't have him suspect that you and I aren't in love."

Belle was taken aback by Bramwell's bold honesty, the way he seemed on edge—*nervous*. It was uncommon for him to appear as such, for typically he was brave, confident, and self-assured.

Belle's heart swelled, and she told the man something she'd never said before. It was an entirely platonic feeling—that she knew—but nevertheless, it was still true.

"Bram, I *do* love you."

A small smile captured his face.

"There's nothing for you to worry about. I'd never spoil our arrangement. You've been nothing but good to me." Belle whispered, claiming his clammy hands in hers. She felt him slightly flinch at the contact—unsure if he enjoyed it or not—and she'd dropped his hands just as quickly as she'd claimed them, eager not to push him any further than he was comfortable with.

"And I love you, Belle Byron. You make me feel like the luckiest man alive." His full lips pulled into a genuine grin, and for a split second, Belle found herself wanting to take a step forward, to stand atop her tippy-toes and plant a sweet, tender smooch along the surface.

She wasn't quite sure if the temptation and deep-riddled desire to be affectionate with her husband would ever quite disappear.

"Lyren Deth was visibly uncomfortable during the toast," Bramwell added, his tone tinted with uncertainty. "He's been kind to you, yes?"

"Of course," Belle breathed, nodding curtly. "He's been nothing but sweet. There's no foul tension between us, I swear of it. You'd be the first to know if there was anyone I was uncomfortable with."

"Besides Topher Hardt and Ithabell Throne," Bramwell dryly teased, earning a small giggle from his wife. "Don't worry, they nearly give me the hives. They're only invited purely for social status."

"I figured as such," Belle whispered, resisting the undying urge to grab Bramwell's hands once more. "Have a lovely time at the opera tonight. I'll be accompanying Henry, Lyren, and Evelin to a nightspot near midnight, if you don't mind."

The woman paused after revealing her plans, suddenly unsure if she should've shared such a thing with Bramwell. She never quite knew how he would react—*what if he said no?*—and almost as quickly as the statement emerged, she wished that she could take it right back.

Instead, Bramwell only nodded.

"I expect you'll be careful. Nightspots in Valen can be shoddy at times. Lyren knows his way around them quite well, he's spent too many nights with too many women in the alleyways behind the clubs. I trust he'll keep you and your sister safe. If not, I'll have his head."

With that, Bramwell delivered a soft pat to Belle's shoulder, and excused himself from the room.

A KISS FROM AN ANGEL

Just as promised, the Byron sisters met both Henry and Lyren on the cusp of midnight in the front foyer of the manor.

The mansion was dark and quiet, the only noise was that of the creaks and groans from the aged structure. Guests were tucked away within their borrowed beds, some still awake, a steadily burning oil lamp illuminating the yellowed pages of old, dusty books.

Several dying candles lit the room, providing only just enough light for both Belle and Evelin to see several feet before them. The young men were crowded by the door, a hushed conversation dancing between their lips as they awaited their dates for the evening.

"You made it!" Lyren lightly cheered, careful not to raise his voice. "Henry boy and I were worried the pair of you wouldn't show."

Henry politely greeted both of the girls, blushing slightly when his stare settled upon a pink-cheeked Evelin. Lyren also introduced himself to Belle's sister, his hand slipping easily into hers as he gave it a soft shake. It took her a moment to snatch her hand from the depths of her three overcoats, for she wasn't used to the bitter breeze that Valen had to offer at such a late hour, and with the sun settled into sleep beyond the horizon, there was no source of warmth to cut through the cold.

"There's fresh flurries outside," Henry announced, readily recalling Evelin's desire to see snow. A gleeful grin immediately captured her features, arms tautly crossed as she begged to see snow for the very first time.

"It's gorgeous, sister. You'll love it." Belle beamed, lacing her arm within Evelin's. She'd seen her first snowfall two months prior, for the very tip of Valen sees snow dreadfully early in autumn, almost completely skipping over the season entirely. It was as if the black manor was eager to be covered in white.

Desperate to be purified.

Just as expected, Evelin was over the moon at the sight of the dainty, white flurries that gently fell from the clouds. There was already a horse-drawn carriage parked at the end of the pebbled path, a sleepy coachman bundled up in three coats, just as Evelin was.

"Evening, Charles." Lyren lightly greeted, shaking the coachman's heavily gloved hand. The older man seemed delighted to be greeted, especially in such an informal way, and he beckoned them into the cabin, which was stuffed with an assortment of warm, cozy blankets.

Evelin's voice filled the carriage for the entirety of the twenty-minute ride, deep-rooted excitement present in her chipper tone as she continued on about the stories that her friend Telly Vaine would tell her about nightspots in Havensworth. At most of the tales, Lyren simply laughed, his knee unintentionally brushing against Henry's on multiple occasions as the Byron sisters sat bundled up together in the bench directly opposite them.

"I have my fair share of tales too, but most of which would scar your innocent ears," Lyren said, motioning towards Evelin. The teenage girl animatedly rolled her eyes.

"I've done things that would make *you* blush, Lyren, I'm sure of it."

"You've only just met me," Lyren slyly countered. "You're severely misguided by what you think would make *me* blush. I had marks on my fingers for days after one of my visits to this particular spot, all due to the old money pearls strung around a wealthy woman's neck."

Belle felt the heat rise up to her cheeks at the thought of Lyren hidden away within the dark, slim alleyway of downtown Valen, his hand around a wealthy woman's throat, his fingers digging into the necklace around her neck.

For a moment, she wondered what it felt like to have his ring-clad fingers latched around *her* throat, and as soon as the visual blinded her, Lyren's baby blue glare met hers, a slight smirk teasing the corner of his mouth, as if he could read her filthy thoughts.

Anxiously, Belle brushed the daydream away, tearing her stare from Lyren's as if to avoid him entirely. Surely, he would be taken aback by the lurid visuals that plagued her mind.

Or would he share the very same?

When the carriage came to a shuddering halt—the horses irritably sighing in response to the below-freezing temperatures—Evelin could hardly contain her excitement, frozen fingers slipping between Belle's as she urged the three of them out into the cold.

"Let's *go!* The Goddesses just know that I need stories of my own to spill to Telly Vaine. I want tonight to make all of her experiences in Havensworth seem insignificant." Evelin exclaimed, dark eyes severely widening at the sight of Valen's most populated nightspot.

It was unlike any type of architecture Belle had ever seen before. It was as if the walls were slapped together by heaping handfuls of mud, sloppily stacked and haphazardly placed. There wasn't a lick of smoothness to the surface, and she found herself wanting to reach out and touch the tan stained surface, to run her frigid digits down the side and caress each and every little curve.

There was not a single window in sight, and if there wasn't such a bold, brazen black door in the stark center of the structure, Belle wouldn't have guessed that it was truly a building at all, but merely a peculiar, endless wall stacked tall.

There were several scanty groups of individuals draped along the entryway, all huddled together and bundled up to their necks in thick, warm attire. Their expressions were revealed by the weak, warm glow of the exterior lamps, hot flames kissing the circular glass. Pinched within most of their gloved fingers were a mixture of lit cigars and pipes, which generated a healthy mix of smoke, combined with the misty clouds of warm exhales.

A burly man donning a red-checkered tie and top hat three inches too tall for his round, petite face was guarding the entrance, black pools for eyes intently studying the quartet as they clambered from their carriage.

Evelin was youthful in appearance and character, and nearly as soon as she'd arrived upon the sealed iron door, the guard had raised a single palm, wordlessly instructing the group to stop in place.

"I'd expect you wouldn't be bringing a child near these parts at such an hour, Deth." the man spoke, his voice nearly a half octave higher than Belle had anticipated. He was neither fit, nor tall—and she was curious as to what he'd even do if a physical altercation had arisen.

"She may not look it, but she's all of eighteen, Cullen. I wouldn't dare risk my reputation by bringing in a child." Lyren slurred, the words slipping so eloquently off of his silver tongue. His demeanor was so poise—so *composed*—as if the world would simply fall to his feet if he'd requested it.

Admittedly, Belle found herself heavily attracted to the trait, and the base of her neck grew hot with blush.

Cullen's dark gaze studied a rigid Evelin, whose hand was still tautly laced within Belle's. It was true, she looked several years younger than her true age. It had proven itself as both a blessing and a curse.

"You trust that she's telling you the truth, then? You'd be willing to take the risk, Deth?"

"Her sister is Lady Hellthorne," Lyren revealed, soft stare swiftly meeting Belle's. The royal wife looked charming as ever—her beautiful, ruby red hair pulled back into a compli-cated braid, one which draped down the length of her back.

It allowed the public to fully view her face, the sharp features of her jaw, the pointed curve of her nose. The abundance of coats that cloaked her thin frame nearly dwarfed her entirely, and once she'd rid herself of them after stumbling inside, she'd nearly shrink twice in size.

Cullen's expression faltered, jaw hung slack as he looked Lady Belle up and down, as if in disbelief. She'd only been on two or three very public outings with the Lord of Valen, one of them being her coronation three weeks post-marriage.

That had been the only time Cullen had laid his own two eyes on the woman, and now he'd realized just how foolish he'd been, for anyone in Valen should recognize that vibrant, red hair from a mile away.

She was royalty.

"My deepest apologies, your lady. It was rash of me to question the age of your sister in such a manner. If you'll forgive me?" Cullen stumbled over his words, as if there were a split possibility that the lady would sever his head clean off of his shoulders if he wasn't forgiven.

Admittedly, Belle wasn't especially fond of special treatment. After all, she was just an ordinary girl from the seaside of Immorium, born to a fisherman, raised in poverty . . .

"I'll inform the barkeeper that the four of you will not pay a single cent during your visit. Even you, Deth. All drinks are on us for my ignorance. I hope you'll accept such apology, my lady–"

"None of that is necessary," Belle interjected, squeezing her sister's hand. "Although, your apology is well appreciated. All I wish is to enjoy a night out with my sibling and my friends."

Evelin's chapped, red lips curled into a playful smirk, a sense of thrill tickling the tip of her throat as Cullen led the four individuals inside.

What they'd stumbled into was entirely unexpected.

Even Henry, who had been bizarrely quiet during the past few moments, had let out a gasp at the sight, a plethora of statements oozing off of his tongue as he studied the scene before him.

Lyren Deth was elated, that much was obvious. He could barely wipe the sultry smirk from his lips as he observed the trio's reaction, their doe-liked gazes desperately taking in the area.

"It's like Eden," Henry announced, his voice moderately raised in order to be heard over the frantic tune played by several string instruments. He was unable to tear his attention away from a surplus of feathery, white wings, which frolicked about the area. Although clearly costumes, the wings looked nearly real, extending outward from each individual's sides by a whopping three or four feet.

They not only donned the backs of women, but of men, also. Gorgeous, beaming, bright white angels, features concealed by varying masks, creative, artistic veils to protect their everyday identities.

On the outside, they were human. Within these walls, they were the angels.

"Not just Eden," Belle began, spotting a heap of bold, black winged creatures. "The Netherworld, also."

It was something Belle couldn't quite believe in—Eden and the Netherworld. Both destinations were spoken greatly of in the Good Book, described in great detail to all of its readers.

Everyone wanted to go to Eden. It was where the Goddesses—Lottie, Lilen, and Liv—all resided, their bums planted in stunning silver thrones, an array of jewels stamped along their skin. Most Pliritans desired nothing more than to place kisses along the smooth, manicured feet of their most adored Goddesses, the women who kept them safe, sane, and fed.

Only, if they even existed at all, most of the population in Minnehel wouldn't succumb to starvation on a daily basis, Belle thought.

If the Goddesses actually existed, there would be no famine.

No war.

No disease.

No wrongful death. Babies wouldn't die in their mothers' wombs, rot the women from the inside out, poison their blood and stop their hearts.

The penniless wouldn't starve, the people wouldn't sin.

"Are these all Pliritans?" Evelin asked, tearing her hand from Belle's. The teenage girl knew quite well that her sister was practically pagan, that the idea of Eden and the Netherworld were nothing but fables told to frighten people into behaving.

Evelin thought much differently than Belle. She, like many others who practiced Plirity, dreamt nightly of meeting the Goddesses face to face on the day of her demise.

"Not necessarily," Lyren shrugged, leading them further into the establishment. "It's mostly just a theme. The light, the dark. Simply put, angels are rather sexy. Are they not? Even the dark ones. *Especially* the dark ones. I've had a few black-winged women and men sit in my lap on more occasions than one."

Belle raised a brow.

Women and *men?*

Her pulse quickened at the thought of Lyren being so open and accepting as she was. How she'd taken such a liking to Florence, another woman.

Sinful in the eyes of the Goddesses.

A disgrace.

Her admiration for Lyren Deth nearly tripled within an instant.

"The Netherworld is nothing to play with, Lyren." Evelin said, her mood slightly dampening. Both her innocence and immaturity had reared its ugly head, but with striking patience, Lyren sweetly countered her statement.

"It's only a costume, Evelin. There's nothing to fret over. Your soul is still in line with the Goddesses, that I can thoroughly guarantee." the blond boy effortlessly spoke, a sweet smile strung along his lips as he reassuringly pat Evelin on the shoulder.

His statement appeared to brighten her spirits, and Henry—who was still trapped within a trance—offered to take all three of her coats from her.

"Can I take your coat, m'lady?"

Lyren had found his way to Belle's side, warm breath dancing along the shell of her ear as he bent downward to meet her tiny frame. She was shorter than him, but only just—for he wasn't the tallest, nor most masculine of men, but every time his bright blue eyes met hers, she felt a burst of adrenaline surge throughout her entire being.

"Don't call me that," Belle softly teased, her little voice barely audible above the music. Still, she offered the man her coat, a burly, black thing made of fur. She watched with wonder as Lyren shrugged out of his own overcoat, revealing a whimsical, ladylike tunic adorned with silken frills. It was brave, what he wore. Belle figured that the attire was relatively common in the Capitol, for the wealthy often dressed quite nicely in Havensworth, but if Lyren had made the decision to walk amongst Immorium's wet soil dressed as such, he'd surely be spoken of for months—maybe even years to come.

The people of Immorium were sullied by the ways of Plirity—masculine men, feminine women. Marriage, often arranged, expected and nearly required. Children always followed.

Be plentiful and bless the earth with your seed.

The scripture made Belle's stomach churn, and she visibly flinched when Lyren's curious fingers met the curve of her clothed elbow.

He took note of her reaction but chose not to acknowledge it out loud. Instead, he simply spoke, "would the Lady of Valen care for a drink?"

Belle grinned. "Something particularly poisonous, if you'd be so kind."

It wasn't every night that the woman had such an opportunity as this, and the thought of going home sober was enough to nearly turn her mood somewhat sour.

Henry and Evelin excitedly excused themselves moments later, skipping hand in hand through a mess of varying angels, disappearing into an abyss of black and white.

The light versus the dark.

A perfect balance.

Just as she'd requested, Lyren soon returned to Belle's stiff side, two glasses of whiskey sloshing about within his clutch. It was evident that the woman felt slightly out of place within these walls, for she'd barely moved an inch since her sister's gleeful departure.

"Don't be so shy," Lyren teased, politely placing the glass into her hand. "Drink up and come dance. You must see the costumes the musicians have on. Their masks are some of the most beautiful artworks I've ever seen, and their talents triumph even that."

Lyren appeared entirely in-tune with his surroundings, and although Belle already knew that he was a frequent visitor, his demeanor proved the point over tenfold. Angels of both light and dark wafted between the pair, moving so gracefully that it almost appeared as if they were floating. The entire aura was nothing short of magical, and the flickering oil lamps that hung from dated chandeliers painted each and every one of their masks with varying patterns.

With a sudden burst of sureness, Belle took a significant swig of her drink, putting back nearly half of the liquid inside. It burned all the way down her throat, and she couldn't help but stick her tongue out in disgust.

The childish reaction amused Lyren greatly, and his lips pulled into a boyish grin, exposing the whites of his teeth. He, too, raised the glass to his mouth, taking an incredibly generous sip as he downed the drink immediately.

Belle watched in awe as he discarded the empty glass with class, politely placing it atop a tray neatly stacked with empty dishes. The tray belonged to a dark angel, a slender man nearly half a foot taller than Lyren, with a feathered, black mask concealing his features.

"Take my hand," Lyren loosely requested, unable to stifle his smile. He rotated his weight between either leg, the alcohol instantly abolishing whatever nerves he had.

"What for, Lyren Deth?" Belle lightly teased. It was her turn to finish her drink, and as the male angel slightly hovered, she felt compelled to hand over an empty glass. With a deep breath, she swallowed what remained, swallowing hard to force every last drop down before placing the cup directly next to Lyren's on the tray.

"I've just told you," Lyren slurred, having to raise his voice slightly to be heard over the screeching violins. "The musicians. They're a sight to see."

Belle took his hand, her remarkably chilly touch instantly warming within Lyren's hot palm. The two weaved between a massive crowd, people from every stretch of Valen—from the upscales, to the suburbs, and even the trenches, it appeared—were all in attendance. Social status didn't quite matter in a place like this.

Belle spotted corsets of every hue, women with deep desires to impress, and evidently didn't mind not being able to breathe. Leather boots, some cracked, others polished, dancing amongst one another, not minding in the slightest how drab or poor the other may be.

It almost truly did feel like a version of Eden within these walls, even with the presence of the dark angels, who slunk about, the tips of their wings gently caressing the shoulders of Valen's people.

Belle spotted her sister in between an array of dissimilar angels, standing nearly in the center of the dance floor. She was opposite a chipper Henry, identical drinks within each of their grasps. They were dancing—heartily, *joyously*—and Belle caught wind of a genuine belly laugh from her younger sibling, one which made Evelin toss her head back on her shoulders, one which made Henry the gardener flush a bright red.

And then, they disappeared. Right into the crowd, blending in with the people of Valen as if they truly belonged. Just a moneyless girl from Immorium, one who shared a bedroom with her younger sisters, and a gardener from Szo Landing, a man only six months younger than Belle, but with the maturity of a thirty-year-old gentleman.

Perhaps little Evelin Byron had found herself an excellent match.

Lyren led the redheaded girl to a brick-lined stage, one which was neatly decorated with an assortment of floral arrangements, all of which appeared to blossom and bloom, even after being torn from their cozy home in the ground.

Just as Lyren had described, a quartet of musicians claimed the stage, the aging, fractured wood beneath their feet visibly shifting with every tiny movement they made. It was probable that the platform would give out at any given moment, but the group didn't seem to care, for they seamlessly played, their bows gliding along the strings at an impeccable pace.

Each of them wore a mask unique to their own self. Three of the performers were men, whereas one of them—the tallest of the bunch—was a woman, with a physique so striking that it made Belle considerably envious.

The lady of the band strut a mask that only concealed her eyes—a gold-plated venetian mask, with a series of differing designs coating the surface. Within her clutch was a gorgeous violin, and her slender, brown fingers were moving so swiftly—so *flawlessly* along the strings that Belle could barely see them.

The pace of the tune steadily increased, and for a moment, Belle locked eyes with the violinist, her lips parted in awe as she admired the musician. The violinist took note of Belle's gawking, and the sight brought a smile to her face.

"She's fantastic, isn't she?" Lyren exclaimed, his voice barely audible over the melody.

"She's so good." Belle said, unable to tear her stare from the woman. She was entranced by how easily she played, as if it came naturally to her. For a moment, Belle wondered if her husband would perhaps gift her a violin, and maybe one day, she would spend her evenings upon that very stage, bright hair pulled back, a mask covering her face.

"Best violinist in all of Elantry, that one is." Lyren added. He spoke several more words, all of which were lost to the music, and when he was able to capture Belle's attention once more, he'd requested her hand in dance.

Shyly, she took it—fingertips barely brushing against Lyren's, as if with uncertainty. He grinned wildly, and claimed her hand whole, tugging the tiny girl close, their bodies numbly colliding.

Belle tripped over her own two feet, the flat of her forehead smacking against Lyren's chin. Instinctively, her free hand climbed up to meet the throbbing spot, a puzzled giggle tickling her lips as the blond boy burst into laughter.

"M'sorry," he playfully slurred, dropping her hand. She took note of where his touch went—how it wandered down her sides, barely brushing the surface of her corset, one that was slightly on the larger side and didn't quite suffocate her as much as some of the others she'd recently worn.

Her pulse quickened, and Lyren's palms flattened against her hips, applying the smallest amount of pressure in a weak attempt to sway her hips from side to side.

"I know how to dance, Lyren Deth." Belle teased, but he hadn't heard her the first time, prompting the woman to nearly shout the statement two and a half more times. The volume of the music steadily increased, and Belle swore that she could feel each tug of the strings jumpstart her heart.

"It's *loud*," she shouted, and Lyren led her into a twirl, spinning her around thrice before pulling her back into his body, a cozy little den, a sweet, comfortable spot.

She molded into his arms like the perfect piece of a jigsaw puzzle, a cardboard painting cut up, divided into a series of odd angles. He was the circular Tab, sticking straight out, waiting for its perfect socket. She was the warm, welcoming Blank, the inward curve, a spot that was made just for the Tab.

A perfect fit.

His hands trailed lower, dangerously so, and Belle's heart leapt into her throat when Lyren barely brushed against the crest of her bottom, the very spot where her corset ended and the silken, smooth surface of her deep maroon dress began once again.

It was a dreadfully large garment—as most of her clothing was, she was smaller than most women her age—but the corset gave it shape, highlighting the way her hips just barely protruded, how her bum gently curved, dipping down to meet her thin legs.

Her relationship with food that torturously taken a toll on her physique, but it wasn't anything new. She'd grown used to it—it was a part of her, now.

"Is this all right?" Lyren lowly inquired, leaning forward to meet her ear. The words were warm against her skin, and Belle couldn't quite mask the goosebumps that arose along the pale flesh.

She nodded, but before Lyren could venture further, Belle increased the pace of their steps—nearly throwing him off course as she directed him into a sloppy form of the waltz, one which didn't quite match the beats of the strings.

"What beat are you following?" Lyren called, frantically meeting her hands in an attempt to steady himself. She only laughed, taking one too many steps to truly define the dance as a waltz, and she could only imagine what her mother would think if she saw her eldest daughter completely butcher a dance that was meant to be elegant as ever.

The pair continued to dance to the beat of their own tune, completely off-key and missing most of the steps. On more than one occasion, Lyren skipped to the tapster, bumping shoulders with several white-winged angels, nearly dropping drinks left and right.

Belle spilled half of her second brandy down the front of her dress, the chilled liquid slipping between her breasts, prompting a shiver to claim her spine. Both Henry and Evelin had joined them by this time in the evening—or early morning, rather—and a giggly, loose-lipped Evelin struggled to rid Belle's dress of the liquid with a deep lavender cloth.

In the end, it was an ebony-winged saint who came to Belle's aid, a cloth soaked with warm water gently massaging the stain in tedious circles. It was a woman within the wings, with hair a frizzy blonde, and green eyes barely visible beyond a duel-horned disguise. The mask completely covered her face, and as Belle studied the woman delicately cleaning her clothed chest, she couldn't help but wonder what the angel's true identity was.

"The stain should be out, Lady Hellthorne," the angel had said, proudly studying her hard work. There was a sopping wet spot along the breasts of her dress, but none of that mattered to Belle, for her expression had almost immediately fell at the angel's statement.

Lady Hellthorne.

So, most of the attendees had known of her identity, after all. Not that it was any secret, but the idea of being just an ordinary citizen of Valen slightly comforted Belle.

Only, she would never be just that.

Royalty would follow her until her dying breath.

With a dress still damp, Belle returned to the dance floor, an additional drink sloshing within her hand as she met the trio she'd come with. Lyren and Henry had been taking turns twirling Evelin around on her heels, a sweet, toothy smile constantly stamped along her lips as she bounced between the men.

There was something special about the way Henry watched her—how his gaze softened, even with his drunken, hazy vision. He couldn't quite keep his eyes off of her, and every time he had a hold of her, Belle watched as his hands politely wandered, careful not to slip too far inward, nor too low.

He was a gentleman first and foremost, but Belle could see his desire—his lust. It was written all over his face.

Perhaps, he and Evelin would fall deeply in love, and he'd convince her to pack up and move out to Valen, where she could visit Hellthorne Manor as often as she desired—have supper with Belle every evening, or a cup of tea to start the day.

It would be bliss, Belle thought, and she was entirely lost in thought when Lyren met her side.

"They're precious, they are," he said, and Belle knew that she wasn't the only one who'd noticed the bond between Henry and her sister.

"Maybe they'll marry, and he'll move her to Valen," Belle added, and the tempo of the music shifted to a slow, sultry tempo.

The crowd instantly shifted moods, and couples fell into one another's arms, noses buried into necks, lips dancing against lips.

Lyren extended his palm, and he took a bow.

"Would a man as myself be lucky enough to have this dance?"

Belle's lips pulled into a smile, and she discarded her barely sipped drink onto a nearby tray, one which was balanced upon the fingertips of another light-bearing angel.

She'd surely see angels in her dreams that night. Whether they be of Eden or of the Netherworld, she wasn't entirely sure, nor did she quite seem to care. Either place seemed like a little slice of paradise in comparison to her drab, everyday life, locked away within a manor with no one to keep her company but the friendly arms of her lover, Florence Smyth.

Not that she was entirely complaining, but the chance to be somewhere entirely different—somewhere *new,* and with the handsome Lyren Deth—was exhilarating.

She wondered if he'd want to go out the following night, and the night after, and then after that.

"Consider yourself lucky then, Lyren Deth. The dance is yours." Belle said, sliding her hand into his once more.

The perfect fit.

Lyren drew her close, and she met his chest with ease. They fell into step as if they'd done it a million times before this very night, and as he held her within his inviting embrace, she couldn't help but wonder—*is this home?*

Or a version of it, perhaps?

Home was Florence Smyth. She'd found comfort—*safety*—within the woman's gorgeous, tender arms. Found home within the smell of the rose scented soap that claimed her skin. Found home within the thick tendrils that trailed down her back, how the curls were coarse to the touch, but Belle could run her fingers through them with ease, not a single knot in sight.

Florence was home, surely, but Belle began to wonder if there were more than four walls to a home—if more than one *person* could be her version of a home.

Surely, there had to be room in her heart for more than just one. The universe felt too open—too *complex*—for a soul to be tied to just one single other. But rather, several. Multiple.

There was room in Belle Hellthorne's heart for more than just one lover, this much, she was sure. And, with Florence's promising approval, and the way she'd even *urged* for Belle to let Lyren in, it confirmed all of her suspicions.

Florence felt the very same.

Her nose found its way to Lyren's neck, the very tip just barely brushing against his shy, soft skin. A thin layer of perspiration claimed the surface—a warm reminder that he was human, after all—and Belle couldn't help but notice just how pleasant he truly smelled. A kind mixture of citrus and earth, as if he'd taken a dip in a lemon bath before dressing himself to the nines in his stunning attire, and then buried himself within a book, the smoky scent of the old pages sticking to his skin.

It was hypnotizing, and Belle couldn't help but flatten her nose against his skin, eyelids fluttering closed as she breathed him in. They'd been rocking back and forth to the tune of an ancient cello, the string instrument only slightly out of tune, a characteristic that made it truly unique.

For a moment, she didn't mind that she was surrounded by people of Valen, who knew her as no one but Lord Bramwell Hellthorne's wife, and how in this very moment, she had her face buried within the neck of someone who was *not* Bramwell Hellthorne.

Most of the regular attendees knew greatly of Lyren—that much she knew—and she had a sliver of hope that perhaps, they wouldn't think much of the scene. Some may even know of his friendship with Bramwell and write the entire thing off as just two friends enjoying one another's company.

But, even Belle could tell that wasn't true by the race of his heart as it erratically beat against her palm, which was cradling his chest.

Swallowing her worries once and for all, Belle succumbed to her drunken state of euphoria, enjoying Lyren's presence as she buried her nose in the curve of his neck. His racing pulse drummed against her nose, eyelids softly fluttering closed as she enjoyed what could possibly become one of the best evenings of her entire youth.

THE CARRIAGE FOR FOUR

The carriage creaked and groaned, a slow and simple journey, a brisk, black night.

Belle could hear the sleepy sighs bouncing between the horses—their disdain for such late travels evident in their vocalizations. They were some of Bramwell's best stallions, but even the best horses often threw fits, acting more human than animal on more occasion than one. Belle always found animals to be so fascinating in that sense—how they, too, could experience emotions so powerful that could considerably compare to that of human emotions.

The moon clung to the sky like a clingy lover, the surrounding clouds engaging in a doting, passionate dance around the circular source of light. It was oddly bright even for this time of night, illuminating the landscape with a beautiful blue glow, highlighting the luscious landscape of Valen's outskirts, a poorly populated place with people very far and few between, mostly cooped up in decades-old cottages with ghastly holes in the roof and decaying wood on the walls.

Belle redirected her attention to the double-benched carriage, with plush, maroon seats that faced one another purely to force social interaction. It was difficult to ignore someone seated just opposite of you, when the only place they had to look was either directly at your face or out of the measly, finger-print riddled window, one that was often concealed by a dense, decorative curtain.

Nearly sitting knee to knee with the lady was Henry the Gardener—exhausted eyes lightly sealed, eyelids occasionally twitching with sleep. His temple laid lax against the wall of the carriage, head persistently bobbing with each and every bump of the road as he sweetly slept. On his lap laid a spent Evelin, her wild, untamed hair draped over Henry's legs, framing her innocent, sleeping expression like an angelic halo. The tendrils were accompanied by the presence of five slender fingers—Henry's fingers, surprisingly neat and clean for such a hard-working boy—and Belle watched as the digits intermittently flexed whilst he dreamt, slightly tightening around Evelin's hair before relaxing once more.

The two had fallen asleep mere minutes into their journey back to Hellthorne Manor, sheer evidence of their merry night. Belle had never seen her younger sister so sleepy—so *fatigued*—but it warmed her heart to see the little woman so comfortable with someone other than a family member, with someone like Henry.

She nearly blushed at the sight of them, a dainty, tooth-filled grin enveloping her lips as her cold knuckles drew upwards to conceal the smile. The individual beside her took notice—for he, too, was still wide, *wide* awake—and she watched with big, doe-like eyes as his knee shifted sideways, softly settling against the pointy curve of her own.

Her pulse considerably quickened, an unsteady beat easing up the length of her throat as her gaze rotated to the side, curious stare settling upon a smirking Lyren. Just like her, he'd had perhaps a *bit* too much to drink, and although they were traveling by horse-drawn carriage, it felt to him as if they were bobbing down the gravel trail on a fluffy cloud.

The thought amused him, and he lowly chuckled—a sound so tiny, so hushed that Belle could barely hear it. If her stare hadn't been locked on him, she wouldn't have known that he'd laughed at all.

"What is it?" she whispered, careful not to stir her sister from sleep.

"Nothing," Lyren lightly dismissed, drawing his knee away from hers. She felt empty at the sudden loss of touch—*cold*—and before she could consider her actions, she'd rotated her knee to the side, settling back against his as if it belonged there always.

He took notice, and Belle swore that she could see a scarlet blush creep down the pale skin of his neck, dipping down into his ruffled collar before disappearing from sight. She wondered if she were to reach out to touch him—to slip her hand between the buttons of his blouse—if she would feel the heat of his blush.

"Thank you for taking us out tonight," Belle said, her tone low and hushed. The last thing she wanted in this moment was for both Henry and Evelin to blink back into reality, for the scene at hand felt fictitious—dream-like. Her fingers dipped within the sleeve of her warm fur coat, and she took the shy skin between her nails, pinching firmly to confirm that she was, in fact, awake.

"I was worried you wouldn't come," Lyren replied, unable to tear his glare from hers. She had the prettiest brown eyes—so big and round—and the man could fathom getting lost in them, dipping over the edge, submerging even his head. He wanted to swim in them—a golden pool of bliss—do backstrokes, float peacefully beneath the surface. Drift away into nothingness.

The night had been full of buzzing energy, an incredible ache pooling deep within Belle's being as she constantly caught Lyren's bright, blue gaze. The way their bodies molded together in dance, the laughter that tickled their tongues. The chemistry was intimidating—something she'd never felt, not even with Florence—and truthfully, Belle found herself riddled with worry of what that could possibly mean.

Florence's words plagued her mind—*I want you to.*

She *wanted* Belle to explore other options—to explore *him.* It didn't make any sense to the redheaded girl, how dismissive Florence seemed of the whole thing, how she encouraged her girl to seek pleasure elsewhere. She wondered what it meant for them, and what would transpire of their relationship if Belle had fallen into Lyren's arms—for as much as she admired the man and couldn't quite deny the aching want for him that set her senses alight, she couldn't lose Florence. What they had was unlike anything she'd ever experienced, and although it was untraditional—*unconventional*—and perhaps entirely inappropriate for the Lady of Valen to even engage in, she couldn't fathom the idea of it ever ending. Of *them* ever ending.

She wanted to hold Florence close until her very last breath.

"Belle," Lyren started, tugging the woman from her trance. She met him with her traditional wide stare, and he felt his pulse begin to race. "I need to be entirely transparent with you, if you'll let me."

Belle sucked in a sharp breath, anxious for what would soon topple off of Lyren's tongue.

"Okay," she spoke. "Go ahead."

Lyren fidgeted in his spot, anxious eyes downcast as he fiddled with the flared, wide sleeves of his blouse. "Belle—*Lady* Belle—this is so rash of me, so *twisted,* and I make myself sick even thinking of it, let alone saying it–"

"Good *Goddess,* Lyren, just say it," Belle interrupted, barely able to contain her trembling.

Lyren briefly paused, and then finally voiced his innermost thoughts. "I've never wanted to touch someone so badly."

There was a fleeting pause. One that made Lyren's stomach tumble so violently that he feared he may spill the contents out directly at his feet. One that made Belle's heart cease to beat and a single bead of sweat to generate along her brow.

I've never wanted to touch someone so badly.

"Belle?" Lyren breathed, tiny tone riddled with worry.

"Touch me," Belle panted, her palm settling upon Lyren's stiff knee.

"W-What?"

"I *said*," Belle began, shuffling out of her cozy coat. A plethora of prickly goosebumps instantly arose upon her exposed flesh, the surface of her chest glowing a bright red as she shuffled towards a frozen Lyren. She removed her hand from his leg and draped her legs over his knees, shaking fingers curling around his own.

"Touch me."

The man gasped as she claimed his wrist, directing his hand *up up up* towards her blushing body. Up past her stomach, frenzied butterflies raiding the organ. Up past her breasts, comfortably concealed by her dress. Up past her rosy chest, gooseflesh covering the surface. By her guidance, the tips of his frigid fingers met her neck—gently coiling around the surface. She encouraged him to hold—to *grip*—and when he applied barely a whisper of pressure to her throat, she airily gasped—lips gently parting.

A wave of warmth flooded through Lyren's core, a miniscule groan threatening to spill from his throat as his bubbly blue gaze grew dark, his own lips parting slightly to silently mirror Belle's expression. He repeatedly replayed the sound she made in his head—over and over and *over*—and he felt himself twitch beneath his trousers, chest blooming with electric sparks as his hand barely shifted against her skin, just enough so that his thumb could creep up the edge of her chin.

He continued on his gentle, agonizingly slow quest up her chin before eventually settling upon the curve of her lower lip, his thumb barely caressing the surface as he lightly pulled it down.

Lyren watched with wide eyes as Belle's eyelids fluttered closed, her warm breath tickling the skin of his thumb. She took his thumb into her mouth, and he sucked in a sharp breath—stunned stare rotating to meet the sleeping pair just opposite them. They were consequently close, and the fact admittedly made Lyren quite irritable.

If only he and Belle could have a single moment completely alone . . .

His mind drifted to that of the nightspot, and how he should've steered her through the rear door when Evelin and Henry weren't looking—how he could've taken her to the same spot he'd snuck off to several times prior, with women he'd never seen again.

Sometimes, he swore that he could still feel the indents of the pearl necklace that one lady once wore, for his palm was wrapped so tightly around her neck, (by her request, of course), that it nearly left bruises behind against his smooth, pale skin.

For a moment, he imagined Belle in that memory—the pearl necklace strung around *her* neck, the whimpers that graced his ears emerging from *her* mouth.

An additional electric shock struck his chest, and he bit back a groan—stumbling back into reality as Belle sealed her lips around his thumb, warm, wet tongue softly sheathing the digit. His forehead crinkled with want, and he tore his thumb from her mouth—urgently latching both palms onto her hips as he maneuvered the petite woman onto the heat of his lap.

Belle squeaked at the sudden shift, and she glanced over her shoulder to view her sister, who was still sound asleep atop Henry's lap, her dreams seemingly uninterrupted. Although she'd confided in Evelin about Bramwell's lack of physical affection, she still worried that her sister wouldn't approve of such behavior from Belle, regardless of her husband's approval.

After all, nothing was natural about Belle and Bramwell's union. It was as if they were married for public appearances. Nothing more.

Lyren handled the woman with skill, positioning her legs on either side of his hips as he urged her to flatten against his lap, wide palms glued to her hardly clothed legs. The fabric of her dress was wonky and askew, exposing a smidge of her left thigh—but none of that mattered, for just as she'd properly located the most comfortable spot, she felt him—stiff, throbbing. Painfully concealed beneath the claustrophobic cloth of his trousers.

A blush crept up Lyren's cheeks, and he shyly grinned—lazy gaze settling upon Belle's lips as he claimed her hips.

"Is this okay?" he breathed, and she nodded; fingers creeping up to meet his cheeky blush. She cradled his face, admiring the way his sparkling azure eyes darkened with each waking second, how she could feel the heat of his bashful blush beneath her palms, the carnal warmth melting her to a puddle of pleasure.

"Bramwell is one of my best friends," Lyren spoke, his shameful stare downcast. He tore his hands away from her hips, furious with his weakness. Belle was Bramwell's wife—the Lady of Valen—and she was currently sat on his lap, the evidence of his arousal pressed flat up against her clothed center.

There was no going back from this, now.

"You saw us in the window," Belle said, urging him to look her in the eye. "Do you think I'd be here—on your lap, in your *arms,* if my husband didn't approve?"

Lyren raised a doubtful brow, pulse racing beneath his chest as he struggled to recall any hint at all that Bramwell had possibly dropped, but his mind was blank. *Empty.* Missing pieces as if it were an incomplete puzzle, a rambunctious child who snuck pieces away when his parent wasn't looking—hiding them in his sock drawer, never to be seen again.

Erased.

"I don't understand?" Lyren spoke, shaking his head. "Are you only married so Bram isn't stripped of his title?"

"Yes," Belle admitted, massaging her thumbs against his cheeks. "He's a different man than most. He wants a companion, not a lover. He knows about Florence and me. He told me that it's okay. That he *wants* me to."

"And what about her?" Lyren added. "Florence?"

Belle blushed at the mere mention of her darling love—*sweet Florence*—and with a small smile, she leaned inward, taking notice of Lyren's sharp intake of breath, and feeding off of it. It amused her, the way he squirmed so easily. She wondered how he'd look naked beneath her in her bed, wearing nothing but the twisted tangle of her sheets, a beautiful bright blush enveloping his fair skin. He was so dainty, so feminine. So *unique.* She'd never met such a man as him, and she loved it—*craved* it. She knew that if she slipped her fingers beneath his belt, his skin would be just as soft and smooth as hers.

"If you want to know the truth," Belle mused, her voice barely above a whisper. Lyren's eyes fluttered closed, shy pants cascading over his slightly parted lips as their noses nimbly collided. "Florence wants you in our bed just as much as I do."

She felt him painfully pulse beneath her, and with a satisfied smile, she met his mouth. Their lips barely collided, a whisper of a kiss, and for a long moment, they stayed just like that. Barely kissing, barely breathing. Just . . . *existing*. Enjoying the way their lips just barely touched, a torturous tease.

Lyren's fingers scaled up Belle's back, tracing miscellaneous, meaningless shapes against the dressed surface as if she were his canvas, and he was a troubled artist.

With one final sigh, Lyren flattened his mouth to hers fully—finally, truly tasting her. It was slow—*sweet*—and the pair just existed in a pleasant trance. He studied the way she felt under his hands—the bumpy slope of her spine, the whisper of her ribs. He wanted to nourish her in every way possible, patiently and with care, for he could tell just by the shape of her lips that she was as fragile as a glass vase, and just one tip, one shove could send her spiraling to the ground in a dozen pieces.

Her lips parted, and she breathed him in—tongues blissfully dancing to a tune they seemingly knew, as if it were a dance that they'd done a million times over. His mouth felt familiar, cozy, *home*. Only, she already *had* a home, and it was Florence—so perhaps, maybe she had *another* home.

Why only seclude yourself within a single four walls when you can comfortably reside within multiple?

After all, there was plenty of room within her heart for more than one, and by just one kiss alone, she knew that she was doomed when it came to Lyren Deth.

There was no turning back.

His hands found her hair, and she moaned, a sound so small, so quiet that Lyren barely even heard it, but when it registered in his brain, he nearly mimicked the sound, for it was so perfect that he could hardly stand it.

The carriage came to a jolting stop, emitting an audible yawn from an exhausted Evelin a mere yard away—and the couple were separated almost instantly, stiffly seated beside each other with heaving chests and reddened cheeks.

Evelin removed herself from Henry's lap, blinking sleep from her eyes as she sloppily attempted to smooth her wild locks back into place. Even through her blurred vision, she was able to spot the blush slapped across Belle's cheeks, and she instantly raised an accusatory brow, gaze flickering between both her and Lyren.

"We've made it back, yeah?" Evelin asked, her voice riddled with sleep.

"That we have, sister." Belle said, purposefully avoiding any contact with Lyren in the slightest.

Do not raise suspicion.

"Great. Let's go inside the manor and get me out of these damned shoes before my feet begin to bruise."

EMPTY PITS OF WHITE

Belle had entered her third consecutive hour of a lovely, dream-riddled sleep when she was irksomely awoken.

Head hazy with exhaustion, the woman stretched an arm outward toward the opposite side of the bed in search of her sleeping sister, but instead, she blindly located nothing but a stiff, cold pillow.

At the absence of Evelin's presence, Belle shot up in the bed, a gasp tickling the tip of her tongue.

Her wild stare struggled to adjust to the absence of light, the oil lamp beside the bed dark and dead. The manor was unbearably spooky in the early hours of the morning, when the sun wasn't due to rise over the cusp of Valen's tallest mountains for another hour. Typically, Belle slept soundly until dawn, but there was a tightness in her chest that she could barely identify, a sharp sting, one that ached and yanked and pulled tighter with every moment that she blindly scanned the bedroom.

She nearly screamed when she saw her.

Stood still beside the bed was her younger sister Evelin, limbs stiff, as if frozen in place. Her jaw laid lax, mouth parted into a dramatic o-shape, ruby red lips cracked and bloody. Oozing. *Raw.*

Her eyes—once a warm, welcoming chestnut—were void of any color, irises absent, pupils erased.

White.

A fearful tremble consumed Belle to her very core, and although the sight before her was admittedly the most frightening thing she'd ever laid eyes on, she couldn't quite tear her stare away.

Her sister, her *blood,* was standing before her—permanently petrified, it appeared—unmoving, unblinking, seemingly unbreathing. Her chest didn't extend outward with steady inhales, her eyelids failed to blink. Her lips—so crusty, bloody, nearly *black*—remained open. *Wide.*

Panic-stricken, Belle maneuvered herself several inches backward upon the mattress, eager to distance herself from the being that looked identical to Evelin, but surely wasn't her, *couldn't* be her . . .

When Belle had distanced herself enough, she finally spoke, her tone low and riddled with fear.

"Evelin?"

Silence.

Unmoving. Unblinking. *Still.*

Eyes endless seas of white, cold, *empty.* She hadn't blinked, hadn't breathed, hadn't *moved.* The only reason Belle was convinced that she was actually standing at the curve of her bedside was because of the sudden appearance of a thin, dainty strand of blood that began to ooze from Evelin's unbearably chapped lower lip. The sore silently burst open, a rush of slick scarlet dribbling down the length of her chin. The tiny red river paused only momentarily at the edge of Evelin's chin, hesitating, before leaving her skin, plunging down to meet the soft rug beneath the frozen soles of her feet.

A violent shake claimed Belle's spine, eyes welling up with tears as she studied Evelin's blank, dead stare. After a fleeting moment, she spoke once more, desperate for some sort of reprieve.

"Evelin, please–"

Belle's statement was silenced by Evelin's abrupt move-ment, one which caused a tiny, terrified yelp to tickle Belle's tongue.

Evelin's bloodied lips sealed, mouth snapping closed with such force that her teeth audibly collided, generating a noise so squirm worthy that Belle instantly grew nau-seous at the sound. If Evelin's lips had opened once more, Belle was almost certain that all of her teeth would be split and severed from the impact, blood rushing from the wounds, gums raw with rage.

The pair sat in silence for what seemed like an eternity, turbulent trembles taking over Belle's entire being as she violently shook.

When Belle's lips parted in preparation to speak once more, Evelin moved. Jarring. Quick. Almost too fast for Belle to see, a movement that she would've missed with a single blink.

Evelin sat cross-legged on the bed, her knees in such close proximity to Belle's that they nearly touched. Her elbows balanced atop said knees, palms crossed, blood-tracked chin sat snug atop her hands. Her scarlet soiled lips pulled into a smile, one so broad, so tall that it nearly touched her blank, snowy eyes, and with every centimeter that the smile rose along her face, the edges of her lips split and cracked.

The sound—the ripping, the *tearing*—the folding flesh peeling away like butter, crawling up towards her eyelids, was a sight enough to truly scar her elder sister for an eternity.

Belle wanted to scream—wanted to *run*—but she remained within inches of Evelin, frigid with fear, limbs locked.

Evelin's sopping wet smile finally met the border of her lower eyelids, and triumphantly, she giggled—a girlish, pure little sound—before finally speaking.

"You're going to die here."

Belle's blood shifted to ice.

"What?" she gasped, knowing quite well what she'd heard.

You're going to die here.

A giggle, a tear, a hollow, milky eyeball tumbling from its socket, a stretched smile splitting the hole wide open.

"Lady *Hell,*" Evelin purred, her voice seemingly magnifying. "Lady *Hell* Lady *Hell* Lady *Hell*–"

The tears freely flowed, now. Belle's defiant limbs thankfully unlocked, allowing her trembling frame to topple from the bed, landing unceremoniously on her back. She released a pained grunt, and when her blurred, tear-stricken stare met the bed, she saw Evelin's upper half draped over the side, palms flat against the mattress, head tilted inhumanly sideways. Only one single eyeball remained, the other tangled up within the blankets atop Belle's bed. Evelin's haunting smile had torn the socket of her eye wide open, as if it had never existed in the first place, nothing but an extension of her sweet, bloody smile.

Belle climbed to her feet, a scream bubbling up within her chest as she vacated the room, refusing to glance back at the horror that had become of her sister.

The woman stumbled into the hallway, not bothering to close the bedroom door behind her, for closing it would just take up too much time, and all Belle wanted in this very moment was to flee, to get far, far away.

Florence's bedroom resided on the entire opposite side of the manor, but she was determined to make it there safe and sound. She wasn't sure if Evelin had followed her—admittedly, she was too frightened to even look over her shoulder and see—but as the woman ran further down the winding halls, she grew dizzy and weak. Her knees buckled, garish tears erasing her line of sight as she fell to the floor, the rough rug leaving burns along her forearms.

"Fuck!" Belle screamed, struggling to stand to her feet. The walls seemed to close in on her—suffocatingly close—and she heard Evelin's voice once more. It ricocheted off of the walls, like an echo, and the sound alone made Belle audibly cry.

LADY HELL LADY HELL LADY HELL

"Stop!" Belle called, palms flattening against her ears. "Stop! Please!"

LADY HELL WILL RING DEATHS BELL

LADY HELL WILL BE A SHELL

Belle forced herself upwards once more, desperate to continue her journey towards a sleeping Florence, stuffed up in her own bedroom for the remainder of Evelin's trip.

She blinked the tears away and continued to run.

Through the hallway, into the upper foyer.

Bramwell's chambers were only several doors down from Florence's own room. His room was vast—oak double doors, brass handles. Belle had only seen the inside of his bedroom once or twice, and it was easily triple the size of her already massive room. She could clearly envision the four-poster bed where Bramwell silently slept, the deep violet curtains swaying in the wind, a bitter breeze easing through the parted window.

She breezed by his room and stumbled toward Florence's. Her fingers met the handle, and a second hand laid atop hers—ashen, gray skin, ghastly, gaping pits over the knuckles, the dead flesh peeled away, muscle absent, nothing but bright, white bone peeking through.

Belle choked on a sob, and her eyelids snapped closed.

It's not real not real not real not–

"Oh, it *is* real," the stranger spoke, their ice-cold breath dancing along Belle's cheek. She could feel the closeness in their proximity—the tip of the entity's nose nearly touching her cheek—but she refused to open her eyes. Refused to look, to *see*.

"Listen here, and listen close, Lady Hell," the visitor said, tenderly unraveling Belle's fingers from Florence's bedroom door. Reluctantly, she obeyed—careful not to open her eyes in the process but allowing the being to remove her touch from the frigid brass.

The entity rasped and wheezed, as if suffering from a wicked case of pneumonia, and Belle swallowed a mouthful of bile, wondering where on earth she'd gone so wrong in life to deserve to be here, at that very spot, in that very moment . . .

"The dead stand below."

What?

Belle felt a fist full of fingers claim her hair, breaths rapidly thinning.

Don't open your eyes don't open them don't–

"If you keep them closed, you'll never see," the entity added, swiftly reading Belle's thoughts, as if she'd said them aloud. Only, she hadn't, for nothing had emerged from her trembling lips but fearful whines.

"Keep them closed, Lady Hell, and you'll never see the dead that stand below."

A hand gripped onto the rear of her scalp, razor-sharp nails penetrating the surface, digging deep. Blood beaded and pooled, drenching the entity's fleshless fingers, staining the pasty, gray skin a violent red.

Belle's lips parted, a pained cry slipping off of her tongue as the entity's hold tightened, nails meeting brain, fluid spilling out.

The faceless entity laughed, curling their fingers into the fleshy mass of Belle's brain, before speaking its final statement: "open wide, Lady Hell, or you too will stand below."

With that, the entity yanked a seizing, screaming Belle backwards, forcing her down into the endless abyss that laid below.

Lady Hell will ring deaths bell.
Lady Hell will be a shell.

ANOTHER LOST,
ANOTHER CLAIMED

H e died in the night.

Topher Hardt's beefy neck met the blade. A twist, a gurgle, a sigh. And then, death.

Hellthorne Manor was no stranger to death.

There was a cackle, one so shrill, so sharp that it made their ears ring. The dead woman within the portrait was laughing—*cheering*. Doubled over, a hand pressed against her side, heaving. She nearly toppled out of her portrait by doing so, tears claiming her gray, sunken cheeks as she celebrated the death of Topher Hardt, who bled out in his bed, his partner laid beside him in a blissful, deep sleep, unaware of the pool of rot that bloomed beside her.

Another soul lost. Another claimed.

When Belle woke, it was to a scream.

Sharp. Shrill. *Mortified.*

She sat upwards in her bed, her nightgown slick with sweat, suctioned to her skin. The once open window was closed, the frigid winter air trapped behind the blurry pane, and Belle was buried beneath a duo of dense blankets, thick and wool. She felt suffocated—*trapped*—and as the morning sun spilled a pool of yellow onto the rug, she nearly toppled out of her bed, desperate to locate the source of the scream.

Evelin was not laid beside her, nor was she upright beside the bed, just as she had been hours prior.

Or so Belle thought.

The memories rushed back, flooding Belle's mind with such force that it nearly blinded her. The rear of her head throbbed, and she snaked her fingers around the bend to meet the source, the very spot where an unknown entity had latched its sharp claws into the surface of her skin, deep into the cavern of her head until it penetrated the loins of her brain.

There was no wound. No blood. No evidence of the attack—nothing but a surplus of haunting visuals that assured her that it had actually happened.

Or had it?

"It was just a dream," Belle breathed, the bare soles of her feet meeting the wood floor. "Just a bad, bad dream. Evelin's using the toilet, she still has both eyes, still a normal smile."

What she failed to notice was the single droplet of blood on the rug beside her bed, a spot she so carelessly stepped over on the way to the door.

The scream emerged again, and Belle broke into a sprint, shuffling down the hall with ease as she met a wide-eyed Clare, arms full of clean linens.

"It's coming from the guest room of Topher Hardt, that man from the Capitol," she said, clutching the linens to her chest. "Follow close, my lady. Ula's searching for Lord Bramwell."

"Have you seen my sister?" Belle asked, following close on Clare's heels. Topher Hardt's guest room was a hallway over from Belle's, and her question went unanswered as the voice of Ithabell Throne suddenly emerged, followed by the low, soothing tone of Bramwell Hellthorne himself.

"We must send for a physician at once! The man has been stabbed!" Ithabell screeched, just as both Belle and Clare rounded the corner.

"No physician can bring back the dead, Ithabell." Bramwell simply said, his tone conflictingly cool in comparison to Ithabell's panicked declaration.

Ithabell was still dressed in her nightgown, typically tamed hair a wild mess, baby blue eyes red-rimmed and wide. Trembles claimed her limbs, and she looked as if she may be sick, a darkening gaze flickering between the lord and his lady.

"Bram," Belle breathlessly began, fingers reaching out to claim her husband's elbow. Unlike the others, he was fairly dressed, as if he'd been awake for hours, now, although it was barely past sunrise.

"My wife," Bramwell sighed, as if out of relief. His warm palm met Belle's knuckles, a sad stare boring into her quizzical gaze. "Topher Hardt's been killed in his bed."

"What?" Belle gasped, brushing past both Ithabell and Bramwell as she charged into the guest room.

Sure enough, a very dead Topher Hardt laid upon the sodden mattress, the linens permanently marred with the mark of death. His eyes were closed, as if deep in sleep, and his date sat upright beside him, still atop the mattress where her apparent lover lay deceased.

She was expressionless—void of emotion. As if Hardt was simply sleeping beside her, instead of purple, bloody, and rotting within his bed clothes.

"Goddess alight," Ithabell cried, joining Belle's side. "Get out of the ruddy room, Amaluna. Goddess *alight,* a man has been *murdered!*"

Belle watched, frozen in place, as Ithabell helped the lady, apparently called Amaluna, out of Hardt's bed. Amaluna barely looked back at the scene, and instead, joined a terrified Clare in the hallway, who was instructed by a shockingly calm Bramwell to escort Amaluna elsewhere, perhaps feed her some scones and a cup of warm tea.

"You shouldn't be seeing this, Belle," Bramwell said, standing beside his wife. He glared at a bloated, dead Topher Hardt, his gaze void of any expression. It was as if the man's death was of no surprise to him.

Planned.

"There's a fucking murderer in these walls, Hellthorne," Ithabell screeched, filing back into the room. "Probably that penniless gardener you dug up from Szo Landing, bunch of inbred freaks 'round those parts, on the mother's teat 'till their own marriage–"

"I won't condone such speech of my gardener, Itha-bell," Bramwell scolded, defending Henry's honor with ease. "Henry is a fine man and would do no such thing. After all, he has no access to the manor, he lives in the quarters with the housemaidens."

"One of their lot could've snuck him in," Ithabell countered, shaking her head back and forth. "The help is always not to be trusted, you respect them far too much for what they're worth, Hellthorne."

"Enough." Bramwell snipped, redirecting his gaze to Belle. She couldn't quite tear her stare away from the murdered man in the bed—the blood, the stench, the *rot*. Her stomach began to do somersaults.

"Your friend, the one who goes by Deth," Ithabell spoke, rounding the bed. "He studies the dead, yes? Conducts autopsies? Have one of your help fetch him at once."

"I'm not entirely sure that an autopsy is needed, Ithabell. The cause of death is quite clear." Bramwell said. He was calm—collected—and the fact seemed to irk Ithabell even further, her eyes contorting into thin slits.

"Belle?"

The voice that emerged from behind them was so tiny—so *fickle*—so innocent, so scared. It nearly sent shivers down Belle's spine to hear it, and instead of the relief that she should feel at the sound of her sister Evelin's voice, she felt nothing but fear.

"Dear dead Goddess Lottie in *Eden*–" Ithabell audibly cursed, snakelike eyes widening to the size of saucers. The color left her face entirely, a sickly, green hue creeping up her cheeks as both Belle and Bramwell twisted their necks to view the source of Evelin's voice.

Within the doorway stood Evelin Byron, youthful limbs clad in a soiled, ivory nightgown, one which was too wide and too long and draped down past her knees.

Slapped across the surface was none other than the very same blood that had erupted from Topher Hardt's neck.

"Hang the wench!" Ithabell cried, her voice cracking. "Hang her by the neck until dead at the Capitol, for Hardt's children to see! Fucking no-good penniless Immorium *trash*–"

"Belle," Evelin wept, her once solid-white eyes replaced by that of her own soul. "Belle, I'm scared."

"Call for the ruddy authorities!"

Bramwell bit his tongue so hard that it nearly bled, blackened stare shifting from a frightened, bloody Evelin in the doorway to that of a red-in-the-face Ithabell, her hands curled into furious fists at her sides.

"For whom, Ithabell?"

"What in the Good Goddess do you ever mean, Hellthorne? Send your penniless little gardener down the hill and gather up every last authority in Valen for the little fucking runt who killed an esteemed member of Elantry's government!" Ithabell exploded, the red color in her face nearly shifting to a bright, bursting purple with rage. She was furious, and Belle was certain that at any moment, the woman would hang Evelin herself by tossing her over the railing of the loft.

"Ithabell, ruddy look at me, will you? Into my eyes." Bramwell impatiently instructed. Ula had stumbled onto the scene at the same time, a mortified expression taking over her features as she steered Evelin Byron from the doorway, blissfully unaware of what she'd done, and instead only worried if she, too, was gravely hurt.

"Bram–" Belle began, but the man silenced her with a raised palm, his focus solely on Ithabell.

Reluctantly, the government official steadied her gaze on Bramwell's, looking directly into his determined eyes as she repeated her request about alerting the authorities down the hill.

"Once again, Ithabell—alert them for *who?*" Bramwell pressed, jaw tightening.

It was then that Ithabell's expression went blank.

Her features softened, the bitter, purple hue along her cheeks fading to a light pink. Her mind became a jumbled mess, thoughts rearranging, the sight of a bloody Evelin in the doorway effectively disappearing from her memory.

"Topher Hardt," Ithabell squeaked. "The authorities need to be alerted of Topher Hardt's death."

Belle stilled, jaw laid slack in wonder as she watched Ithabell appear to stumble over her words, her thoughts a blurred mess.

What had just happened?

"I think it would be wise for you to do so yourself, Itha-bell," Bramwell began, breaking his intense eye contact with the woman. He blinked several times, eyes slightly watering. "Take one of my carriages, a man named Charles would be delighted to take you down the hill. Tell him Topher Hardt has been found dead."

"Someone must've killed him–" Ithabell stammered, forehead wrinkling in worry. It was as if she knew of the answer she so desperately craved, but it was just without of reach—tucked away in a spot that she could not quite see.

"Leave the investigation to the authorities," Bramwell urged. "For now, go find them. Return to Havensworth soon after. Rest, relax, and breathe. You are safe, Ithabell."

Ithabell's lips parted and then snapped shut. She glanced once more in Topher Hardt's direction, eyed the murdered man up and down, and then abandoned the room entirely, beginning her mission to fetch the authorities at the bottom of the hill.

"Come with me," Bramwell said, interrupting Belle's racing thoughts. He offered her a hand, but she refused to take it.

"What the fuck just happened here, Bram?"

Bramwell shrugged, abandoning Belle within the rot-filled room. Topher's body was beginning to stink, and the sight and smell alone was suddenly overwhelming. Belle turned on her heel, filing out of the room and following close on Bramwell's heel. He appeared to be in a rush, shuffling down the hallway with long, steady strides as he anxiously ran a hand through his hair.

"Bramwell, I'm ruddy *speaking* to you–"

Bramwell sharply paused, spinning on the heel of his foot to face a clearly distressed Belle, who unintentionally ran directly into his front, her nose colliding with his firm chest.

"I won't ever do it to you," he said, features instantly softening at the sight of his wife. "Never. I swear it."

Awestruck, Belle stood before him, unable to conjure up a word, a sentence, a sound, *anything*. She just stood there, dumbfounded, lips parted, eyes widened.

Bramwell delivered a gentle pat with the palm of his hand to her shoulder, and with that, he left. Resuming his lengthy strides down the hall, disappearing from sight.

"Lady Belle?" Ula whispered, politely tapping the frozen woman's shoulder. "Would you like to see your sister?"

# THE EXORCISM OF EVELIN BYRON

Word spread like an untamed wildfire of Topher Hardt's death around the Capitol, and most of Havensworth was up in arms. The details were scarce, and the only witnesses—both Ithabell Throne and Hardt's nearly mute lover, Amaluna, could barely recall what had happened. They'd both spoken privately with Bramwell Hellthorne before traveling down the hill to locate the authorities, and after their brief conversation, they simply left Valen altogether—nothing but the clothes on both of their backs following them back home, their trunks forgotten in their respective guest rooms at the manor.

Lyren Deth personally delivered both a death certificate and an autopsy report to Havensworth a day and a half following Hardt's demise. He was clad in a fine navy suit, a sleek black bowtie, and with his silver-blond curls politely pulled away from his features.

It was perhaps the simplest autopsy he'd conducted to date, and the Capitol of Elantry thanked him sincerely with a hefty, fat check—one which he could survive off of for an entire year, if he chose to not work.

He was sure to run the paperwork by Bramwell before he left, his penmanship clean, dark, and bold, explaining in the most uncomplicated terms how Hardt's death had come to be.

DEATH BY FATAL OPIUM OVERDOSE

The bloody sheets were burned, the housemaidens minds were scrambled, and the only individuals who knew the *true* story of Topher Hardt's untimely (but rightful) death were those most deserving of knowing such information.

Before abandoning the city of Havensworth, Lyren was sure to pay a respectful visit to his sister, and then, he was on his way back to Valen—back to Hellthorne Manor, back to the place he now considered home.

It was nearly three days following Topher's death that the Holy Man of Plirity Enny Koe arrived upon the manor's wrought iron gates.

He'd been visiting family in Westcastle when the letter arrived, a desperate plea for help from the Lord of Valen himself.

It had been years since Enny had been called for such a task, but as one of the only true Holy Men of Plirity still living in Elantry, it was his sole duty to do his absolute best to please not only the royal family, but to rid their family member of her evil spirit.

He found the demon infested lady laid upon a dusty sofa in a sitting room, several anxious individuals surrounding her.

"Koe," Bramwell spoke, his tone riddled with relief. He took the Holy Man's hand in his, shaking it firmly. "Thank Goddess you made it here safely and so soon, I'm not sure how much longer she can live with it."

"Grief, how old is she, my lord? She looks dreadfully young." Koe observed with a frown. His gaze flickered over to the woman sat at the foot of the furniture, eyes red-rimmed with tears, gorgeous red locks braided down her back. She looked helpless and stricken with dread, a peculiar emptiness existing behind her once lively gaze.

"Eighteen," Bramwell revealed. "She's my wife's sister. I believe that Velveteen has a hold of her, Koe, just as she did of me."

Koe's features paled.

Velveteen.

The fourth sister of the Goddesses.

The outcast. The sinner.

The topmost demon of the Netherworld. The Queen.

He remembered Bramwell's exorcism well—the boy was just barely ten—but that was a memory for another day. It wasn't every day that a child so young could be capable of summoning the Queen of the Netherworld, and with such ease that it frightened the Holy Man still to this very day.

"Velveteen must thrive within these walls," Koe murmured, studying Evelin's blank, unblinking stare. "There's something that grounds her here. She wants to be here. *Live* here. Possession is her only way of truly being one with the manor."

You *ground her here, Lord Bramwell. Her summoner.*

"None of that garbage is even *real,*" Belle blurted, a small sob cascading up her throat. "Not the Goddesses, not the Queen of the Netherworld, none of it. My sister is *sick,* and you're just turning this all into a ridiculous religious Pliritan nightmare–"

Florence's palm clamped down on Belle's shoulder, as if to softly shush her. It worked, and Belle's lips instantly sealed—watery stare glancing over her shoulder to view Lyren, who was pacing behind the sofa, his nails nudged between gnawing teeth.

"I'm sorry to hear of your lack of beliefs," Koe sighed, flashing a sympathetic stare in Bramwell's direction. The lord ignored it.

"If you're just here to insult the Lady of Valen, you'd better just leave–" Lyren cursed, the statement muffled by the presence of the fingernail pinched between his teeth.

"Lyren," Bramwell warned, and his friend fell silent, continuing his relentless pacing.

Koe, the Holy Man, set his briefcase down on a nearby table, shuffling out a worn and beaten copy of the Good Book, one that had been read and reread so many times that the ink on several pages began to bleed from the persistent presence of clammy, moist fingers. Belle, Bramwell, Florence, and Lyren all watched with curious, widened eyes at the religious man wormed his wide shoulders out of his thick coat, discarding it with ease beside the forgotten briefcase. The individuals in attendance were the only ones that knew of the true conditions of Topher Hardt's puzzling demise, and although Belle continuously insisted that her sister simply *couldn't* have murdered a man with such ease, the others weren't so sure what to believe. Lyren was the only one who appeared to genuinely agree with Belle's claims, for the portrait of a dead girl had haunted his mind every night before bed.

He knew what he'd seen, and Belle had now seen something, too.

"Velveteen," Koe weakly began, knowing quite well that the entity was temperamental. She hardly responds to her given name, unless her mood was particularly playful.

"Are you here with us now, Velveteen?"

There was a stiff pause. No one seemed to breathe, for even the tiniest of sounds seemed like a nuisance in that very moment.

Evelin Byron hadn't moved—nor had she blinked, *breathed,* even—but there was a noticeable shift. A whisper, a chill, a significant drop in temperature. The weak, flickering flame within the fireplace promptly extinguished, leaving behind nothing but puffs of black smoke, weak remnants of the fire that once brightly burned.

"Do you feel that?" Florence whispered, a sharp, stabbing pain piercing within her chest, dangerously close to her briskly beating heart.

"Goddess alight," Lyren murmured, a palm steadying against his own chest. "My chest hurts."

"She's here, isn't she, Koe?" Bramwell breathed, a familiar sensation flooding his limbs. It was as if the forgotten Goddess was an old friend—a parental figure, perhaps—and the lord nearly fell to his knees as the sensation swallowed him up whole. He knew, then, that the entity had awoken within Evelin Byron, the sweet soul of Belle's little sister being brutally shoved aside.

She was a host, nothing more.

Koe studied Evelin's frozen frame; her red-rimmed eyes unseeing, unfeeling. She still hadn't moved, and although every individual within the room could feel Velveteen's presence, it was as if the demon wasn't even present at all.

Only, Koe knew better. She was cunning. *Sly.*

Velveteen liked to play with her food.

When the voice emerged, Evelin's lips hadn't even moved. It was her voice—soft, sweet, shy—but although it sounded the very same that it had since Belle could remember, it was different. Off. *Wrong.*

"You know what I want, Enny Koe. Nearly two decades it's been since we've spoken, hasn't it been?"

Belle's hand crept up to meet Evelin's elbow, only to recoil almost instantly, a gasp tickling her tongue.

Evelin's skin was bone cold, as if she'd been dead for days.

"Leave us," Bramwell breathed, swallowing thickly. When no one budged, his fingers curled into furious fists, darkening stare meeting a horror-stricken Belle upon the sofa. She was the only one to have seen Evelin in her possessed state—the way she looked, how she *spoke*—that very same night she'd apparently killed Topher Hardt in his sleep. The memory haunted her, and although her sister persisted that it was only her—*it's me, Belle, I promise you, swear to the Goddesses, nothing is inside of me but me*—she simply *knew* better.

She didn't believe in Plirity. She didn't believe in the Goddesses, nor their fallen sister, the one who had fallen from grace and burned beneath the ground.

"Bram–" Belle started, shaking her head from side to side. Although she'd refused to sleep next to Evelin for three entire nights, the sheer thought of abandoning her flesh and blood in this very moment was nearly enough to make her scream.

"Long live Goddess Lottie, if the three of you don't leave, I'll escort each of you out by force–" Bramwell seethed through gritted teeth. It was a rare sight—Bramwell expressing anger—and Florence reassuringly grabbed her lover's hand, whispering a series of reassurances against Belle's cheek.

"We'll keep your sister safe, m'lady," the Holy Man assured, smiling sweetly. He seemed sincere enough, but Belle hardly believed in Plirity to begin with, and being in the presence of the *holiest man in all of Elantry* almost made Belle's skin crawl.

Somehow, he was more terrifying to her than the entity that currently occupied her sister.

"This is horse shit," Lyren cursed, reluctantly following on the two women's heels as they headed for the exit. "We all know there's something sinister within these walls, Bram. I've seen it, now Belle has. You might as well just let Florence finally see it, too. No one believes it until they see it with their own eyes. The manor is fucking *cursed*."

"Duly noted, Lyren." Bramwell bitterly dismissed, barely looking his friend in the eye as he, Belle, and Florence vacated the sitting room.

The Holy Man waited several moments before speaking, his gaze still fixated on an unmoving Evelin. She'd only spoken once, and not again since her audience's departure. She liked to put on a show, and he knew that the dark Goddess wouldn't be pleased by their absence.

"Your wife isn't a Pliritan?" Koe spoke, ignoring Velveteen's presence. She was still in the room with them—that much was evident by the steadily dropping temperature—but he only ignored her existence, hoping that it would make her squirm.

"She's not," Bramwell confirmed, side-eyeing a frozen Evelin. "I wasn't either, until I summoned Vel."

Vel.

A girlish giggle cascaded up Evelin's throat, a trail of spittle coating her lower lip as she tried to hold it in. The Byron girl was fighting her, but Velveteen was far too experienced, and centuries older.

It was then that the teenage girl rose.

Her movements were inhuman and quick—there one second and gone the next—with speed so precise that it made both Koe and Bramwell dizzy.

When she finally made her presence known once more—the audience flustered by her momentary absence—Velveteen simply laughed, her own deep, dark tone dancing along Evelin's tongue. The young girl fought good and hard—she had such strength that even Velveteen found herself considerably impressed—but it had been a dreadfully long time since the demon had ten fingers and ten toes, and after all, Hellthorne Manor was her most favorite place to be.

Heads turned, and Koe gawked, his stare glued to the corner of the room, where Evelin's body lay suspended midair as if by a set of strings. Her legs and feet dangled, bare toes pink and cold, arms laid lax along her sides. With shoulders slumped and long, unruly locks draped over her eyes, Evelin's possessed lips pulled into a sinister smile—one so large that it tore the chapped, fleshy corners of her lips open wide, angry, red muscle occupying the spots where her once unblemished cheeks previously laid.

The Holy Man appeared mostly unbothered by the sight, as if there wasn't a teenage girl floating within the air, with a smile so large—so *ghastly*—that it had torn her face completely open. He averted his stare from Velveteen's vessel to meet the anxious expression slapped across Bramwell Hellthorne's aging features.

"You know what she wants, my lord," Koe said, glare rotating between Evelin's unchanging expression and Bramwell's pouted lips. The vessel giggled once more—sweet and soft—and it almost appeared as if her pale skin had a warm, pink glow to it.

A blush.

"I've wanted him since the day he was born," Velveteen revealed, unaware of Evelin's twitching fingers. Koe took note of the slight movement and knew immediately that it was the Byron girl buried within attempting to overthrow her captor.

"The little *bastard* boy," the evil Goddess continued. "Valen's *forgotten prince.* Mummy let you suck the teat until you were ten, Daddy wanted you *dead.*"

Bramwell swallowed a mouthful of bile, unwelcome childhood memories flooding his vision.

"You wanted *me* as your Mumma," Velveteen added, oblivious to the way Evelin's knuckles curled inward, attempting to form a fist. The Byron girl's body seamlessly floated across the room—leisurely, *slow*—the eerie, blood-sodden, flesh-torn grin still snaked along her mouth. She hadn't blinked a single time, beady black pupils consistently studying a fidgeting Bramwell.

"Vel–"

"*Enough* with the pet names, my lord," Koe scolded, disgusted by their apparent intimacy. Back in the day, Bramwell was rather reluctant to be exorcised—in fact, he'd sobbed and screamed, *begged* for the Holy Man to leave. It was his father—the previous Lord of Valen—who had insisted upon it, said that the bastard boy had cursed the manor to the Netherworld by conjuring up the most sinful being of all.

Perhaps, the late lord had been right.

"Don't you see it, *Holy Man*?" Velveteen cheered, a trail of pink tinted drool dripping down Evelin's lower lip. Her teeth still hadn't parted once, nor had her mouth moved. She was frozen solid—a statue, a figurine.

Velveteen's pretty little doll.

"Enough of your games, Velveteen." Koe said, wedging his thumb beneath the flimsy flap of the Good Book. He tore it open with ease, blindly navigating the memorized pages as he'd done countless times prior. The book wasn't needed—he knew every word by heart—but having it in tow meant that he had all three of the Goddesses behind his back, their protection shielding him from the dangers of the impending exorcism.

"Mummy's *little boy*," Velveteen cooed, and Evelin's ghoulish grin disappeared. The skin sealed, the muscle vanished. Her wicked black stare softened, a gentle blue hue overcoming the irises, and the soles of her frigid feet meet the rug, toes curled in comfort.

Bramwell barely breathed at their close proximity, and Velveteen's vessel curled her fingers around the lord's elbow, her nose burying itself into his chest. She inhaled deeply—eyes tipping upward, rolling back into her head—and sighed, as if she was finally home.

"Mumma's missed you," Evelin's lips revealed, but it was not her voice that had emerged.

"Bramwell," Koe warned, locating the very first passage required to complete the dispossession. "Don't fall for it, she's cunning—*evil*. She's working her way into your head again as she did all of those years ago–"

"Don't forget the precious gift I gave you, sweet boy," Velveteen said, the statement just barely audible to anyone's ears but Bramwell's. Her lips were mere inches from his neck, ice-cold, deathly breaths tickling his flesh, igniting patches of prickly goosebumps.

"By my Goddesses Lottie, Lilen, and Liv, I do call upon thee to aide in the banishment of the wretched, evil, forgotten sister called Velveteen–"

"Be a good boy and show Mumma just how talented you are," the Goddess said, trailing Evelin's fingertips along the curve of Bramwell's jaw. He was tense—unyielding—but he could never deny the soft spot that he harbored for the Goddess, for everything she spoke of was the truth.

She'd raised him.

"Brammy," Velveteen urged, cradling his cheek with her vessel's cold palm. "*Use* it."

"*For to save the soul of one Evelin Byron, devoted and beloved daughter, sister, friend, a woman worthy of an eternal existence among the Goddesses, only following a lengthy life, where one would bear children for the Goddesses, a gift of life and love–*"

Bramwell's hand layered over Evelin Byron's, and for a moment, he felt the woman within wiggle her fingers—*I'm in here*—and although he knew deep within his being that Velveteen belonged somewhere other than within this particular vessel.

"I'll do it," Velveteen whispered, effortlessly reading his thoughts. "She'll go mad, but your little wife will have her sibling back. I'll do it, Brammy, if *you* do it."

Koe continued his speech, determined to rid Evelin Byron of the pesky demon that was Goddess Velveteen, going on about Evelin's right to her own body, her own existence, her own soul, which was already tainted—*ruined*—by Velveteen's presence alone.

"Bramwell, take my hand," Koe urged, desperate to reach the final chant. *He was so close.*

Velveteen's vessel grabbed Bramwell's open hand, fingers slipping between his, and with one final breath, she pleaded: "*now,* baby."

The lord obeyed.

The Holy Man Enny Koe met Bramwell Hellthorne's deadpan stare, the soul that once laid beyond his kind orbs seemingly nonexistent.

No...

"Look at me one last time, Holy Man Koe." Bramwell said, a slight snicker in his tone, and under his breath he muttered the simplest word, one that he'd said many times prior, one which made Velveteen burst into a fit of nearly uncontrollable giggles.

Morte.

The Holy Man's heart exploded within his chest.

HELLFIRE

Belle never saw the Holy Man leave.

Whatever the religious man had done, it barely seemed to work, for her younger sister had fallen into a fourteen-hour slumber following her exorcism, only to awaken in a fit of screams in the very same sitting room where the event occurred.

She was inconsolable—terrified beyond comprehension—and within moments of being conscious, she'd snatched up a decorative, floral-stamped knife from the tray of half-eaten scones, a thick layer of jelly still coating the silver blade, and she'd plunged it into the supple skin of her left wrist.

Through a mass of tears, Belle snatched the blood-ied blade away, but to her dismay, the wound was rather deep—*gushing*—and she'd tripped over her own two feet while calling out for her husband.

"I love you more than words," Belle wept, her tear-soaked face buried within Evelin's unkempt hair as Ula tended to her wound. It was only moments later when the younger Byron girl began to scream again—arms flailing every which way, legs furiously kicking at the housemaiden who only wanted to help, and with that, Ula had thrown her arms up in sur-render, refusing to treat Belle's sister any longer.

"We must send her to the Capitol," Bramwell muttered, a barely drank glass of scotch pinched between clammy fingers. Both he and Lyren hovered the open door to the sitting room, their stares fixated on a hysterical Belle beside her manic sister. Regardless of what Belle did, Evelin only screamed, sobbed, and acted violently—*viciously*—begging her elder sister to end her life.

"What in the Goddess Lottie happened to her, Bram?" Lyren breathed, sympathetic tears pricking at the corners of his eyes. Only hours prior, he'd had to hold a distressed Henry back after breaking the news to him about Evelin's condition.

It was difficult to believe that only nights prior, the four of them had such a wonderful time at the nightspot.

No one quite knew that it would be Evelin's last night fully alive.

"Something died inside of her during that exorcism," Bramwell said, not fully fibbing. He was right, Evelin mostly had died following Velveteen's release from her mortal body. She was breathing, yes, but that was the extent of it.

Evelin Byron was good as dead.

"Bram–"

"If we don't send her to the Azyl in Havensworth, she'll be dead come morning. She'll put another jelly knife to her skin, only this time, her throat. She'll be safe at Azyl. They'll monitor her there." Bramwell explained, openly frowning when Evelin began to beg Belle for death once more.

"Keeping her alive almost seems unjust," Lyren said, mindlessly running his fingers along the front of his throat. "Everyone at Azyl is beyond mad. She'll be surrounded by nutters."

He knew well of Azyl, as did most of the country. There were others like it, but none as esteemed. The Azyl of Havensworth only accepted the highest quality doctors, for those individuals who were typically sent all the way to the Capitol for treatment were most likely regarded as *good as dead.*

"With all due respect to my dear wife, I'm saddened to say that her sister herself has become quite a nutter." Bramwell said, waving another housemaiden over. He instructed the woman to ready the carriage and ride with Evelin to Azyl in the Capitol of Elantry, the safest place for her.

"What if we just send her home? Back with her parents?" Lyren weakly suggested, but even he knew that was not wise.

"She'd kill all of them and herself," Bramwell countered. "Now, if you don't mind, I could use your assistance in escorting Evelin Byron to the carriage, as well as your help with Belle. She won't let her sister go peacefully, that much I know."

It had been four hours since Evelin left by carriage for Azyl.

Four hours since Belle said goodbye to her little sister for what would unknowingly be the very last time, for Bramwell wasn't entirely correct. Although Azyl *was* the safest place for Evelin to be, with medics so skilled that they'd saved a generous amount of mentally ill patients, not one of them could help poor Evelin Byron, for she was not ill.

She was a dead girl in a living, breathing body.

She'd last a number of months—nearly two full years—before tearing out her own throat with the razor-sharp edges of her fingernails, which had been meticulously bitten and shaped by the assistance of her gnawing teeth. When a medic had reached her room, there was a river of blood from her pillow to the cold, concrete floor, and a pair of ornate, neatly typed letters with bold, black ink were crafted by a drowsy doctor with a leaky, snot-filled nose.

The pieces of parchment were tucked away into respective envelopes, addressed appropriately, and mailed by carriage, arriving first to Valen, and last to Immorium.

Only, this event wouldn't occur for another twenty-or-so months, and a disconsolate Belle Hellthorne laid trapped beneath several blankets, cheeks reddened with sorrow, eyelids heavy with sleep.

Even she could not predict what was to come, and Evelin's forthcoming death would be trivial in comparison to the times that laid ahead.

She'd rarely rise from her bed in the days to come, but no one dared to breathe a word, for the Lady of Valen was busy grieving a girl whose heart still beat.

Bramwell sent a neatly typed letter to the Byron family, explaining in as much detail as he saw fit of the events that had transpired within Hellthorne's walls. He omitted the most gruesome details and explained that he would be responsible for supplying the funds for Evelin's admittance to Azyl, an institute that would require three years' worth of her father's salary for only six months of treatment.

He spent several nights following Evelin's departure hovering Belle's parted doorway, a glass of alcohol traditionally held within his clutch, kind, dark eyes studying the sobbing woman buried beneath the sheets. A small part of him ached to enter, to take a seat at the corner of her mattress, to lay a comforting palm upon her shoulder. Only, his guilty conscience prevented him from doing such, and instead, the flats of his feet remained planted, a frown etched along his mouth as he watched his wife come completely undone.

He could nearly hear Velveteen's voice within his ear—*Mumma's good boy*—and the lord found himself wandering down the hallway of Belle's wing, curious stare raking the walls. He knew it was here—Lyren had revealed its origin—but as Bramwell paced up and down the hallway three times over, he failed to find it.

He failed to find *her*.

The portrait of a dead girl.

Velveteen's portrait.

He arrived upon the edge of the corridor, a dissatisfied ache present within his chest, and when the manor went quiet, he swore that he could hear the faint rattle of rusted chains echo beneath his feet, buried deep within the bowels of the mansion.

"Straight to the hellfire," he muttered, and with a sigh, Bramwell brought the liquor glass to his lips and swallowed its contents with one large swig before retiring to his own individual quarters for the night.

BREATHE ME IN

Belle slept with the lights on every night since Evelin's departure.

When the oil would run out, her heavy eyelids would tear open, the whites of her eyes red and bloodshot, and she'd shuffle out from under the covers, swiftly lighting the lamps with such urgency that it made her legs shake.

Florence seldom slept, either. She'd offered her love some space, but Belle only refused, fearful of spending the evenings alone after waking up to witness a possessed Evelin upon her bed.

she wasn't possessed, lovebug

she's sick, lovebug

Florence refused to acknowledge the fact that something was sour within the manor's walls, and regardless of how much evidence laid before her feet, she always had some sort of logical explanation, some type of excuse.

perhaps Evelin was poisoned or drugged during your night escapade

Her ignorance jammed a wedge between the pair, and although Belle felt somewhat betrayed by Florence's lack of understanding, she was petrified of being alone in her own room for too long. Thus, she kept Florence close by—their conversations brief, their affection sparse. Surely, she still loved the woman, but the lady just wanted to be heard, to be *understood.*

Lyren Deth believed her.

On the sixth night following Evelin's departure, Belle was woken at the cusp of midnight, a bitter chill cascading down her spine as she repugnantly gasped.

Florence was still sound asleep beside her, a dream so pleasant dancing behind her eyelids that she never wanted to wake, whereas Belle shook from head to toe in pure terror, tear-filled eyes fixated on the four red, weeping walls.

Gallons upon gallons of thick, blotted, nearly black blood slipped through the cracks in the ceiling, draining down the walls at a snail-like pace. It stained the paint, tainted the collectibles. Dated paintings were soiled—*ruined*—drowned in the blood of the manor.

Belle pulled the blanket up past her nose, doe-like eyes unable to tear away from the scene. She'd never seen so much blood in her life—chunky, black, *rotting*—and the scent was overbearing, one so strong that it singed the tiny hairs within her nostrils.

She blinked back tears, and with shaking fingers, she nudged Florence's shoulder, wordlessly waking the woman.

"Bells?" Florence whispered; voice laced with sleep. She hadn't yet opened her eyes, and Belle audibly gulped as the thick sheets of blood finally reached the edge of the carpet, dipping down deep, staining it forevermore.

"Blood," Belle breathed.

Florence's eyelids shot open, a worrisome stare studying the room as she struggled to see exactly what Belle had meant.

All that she could see was the faint flicker of the oil lamps painting lively portraits along the walls, the raging flames burning indefinitely.

"Where's the blood, baby?" Florence cooed, her chest aching with worry. She wanted to believe that Belle wasn't as insane as her sister, but this wasn't the first time that Belle had cried over something nonexistent.

"The walls, Flo," Belle pressed, shaking her head back and forth. She met Florence's sympathetic stare, and she immediately knew that the woman did not believe her.

"How do you not see it?" Belle spat, unintentionally redirecting her anger towards her lover. "It's *everywhere.* The walls are ruddy *covered* in it! It *reeks!* It smells of *rot!* It's as if someone's been murdered in the attic!"

Florence's palm met Belle's cheek, but the smaller woman only tore it away, frustrated beyond belief.

"Why don't you believe me? Do you think it's all made up? Do you think Evelin wasn't possessed? That she, in her right mind, *murdered* a human being? That Lyren was fibbing about the dead woman in the portrait? This manor is *sinister,* Florence. There's a wickedness within these walls that I can't even begin to comprehend, and by Goddess I'd be lying if I said I wasn't terrified to exist in this mansion every single day."

Belle blinked, and the blood was gone. There was neither a drop, nor a stain, and the absence of it was enough to make her scream. Loud.

"Bells!" Florence exclaimed, shuffling towards the distraught woman. She clamped a hand over Belle's gaping mouth, a series of coos slipping off of her tongue as she took the younger woman into her arms. In the best way that she knew how, she comforted the terrified girl with a series of kisses and comforting sweet nothings whispered against the fiery red edge of her hair.

"I'm scared," Belle said, resting her forehead against Florence's. "I'm ruddy *terrified,* Flo. I want to feel safe here, but something feels so sinister. So *wrong.* I don't even know how I feel about my own husband, nonetheless–"

"Bramwell is an amazing man," Florence immediately countered, a stern stare meeting Belle's. "He'll care for you until his dying breath. That much, I know."

Belle didn't appear entirely convinced.

"There's something not right about him, love. Odd things happen around him—*with* him. People forget things. People *die.* He's a cursed man, isn't he, Florence?"

"No," Florence said, trying not to grit her teeth. "Not even close. He had a rough childhood. He was a bastard child. He was unwanted, uncared for. He found comfort the only way he knew how. He's not cursed; he's *blessed.*"

Before Belle could pry any further—*what in Goddess Lottie did any of that even mean?*—there was a knock at the door, and sure enough, the man himself, Bramwell Hellthorne, poked his head around the corner.

"One of the night guards informed me of a disturbance," he explained, wide limbs clad in a pair of strikingly ordinary loose-fit pajamas. It was the most casual Belle had ever seen him.

"Night guard?" Belle asked, a brow raised. Bramwell had already eased himself fully into the room, hands stuffed within the pockets of his puffy pants, sleepy stare studying the two women cuddled up within the bed.

"I hate to intrude on your privacy, my darling, but I've been on high alert since your sister's departure and Topher's death. I appointed several night guards to stand watch within the manor, mainly downstairs. None ever enter your hall, for your privacy is important to me." Bramwell explained, his voice husky and low, exhausted, even.

"Evelin killed Topher in her possessed form," Belle said, shifting uncomfortably beside Florence, whose arms were still draped around Belle's shoulders. "With her at Azyl, there's no need for such security. Unless, of course, you're aware of the sinister threats that reside within these walls, just as Lyren and I have described?"

Florence stiffened, and Belle took note. She was tired of acting as if she was hallucinating—*dreaming.* Everything she'd seen was real, whether or not anyone else could see it, too.

Belle wasn't insane. Not even the least bit.

"You're right," Bramwell said, and Florence's jaw dropped. He edged closer to the bed, taking a hesitant seat at the very foot of the mattress, as if unwelcome. "There's something sinister within these walls, certainly. Did you really suspect that a gothic mansion such as Hellthorne estate would be full of rainbows and lilies and light? My father was a terrible man, a violent man. He enslaved people, tortured people. He locked me away for years in a bedroom with not a single window. Evil resides within these walls because of him. I should've told you what you were getting into before moving you to Valen."

"Bramwell, you can't be serious," Florence interjected, tearing her touch away from a slightly satisfied Belle. "You know that's all a fib. Your father is dead, Velveteen the *demon* doesn't exist, nor do the Goddesses. I know better, and you know better. Playing into these fantasies will only have Belle beside her sister in Azyl strung out with insanity in no time."

Bramwell sighed, weakly tossing his hands airborne as if in surrender. "You're right, Florence. The very last place I'd want my wife is within the walls of Azyl, although they'd take wonderful care of her as they will her sister."

Bramwell redirected his attention to a now thoroughly confused Belle, fresh tears flooding her eyes as she wondered who to believe.

"My sweet Belle, whatever it is you see, or hear, or touch, even if it is not there, just know that I will always believe you, sympathize with you, and support you. There are mysteries in this world that no one can truly explain, and although Florence is right, the tales of the Goddesses, of Velveteen, of demons and spirits and ghosts are nothing more than falsified fabrications of unexplained realities, I will never make you feel as if you are lesser than for believing in such."

Bramwell extended a hand, urging Belle to lay hers within his wide, warm palm. A peace offering.

She hesitated, a single tear easing down the slope of her flushed cheek, and she rotated her stare to meet a content Florence, a small smile strung along her lips.

She'd never felt more lost and confused in her entire existence.

Exhausted with the back-and-forth banter between a seemingly secretive Florence and an unreadable Bramwell, Belle gave up entirely, taking Bramwell's hand in hers before softly squeezing.

"Okay," she said, and that was that.

Bramwell bid the pair goodnight, and left Belle to her thoughts, a sleepy Florence tangling her legs within hers.

"Hey," Florence cooed, dainty fingers dancing along Belle's jaw. Their eyes met, and Florence sighed, a look of clear disappointment painted along her lover's features.

"I'm sorry," Florence said, caressing the sharp curve of Belle's chin with the flat of her thumb. "I really am. You're terrified, and all I've been is dismissive. A lot has happened recently—with Bram, with your sister, with the manor. Just know that you have me, you'll always have me, and even if I don't understand—if I don't *see* or *hear*—I'll always listen."

Belle's pouted lips turned up into a small smile, another tiny tear escaping from a drowsy eyelid as her forehead met Florence's, followed by a tender, short-lived smooch.

"I love you," Belle said, and the woman opposite her smiled—big, bold—before kissing the red-haired woman several times over, soft lips straying from Belle's, wandering along her chin, her cheeks, her forehead.

"And I love *you*," Florence replied, planting one final kiss upon Belle's lips. "I'm lucky to call you mine, even if it's just within these four walls."

"I'm yours even outside of them," Belle confirmed, knotting her frigid fingers around Florence's warm wrist. "Even on Bram's arm, I'm yours. Even with his name, I'm yours. *All yours.*"

"Forever," Florence breathed, and she urged Belle to lay back down, the tiny girl resting her head upon Florence's sturdy chest, the steady beat of her heart putting Belle to sleep.

ROUGH WATERS

On the ninth day, Belle wandered down the iron spiral staircase in nothing but a warm hefty gown, pale feet bare and freezing, toes flushed a violent red.

She was met by a chipper Clare on her way to the kitchen, whose gaping gaze was startled to see the lady up and out of bed after what seemed like an eternity.

"My lady!" Clare cheered; nimble fingers threaded within her hair as she sloppily braided it down her back. "How are you feeling? Do you need anything? Have you not been brought any breakfast?"

"I wanted to come help with breakfast," Belle revealed, smiling sweetly. Her feet were freezing upon the aged wooden flooring, and Clare took notice of her lack of footwear, her thin lips pulling into a frown.

"Lady Belle, you should really be wearing socks or even some shoes, the manor is freezing this morning. There's a blanket of snow beyond the windows, so white and bright that it's blinding." Clare said, drifting along the wooden floorboards with such elegance and ease that she almost looked unhuman.

A ghost.

Belle shoved the intrusive thought to the very depths of her mind, observing the housemaiden closely as Clare approached the big, broad windows, arms raising above her head to claim the weighty mahogany drapes. She tore them open to reveal the most breathtaking view.

She was right, overnight Valen had been buried in the thickest, most powdery blanket of snow that Belle had ever seen, and she audibly gasped, for the sight was magical—*beautiful.* She crept towards the windows, fingers dancing along the cold glass panes as she ogled the view from the manor.

Nearly everything was buried beneath the snow—all besides a patch of impossibly tall poppies, a deep crimson hue, and although Belle didn't know much about plants, she *did* know that poppies hardly blossomed in harsh, wet environments, but it appeared as if these blood-red florals continued to thrive, even amongst the snow.

"It's stunning, isn't it, Lady Hellthorne?" Clare said, planted directly beside Belle. She, too, seemed to be in a trance, as if she hadn't worked for the manor for just about six years, as if she hadn't seen the stunning sight every winter like clockwork.

"Jeanne's been baking some," Clare revealed, resting a hand on Belle's bony shoulder. "Why don't you wander back up to your wing, I'll have someone bring you up breakfast shortly."

"But I wanted–" Belle stuttered, but the housemaiden didn't let her finish.

"The kitchen is no place for the Lady of Valen," Clare smiled, but there was something strange, something *sinister* behind her seemingly normal grin. Typically, Clare didn't say much to Belle—she hardly paid her any mind at all—but this morning was out of the ordinary, and the fact made Belle's skin slightly crawl.

"I'm just a seaside girl from Immorium," Belle muttered, shrugging her shoulder out of Clare's gentle hold. "I'm royalty by marriage, and only just. But it appears that I am not wanted among the housemaidens, so I'll obey your wishes."

She half expected Clare to profusely apologize—to ramble on about how Belle had just misunderstood her, how she'd misspoken, how what she said was out of line. Only, Clare did none of those things. Instead, that same, empty smile claimed her features, and the housemaiden nodded, curtsied, and abandoned Belle within the foyer, the flowing tail of Clare's pale blue dress dipping from sight.

What in the name of Goddess Liv was going on around here?

Belle took her time venturing back to the lonely halls of her own wing, curious fingertips trailing along the textured walls, a forefinger tracing the dissimilar shapes along several painted portraits. She took a peek beyond several sealed windows, poking her head around the thick drapes, and she located Henry outside near the blood-red poppies, his gloved fingers curiously caressing the floral arrangements. She wanted to knock on the fogged pane of the window—to wave, to smile—but she knew that Henry too was in an odd mindset following Evelin's episode. Belle wondered how often he thought of her sister, if he blamed himself for her ruin. No one besides Belle, (and possibly Lyren), even seemed remotely convinced that the Byron girl was possessed—*not herself*—and instead, most assumed that she was simply ill in the head, a sickness that could be cured at Azyl, the institution for the psychologically diseased.

She passed by one of Bramwell's night guard's—who, oddly, was still within the mansion during the day—and Belle offered the big, burly man a warm smile, one which he failed to return. He was wide-shouldered, with shy, scruffy blonde hair strewn along his pink features. He was dressed rather unusually—a style so outdated that it almost resembled something a guard from the 1820's would adorn—and as he strut right past Belle without a single word, she took a second look, her neck craned slightly to glance over her shoulder.

The night guard had disappeared.

Belle paused, the blood within her veins shifting to ice as bile crept up her throat. She'd seen him, surely, but when she'd stolen another look, it was as if the man had never even existed in the first place. Vanished into thin air, slipped into the floorboards, burst into an imperceptible cloud of dust.

"What in Goddess name," Belle mumbled, anxious to continue onward. She never quite knew what she'd see around the manor, and everytime she blinked, visuals of Evelin's pearly white stare invaded her vision—the sopping, sanguine grin. The bloody nightgown.

Then, there was a whisper.

A hiss.

Initially, the woman wasn't entirely sure of its origin, that was, until she'd stumbled toward the wall, an ear flush against the surface—waiting, *listening.*

It led her towards the fifth bathroom in the west wing—*Belle's wing*—which was a good walk down from her bedroom.

The low hissing buried within the walls increased with each passing step, imitating a language the woman didn't know as she curiously followed. Her right ear never quite left the surface, trembling fingers grazing along the wallpaper. She narrowly missed the portraits, unintentionally shifting several from their cozy homes, only to briefly pause to realign them. She paused at the sight of one in particular.

It was of a woman—young, possibly around Belle's age—who was stiff against a brown chair, the ruffled sleeves of her gown concealing both her hands and arms. She looked relatively normal, until the woman noticed her eyes.

Bleak.

Dead.

Belle gasped, tearing away from the portrait in fear. The girl in the painting looked completely and utterly *dead*, and just as Lyren had told both her and Bram, the portrait *did exist*. Only, it wasn't hung in the same spot that he'd shown them before. No, it was considerably further down the hall, much further than where Ula had found him unconscious on the floor.

Belle's heart jumped into her throat, and the shy, soft voice returned—a series of hissing tones—and with trembling legs, she abandoned the eerie portrait altogether, desperate to never see such a terrible thing ever again. She shelved her plans to tell Bramwell of its existence in the very back of her mind, a thought that she'd come to forget, and continued onward, curious to find the origin of the voice beyond the wall.

The volume increased considerably as she approached the fifth bathroom, and it almost seemed excited—*anxious*. Her fingers gently collided with the circular brass handle of the sealed door, and the voice nearly exclaimed with glee, causing Belle to visibly flinch, widened eyes glancing around at her surroundings.

She was completely alone.

She tore her hand from the knob, and the voice shrieked—angry, *cold*. Belle's palms met her mouth, parted into an o-shape, and she took a large step backward, bile rising up the slope of her throat as the unrecognizable sound increased with each passing second, calling, *beckoning* her back toward the door.

Open me.

"Oh, good Goddess," Belle cried, unable to stifle the fearful shakes that consumed her core. Her curiosity had completely vanished, replaced only by true, intense fear that made her blood run cold.

Nothing about the manor was normal, and just as Bramwell had said, Belle truly began to believe that at its very core, pure evil beat through the veins of the home, bleeding down the walls in a sickly, black goo. She could still see the blood, the way it dribbled down the four walls of her bedroom, how it pooled along the floor, stained the carpet a sickly red.

The voice shrieked once more, and Belle lurched forward, shaking fingers latching around the warm handle as she twisted it open.

The portal opened, and the sound silenced—leaving behind nothing but a dull ring within Belle's ears. She gasped, but not due to the lack of noise, but what laid within the room.

Similar to her individual bathroom, this particular space was spacious and wide, accented with a plethora of ebony stained wood. Directly parallel to the door sat a hefty clawfoot tub, the basin a cool white, whereas the feet were plated with stunning gold.

The tub was occupied.

"Belle?"

An inquisitive azure stare met Belle's frozen features, blond hair newly washed and tickling the curve of his chin. Lyren shifted slightly in the bath, the water surrounding his pale frame gaily rippling, creating soft, sweet waves that met the rounded surface of his exposed knees.

"Lyren, I–"

"No, it's okay," he lightly pressed, reaching an arm out towards her. Warm water slid from his skin, decorating the tile in diverse variations of circular shapes. His fingers parted, beckoning her forward.

Come.

"There was a voice–" Belle stammered, desperate to plead her case, to make her seem less like a creep for peeping on Lyren in the bath, but the man didn't seem to mind.

Instead, a jaunty grin snaked along his lips, exposing his abnormally white teeth, canines pointed and sharp. He enjoyed watching her squirm—the way her cheeks flushed, the color draining down her neck. How her stare shifted uncomfortably towards the wall, desperately avoiding the sight of his lanky self in the tub, *thoroughly* aware of the pile of discarded clothing unceremoniously tossed upon the floor—forgotten, unneeded.

"I was thinking about you," he admitted, confident in his confession. "About the window. The carriage ride. The way you've avoided me for days, especially since Evelin's departure."

Belle shifted in her spot; gaze glued to her bare feet. He was right, she hadn't seen him in days. Evelin left over a week ago, and her sister's presence was a perfect excuse to avoid the man, but now with her gone, her excuse was null. With him evidently living in the manor full-time now, there simply was no avoiding Lyren Deth. Hellthorne Manor was massive, but the hallways all led to one common place, and apparently, that place was *him.*

Admittedly, she'd barely had time to think about the brief moment they'd shared within the carriage. It seemed like an eternity had passed since then—nothing but an eternity of horror immediately following. It was difficult to think of anything besides Evelin's nightmarish episode and the repetitive incidents that seemed to occur almost daily.

"Close the door, will you? You're letting in a draft." Lyren said, arm still extended in Belle's direction.

The heat returned to Belle's face in the form of a furious blush, and without a sound, she snapped the door closed, still firmly avoiding the man in the tub.

She wanted to tell him all about the voice—the way it hissed, spat, *seethed*—but none of that seemed to matter anymore, for it had vanished completely, as if it never existed at all. Only, she knew better.

She wasn't crazy.

"I think about the window often," Lyren openly admitted, lowering his arm when Belle failed to step forward and take it. "That was the first time I truly, fully laid eyes on you. The way your pale skin shifted beyond the frosted glass, how I could see a pink blush crawl up your neck when you realized that I was watching."

Belle felt that very same blush start to creep along her chest, and she met Lyren's glare—sultry, sweet, *wanting.*

"Perhaps I shouldn't be here–" Belle stammered, gaze flickering between the closed door and Lyren's achingly nude form buried beneath the stagnant, rose-scented water.

"Get in the tub, Lady Hellthorne." Lyren said. It wasn't a request—it was an order.

He didn't have to tell the woman twice.

Belle lifted a leg, clambering into the decorative basin to meet a buzzing, blush-ridden Lyren, his pale skin reddened with warmth. He could feel the heat of his carnal desires creep up his spine, and with unblinking eyes, he watched Belle climb into the bath with him, her tiny form still clad in her dense morning dress.

She immediately settled upon his lap—nothing but the bulky, drenched clothing of hers separating them. Even through the thick fabric, the woman swore that she could feel Lyren brush up against her inner thigh, his cock painfully pulsing beneath the fragrant waves.

The bath water wildly shifted from Belle's sudden entrance, sloshing over the curved edges of the basin before flooding the floor. It made a dreadful mess, but the pair didn't quite seem to care.

Lyren's palms found Belle's cheeks, a single thumb dipping downward, delicately trailing along the pouted pink flesh of her lower lip. He couldn't blink—couldn't *think*—for the Lady of Valen was on his lap once more, just as she was in the carriage several nights prior, only this time, there was no concealing his aching erection.

"Kiss me, m'lady."

Their mouths met in a hurried frenzy—teeth clattering, a series of giggles tickling one another's tongue. She tasted of lemon tea and the flavor made Lyren dizzy, eyes tipping up into his skull as he basked in all things *her*.

"I told you not to call me that," Belle murmured, barely tearing away from his kiss to utter the statement. She refused to allow him any time for a response, for her mouth had claimed his once more, eager and determined.

She became achingly aware of the heavy garment draped around her lithe frame, and she was eager to rid her limbs of the pricy fabric—to tear it *off off off*...

"Help me," she whispered, trembling fingers tearing at the sleeves of her gown. Lyren wordlessly obeyed, looping his bare fingers—*had Belle ever seen the man without his rings before this very moment?*—around the dense material.

There was a yank—a *tear*—and Belle couldn't help but outwardly gasp—*you've fucking torn it, you have*—widening stare shuffling toward the source of the sound. She saw the rip in the fabric, the way he'd so seamlessly torn the sleeve, and she gasped once more when he mindlessly rid her shoulder of the dress, exposing the white skin beneath.

"Lyren–"

"I'll replace it," Lyren dismissed, tearing his lips from hers. Belle barely had a moment to breathe before he found the slick skin of her neck, teeth gently nibbling along the soft surface.

I'll replace it.

Oh, what a luxury—to hoard riches and wealth, to have the ability to purchase such an elegant, expensive gown at the tip of a hat.

A gown her father would work nearly half a decade just to afford.

Her attention had drifted, and Lyren took note—soft, plump lips detaching from the curve of Belle's neck.

"Are you all right?"

Eager not to soil the moment with the bland discussion of finances, Belle redirected her focus, lengthy nails burying within the light blond tresses of Lyren's thick, healthy hair, before finding his scalp. Gently, she massaged the surface, earning a throaty groan from the man as he shifted ever so slightly beneath her clothed hips. He tried—but failed—to hide his rock-hard length, which was separated from Belle's burning core by nothing but the fabric of her ripped and ruined dress.

The action was innocent and sweet, but Belle enjoyed how it felt pressed up against her. It was a mostly foreign feeling, a sensation she hadn't felt since her youthful events with her teenage lover, Dalbir.

Lyren remembered their conversation from the carriage ride, one that revealed Bramwell's apparent abstinence. The thought brought him to a pause.

"Have you ever . . ?"

Belle nudged her upper half out from the confines of the dress, exposing the stark white skin that lay concealed beneath. The torn material collected around her partially submerged self, circling her lower stomach like the waist of a loose, ill-fitting skirt.

"I'm not free of sin," she said, untangling her bright red hair from her messy, unbrushed braid. She shook her head from side to side, her knotted curls drifting down to meet her middle, the ends delicately dancing along the surface of the water. Her hair was a dreadful, matted mess from sleeping in her braid, so much so that not even her fingers could detangle the knots.

Lyren found the sight of her messy, tangled hair rather amusing—*human,* even—and he recalled how many times he'd encountered women from the Capitol with perfectly polished hair. Women who'd bat his wandering hand away if he'd gotten too close.

Belle was different. She was ordinary, through and through—nothing at all like the people who walked the streets of the wealthy Havensworth, or even the upper class of Valen, which was full of snobbish women who would shun the Lady of Valen for appearing so unpolished.

"We'll be a right pair in the Netherworld, won't we, then?" Lyren teased, peppering soft, sweet kisses up the column of Belle's throat. "With Florence in the mix—a sweet, sinful trio."

Trio.

Their lips met once again—a feral frenzy—and Belle almost forgot how to breathe. Lyren's touch wandered, starting at the nape of her neck, the flat of his thumb just barely applying pressure to her chin, urging it downwards, prying open her mouth. His tongue slipped in with ease, if it belonged there, and she grew dizzy with want, heat pooling down at her core as she began to throb.

Suddenly, the fabric of the dress separating their groins was nothing but a nuisance.

His fingertips trailed south—slowly, as if out of caution—and he traced the bony indent of her chest, politely avoiding her bare breasts, not wanting to touch her in places where she may not fully consent to being touched.

Belle was too wrapped up in all-things Lyren to even move, his tongue busy exploring the warmth of her mouth. Between his shy, curious touch and the way his breath felt along her tongue, she could hardly form a coherent thought, let alone command her brain to move a single limb. Instead, her hands laid entrapped within his hair.

She tugged, and he groaned—his touch disappearing beneath the pleasantly scented water, coiling tightly around her submerged (and still sadly clothed) waist.

Her fingertips wandered, grazing along his upper arms, and when she stumbled upon something strange, her eyes flew open in wonder.

The skin was rough and raised beneath the soft pads of her fingers. She ran the tip of her index finger along the surface, following the marks, easing up the ladder. It was peculiar—unlike anything she'd ever felt—and Lyren's breath hitched when she tore away from his kiss to inspect the tainted skin.

She squinted, studying the surface of his skin, and was met with a winding stepladder of healed scars that claimed a majority of the upper portion of his arm. She hadn't even noticed them before, for they were just barely a single shade paler than his actual skin tone, but now that she was up so close—so *personal*—she could see them all.

Lyren remained silent as she shyly inspected his skin, and she was stunned to find that his other arm was almost identical to the first. Only that side wasn't quite as invisible as the other.

There were moderately fresh wounds near the tip of the haphazard ladder, only a mere inch from his shoulder, and the skin was angry and red, cracked and dry. She wanted to feel the newer ones, but her mouth ran dry at the sight, and she felt frozen—*numb*.

She wanted to ask, but she couldn't quite find the right words to say. Lyren's stare met hers, a soft twinkle in his eye. His palm cupped her cheek, and he drew her close, pausing only slightly to breathe her in, before giving himself to her fully with a long, lustful kiss.

"Get me out of this damned dress," Belle pleaded, tearing away from his intoxicating kiss.

"Take me to your bed, then," Lyren said, fiddling with the drenched dress. "I want to see you laid out all pretty for me."

Belle paused, achingly aware of the more than several steps that it would take for the pair to arrive upon her private quarters. Sure, the entire wing belonged solely to her, but the housemaidens had a bad habit of *wandering,* and what would they think if they saw the Lady of Valen stark nude, trotting hand in hand with an equally naked Lyren Deth, Bramwell's best pal?

The only one who will see you will be the portrait of the dead girl.

A shiver claimed Belle's spine, and she met Lyren with a wordless nod. He helped her from the tub, assisting the woman in ridding her goosebump riddled frame of her saturated clothing. When she stood before him in nothing but her undergarments, she felt suddenly insecure—*odd.*

As if he hadn't already seen every inch of her pretty, pink cunt beyond the frosted window of her bedroom.

Belle was so wrapped up in worry and insecurity and panic that when she finally fixated on the situation at hand, she discovered that Lyren Deth was standing before her entirely naked. He was still hard—visibly throbbing—and shockingly bare of any hair, nothing but a dainty puff of peach fuzz surrounding his dick.

"You're so–"

"Feminine?" Lyren lightly mocked, as if he'd heard it several times over. On the outside, he seemed mostly unphased by it, but to most Pliritans, a feminine man was insulting—*sinful*. Belle could almost bet Bramwell's entire fortune that Lyren had heard nearly every insult in the book from more than several unruly followers of the Goddesses.

"Gorgeous," Belle breathed, smiling sweetly. She yanked the drain from the tub, careful not to slip on the wet mess they'd made all over the tile.

When the bath was good and empty, Lyren extended a hand, a pearly-white smirk slithering along his lips. "Come, Lady Belle. Let me worship you like Paio worshiped the Goddess Lottie on the sixth day of Eneve."

THE SIXTH DAY OF ENEVE

As foretold in the Good Book of Plirity, there was a time in the golden days of the Goddesses where their sovereignty was tested.

Before man walked the grounds, the royal deities and their mythical beings roamed the planet. For hundreds of years, all went considerably well—people loved the Goddesses, *adored* them—but over time, some had come to question their reign.

Disciples grew distant, hungry for change, curious of the power the golden thrones held.

The shift led to divide, which tumbled into war—Goddess Lottie leading the light, and the fallen divine called Velveteen dominated the dark. The conflict spanned decades, wiping out hundreds of thousands of supernatural folks, leading to their extinction.

The land was tainted—*maimed*—and the three royal sisters—Lottie, Lilen, and Liv—crafted a safe haven for those who still remained, a place where eradication, death, *despair* would be impossible.

A spot where the darkness could never penetrate.

Thus, the Goddesses abandoned the land, and took with them all of the light-bearing souls that remained, transporting each and every one to Eden, a land where only the light could penetrate.

Abandoned, starving, and left to die on a planet unfit for the dark, Velveteen and what remained of her vile, abominable army dug deep, crafting a sanctuary of their own—one where they'd be comfortable, safe, and free to sin. Thus, the Netherworld was born, and they, too, abandoned the land, leaving it barren—*empty*—until nearly a century later when the first woman would blossom from the ground, and the rest was history.

There were celebrations following the creation of Eden, and one ceremony lasted eleven days—the days of Eneve.

The days of Eneve were spent with constant worship of the Goddesses—the three Queens who saved the lives of the light bearers who remained. All were thanked—abundantly so—and they gave up food, pleasure, and sleep solely to spend each of the eleven days on their knees before the golden thrones. Women brought fresh babies as gifts, eager for their children to be granted white, fluffy wings and grow to become warriors for the women. Men kissed their feet, fed them bread, grapes, and cheese, dedicated their bodies and souls to the three sisters indefinitely, a way of thanking them for eternal salvation.

One man, in particular, was called Paio. He had just barely blossomed into a man, his parents and siblings lost to the war. He was one of the last few of his kind, with a generous ability of curing even the sickest of the sick, and he'd fallen for Goddess Lottie—*hard*.

According to the Good Book, on the sixth day of Eneve, Paio had approached the Goddess with hopes of worship, pleasure, and peace. She took kindly to him, and for the first time since the festivities of Eneve had begun, she rose from her throne, slipped her hand into Paio's, and abandoned the House of Holiness, leaving behind thousands of worshipers still on their knees.

What is written in the scripture is subjective, but it has been foretold that not only did a young Paio worship the Goddess physically, but also doted upon her for an entire day, from sun-up to sun-down. It wasn't until the seventh day that Lottie returned to her throne, a murmur of a baby swelling within her belly, and the daughter of the pair, Yenevieve, would be the first child born of Eden.

It was a tale passed down through time—written and rewritten within the pages of the Good Book—but Belle always found the story to be quite silly. Countless times during worship as a child, she'd openly mock how someone as seemingly average as a young man like Paio couldn't possibly impregnate a *literal* Goddess, and her mother would scold her over and over and over.

The word of the Good Book is the only true word.

So, although Belle never quite cared for the story of the sixth day of Eneve, the way Lyren so simply quoted the sacred writing turned her legs to jelly, for admittedly, she'd always wondered what it would be like to be worshiped as intensely as Goddess Lottie had been.

She could hardly wait.

It wasn't unusual for Belle to wander the halls of the manor; Florence knew this much.

The residence mirrored that of a grandiose castle, and although Florence herself had lived on the property for a solid decade, even she was unaware of every little secret that Hellthorne Manor hid within its thick, dusty walls.

So, when Belle wasn't in her bedroom when Clare had brought up breakfast—a tray filled to the brim with sausage croissants, jelly, and juice—Florence wasn't entirely surprised. Clare didn't dare question Florence's presence—or Belle's absence—and she simply placed the tray on Belle's bedside table and excused herself from the room.

Florence was fiddling with the bouquet of wilting flowers (gifted to Belle by Bramwell following Evelin's frightening exorcism and sudden trip to Azyl in Havensworth) when she heard a disturbance in the hall.

Not just one voice, but two—hushed chuckles, soft footsteps. Often, the housemaidens would frolic about the halls between duties, sharing secrets they'd overheard from Bramwell's meetings, but this was different.

One voice was certainly female, while the other sounded deeper, lower. *Male.*

Florence raised a curious brow, and as she took a step towards the parted doorway, she was met with two gleeful individuals, both stripped bare of their clothing.

"Belle?" Florence gawked, sweet stare considerably widening at the sight of her lover laid bare before her, pale skin flushed a soft pink, lips pulled into a wide smile. She was hand in hand with Lyren Deth, who was also entirely nude, a similar expression slapped across his features. He was smoother than she'd envisioned, dainty patches of hair barely claiming their respective spaces along his body.

At the sight, Florence couldn't help but smile.

Oh, what a sight.

"Well, then?" Florence began, unable to stifle her smirk. "Best shut the door, unless you want a nosy Ula or Clare to see something they shouldn't."

"If we're lucky, only Jeanne will see," Belle countered, referencing the mute housemaiden. "She wouldn't breathe a word, no matter how shocked she may be."

Florence lowly laughed, and with an outstretched hand, she beckoned the couple inward, promptly sealing the door behind them before latching the lock.

A trio of dissimilar giggles ricocheted off the walls of Belle's bedroom, and Florence fell into Lyren's arms, mouths delicately colliding, lips pulling upward into identical, toothy grins.

"Eager, much?" Lyren teased between breathless pecks, and Florence's cheeks flushed, for she was never one to shy away from her desires.

"I've been wondering when I'd finally see you in Belle's bed," Florence said, buzzing fingers fiddling with the buttons on her dress. Belle's cool, tender touch met hers, and with ease, she assisted the woman in shedding herself of her own clothing, joining the pair in their nakedness.

"Our bed," Belle corrected, and her lips found refuge upon Florence's bare shoulder—licking, nipping, sucking—whereas Lyren's effeminate frame rocked against Florence's partially clothed self, her day dress bunched up around her waist, aching to be shed—*forgotten.*

"This feels like a fantasy," Lyren cooed, hungry gaze shifting from a moderately winded Florence to a pink-faced Belle, a rush of blood pooling within her cheeks.

Florence's fingers met the unblemished surface of Lyren's forearm, and with a little smirk, she pinched the skin—*hard*—and he tore away with an impish yelp, only to be silenced by Belle's mouth.

She swallowed his shout, a low purr vibrating along her tongue as she snaked it into Lyren's open mouth. They were a tangle of limbs and sighs, and Florence finally rid herself of her dress, kicking the clothing aside along with her shoes.

She encouraged the snogging twosome to take several steps backwards, where they'd tumble onto the mattress in a mixture of sweat, skin, and heat.

Belle and Lyren barely broke their kiss as they blindly followed Florence's lead, and Lyren's back met the warm, fleecy duvet, silvery blond locks sprawled around his head like a lovely aura.

An angel.

Belle sat neatly upon his lap—their warm groins meeting with ease—and Lyren outwardly groaned, beautiful blue eyes disappearing beyond fluttering lashes, fingers knotting within the sheets. He nearly whined when Belle's needy mouth met the flat of his neck, and his rushing pulse drummed against her lips. It was overwhelming—*dizzying*—and Florence's hands met his hair—gentle, nimble strokes—and she combed through the locks with ease, fingertips massaging his scalp, eliciting a thick moan to emerge from the depths of his chest.

"Good *Goddess*," Lyren groaned, craning his neck to meet Belle's lips once more. He was hungry with want—*need*—and she was so warm and so wet and so—*fuck.*

His hard, aching length throbbed against Belle's center, and she whined upon his tongue, teeth biting down—*clamp-*

ing—leaving little marks behind along her swollen lower lip, blood rushing to the surface. *Pooling.*

It hurt, and she loved it.

"This is so beautiful," Florence purred, still running her fingers through Lyren's hair. "You're *both* beautiful."

Belle blushed so fiercely that she wondered if her milky white cheeks would forever hold the sweet scarlet stain, and she pulled away from a greedy Lyren—his tongue lustfully lapping at the petite bubbles of blood along her lip—and met Florence's kiss. Belle's blood was metallic and sweet—a strangely sensual concoction—and Florence went woozy at the taste.

Drinking her lover's blood—such a sinful, disfavored action. She'd never quite believed in the tales of the night stalking bloodsuckers, but when the diminutive drops of Belle's bright red blood tickled Florence's tongue, she dreamt of being within one of those aged fables.

If drinking her partner's blood was sinful enough to send her to the Netherworld, she'd drink it by the glass.

"Let me have another taste," Lyren longingly requested, ivory flesh slick with sweat, blue stare hazy with want, with *need.*

"We're no better than those damned bloodsuckers our parents told us fables about," Florence teased, and the three of them shared a breathless chuckle as Belle's mouth met Lyren's.

It felt venereal—*ritualistic*—and yet, it seemed familiar, as if the three had done this very same thing dozens of times before. Wandering hands knew exactly where to touch, where to grab, where to *spank*. Florence taught Lyren just how to snake his pretty ringless fingers around Belle's throat, to apply the amount of pressure that the redheaded girl liked just right, and when she sighed, Florence and Lyren joined in with a chorus of groans.

Lyren rutted upward against Belle's heat, the head of his hot, pulsating dick locating the curve of her clit. She outwardly gasped, a single hand claiming his hair, whereas the opposite gripped onto Florence's wrist.

She wanted to feel all of him. Every inch, every pulse, all of the wet warmth. She wanted it all, and she wanted it *now*.

Belle's palm met the center of Lyren's chest, nails curled inward, angry red crescent moons etched along his otherwise smooth skin. With a groan, Lyren lifted his hips ever so slightly, a wordless beg—a *plea*.

"Tell me," Belle cooed, a taunting tone. "Use your words, pretty boy. Tell me—tell *us*—just exactly what you want."

"Goddess Lottie in Eden," Lyren slurred, beside himself in pleasure. He was blinded by it—*consumed*. Trembles tickled his knees, a rushing pulse buried beneath flesh, muscle, and bone. An eager bird, desperate to flee from its skeletal cage.

"The Goddesses can't save you, now," Florence teased, her voice laced with seduction, and she and Belle exchanged glances, giggles tickling their tongues. "You'll have to beg on your knees for seven days and seven nights after we're done with you, Lyren Deth."

The maidenly man beneath Belle's hips writhed and whined, a series of begs slipping off of his lips so quickly that they were barely legible. The women lightly laughed once more, and Belle audibly requested Florence's assistance.

Her hips shifted—her weight distributed amongst either leg as she rose off of Lyren's lap, but only just—and naturally, as if he'd routinely done it a thousand times before, the man's hands found her sharp, pointed hips, clamping, squeezing.

Marking.

He watched with wide eyes as Florence's arm weaved around Belle's body, her lovely aristocratic fingers encircling Lyren's prick, and he nearly cried upon contact. He was painfully aroused by now, desperate for release, but their game had just begun, and if he were to please not one, but *two* stunning women at the very same time, he'd have to concentrate. *Focus.*

Focus, Lyren.

Fuck.

"Easy, now," Florence purred, gradually grasping him. Lyren watched, unblinking, as the woman lined him up with an aching, pulsating Belle, her desire nearly dripping down her legs.

She guided him inward—slowly, *tortuously*—and Lyren tossed his head back, damp, silver locks wild and awry, eyelids squeezed tightly shut. The muscles beneath the skin of his stomach tightened and flexed, and Florence's mouth met his as Belle took him in to the very hilt.

Florence swallowed Lyren's guttural groan with pleasure, and she clamped a hand over his own, which still firmly held onto Belle's hip, as if for support. His nails curled inward, creating a sensual soreness that only made Belle's chest grow hot, and the three wriggled and whined within unison, a dance only they knew.

By the very first roll of her hips, Lyren grew greedy. She was moving at a pace so achingly slow that it made him impatient.

More more more.

His mouth strayed from Florence's, and Belle was suddenly on her back, a motion so swift and slick that both of the women went dizzy. Lyren barely missed a beat, swollen, red lips diving down to meet Belle's gaping gasp. He drove fully into her, pausing only briefly to gauge her reaction—*whiny, whimpering, wet little mess*—and he fell into a pleasant rhythm, with thrusts so deep and full that Belle outwardly squeaked every time he sank completely in.

Blissful blurs clouded Belle's vision. She couldn't speak, she couldn't *think*—for Lyren was fucking her so hard and so well and *good Goddess Lottie in Eden,* she'd *never* felt such a sensation as this. The only other man she'd been with was purely experimental—dreadfully inexperienced—but Lyren was vastly different. He was experienced—*determined.* He knew where to touch, where to kiss, how to move. He swiveled his hips just as his mouth met Florence's bountiful breast, and Belle cried, fingers tangling around her favorite lady's wrist, clinging on for dear life.

The three were a knotted mess of limbs and sweat and warmth, and to an outsider, it wouldn't be entirely clear where one individual began and the other ended, for Belle had been moved once again, dizzyingly quick, her knees flush against the mushy mattress, face buried within the sheets. Lyren slipped back into her warmth with ease, as if he'd done it plenty of times before, and as a chorus of moans traveled up Belle's throat, she felt the tip of Florence's tongue lap at her clit.

She didn't know how—she was too weak, too woozy to even lift her head up to see—but Florence had managed to position herself between Belle's legs in just the right way, her mouth suctioned to Belle's clit, whereas Lyren gracefully and skillfully fucked her senseless.

"F-Flo," Belle whined, unable to form a coherent sentence. She wanted to scream—to beg, to whine, to *explode.*

Lyren only laughed, breathlessly, and his fingers tangled within Belle's unkempt hair, pulling her head slightly back, a pleasant twinge of pain radiating down her neck.

"Such a good little kitten," he said, and she whined in response. Florence's fingers had joined her tongue, pointer finger delicately massaging the very place where Belle and Lyren lay conjoined, and it took everything in his willpower to not combust entirely at the sensation.

"Kitten?" Belle countered; the nickname unheard of to her. She was so young, so *unschooled,* and Florence was never much of a talker during sex, for her mouth was typically occupied for a majority of the time.

"Is that okay?" Lyren panted, pressing a weak kiss to Belle's shoulder blade. He could feel himself reaching a peak, but he wasn't finished. He *couldn't* be finished.

"Say more," Belle innocently replied, burying her face once more into the sheet.

Lyren couldn't help but smirk, his filthy influence evidently rubbing off on the lady, and he suddenly stilled, filling Belle to the brim, his balls warm and cozy against her. Puzzled, Florence ceased her actions, kisses straying along Belle's inner thighs, as Lyren's lips met Belle's ear.

His warm pants sent shivers down her spine, an array of goosebumps coating her white flesh.

"Be a good little kitten and cum nice and hard for us."

Belle gasped, and Lyren redirected Florence's face to her lover's little cunt, his thrusts full, calculated, *determined*. He took note of Florence's pace, and followed suit, mimicking her skill with such preciseness that bright, bursting stars began to raid Belle's vision, blinding her momentarily.

"That's it, sweet girl. Cum for me. Let me feel." Lyren slurred, her walls clenching around his cock. She was incredibly close—he could feel her climax building with every swift stroke—and when he drove fully into her one last time, she clenched around him. *Hard.*

He groaned—deep and dark—and without missing a beat, he withdrew, painting the ivory surface of her back with the essence of his passion.

Florence's tongue instantaneously met Belle's soiled skin, flattening along the surface as she cleaned up every last drop of the evidence, a sight so rousing and wonderful that Lyren's cock jolted and throbbed, and he nearly came dry.

Eventually, the constellations along Belle's lids ceased, and she blinked back into consciousness just as Florence rolled her onto her back, a lively laugh tumbling off of the gorgeous girl's lips.

"Here," Florence whispered, cupping Belle's cheek. "Taste him."

Their lips lazily met, and Florence's tongue dipped into Belle's mouth, the savory flavor igniting Belle's senses. She'd never tasted such a thing, and if asked to describe what it tasted of, she wasn't even sure if she could accurately depict it. It was inimitable—*lovely*—and she couldn't wait for more.

"Fuck," Lyren wheezed, his softening dick still throbbing, electricity consuming his core. "That was brilliant."

Belle beckoned him closer, and the three curled up within one another's warmth, legs a tangled mess, lips languidly meeting, exchanging sweet smooches. Belle laid in the middle, so tiny between the two of them, and she felt her heart swell several sizes too large.

"A right trio in the Netherworld we will truly be."

THE PEOPLE OF VALEN

When the lady of the house didn't appear for lunch that afternoon, several brows were raised.

Although she rarely ate what was on her plate, she was typically in attendance, small talk bouncing between herself and Bramwell as he'd sip in his soup and snack on his crackers.

But today, he'd sipped his beet soup alone. He'd pinched the crackers between his fingers, watch how they crumble and crack, the dust showering his fingers, the severed pieces coating the tablecloth.

"Florence hasn't been seen since supper last night, but that isn't entirely unusual," Clare gossiped, her tone just loud enough for Bramwell to overhear. She and Ula were cleaning off the dining table, exchanging accusatory stares within one another's direction, and Bramwell was busy at the window, the drapes gently parted, a burning cigar pinched between his grasp.

A soiled sheet of snow claimed the grounds, melted and moist, and the red poppies were droopy and depressed, a peculiar sight.

The lord sighed, took a drag from his cigar, and tuned back into the housemaiden's gossip.

"What's even stranger is that Lyren Deth never came down for breakfast *or* lunch. That, my friend, is *highly* unusual. The man eats like a teenage boy, that one does."

"I wouldn't be surprised if we found Florence in a broom cupboard with the chap. She's always battered her eyelashes at him extra hard, for years now. She thinks we don't notice. We do. Or at least *I* do."

"*Really?*" Clare gasped. "You don't say? I always took Florence for the unusual type. Lonely. Not curious about love or affection. She never seemed the type."

"She's certainly the type," Ula countered. "Put her and Lyren in a room together and latch the door shut, they'll be shed of their clothes within moments. That, I'd put money on."

"Last I heard, you'd been borrowing money from that brother of yours who lives down in Gylsea," Bramwell said.

Both of the housemaidens fell silent, only the clinking of glasses and the shifting of unsteady feet filling the room. The lord still hadn't turned to face them. Instead, he kept his focus on the cliffside before him, the gorgeous view of Valen beneath a blanket of snow, the tiny, ant-like, barely visible forms of the townspeople frolicking about below.

He was due down in town within the hour, with his legal wife on his arm.

When neither housemaiden replied, Bramwell spoke once more.

"It would be wise of you both to limit the gossip that tickles your tongues. The Goddesses don't take lightly to such a sin. I'd hope to see you both within the clouds of Eden when the day comes."

Ula audibly gulped, eyes wet with tears, and the two women stiffly curtsied when Bramwell exited the room, the butt of his cigar burning at their feet.

It was the very first unsatisfactory encounter that either housemaiden had ever experienced with the young lord, and as Clare bent down to claim the cigar before it could burn a sightly hole into the rug, she couldn't help but cry.

Bramwell made his way to Belle's quarters, and out of familiar habit, he scanned the hall the entire way to her bedroom door, wondering if he'd ever lay eyes on Velveteen's portrait.

It was apparent that she didn't want to be found.

Seeing her hidden within Evelin Byron's eyes was the closest Bramwell had been to the demon in what felt like a century. Before her possession, he wasn't even certain that her presence even existed within the walls of Hellthorne at all, but now, he knew better.

Velveteen had never left.

He paused before Belle's door. The wood was thick—*binding*—and although he couldn't hear more than a whisper of what lay within, the lord knew quite well what he would encounter when he circled his fingers around the knob.

His voice emerged before his slender frame—a courteous warning—and Lyren fell from the bed, his pale skin, slick with sweat, meeting the aged rug. Florence's legs were still parted—suspended midair—the perfect shape of Lyren's slim shape. Belle had a single leg draped over Florence's heaving stomach, her dainty fingers tangled within her lovers knotted, unbrushed locks, both of their lips stained red with want.

Bramwell couldn't help but grin.

"My lady," he began, gaze settling upon a frozen Belle, her chest heaving. Lyren still hadn't risen from his hidden cove beside the bed. "We are expected at the bottom of the hill by our people. I was hoping you'd be dressed by now; we're already running behind."

"Oh *Goddess*," Belle cursed, tearing herself from Florence's flushed frame. "I'd completely forgotten, Bram, I'm so sorry–"

"Wear something black," Bramwell interrupted, still visibly unphased by the entire scenario. "Have Florence help you tie your hair into a braid complete with a black bow. The women of Valen determine authority by the complexity of a lady's braid. Florence knows what I mean."

"Yes, my lord," Florence whispered, nodding curtly, quick to cover herself. She knew that Bramwell didn't mind her relationship with his wife, but to actually see—to *witness* it all—admittedly, made her slightly terrified. She wondered if perhaps he would revoke the privilege immediately, out of jealousy, or spite, perhaps.

"Enough with the formalities, Florence. I am no longer your guardian, but simply your family." Bramwell said, brows furrowed. "And Lyren?"

The room stiffened, and Belle's jaw dropped, bottom lip quivering in fear as the two women rotated their stare to meet a blond, blushing Lyren, who crept up from beside the bed, a trembling palm cradling his privates.

"Bram, I'm so sor–"

"Bring Florence to town with you on your arm," Bramwell calmly interrupted. His eyes were warm—*kind*—and Lyren couldn't quite tell if his long-time friend was furious with him or not.

"You'll be joining Belle and I on our trip, with Florence as your date. You know how much the people of Valen respect and love you, Deth. You've always taken wonderful care of their dead. They'll be overjoyed to see the woman in which you share your space, even more so to see that it is my ward. Some may be, at least. Others may reek of jealousy, I fear."

The lord lightly laughed and rotated his eyes back to meet a bewildered Belle, who was now seated on the very edge of the mattress.

"I expect the three of you by the carriage in a quarter hour. We mustn't keep the people waiting much longer. Grab your thickest coat, the wind today is rather unkind."

With that, Bramwell left—closing the door tight on his heel, and the trio breathed in unison, exchanging per-plexed stares.

"He may kill me," Lyren whispered, his chest aching with fear.

Belle stood from her spot, rounding the foot of the bed to stand before an anxious Lyren, his softened dick still shielded by the skin of his palm.

She placed a hand on his chest—hovering his heart—and his frantic pulse drummed against her fingers.

Belle leaned forward, her lips barely brushing his, and with the most genuine, sincere tone, she whispered a haunting statement against his open mouth: "If he ever tries, I'll stick a blade in his neck."

The carriage ride down the hill lasted barely fifteen minutes but felt close to fifteen hours.

No one spoke. Not a single word.

Florence was dressed in a lovely powder blue coat with rhinestones for buttons. She sat knee to knee with a stiff Lyren Deth, his blue gaze glued to the fogged, frozen window, bottom lip drawn between gnawing teeth, nearly severing the raw, cracked skin open.

As requested, Belle was dressed from head to toe in a striking black gown and matching overcoat, a complex, textured pattern drawn along the surface of the fleece. Her deep red hair was pulled to the back of her head in an intricate braid, finished off at the bottom with a lovely long bow.

Every time Belle blinked, she swore that she could still see Florence's legs laced around Lyren's hips, the way their differing complexions looked so lovely—so *right*—all wrapped up together. She'd stolen countless kisses from the pair as Lyren struggled to contain his sloppy thrusts, how he'd chuckle against Belle's mouth as she told him over and over again just how gorgeous, how *regal* the man was.

It was *her* who was royalty, but she firmly believed that Lyren should be the one wearing the crown.

"Stay close," Bramwell murmured, interrupting Belle's daydream. "Most of the townsfolk admire you, but there are some who may not. Never once let go of my arm. Do you understand?"

The carriage door opened, and the group was met with a blinding gust of wind, one so wet, so cold that it cut through straight to the bone. Belle couldn't help but shiver, for she wasn't sure if she'd ever adapt to such bitter temperatures.

Bramwell offered her a hand, helping her step down from the carriage as a soft roar tickled her ears—a chatter of voices, the sound of her name over and over—*My lady! My lady! My lady!*—and she couldn't help but smile, for she was finally outside of the manor, and met by people who adored her, who *worshiped* her.

They were at the townscenter, a stunning, sleek white building that stood seven stories tall, ancient architecture that withstood the test of time. The giant triangular pillars towered over the crowd, and Belle admired the building in awe as she tightened her hold on Bramwell's elbow, knuckles flushed a gaunt white. Rosy red vines adorned with a whisper of gold encircled each pillar—a handmade decoration created by the hardest working hands in the land, no doubt—and Belle gawked at the sight. She'd never seen such an elegant, wonderfully decorated building before, and she wondered just what all lay within its walls.

They were led toward the steps of the monument, the very center of Valen, and she occasionally glanced over her shoulder to view both of her lovers, who trailed close behind. The tips of Florence's fingers trailed mindless shapes along the sleeve of Lyren's arm, and his silvery blond, windswept hair wouldn't quite stay out of his eyes regardless of how hard he tried.

Bramwell assisted Belle in climbing the stairs, and once they reached the top of the ten-step, they paused, turning around to face the growing crowd of Valen's inhabitants. Florence and Lyren took their place three paces behind the royal couple, still arm in arm, their faces masked by forced smiles.

Most of the Valen townsfolk were dressed in their best. Little girls wore tight-knit braids, accented with sleek, inky black ribbons, identical to Belle's. A father claimed his youngest girl in his arms, placing her atop his shoulders, her gap-toothed teeth on display as she pointed a finger at Belle and exclaimed: "there she is! The lady!"

Belle blushed, squeezing Bramwell's arm as hard as she could as her husband delivered a reassuring pat to her ice-cold hand. He scolded her in a hushed tone for failing to wear gloves, and before she could come up with a witty counter, the curly-haired man with a wispy mustache at the foot of the steps announced their presence.

"Introducing his elegancy, Bramwell Hellthorne, Commander of the Swift, son of his late majesty Ayer Tannisty Hellthorne II and her ladyness Sorrel Evaniene Alesek Hellthorne, the leader of the Val, our lord of Valen. On his arm, Belle Diantha Byron Hellthorne, the daughter of Hemlock Ere Byron and his darling Gladys Janeen Byron, daughter of the sea, girl of Immorium, the lady of Valen. They are accompanied by Valen's very best, Lyren Deth and Florence Smyth, Lord Bramwell's ward."

The crowd erupted into a deafening cheer, and for a moment, Belle felt numb. She'd only heard the formal introduction once, shortly after their wedding and during her initial arrival to Valen, but to hear her name followed by so many formalities seemed so strange, so *foreign*.

Belle Diantha Byron Hellthorne, daughter of the sea, girl of Immorium, the lady of Valen.

"It is a privilege to stand before the most wonderful people of Elantry," Bramwell announced, unable to mask his joy. It was evident that he loved the attention—*craved* it even—and Belle wondered why the pair didn't wander down into town on more occasions.

"I may be speaking purely out of bias, but I believe the occupants of Valen are the kindest of the country."

Laughter consumed the crowd, and an additional gust of icy wind caused Belle to shiver within her boots.

"It's been far too long, my friends. I apologize for the long absence of my wife and I. As you all suspect, we've busied ourselves with the wonders of our first year of marriage, and time has been lost on us. We hope you'll find it in your hearts to forgive our lack of appearances as of late."

The crowd cheered and cooed, their individual words lost among the masses, and when they finally began to quiet once more, Bramwell continued with his speech.

"As many of you have heard, there has been a tremendous loss in the Capitol. Topher Hardt's passing has stunned even those along the sea, who were never quite blessed by his presence. It is always such a travesty to lose someone of such importance in our country, and Topher Hardt was certainly of great importance to our government."

"It is important for us to recognize the true threat that the abuse and overconsumption of opium, and other illicit oddities. Valen has always been a cleaner city, far cleaner than the streets of Havensworth, and I intend to keep it that way. The safety of our people, the *health* of you all, is of my utmost importance. I've been conspiring with the government on ways that we can create a safer country for all of us to live and thrive."

Once more, the crowd cheered. Bramwell seemed well liked, and the sight made Belle's heart slightly swell with joy.

"There have been whispers beyond the hills of riots forming within the Capitol," Bramwell said, and the crowd fell silent. Deathly silent. Belle's breaths stilled, for she feared that with every exhale, she would be heard over the deafening quiet.

"There are groups in Elantry who wish to oversee the government, and Topher Hardt's death has created somewhat of a gap for these groups to file in. It is imperative that the people of Valen do not contribute to such acts. We are a city of royalty, not of politics. Although the government rules over my status, it has been tradition for generations that Valen follows in the footsteps of the royal family. Trust in me, my people, for I will not lead you to war. But be advised, for when the night is black and the city begins to sleep, a war is coming. We mustn't let it reach our borders, nor should we allow the toxicity to fester within our walls."

Belle barely breathed.

"Any mention of involvement with these vigilante groups will be punishable by the full extent of the royal law—banishment. Do not turn our home sour in the name of a political game. Keep Valen true, pure, and royal, as it always has been, and must continue to be. There is a reason our city is admired to such a high decree—for even the people of Havensworth wish they had what we have. Let us not forget our roots."

Bramwell concluded his speech with a firm nod, and the town began to roar—applause, cheers, cries.

It was evident that Lord Bramwell Hellthorne could do no wrong, even by threatening to punish anyone who attempted to disagree with Elantry's government.

How could they all so blindly follow?

With her lips sealed in a thin line—barely teetering that of a frown—Belle glanced in Bramwell's direction, slightly sickened by the stupid grin that claimed his features. She was under the impression that he despised Elantry's government, but it was evident to her now that he was just one of them after all, regardless of how much he'd claimed not to be.

What good was a lord who didn't have any interest in positive change for not only his people, but all of the country's population?

Perhaps Bramwell Hellthorne wasn't as wonderful of a man and leader as Belle originally thought.

"We best be going now, little love," Bramwell spoke, his tone barely above a whisper, the curve of his lips barely brushing the frozen shell of Belle's ear. She'd slipped into a temporary trance following his speech and had barely noticed that a majority of the crowd had fallen to their knees in the form of a kneel. The people of Valen formed a perfect path straight to the open door of the royal carriage, a low murmur of prayers tickling their tongues as the man who announced both Bramwell and Belle's professional titles extended a hand.

"Back to the carriage, my lord and lady?" he offered, lips pulling into a gap-toothed grin. A stunning silver collar claimed his neck, but barely concealed the swirls of deep dark ink etched along the surface.

"To your feet," Bramwell called, ordering the townspeople up from their worship. "I am no man to worship, I've told you all plenty before. My father before me expected such treatment, but never will I, for you shall only kneel before the Goddesses on your day of judgment, and not an ordinary man with an extraordinary title such as myself."

With a collective sigh and several chuckles, the people of Valen obeyed, shuffling to their feet as the Hellthorne's descended the stairs, followed close by both Lyren and Florence, who had both been so silent that Belle had nearly forgotten their presence.

The quartet was halfway down the parted path when a woman hopped into the center, blocking both Belle and Bramwell from proceeding. Her entire appearance reminded Belle of her Immorium roots—gray rags that clung to the narrow woman's frame in all the oddest places, seemingly weighing her down. She was incredibly tiny—even smaller than Belle, if that were even possible—and her bloodshot eyes were wet with tears, button-like nose a ruby red, chilled cheeks stained with salty tears.

"My *lord*," she spat, swaying from side to side. She was unsteady on her feet, and Belle was certain that if she placed her palm flat against the woman's forehead, she'd surely topple backward.

Several iron-clad members of Valen's armed defense instantly stepped in—swords drawn from their belts—and Belle outwardly gasped, nearly tripping on her own two feet as she attempted to take several steps back from the scene. Her backside collided with Lyren's front, her heels mistakenly stepping on his toes as a series of hushed apologies littered her lips.

Florence had told her plenty of the brave men and women who served in Valen's defense, but she'd never actually encountered them before. In fact, she wasn't even aware of their presence up until this very moment, for they'd done a stellar job of blending in with the crowd.

"Stand down," Bramwell ordered, tearing his arm from Belle's. He extended it to the strange woman instead, a soft grin snaked along his lips.

The soldiers obeyed, sheathing their weapons, but refusing to take a single step back. The woman appeared mostly harmless, but even the most innocent could harbor ill intentions.

Lyren's fingers gently danced along Belle's clothed elbow, a small sigh dancing along his tongue as he weakly attempted to conceal his affection. He was there to show off *Florence,* not the Lady of Valen, and almost as quickly as he'd touched her, he tore his hand away before softly urging her forward back by Bramwell's side.

"My apologies, madam," Bramwell spoke, enunciating each word so that those in attendance could clearly overhear. "Is there something I can assist you with? Or perhaps, my lovely lady can?"

He slipped his hand into Belle's without missing a beat.

"I know it was you," the woman seethed, trembling from head to toe. "It was *you.* You killed my mother. You *slaughtered* her at your own wedding!"

The crowd turned to chaos—all, mostly in defense of their wonderful lord—phrases such as *he was dismissed of all charges* and *the lord could never* and *you filthy little liar.*

"Don't let him get his hooks in you, missus," the woman added, an exaggerated gasp easing up her throat as the guardsmen shuffled forward, hooking their arms beneath the pits of hers.

Belle's wide, watery gaze remained fixated on the frantic woman, who had been lifted from the ground with ease by two of Bramwell's men.

"Nothing ever dies at Hellthorne, m'lady! Not unless he commands it!"

"Bram," Belle urged, a tremble present in her tone. "What is she talking about?"

"Nonsense," Bramwell easily dismissed. "My fine woman, look at me, won't you?"

The woman continued to struggle within the locked arms of two broad, burly men, but did as she was told. Her beady black eyes locked directly onto Bramwell's, and with a rotten-tooth smile, she waited.

"Go on," she urged, lips forming into a purse. She spat in both Bramwell and Belle's direction, barely missing the pair by half of a centimeter. "Try your little charming witchcraft on me. It won't work. Not like it did for my Ma."

Belle's breaths thinned.

Witchcraft.

The other surrounding guards began to usher the crowd away, urging them to return to their homes, their duties, or their hobbies. Some had their curiosity piqued, especially at the mention of witchcraft, but most swiftly denied all claims, repeatedly labeling the woman as a liar through audible shouts.

"Lyren," Bramwell began, squeezing his wife's palm. "Take the girls back to the carriage. It's important that I speak to this woman about the misfortune of her mother's untimely demise."

"No," Belle murmured, refusing to take Lyren's arm. "No. I'm your wife. Whatever you say to her, I want to hear. Her mother died at *my* wedding, too."

"Belle," Lyren urged, but was silenced by a simple raise of Bramwell's hand.

"Escort Florence, will you, Lyren?"

Lyren wordlessly nodded, concern etched along his features as both he and Florence silently bid them a farewell before retiring to the carriage straight ahead.

"Try it," the strange woman exclaimed, writhing within her captor's grasp. "Do it. Kill me like you did my poor Ma."

"Will you look at me, my dear woman?" Bramwell kindly urged, appearing unphased by her rash accusations. "Right into my eyes, as a proper lady should."

She did as she was told, staring deeply into Bramwell's eyes as her grin grew wider. "You gonna do it, my lord?"

"Do *what,* my dear madam?" Bramwell asked, his tone reeking of confidence.

The woman paused—only briefly—before bursting into a fit of giggles. "Kill me just like you did my Ma."

Belle felt her husband stiffen beside her, as if out of shock. It was evident that whatever he was trying to accomplish, it hadn't worked.

Not on her.

"I *told* ya," she began. "Your magick doesn't work on me like it did her."

Bramwell frowned.

"Take her to the jailhouse," he instructed. "Let her sleep off this fever. Be sure she's fed plenty of broth and bread."

"Yes, my lord," the faceless guard said, his features concealed by a thick plate of facial armor.

"The dead *never truly die,* my lady," the woman said once more, desperately attempting to claw her way out of her trap. "No one really dies up at the manor. *No one.*"

The woman met Bramwell's unblinking stare one last time, and Belle could've sworn that she heard her husband mutter beneath his breath. A single word, one she'd never heard.

Morte.

The mad woman only laughed, clearly pleased by the situation, and Bramwell led his wife back to the carriage with a sigh.

Belle would etch the letters of the strange word along Florence's flushed flesh later that evening, using nothing but the very tip of her fingernail, gentle and soft. Her lover would be deep in sleep, youthful appearance partially illuminated by the steady flicker of a burning oil lamp, and along Belle's waist would be a strong, sturdy arm, pale and hairless, belonging to that of none other than Lyren Deth, shy snores slipping between parted lips.

She would lie awake for hours to come, stuffed between her two lovers, mind fixated on the mad woman at the town-scenter. How she was so adamant, so *feral*.

The single word Bramwell spoke, the disappointed look in his eyes when the guards took the woman away, the woman who still lived, still breathed.

Belle sighed, and let the word slip off of her tongue.

Morte.

THE SUMMONING
NINETEEN YEARS PRIOR

A boy of ten.

Eyes a warm, russet brown. A hue identical to that of his fathers.

The father that did not live within the manor's walls, but rather, the towering, muscular lad who'd manned the grounds since the eve of his sixteenth year of birth, following in his own father's footsteps, as well as his father before him. He, instead, resided in a warm, cozy log cabin with a steadily burning fireplace against the cusp of the cliff, overlooking both the Manor and all of Valen, a view that always took his lovers breath away every time she sat in the old, wicker chair on the aging wooden deck.

The old lord of Valen knew those eyes were not his from the second they opened—with swollen, tiny pink cheeks and little red lips parted, a cry toppling off the little child's tongue. The baby took one look at his false father and the lord knew—for his own eyes were as blue as the sea, such a stunning, striking hue—and his own kin would've surely inherited the very same eyes that had been passed down for generations.

After all, every man of Hellthorne blood had those very same baby blue eyes.

His wife had assured him that the color would change—*the eyes of an infant are not the eyes of the man*—but ten years later, his eyes were the very same. Brown, like the earth. The warm, wet dirt on a chilly spring morning.

There were no windows in his room. The room wasn't much of a bedroom at all, really. It was a stuffy old space up in the south tower, with horrid ventilation and a con-siderably bad rat problem. They'd managed to stuff a decent four-poster bed into the cramped chamber, as well as some books, several oil lamps, and a rug. A tiny hole in the ceiling grew wider each winter, and as a ten-year-old Bramwell Hellthorne laid buried beneath the dusty blankets of his bed, he was able to watch several fresh flurries flutter into his room.

His mother—a kind woman named Sorrel, who he loved with his entire being—was due back any moment he'd hoped, and with a rumble of his stomach, he wondered what she'd bring up for him to snack on. Yesterday, it was bone broth with stale biscuits. The day before, a hefty bowl of fruit. The only thing that truly kept him healthy was the milk from her breast.

It had been years since he'd seen the man who was labeled as his father. He was called Ayer II, and he was an awful, mean man who hated Bramwell with all of his being. He'd never said the words to his alleged son, but Bramwell knew better—he knew by the venom in his voice, the darkness in his eyes, the bright red shade that claimed his cheeks.

It was Bramwell's seventh birthday the very last time he saw Ayer, the man who he was told was his father. There'd been an argument between his parents—his mother had burst into tears, his father laid hands on her. It was the last time the boy had been down from his room, the last time he'd sat at the dining table for a meal.

There'd been a word thrown around that night, one Bramwell had never heard, but he knew it was rotten, whatever it meant, for when it slipped off of his father's tongue, it was as if the man had spat out a mouthful of venom, his face so red that it was nearly purple, his blue eyes black with rage.

Bastard.

Thus, the bastard stayed in his room up in the attic, where the hole in the roof grew with each passing winter. He spent his days reading every dusty book on his shelf from cover to cover, often rereading those about magick and witchcraft and the Goddesses.

He knew that his parents were special. Royalty, even. It was written in one of his books.

His surname—*Hellthorne*—dated all the way back to the 1500s, as detailed in *Valen, A Comprehensive History*. It was a beefy, 800-page novel that covered every little detail of his hometown from the very beginning, and he'd fallen in love with the town he'd never even seen.

Near the rear of the book, the pages included details of his father's birth—how he'd been born to Ayer Tannisty Hellthorne I on a blistering hot summers day, how his mother nearly perished during childbirth, and would remain bedridden until her final days.

It would be thirty years following the ending of the book until the first Ayer Hellthorne would perish, and Bramwell's father would claim the throne. Barely a year following, his lovely, wedded wife Sorrel would produce a son, one with eyes so brown that they were nearly black, and from that day forth, the town of Valen had been told that the boy breathed six breaths, and then had died.

The boy was ten, and his true father still lived.

Still sleeping in the cottage by the cliff, wandering out only to perform his duties, nothing more, nothing less. The years had been hard on him, winters even harder. He'd gained one hundred and fifty pounds easily since Bramwell's conception, sprouted a speckled gray beard, a belly nearly too large for his tunics.

Occasionally, he and Sorrel would lock eyes—a somber stare, a yearning heart. She mourned the man he once was, such a handsome lad gone to waste, but she knew it was difficult for him to see her on Ayer's arm instead of his.

She hadn't snuck down to his cottage since the eve of Bramwell's first birthday, and he was certain that she never would again.

Solemnly, the groundskeeper glanced upward toward the south tower, icy flecks of fresh snow littering his vision. There wasn't a window, but the wood panels that made up the four walls were thinning by the day, and when he looked just right, he could catch an orange flicker of a raging oil lamp.

He knew his son was up there. Banished by the lord of Valen, the bastard son held prisoner. When he dared to venture down to town, to slip down the bottom of the hill, he heard the stories. How Lady Sorrel failed to produce a viable heir to the throne, how Lord Ayer II would be the final

Hellthorne to rule Valen, for following his death, there would be no next of kin to take over.

Only, the groundskeeper knew better. There *was* an heir to the throne, and he was locked up in the south tower, rotting away the days as if he never existed at all.

His son.

"Happy tenth year, my son," the groundskeeper whispered, blinking snow from his eyes as he studied the looming tower.

He would fall from the cliffside less than ten minutes later, arms outstretched from side to side, russet brown eyes tightly sealed, a single tear easing down the slope of his wind-chilled cheek.

The weather would bury his body, and when summer would come, he would be nothing but rot and bones.

There was a knock at the door—a trio of taps—and Bramwell's lips upturned into a smile as his mother stepped inside. She was dressed in a lovely blush nightgown, with light lace sleeves, and her blonde hair was pulled back into a thick braid, finished off at the bottom by a sleek black bow.

"My darling," Sorrel cheered, latching the door closed behind her. She was careful not to make too much noise.

Bramwell's smile turned to a frown when he realized she had no food with her.

"Mother, I'm starving," the boy whined, a hand reaching down toward the flat of his belly. He was worrisomely thin, wasting away, and the sight of her malnourished son pained Sorrel, but only barely.

The older he grew, the more he resembled his father. His *real* father.

"There were no leftovers from supper," she fibbed, her belly full of bacon, leek soup, and bread. "It'll just have to be a bit of milk for tonight."

"But it's my *birthday*," a young Bramwell whined, shivering beneath his blankets. "And it's so cold, Mother. Don't you feel how cold my room is? Maybe the servants can build a fireplace, like the one in the sitting room."

"It's too dangerous to have a fire up this high," Sorrel said, taking her spot on his bed. "Father wouldn't want your tower catching fire, we'd lose you with it."

"Father hasn't let me leave this tower since my seventh birth year," Bramwell muttered. "Father wants me gone."

"Father has just been having a difficult time," his mother weakly defended, slipping a breast from the comfort of her dress. "It's a difficult job ruling an entire city, my dear. He is very busy, very stressed, and very tired. Just as you age, he does as well, and so do I. He just celebrated his fortieth year, and difficult times lie ahead at such an age."

She beckoned Bramwell forth to eat, but suddenly he didn't feel very hungry. He wanted food—*real*, substantial food—something he could pick apart, feel its warmth, taste the flavor. Not the milk from his mother's breast.

"I want a *real* supper," Bramwell begged, taking hold of the fabric of her dress. "I'm not an infant. I'm not a *child*. I'm old enough to eat and I don't need to suckle from you anymore."

"Bramwell," Sorrel snipped, brows knit together in frustration. "You are but only ten, still a child, still a boy. Still *my* boy. You'll let me feed and nourish you until I see that you no longer need it."

Defeated, a young Bramwell obeyed, and when his belly was only moderately full and he was sick of his mother's presence, he dismissed her, eager to be left to his books once more. The oil was running low in his lamps, but he didn't dare ask his mother for a single favor, for it was his birthday, and she couldn't even be bothered to sneak him up a plate of food.

It was far after midnight when Bramwell crept from his bed, socked feet gliding along the creaky, wooden floor as he approached the dilapidated shelf full of books in the very back corner of his room.

The shelves were crooked and sad, bent by the weight of old, dusty books. Most of them Bramwell had already read. Several times over, even.

There was one—buried at the very bottom, hidden beneath the folklore of bloodsuckers and seven-foot wolves—he located a book he'd never read before. It was old, worn, tattered. A fabric cover, red as blood, with two simple words etched along the front in silver ink.

QUEEN MOTHER

He had no idea what it meant, but the book always intimidated him. Every time his fingers hovered the spine, he'd felt an unexplainable sense of dread creep up into his bones. Thus, it was forgotten.

Until now.

He peeled the dusty book from the shelf, a small cough toppling from his tongue as the particles went airborne. With curled fingers, he tore the book open, revealing the thin, yellowed pages within.

The drawings were demented—*dark*—unlike anything a youthful Bramwell had ever seen before. A nude woman with sopping wet fangs, a forked tongue snaked along her chin, nothing but black slits for eyes. Her form was small and lean, a rack of ribs visible beneath paper-thin skin, breasts round and robust.

It was an exquisite drawing, and as Bramwell flipped through the wilting pages, his eyes continuously widened. The visuals were morbidly stunning, and he couldn't help but begin to read some of the mysterious text etched along the pages.

Regina mater ut surgis

Bramwell whispered, struggling to pronounce the foreign tongue. The statement was scribbled in splotchy red ink beneath another intricate drawing of the nude, fanged woman, a wet, beating heart held within her claws.

There was more writing on the next page. It was curious—*fun*—and Bramwell had always taken a liking to learning new things, and this language was interesting beyond belief.

Protege me tua sapientia

Another page, another drawing, more scripture.

Nutri me lacte pectoris tui

He knew that he was surely mispronouncing most of the text, but that didn't matter to the young boy, for he couldn't quite turn the pages quick enough. If only there was a way he could translate the new tongue he was coming to learn.

*Exsurge ab inferis et suscipe
me sicut tua.*

It was then that the scripture suddenly stopped, one final word messily etched across the center of a blank page.

Venire

A single snowflake landed atop the tip of Bramwell's nose, easing in through the miniscule hole in his roof, and with knitted brows, he shuffled through the pages once more, desperately in search of more statements. Only, there were none. Only drawings of the peculiar woman, scenes of chaos and anguish, melting places and weeping faces.

His fingers buzzed from the cold, numb to the bone, and he snapped the book shut, placing it back in its rightful spot on the shelf.

As the boy slept that night, the manor came alive.

An ancient portrait, one that had been hung along the walls since the 1600s, began to shift. The woman within was

cold, bleak, *gray.* Eyes empty, unseeing, unfeeling. Fingernails formed into claws; canine teeth stretched into fangs.

She clambered from the frame, landing on the rug with
a dramatic *humph,* blood and mud and rot dripping from
her gown, soiling the ground.

Her strides were long and silent, calm and calculated,
and when she reached the south tower with the latched
door, she opened it with ease, decaying fingers encircling
the frigid brass handle.

Buried beneath a plethora of blankets was the young
bastard boy, just barely ten, dreams dancing along the lids
of his eyes. A soft snore tickled his pillow, and his stomach
rumbled with want, igniting a fire within her chest.

Her figure began to shift.

Dead fingers transformed, shedding their rot, becoming anew. Perfect pale skin stretched along her arms, pointed fangs retracting within her mouth, filing down into
pearly white teeth, a black tongue turned pink.

When she sat beside the boy in the bed, she'd been
completely made anew—a dashing green gown, silken
black hair, golden eyes glimmering with life.

"My son," she spoke, a warm hand claiming Bramwell's
shoulder.

The young lord shifted and woke—sight riddled with
sleep. The woman before him was a stranger, not his mother,

but instead of filling with fear, he almost felt comfortable. *Safe.*

"Who are you?" Bramwell asked, placing a hand over hers. She was warm. *Welcoming.*

"I am your mother, now," she said, smiling sweetly. She was the most gorgeous human the little boy had ever seen, for he hadn't seen very many humans, beside his parents and the servants that wandered Hellthorne Manor, but she was surely the prettiest of them all. Perfect, nearly. Not a single flaw.

"My mother is called Sorrel," Bramwell said, her name tasting of venom on his tongue.

The woman's smile did not waver.

"The woman does not deserve you, little Bram," she whispered, squeezing his hand. "Let me be your mother. My name is Velveteen, and I'm going to love and care for you with every bit of my soul. This I promise, now and forever, as long as you'll have me."

Bramwell paused, suddenly unsure of the situation, but the woman named Velveteen took notice, and she threw up a single finger, excusing herself from the room. Within moments, she returned, a shining silver platter topped to the brim with elegant eats in tow.

Bramwell's eyes nearly bulged out of his head, an enthusiastic gasp tumbling from him as he threw the covers off of his bed. He giggled with glee as Velveteen placed the tray atop his mattress, an assortment of eggs, sausage, fish, cheese, biscuits, and two cups of steaming lemon tea lined along the surface.

"Happy tenth year, sweet Bram," she cooed.

"Thank you," Bramwell beamed, unsure of what to eat first. His cheerful gaze met hers, and without hesitation, he accepted her proposal.

"Please never leave me, Mother."

She smiled. "Never, my sweet."

HIS, HERS, AND MINE

Bramwell had requested the presence of all three lovers on a bitter Tuesday morning.

He was already sipping from his third cup of steaming lemon tea when Belle, Florence, and Lyren strode into the dining hall, their eyes all riddled with sleep.

It was evident that they'd been up all night.

"Friends!" Bramwell cheered, rushing to his feet. His knee clipped the curve of the table, and the wooden legs shifted with an obnoxious groan.

Belle visibly flinched at his peculiar greeting, and she took a step forward to meet her husband with a half-armed hug, her lips placing a brief peck on his cheek.

"Good morning, husband."

"Oh, no need for formalities within these walls, Belle. Just Bram is and will always be fine." Bramwell pressed, his tone littered with false positivity. "I've been waiting what seems like hours, I take it you've all overslept?"

"Bram," Lyren began, taking the seat closest to Bramwell's. He shyly settled into the chair, nudging his plate full of eggs, grilled white fish, and chopped potatoes further from him. The sight of food alone turned his stomach somewhat sour.

Both Florence and Belle also claimed their own chairs. Florence was the first to pick at her potatoes, and Belle sat with her hands in her lap, stomach irritably growling in protest, her head swimming with worry. She needed to eat—this much she knew—but she wasn't sure if she could muster up the mental strength to lift her arms above the table to grab her silverware.

"Yes, Lyren?" Bramwell chirped, stuffing his mouth full of potatoes. He'd been kind enough to await their arrival, leaving his plate—and the others—considerably cold.

"It's been a week since you discovered us," Lyren began, the urge to vomit swiftly arising. He knew the topic could not be avoided any longer.

"Belle, please try and eat. You only ate half a biscuit and a few berries yesterday. Seeing you wither away worries me deeply. I want you to be healthy and strong." Bramwell said, ignoring Lyren's statement.

"Bram, I'm fine," Belle murmured. She took her finger and pinched it, nausea bubbling up within her belly as the sight and smell of food made her woozy.

"Bram, we can't keep ignoring the subject. If you'll have me banished from the manor for my actions, just do it already. The wait is agonizing, it's turning my stomach sour at every hour." Lyren spilled, fiddling with his fork.

It was true. He'd spent most of the previous night wrapped up within Belle's arms, sobbing softly into her chest. The guilt he felt was immeasurable, regardless of how much reassurance both Florence and Belle gave him. He needed to hear it from Bramwell's mouth, not theirs. He needed his blessing.

He needed his best mate's permission to fuck his wife.

"I'm not entirely sure why you'd think your banishment is on my mind," Bramwell began, swallowing thickly. "If you wish to leave Valen and return to Abler Black, do so on your own accord. Don't pressure me into banishing you from my land."

Lyren grew impatient. It seemed as if his friend was merely tiptoeing around the subject.

"Bram, I'm fucking your wife."

Florence dropped her silverware.

To Belle's horror, even Clare heard, for she was standing in the doorway with a tray of piping hot lemon tea and a plate full of extra cubes of sugar, just the way Belle liked it.

The housemaiden dropped the tray, showering the floor with steaming tea, glass shards, and crushed sugar cubes. The boiling liquid missed her legs only barely, and she had both palms over her mouth in shock.

"Clare!" Bramwell exclaimed, more startled than angry, and he stood to his feet, crossing the room in only three long strides as he came to his housemaiden's aide.

"My lord, I'm dreadfully sorry," Clare stuttered, unable to tear her stare away from a flushed-face Lyren, who was turning greener by the second.

"Look at me, Clare," Bramwell pressed, a forefinger meeting the tip of her chin, directing her sight. Their eyes met in a rush, and when she opened her mouth to speak, her recent memories were swiftly erased.

"My lord—*my lord!*" Clare cried, frightened by the sight of the tea tray scattered along the floor. "My apologies, sir, I can't quite recall how I'd done this! I must've . . . must've lost consciousness . . . briefly. I'm not entirely certain, I'm afraid. Oh, my lord, please forgive me, are you burnt? Are you hurt?"

"Clare, my dear," Bramwell cooed, a palm steady on her shoulder. "Deep breaths, dear. Go rest. Take the rest of the day off. Start the next morning fresh and new and fully rested."

The housemaiden bit her lip and nodded curtly, insisting that she clean up her spill, but Bramwell refused. She met the trio's glares, and for a split second, Clare could've sworn that she'd heard Lyren say something, but she just couldn't quite recall what it was.

When a sniffling Clare disappeared beyond the door, Bramwell took his seat once more, briefly meeting both Florence and Lyren's stunned stares. It only took a moment for each, but he'd done the very same thing that he did for Clare, and the only person in the room that had any memory at all of Clare's accident and Lyren's confession was Belle.

What the fuck?

By now, it was evident to Belle that Bramwell was no ordinary human being. He was magick—*a witch.*

Belle's mind wandered back to their visit down to the townscenter, with the deranged woman claiming that Bramwell had—in fact—murdered her mother.

He seemed so sweet—so *kind*—for Belle would've never thought that the man would hurt a fly, let alone kill someone in cold blood.

But then again . . .

If he's able to wipe one's memories by a single stare, perhaps the deaths he's caused weren't in cold blood, for he never had to lay a single finger on any of them at all. Just a look—a stare—was enough.

Morte.

Belle choked back a gasp, her pulse racing within her chest as Lyren shook his head from side to side, his thoughts a jumbled mess.

"Bram, I need to tell you–"

"About how you're pleasuring both my wife and my ward in the wee hours while I sleep?" Bramwell interrupted, his tone light and playful. He seemed amused by it, even, and if it were even possible for Lyren's white skin to appear even paler, it did.

"Lyren, you are my oldest friend. My *best* friend. I owe you an explanation. I owe you the truth." Bramwell said, sighing softly.

Belle's stomach went sour by his words. Everything the man said just reeked of venom, now. There was nothing good about Bramwell Hellthorne, nothing kind. He was a coward who hid behind lies and deceit. He stole memories—*moments*—directly from those he cared for—loved, even—in a wicked abuse of power.

"The truth?" Lyren stuttered, toying with the handle of his silver fork.

"Nothing but," Bramwell said. "Belle and I married to please the Capitol. My father turned the Hellthorne name considerably sour, so they've been on me since the day they discovered my existence, and when time continued to tick and I hadn't taken a wife, they became impatient. As *royal* as I may be, they do still stand above me, and if needed, they have the power to strip me of my title. Of my rights."

"So, your marriage is–"

"–purely political." Bramwell finished with a nod. He met Belle's empty stare with a shy smile. "Not that I'm unhappy with Belle's presence. I couldn't have asked for a better wife. But our relationship is nothing but an image, and it would be unfit—*unjust*—to ask Belle to remain faithful to me when our marriage is not of love, but of politics."

There was a pause, and everyone seemed to hold their breath.

"Therefore, if both you and Florence see fit to lay with my wife at night, I wholeheartedly approve. I could think of no better people than both of you to keep Belle's bed warm."

Both Lyren and Florence were floored. Florence already knew that Bramwell approved of her arrangement with Belle, but to hear him approve of the *three* of them? It was almost baffling.

"All I ask is that she remain on my arm and my arm only for public appearances," the lord added, taking a small sip from his cup. "What happens within these walls is for the Goddesses to judge, not me."

"Are you certain of this, Bram?" Lyren asked, unable to catch his breath. He'd never expected his friend to be so lenient with such a matter, but admittedly, he felt an overwhelming sense of relief, for he'd grown to adore the little redheaded girl more than he could fathom, and the thought of seeing her and not being able to touch her, to kiss her, to *fuck* her, would've been enough to force Lyren out of Valen permanently.

"Take care of my wife, you two," Bramwell said, finishing off his plate. "Or I'll have both your heads."

AUTOPSIA

Lyren returned to work on a brisk Monday morning.

He nearly had to drag his feet to the carriage, for Belle's bed was impossibly warm and cozy, such a beautiful, blissful state of being. Belle had blinked into consciousness whilst Lyren dressed, for as quiet as he'd attempted to be, he'd still woken her, and as Florence continued to snooze, the lady extended an arm, reaching out for her lovely blond lover.

"I must go, my lady," Lyren lowly teased, knowing full well that Belle despised him using her title.

"Not without a final kiss, Mister Deth."

Thus, he fastened the buttons of his blouse, and crawled back into bed, needy lips crashing against Belle's, a petite whimper crawling up her throat.

She decorated his hairless cheeks with a plethora of open-mouthed pecks, dipping down onto the flat of his neck, licking, nipping, sucking. Lyren's eyelids fluttered closed, and he whimpered, growing stiff and hard beneath his sleek black slacks.

"Bells," he whined whilst palming his throbbing self. "I have to *go.*"

"It isn't fair," Belle muttered, replacing his hand with her own. He gasped, and she mewled—satisfied by his reaction. "You can stay here at the manor forever. You don't need any money, you don't need to work. There's no need for any of that here."

"I wish I could, but I can't, Bells. I have an obligation to uphold. I have a career. I *miss* working," Lyren countered. It was true, he was itching to slice open the dead, examine their innards, discover the secrets that lie buried beneath their flesh.

Belle's lips turned to a pout, and Lyren placed a loving kiss upon them, amused by how innocent, how *lovely* the woman looked.

"Fine," Belle grumbled. She began to untie his waist. "Let me taste you one last time before you go."

Lyren arrived at town later than he'd anticipated, and when he'd stumbled in through the bulky doors of his practice, he was out of breath.

He called the place *Singlebells,* named after his mentor, the late Yves Singlebell, once the best death examiner and forensic pathologist in all of Valen, until he lost six fingers in a fire incident. Yves succumbed to a deep depression following his undesired retirement, and shortly before taking his last breath, he asked Lyren Deth—who had only been twenty for thirteen days at the time—to take over his practice.

Singlebell slit his throat with a kitchen knife the very same evening.

It was a pleasant little building crunched between a shoemaker run by a seventy-year-old Elleen Woodsall and a bookseller that consistently rotated its staff. The structure was bright and airy, a plethora of windows claiming the walls, some accented with breathtaking panes of ornamental stained glass, commissioned by Singlebell's daughter. The young woman adored artwork, and often enjoyed sharing her passions with her father, incorporating most of it into his practice.

It was refreshing to be surrounded by so much color and life while working with the dead.

Lyren discarded his overcoat and slid into the examination room, which was currently occupied by a frumpy man, mid-thirty, wearing a bloodstained off-white apron, hands stained with the mark of death.

Before him on a wooden table was a girl—no older than thirteen, it seemed—her chest cavity opened wide, skin secured by pins.

"Young one, she is," Lyren frowned, saddened by the sight. It was always a sad, unfortunate day when a child was brought to his practice.

"Lyren, m'boy!" the man exclaimed, tossing his bloodied hands midair. "By Goddess, it's been ages, it feels. Thought you wouldn't be back 'till after Yule."

"Glad to see you too, Darce. Many thanks for keeping my practice running during my absence." Lyren smiled, nodding curtly in Darce's direction.

Darce Dego trained by Lyren's side for several months with Singlebell, before his mother ran a fever that never went down. He left to care for her, and after she died, he couldn't find it in his heart to view a dead body—not for many years, that is.

Now, he served Lyren's practice when needed, paid fairly, more than plenty to keep him fed and warm during the months he went without work.

"I wouldn't have minded another five weeks of cutting people open, truthfully," Darce mused, stepping toward the sink. "Come Yule there'll be people dropping like flies. The holiday claims so many souls, it's a peculiar thing."

"A certain sadness claims the lives of many during the celebrations," Lyren said, shuffling through Darce's hand-written paperwork. The deceased girl was called Noreen, aged eleven, and her parents requested an examination under suspicion of poisoning.

"Poisoning? A girl of eleven being poisoned?"

"Had a cousin who didn't like her much, they say," Darce replied, scrubbing Noreen's blood from his hands. "Rotten teenage girls, little bratty things. I never liked my brother much, but I wouldn't have dreamt of slipping him something to make him sleep forever."

"They'll be pressing charges, I presume? If we find something unsatisfactory?" Lyren wondered, swiftly scanning over Darce's fairly neat penmanship. He'd just begun to inspect the stomach, just barely slicing it open before Lyren showed up.

"Her mother is pushing for death," Darce said. "Her sister argues that Azyl would be a better fit. She just wants her child to live, understandably. The suspect is barely fourteen, still a kid."

"Old enough to commit murder, old enough to reap," Lyren murmured, snatching a clean apron from the nearby table. "Let's get this stomach of hers open, see what's inside. Your writing's better than mine, best we be able to read what I find come morning. Grab some ink, let's get started."

"Fifty-two grains of arsenic in that poor girls belly. Unbelievable."

"Where the ruddy hell would a child of fourteen obtain so much arsenic? It's almost comical, really. Perhaps she waltzed to the market and purchased some from a little old lady too blind to read labels of what she's selling?" Darce said, shuffling through his pockets in search of three additional silver coins.

The woman manning the lunch wagon appeared un-enthused, a single, bushy brown eyebrow snaked above green eyes as she handed Lyren his lunch. Darce was three coins short, and when his pink-stained hands failed to produce any silver, Lyren fished them from his own pocket, shuffling them into the woman's open palm.

"Thanks, pal," Darce grumbled, collecting his over-priced ham sandwich and mince pie. It was the best cart in town, but the food cost what seemed like a fortune to the lower-class inhabitants of Valen.

To Lyren, it was just a few of many silver coins he harbored.

"Noreen's mother will be pushing for that kid's death, you know," Darce said, taking a seat beside a starving Lyren, who had already consumed two of his boiled eggs.

"Surely, but the court of Valen will have words, I'm sure. It's rare to see a sentence so harsh for a person so young, especially a woman. She's nothing but a girl, they'll be hesitant to even send her to the jailhouse out of fear of what some of the men inside would do to her."

Lyren shuddered at the thought of a tiny teenage girl in chains, surrounded by vicious, violent criminals who hadn't felt the gentle touch of a woman in years. If she'd been sent to rot in Minnehel's prison, she wouldn't make it longer than a month at most.

"Will you take the stand if it goes to trial? Defend the poor girl from an ugly fate?" Darce asked, barely picking at his sandwich. He felt for poor little Noreen—the small dead girl whose blood stained his hands—but the thought of sending *another* child to a certain death would only stain his soul an even darker shade.

"Afraid not," Lyren countered, finishing off the last of his eggs. "All I do is cut people open. The legalities and politics behind it all is beyond my qualifications. I refuse to be a part of it."

The pair finished their lunch in silence before marching down the pebbled road back to the practice. It was dreadfully cold, but with no fresh snow, nothing but stale chunks of ice and slippery roads beneath their feet.

Lyren started a small log fire in the sitting room to warm up the place, and Darce collapsed against an aged, squeaky chair. Although they'd discovered the truth of Noreen's demise, there was still much to be done with her body before the burial, and since Lyren's sudden departure, Noreen was the twenty-seventh body Darce had worked on alone.

"What kept you gone so long, Lyren? I've never expected such a leave of absence from someone as yourself. By Nether, half the time, I'd have to beg for some work, ruddy drag you out the doors for a day off, and suddenly, you disappear for weeks upon weeks?"

Lyren took a seat upon the sofa closest to the fireplace, hands outstretched in search of warmth. "Troubled times, Darce. Strangest I've endured in a while. Lord Hellthorne was kind enough to offer me room and board while I recovered."

"Was odd seeing you at the townscenter after so long, standing all proud behind the lord and his lady, and with a woman on your arm, no doubt! Not too ill to take that lass to bed, now were you?" Darce teased, picking at the severed skin around his nails. He examined the flesh—how it shone a shy pink—and wondered how many days it would be until the remains of poor little Noreen washed away for good.

"Even the sick need company at times," Lyren mused, blushing slightly. He knew that Darce was referring to Florence, but what he didn't know was that Lyren had the company of *two* elegant, breathtaking women every evening. Two ladies who couldn't keep their hands—*or their mouths*—off of him for longer than half a day.

He twitched within his trousers, and slyly shifted in his seat, careful not to alert his coworker of the arousal coursing through his loins.

"She's beautiful, I'll give you that," Darce said. "Something like Flora? Florentine?"

"Florence," Lyren corrected. "Florence Smyth. Lovely lady, that one. Lord Bramwell's ward. She's had her eye on me for years, or so she says. Was only a matter of time before I got tangled up in her sheets."

"The *ward?*" Darce gawked. "You're fucking his daughter?"

Lyren shot Darce a bitter glare, daggers digging deep into the older fellow's chest as he tossed a hand up in surrender, immediately regretting his outburst.

"He was her guardian, not her father. They are cousins, nothing more." Lyren said, adding an additional log to the fireplace.

"Well, then," Darce grumbled. "You planning to court her, then? The nighttime whore Lyren Deth finally going to settle down and pump out a few little ones?"

Lyren's lips upturned into a smirk, the thought of his child blooming within either Florence or Belle's wombs, (or, perhaps, *both* of their wombs), created a warm, fuzzy feeling inside of his chest. He'd never quite imagined himself as a father up until that moment, but to see both of his ladies swollen with his offspring excited him.

His ladies.

"You're in love, kiddo," his coworker teased, groaning as he stood to his feet. "Can see it in those eyes. You're envisioning a life with that girl ain't ya? Thinking of how sweet she'd look all swollen in the belly."

"Perhaps," Lyren breathed, and he beckoned Darce back into the examination room so they could finish their work on Noreen, and both retire home just in time for supper.

HELLTHORNE, A HISTORY

Belle had never seen the manor filled with so much color.

During Yule the prior year, Hellthorne Manor didn't have much joy to offer. Several bleak wreaths, a single, weeping tree.

This year was different. Bolder. *Happy.*

She even caught Bramwell helping Clare hang up a strand of ruby red ribbons, encircling the banisters of the stairs in a gorgeous glow. The red looked dashing opposite the black, and Belle's eyes lit up when she spotted wreaths as tall as herself lined up along the wallpaper, itching to be hung.

"Oh, Goddess *Lottie!*" she exclaimed, taking the steps two at a time as the lengthy train of her silken lilac day dress flowed behind her like a cape.

"Good morning to you too, Belle," Bramwell beamed, thoroughly amused by her glee. "Florence is in the kitchen snacking on blackberry scones as they bake. Henry's due in anytime to hang some of these wreaths on the windows—damned things are heavy as all—and Ula's gone to fetch some ornaments for the tree, if you'd be interested in decorating some."

"I'd be honored!" Belle exclaimed, clapping her hands together. She'd always helped her mother decorate the tree for Yule, and although it was usually one of the cheaper, more drabby looking plants of the lot, it was always such an exciting time for Belle and her sisters.

Thoughts of her family plagued her mind suddenly—a holiday season spent without not one, but *two* of their daughters—how Belle wasn't there to tie knots in the ribbon, how Evelin wasn't present to arrange the candles.

Evelin.

Alone at Azyl for Yule. Unaware of the season, presumably. Bedridden, at best. Eyes empty, cold hands.

Belle wondered if her sister even remembered her own name.

"Cheer up, my sweet," Bramwell urged, noticing her sudden shift in mood. "I've got a box full of ribbons needing tying, and unless you want Jeanne to steal them from you, you best come over here."

Belle squealed, digging her hands deep into a box full of rosy red ribbons, a material so soft and slick that it slid straight through her fingers. The quality was high-class, far superior to the cheap ribbon her family reused each yearly Yule, and she ran it along her skin—slowly, curiously. It was as gentle as the silk she wore to bed.

"Only the finest ribbon for Lady Belle," Ula said, her winged lashes batting. "May I?"

Belle wordlessly nodded, shuffling several strands of ribbon into the housemaiden's hands as the pair of them began to tie them into knots.

"Lord Bramwell's bringing in some new help," Ula casually revealed, admiring Belle's handiwork. "Excellent knot, my lady."

"More housemaidens?"

"Three more, I believe. With Lyren Deth living in the manor full time, there's more to make, plenty to bake. Jeanne's getting older by the second. Henry, the gardener, is taking on the title of groundskeeper and is moving from the servant quarters to the old cottage by the mountainside. This house hasn't had a groundskeeper since the man named

Gawain, but he was employed during Lord Ayer II's time, far before any of us came to the manor."

It was the most Ula had ever said to Belle since her arrival. In fact, the lady had never spoken more than a few words at a time to the housemaiden, and there she was, gossiping as if they were old friends.

"Who was Gawain? I've never heard that name before." Belle wondered, and Ula handed her several glass ornaments, hand-carved and seemingly new.

"Son of Aloysius, the previous groundskeeper, who was the son of Edvard, the groundskeeper before him. The Baspben family served the Hellthorne's for years and years, the first-born son inheriting the role. Gawain was the final groundskeeper, he died when Lord Bramwell would've been about ten. No one knew of the little lord, then. He was Lord Ayer II and Lady Sorrel's secret son."

The housemaiden handed Belle another ornament.

"Gawain just disappeared one day. Nowhere to be found. Didn't report for duties for several days. Lord Ayer II was not as kind as our new lord, he was bitter—*mean*. I'd never met him, but the stories told all around Valen were enough for me to feel as if I had. When the snow finally melted come spring, they found the groundskeeper buried at the bottom of the mountain, nothing but bones left. He'd fallen off the cliff."

"Goddess alight," Belle gasped, horrified by the thought. "Why did they never bring in a new groundskeeper?"

"Gawain never married. Never had a child. There wasn't a Baspben to pass the role down to, so it just fizzled out. Died with him. His cottage was left to rot. Henry's been busy cleaning it out for days, I bet you can imagine the smell. There was still food in the pantry, dirty linens on the bed. Lord Ayer II's been gone over a decade, and Lord Bramwell saw fit to appoint Henry as groundskeeper."

The pair fell silent, working hand in hand on hanging ornaments on the tree. Belle's mind reeled with what she'd learned, visuals of a rotting skeleton being found at the bottom of Valen's highest hill sending a shiver down her spine. She'd wondered how on earth the man had managed to fall, as he'd lived and worked so close to the edge for most of his life, and something deep within her spirit began to wonder if it may have been intentional.

After all, it was no secret that Lord Ayer II was an awful man.

"There're books all about Valen and its history, even the history of this very mansion, in Lord Bramwell's sitting room. I'm sure he wouldn't mind you doing some light reading, especially of the land in which he came. There's a lot to learn about the royal family, stories and tales that'll entertain you from dusk to dawn, surely." Ula said, finishing off the last of the ribbon.

"Thanks for talking to me, Ula," Belle smiled, grabbing the housemaiden's hand in hers. Ula softly flinched, but eased into the lady's hold, her frigid fingers cradling Belle's warm touch.

"It's been a pleasure, my lady," Ula gushed. She pulled her hands away, wiping them along the ivory fabric of her apron as she collected the empty box.

As the housemaidens continue to prepare the manor for the festivities of Yule, Belle took refuge within Bramwell's sitting room, a crackling fire dancing within the fireplace, her long nose buried within the yellowed pages of a book.

It told tales of Hellthorne Manor, from the earliest days recorded of the Hellthorne family, and Belle was beyond intrigued. All she'd ever known about the Valen royalty was of the stories she'd heard from others—her father, mostly, for he'd practically worshiped the family for as long as he's lived—but it was so much deeper, so much *darker*.

The first recorded presence of the Hellthorne name was in 1503. Valen wasn't fully formed yet, merely an idea. A cluster of families in cottages, a sense of belonging. The country of Elantry was still exceedingly fresh—officially founded and settled by immigrants who claimed the land as theirs—in 1488, and the only true town was that of the Capitol, present day Havensworth. Only back then, they just called it Haven, or the Capitol.

Ragmeihl Hellthorne was the first of his name. He was born of the land, of natives rather than immigrants, and when those from the Capitol attempted to claim the land of present day Valen as theirs, it was Ragmeihl and his army who had prevented them from doing so.

Thus, Valen was named as such in 1507, a separate entity from Haven. It was shortly after Ragmeihl's success and Valen's formation that the community appointed him as their leader, and he became the first Lord of Valen.

A mansion was commissioned in 1510, and by 1515, Hellthorne Manor was fully erected. Ragmeihl—thirty and three years at the time—took his first wife two months following the completion of the manor, and mere weeks following, she grew round with his seed.

Elantry became a proper country in 1522, conquering as much land as the eye could see, forming places like Minnehel, Immorium, and Westcastle. The Capitol grew greedy—*hungry*—and wanted the entire continent under one single government. By 1548, Valen was invaded once more.

Only this time, Ragmeihl was unprepared. He had aged significantly—now sixty and six—and he'd slowed with age. His back ached; his feet swelled. His eldest son, Naras, was perfectly half his father's age, and even had three daughters of his own.

Neither Naras, nor Ragmeihl, were ready for what invaded Valen. The armies were weak, the loss of life was abundant. Valen was forced to surrender, and as a kindness, the government of Elantry continued to observe the Hellthorne family as Valen royalty. Only, royalty fell below the government and seemed nearly useless—*silly*—after they forcibly joined the country.

Belle skimmed through dozens upon dozens of Hellthorne names. After joining Elantry, their status almost appeared meaningless. Originally the leaders of Valen, now reduced to just titles—titles that could be easily stripped by the Capitol if deemed necessary.

Belle recalled how Bramwell mentioned the government's power over him, how he'd been threatened—*forced*—to marry, for entering his thirtieth year without a wife would mean the end of Valen royalty.

Now, there was talk of an uprising. Topher Hardt's death sparked a new light for rebellions. Many were exhausted with the way Elantry was run. There were only four wealthy cities—Havensworth, Valen, The Shores, and Westcastle. The rest, significantly lesser than.

The lady had just begun reading about Lord Ayer II, Bramwell's father, when her husband silently entered the room, startling her half to death.

"Good *Goddess,* you scared me." Belle whimpered, snapping the book closed. A plethora of dust littered the air, tiny particles dancing within the firelight, and Bramwell took a seat next to her on the sofa, a curious stare settling upon the object in her hands.

"Interesting story, isn't it? Who was your favorite lord?"

Belle absentmindedly ran her fingers through her hair, avoiding Bramwell's eyes as she flipped the book back open to reveal its contents. It was a hefty piece of work, and she was surprised by just how many Hellthorne's had lived within these very walls.

"Lord Ragmeihl, I think."

"The first of his name," Bramwell commented. "Strong leader. A warrior, even. Lived until the eve of eighty, unheard of for the early ages. He'd outlived his own son."

"It took Naras seven tries to get an heir," Belle acknowledged, amused by the thought. "He just kept having girls. His poor wife probably hated the man after so many painful births."

Bramwell chuckled, wedging a cigar between his lips. "Stories say she wasn't very fond of him, no. Would you be, after baring seven of his children?"

"Goddess, no."

"Hesperius and his thirteen bastards always tickled me," Bramwell added, his voice muffled by the cigar. He struck a match, lighting it with ease, before reaching over to claim the book. Instead of tearing it from Belle's hands, he thumbed through the pages as it sat within her lap, clearly in search of something specific.

"Here. 1701. Lord Hesperius confesses to the birth of thirteen illegitimate children, on top of having *eight* with his own wife. If you thought Naras's wife hated him, just picture poor Kyota. She nearly died giving birth to two of them, lost a fair bit of blood."

"The Capitol wants us to make a baby," Belle flatly said, head hung low. She'd just read an alarming amount of information about Elantry's government—the sheer power it held, even over the royal family—and the idea of Bramwell being stripped of his status due to their lack of intimacy terrified Belle.

"That they do," Bramwell voiced. He seemed unphased. "There're other matters keeping them busy at the moment. The rebellions, the impending revolution. Most of the country is severely unhappy with how things are handled. Valen wants to secede entirely."

"Do you want the city to secede?" Belle interrupted, tucking her feet beneath her. She suddenly felt ice cold, even with the fire roaring nearby.

"That would give me a fair bit of power," Bramwell sighed. "Responsibility I'd never even thought of. It's hard working running a country. All I mostly do is handle the local work and look pretty."

Belle snorted, fingers still fidgeting within her hair. It was dreadfully oily, and she needed a fresh bath, but Lyren wasn't due home from work until dusk, and she preferred it when he washed her hair for her. There was just something about the way his nimble fingers massaged her scalp, how he parted her lengthy, luscious hair into thirds, rubbing the soap into each and every strand with precision.

"Your father was about your age when you were born, wasn't he?"

Bramwell took a long drag off of his cigar.

"That he was."

"You'll eventually need an heir."

Bramwell sighed. "I will."

There was an uncomfortable silence. A painful pause. So many things that Belle wanted to say—the witchcraft, the *magick*, the *killing*—so many things she'd continued to bite back, to swallow, to hide.

"All we need is one night," Belle cautiously began, unsteady fingers working diligently at a pesky knot in her hair. "One night, and you can make me forget it ever happened. It's my only duty as Lady of Valen. To give you a son."

Bramwell's blood turned to ice, eyes darkening severely as he shot Belle a warning glance. Her mere mention of his abilities made his stomach churn, and he knew that one day, he would regret never once charming the girl.

"I told you I'd never use it on you."

Belle rose from her seat, the book of Hellthorne ancestry falling to the floor in a fanned-out heap as she fell to Bramwell's knees. Her palms flattened against the bend of each leg, doe-like eyes wide and round as she looked up at her husband.

"We have to do this, Bram."

Bramwell stood to his feet, bitterly brushing by the woman on her knees. She toppled backward, landing awkwardly against her bottom as he put out his cigar on the wobbly wicker table.

"Goodnight, Belle."

"The sun hasn't even set–"

"Good ruddy night!" Bramwell seethed, cheeks flushed a fiery red. His hands formed into fists at his sides, back bitterly hunched, spittle seeping from his lips.

Belle instinctively crawled backward on her hands and knees, desperate to get as far away from the angry man as she could, and when Bramwell left the sitting room and slammed the door closed on his heel, she burst into tears.

Several paintings came loose from their nails, easing off of the wall, meeting the floor with a sharp *thwap*. Belle aggressively flinched, somber cries ricocheting off her tongue as she curled up into the smallest ball imaginable atop the mahogany rug.

Perhaps, it truly was possible that Bramwell killed those women at the wedding.

Possible.

Probable.

Definite.

She was married to a murderer.

THE DAYS OF YULE

Every Thursday since her sister's departure, Belle had written Evelin a letter.

The lady sat hunched over a weighty wooden desk, wavy hair dangling over her shoulder, legs strung up beneath her bottom. She'd filled up half a piece of parchment within minutes, detailing every little thing about her life as of late, nearly knocking over the ink fount every time she reached for more.

There's a secret I'd never told you, one which you deserve to know.

Hot tears teased the innermost corners of Belle's eyes as she paused, reading the last line she'd written several times over. She wasn't even sure if Evelin was reading any of her letters, for she never received any back.

She spilled all of her secrets onto that parchment—how she'd fallen in love with Florence shortly after arriving at the manor. How they'd taken Lyren into their bed with them.

I'm in love with him, too. I just haven't told him yet. I'm not sure if I even should.

Belle paused, realizing then that it was the first time she'd ever admitted her true feelings for Lyren. They'd been bouncing around within her brain since the very first night they'd spent together—that sweet kiss in the carriage on the way back from the nightspot—right in front of a sleeping Henry and Evelin. Her sister had been *right there*. Nearly *caught* them.

Now, she'd never even know the truth, regardless of what the letter said. Belle knew better. She knew that her sister was gone. Her heart still beat, blood still rushed through her veins, her eyes still wandered, but her soul had left.

As much as she doubted Plirity and the existence of the Goddesses, Belle only hoped that perhaps they *did* exist, and that her sister's soul was up in Eden, being pampered daily by the Queens in which she worshiped.

I love you always, Evelin.

Goddess Be.

Belle

Belle sealed the letter, the Hellthorne sigil in black wax, and took it downstairs, dropping it in the box full of outgoing mail.

"My love," a small voice emerged, a hand on her shoulder. Belle flinched only slightly, then sighed—immediately calmed by Florence's presence.

"Another letter for Evelin?"

"Yes," Belle admitted, almost embarrassed by the fact. Everyone in the manor knew of Evelin's condition, and to an outsider, it may seem silly to send so many letters to someone who couldn't even read them.

"Do you think someone else at Azyl may be reading these? Since Evelin can't?" Florence wondered, a sense of worry enveloping her bones. She'd never pried when it came to the contents of Belle's notes, but a part of her began to fear that there were secrets within the parchment that should never leave the cliffside.

"No, I don't think so." Belle's head hung low, and she coiled her arms around Florence in a tight, tear-filled hug.

"My love, you need to try and eat something. I can feel your stomach rumbling against mine." Florence purred, threading her fingers through Belle's wavy locks. "There's fresh oranges and blueberry biscuits ready. Lavender tea, extra sugar cubes, too. Nourish that beautiful body of yours for me, please?"

Their eyes met, a deep sadness hidden behind Belle's deep-set brown eyes, and the little lady nodded, excusing herself to the sitting room where her breakfast sat waiting.

Florence hung back for only a moment, ensuring that Belle had rounded the corner before snaking her hand into the box of outgoing mail. She snatched the letter meant for Evelin Byron out of the box and tore it into fourths, shoving the remains into the heel of her shoe.

"Our secrets shall never leave these walls."

It was tradition for the royal family to host a Yule ball on the eve of the holiday.

A tradition that ended with Lord Ayer II's reign, and Bramwell never quite picked back up. Until the most present Yule, that is.

Hellthorne Manor was flooded with folks dressed in their very best—stunning silver, glittering gold—laughter ricocheting off the ancient walls as guests walked arm in arm through the broad double doors. The people of Valen hadn't seen the inside of the manor since before Bramwell's birth, when his mother was still round with pregnancy. She'd barely fit into her custom sewn gown, such a lively green hue, and the people had fawned over her precious form, the idea of the arrival of a new Hellthorne baby bringing tears to most of their eyes.

But then, the baby died—or so they said—and the Yule ball at Hellthorne Manor was no more, a tradition that originally began with Lord Jynolvene in 1632, and ended with the stale and bitter Lord Ayer II, a man most disliked, but nevertheless bowed to, as they were expected to do.

"I never thought I'd see the inside of Hellthorne Manor with my own two eyes," a blacksmith named Godwin had said, his voice croaky and hoarse, a red blush creeping up his neck. He'd been directly beside a finely dressed Belle when he'd let the statement slip—not even aware of her presence—and when the blacksmith heard the tiny woman release a friendly chuckle, he outwardly gasped, large eyes formed to the shape of saucers.

"My lady!" he exclaimed, taking a single knee. His date—a slightly younger woman with loopy black curls and catlike eyes—also fell into a bow, nearly tripping over her handmade gown in the process.

"Oh, that's not needed," Belle cooed, her tone smooth like honey. She looked stunning—glittering silver eyeshadow drawn along her eyelids, bright red hair draped along her shoulders in lengthy, drawn-out waves. It was the first time she'd worn her hair out of a braid in the presence of the townspeople, defying tradition.

"Your dress is beautiful," the blacksmith's female guest complimented, looking Belle's attire up and down. Unlike the dark black hue she typically adorned in public, Belle was dressed in all white—a color so bright that it resembled a patch of freshly fallen snow.

It was perfect for Yule.

Belle's lips snaked into a smile, and she offered the regular townswoman a hand. "Thank you, sweet soul. Would you care for an escort to the ball room? I've just heard they've brought out plenty of fresh rose wine. The housemaidens made it fresh just this morning."

The blacksmith's date looked stunned—plump, glossy lips pulled into a gawk as she tore her arm from Godwin's and eased her hand into Belle's. Her touch was as cold as ice—a perfect pair to her bright white dress—and a shiver ran down the woman's spine, unblinking stare rotating to meet the blacksmith.

"Go," he urged, nodding curtly. "I'll find you in the ball-room."

So, she went. Hand in hand with the Lady of Valen, a frantic burst of butterflies dancing within her aching stomach. She hadn't eaten since breakfast—just some jam and toast—and being so close to royalty made her woozy and unsteady on her feet.

"Don't be so nervous," Belle said, lacing her fingers through the strangers. "I'm only a girl from the seaside. I'm only royalty by marriage. If there's anyone you should be nervous around, it would be my husband. He's royal by blood."

The lady lightly laughed, and the townsgirl could do nothing but anxiously grin. She feared that if she opened her mouth, bile would spew straight out onto the perfectly polished floor.

"Tell me your name," Belle urged, nodding at each of the passersby as she led the townsgirl through the manor's packed front hall. The people seemed to part for the pair—effortlessly so—creating a perfect path straight to where the ball was held.

"Xylia," the townsgirl revealed in a singsong voice, one so dainty and sweet that it almost brought a blush to Belle's cheeks. The woman was precious—barely twenty herself, it appeared—and the lady wanted nothing more than to make her esteemed guest feel welcome within these horrific halls.

None of them knew the terror that truly resided within the manor. The trails of crimson down weeping walls. The portrait of a dead girl. The whispers within the pipes.

The evil, demonic possession of her little sister.

The messy murder of Topher Hardt.

"What do you do for work, Xylia?" Belle wondered. The Towns girl's palm was slick with sweat, dampening Belle's icy touch by the minute, but she didn't mind. Not even in the slightest.

"I've just turned nineteen, and I want to be a writer," Xylia shyly explained, a raging red blush claiming the brown skin of her cheeks. Eyes all immediately fell on her, envy slapped across the features of several women as they observed her walking hand in hand with the most esteemed woman in all of Valen. It was a privilege to merely be in Lady Belle's presence, but to hold her *hand?*

"Do your parents support your dreams?"

"Not particularly," Xylia murmured, her eyes twinkling beneath the plethora of burning candles. The manor was beautifully decorated—wreaths and bells and candles alike—with more ornamental trees than she could physically count, each dressed to the nines with dried fruits, ribbons, glass trinkets, and twigs. The candles draped along the banisters appeared to float in place, illuminating the crowd with such a brightness that just didn't seem possible.

"It's just gorgeous in here, isn't it, Xylia?" Belle said, admiring the decor. She couldn't quite get enough of it. Both her and Ula decorated dozens of trees together—tying ribbons until their fingers ached, draping dried fruit along prickly branches. The new housemaidens had taken quite a liking to the lady, and admired her desire to help, forming what seemed to be a sort of friendship with the girl from Immorium.

Friendships that an envious Florence wasn't particularly fond of, Belle learned.

The ballroom was packed when they arrived.

An overabundance of varying colors clouded their vision, laughter filling the void. A string quartet sung a beautiful melody, a pianist picked at white and black keys. Housemaidens weaved in and out of the horde, sparkling drinks and simple eats balanced upon doily covered trays.

One of the newest housemaidens, a woman of twenty and six who went by the name Keahi, couldn't help but smile when she saw Belle, for the two had decorated three trees after Ula injured her index finger.

"Good evening, my loveliest lady," Keahi greeted, a splotchy pink stain present on her lily-white apron. "A glass of rose wine for you and your friend?"

"For me, yes. Xylia, a glass?" Belle asked, nodding curtly as Keahi handed her the drink.

"None for me, no," Xylia lightly dismissed, slightly ashamed of denying her lady's offer. Belle seemed unphased, and the help only continued to smile.

"Not a problem at all, Xylia. Pleasure to make your acquaintance. There's lavender tea floating about the room, carried by another housemaiden called Tove. Hard to miss her, she's got hair as white as snow, just like our lady's gorgeous gown."

Keahi then disappeared into the mass, and Belle finally dropped Xylia's hand.

"It was a pleasure to escort you to the dance," the lady said, taking a small sip from her wine. "I'm afraid it may be difficult to find your date in this mess, but I wouldn't mind having you follow along. I just want to find some friends of mine."

"Are you sure?" Xylia croaked, still overwhelmed with anxiety. She wasn't entirely sure how to act around the Lady of Valen, for she'd only ever seen Belle and Bramwell from afar, tucked away within the crowd. Only now, she had no choice but to speak to her, to create *conversation*. Xylia only had few friends of her own, the idea of finding a friend within the lady was just beyond comprehension—even if the friendship only lasted a single night.

"Positive," Belle smiled, finishing off her wine with a large gulp. It appeared as if she, too, was rather antsy. "You've seen Lyren Deth, haven't you? Either around town, or at our last visit?"

Xylia nodded. "He works on our dead. My brother speaks highly of him."

Belle briefly blushed. "Yes, it seems as if many speak greatly of him. He's here with his date, Florence Smyth. She was on his arm last, I'm sure you saw. Tell me if you see them, I'm looking for them both, but this crowd is just monstrous, it almost makes me jittery to be around."

"Me as well, my lady," Xylia smirked, and the pair set off in search of both Lyren and Florence.

They were unaware that the two individuals in which they set out in search for, had already spotted them—for Lyren and Florence had been arm in arm just barely behind Belle and Xylia as they navigated the manor. The sight of Belle's generosity had brought a sincere smile to Lyren's handsome features, whereas Florence couldn't quite tear her stare away from Belle's hand, which had been tangled within a strangers.

"You're stiff as a board, Flo," Lyren cursed, his inner elbow aching.

Florence wore a stunning evening gown, an impressive shade of sunny yellow, and it was a perfect complement to the hue of her skin. She looked breathtaking, and before the pair had even made it downstairs, they'd snuck into the second study, a room seldom used, and Lyren bent her over the edge of an unsteady chair, the unique woodwork etching intricate shapes into Florence's upper arms. She'd mewled and whined with every sloppy thrust, and Lyren barely pulled out in time, finishing within his hand, careful not to leave any evidence behind.

"Have you ever seen that girl before?" Florence hissed, her blood turning to ice.

"She's just another townsgirl," Lyren lightly dismissed, threading his fingers through Florence's. She squeezed—*hard*—and he nearly yelped, brows furrowed in bewilderment as he shot her a quizzical glare.

"Flo, are you jealous of that girl?"

"Don't be absurd," Florence dismissed, eyes rolling within their sockets. "Jealous of some ordinary townsgirl with a hand-me-down dress? Please."

"Don't be so unkind, Flo." Lyren kindly scolded, careful not to offend the woman.

Florence's muscles went lax, and she released a strained sigh.

"I'm sorry, you're right. It's just . . . what says she won't take a liking to her, too? I don't want to share our bed with another."

Lyren paused, apologizing to the couple who nearly collided with their backsides as he directed Florence off to the side of the parlor, directly beside a crowded table adorned with an assortment of jewels, candles, and ornaments.

"Listen to me, my love," Lyren whispered, a warm hand cradling Florence's cheek. "Both Bram and Belle are the hosts of tonight, and everyone is just begging for a single interaction with them. Belle's been locked up in this house with nothing but the company of us, Bram, and the servants for over a year. Let her make friends. Let her socialize. She's not going to cast us aside just because she met someone new to share her time with."

Tears pricked the corners of Florence's eyes, and Lyren wiped them away, his lips brushing against her forehead.

"Don't be jealous, Flo. She is ours, and we are hers. Let the girl make friends. She deserves to."

Their stares met, and a statement slipped off of Florence's lips with ease, one she'd never uttered before this very moment, one she wasn't entirely sure if she should say at all.

Lyren weakly smiled, kissed her once, and took her hand. With words unspoken, the pair filed back into line and headed for the hall.

BLOOD MOON

Belle had already downed three glasses of rose wine by the time Bramwell made his speech.

The blacksmith, Godwin, took an entire hour to locate his date Xylia, who at that point, had already met both Lyren and Florence, and had drunk an entire cup of warm lavender tea.

Belle had introduced the townsgirl as her friend, and Florence struggled to swallow past the pesky lump of bile in her throat as she shook Xylia's hand.

"Promise me you'll visit my mother's bakery? I'm there six days out of the week," Xylia had said, just before Godwin tore her away for a dance.

"I swear it," Belle answered, and she watched as the townsgirl disappeared into the crowd.

Belle barely listened to the speech her husband had made, for she couldn't quite tear her eyes off of both her lovers. It had become exceedingly difficult for the woman to mask her emotion, and she was almost certain that her pupils had formed into dainty little hearts at the sight of the pair, a beaming pink aura surrounding her skull.

She was in love.

Florence knew how she felt about her. The words had oozed from her lips an abundance of times. She said it every night before bed, peppering kisses along Florence's warm, naked flesh, etching the statement into her skin. She whispered just as the woman woke, a nose buried within coiled black hair, a thumb caressing pouted lips.

It was Lyren who didn't know.

Belle had said it, but she wasn't entirely certain if he'd ever heard it. She was careful—*cautious.* She'd wait until his soft snores would shower the pillow, and then she'd say it. A whisper. A secret.

His lips would paint portraits along her bony spine, and she'd mouth it—hushed, silent. Her fingers found his sides, and she'd spell it. Gently, slowly. An invisible statement scratched within his skin.

"It's been a blessing from the Goddesses above to have you all in attendance this evening," Bramwell's voice boomed, and Belle claimed another glass of rose wine from Keahi's tray. The housemaiden's brows pulled together in worry, for she was well aware of Belle's condition, her lack of nourishment, the abundance of alcohol sitting on her stomach.

Florence and Lyren stole several small kisses, and Belle's stomach turned sour, gaze darkening as she sipped her wine. She steadied her glare on a beaming Bramwell, who stood tall on a pedestal, towering above everyone in the room. He was dressed in an outfit she'd never seen before—a dashing scarlet frock coat, slim fit, falling just to the tip of his thigh. The Hellthorne sigil was threaded along the lower sleeve in deep black thread. His waistcoat was blacker than the night sky, accented with ornate white specks that reminded Belle of the stars that dangled within the clouds.

He looked absolutely dashing.

For a murderer, that is.

Belle finished her fourth glass.

She was light on her feet when she was beckoned forth for a royal dance. The crowd parted, creating an open circle, and the lady nearly emptied her stomach all over her shoes as she approached a grinning Bramwell, his arm outstretched in search of hers.

"My wife," the lord announced, proudly so. He took Belle's hand in his, and drew her close, guiding her through the steps of a dance she barely knew. The string quartet played to the tune of a gorgeous love song, one that Belle had heard once before at her own wedding, and halfway through the royal dance, the guests began to sway to the tune.

"Tonight, the moon will fill with blood," Bramwell revealed, his voice barely above a murmur. Belle's brows raised in wonder, and he spun her around.

"I've heard of it," Belle said. "Only once. When I was a child. My mother told me of how the moon would fill with blood when the witches boiled a new brew, and the blood-suckers had risen from their tombs."

"Your mother is a smart woman," Bramwell answered, pulling Belle close. "Blood will be shed tonight, Belle. Best if you stayed in. Avoid any nightspots, any mingling. The last Blood Moon, Valen lost thirteen of its own."

Was it because you'd killed them?

"I have no plans to leave the manor tonight." Belle said, and Bramwell did not reply. They finished their dance with a bow, and the lord dismissed her, eager himself to go mingle with his people.

Curious thoughts poked and prodded at Belle's brain as she weaved within the crowd, drunken vision eagerly searching for a single sight of either of her lovers. It seemed odd how Bramwell spoke of the moon, how it would flood with blood, and although she'd never quite believed in the fables of witches and bloodsuckers, she wondered now if perhaps, he could be both.

Magick existed, that much she now knew, and it made her question the stories of the Goddesses—tales she always easily dismissed, that now seemed quite possible. If witches walked among them—resided within the very walls in which she lived—the idea of three Goddesses watching over them wasn't entirely far-fetched.

Her stomach lurched, and she stumbled in her shoes. A new housemaiden by the name of Tove nearly dropped her tray trying to catch the lady, the steaming lavender tea spilling over the sides of their designated cups.

"My lady, are you all right?" Tove queried, a hand resting on Belle's elbow. "You're drunk, my lady. Come with me, let me get you some bread to sober you up."

Belle nodded, and followed the housemaiden out of the ball room, her ears ringing with every step as the violinist increased the pace of the current tune, a shrill, shrieking sound that made the lady's head spin.

The laughter faded to a muted mumble, and Tove led a drunken Belle to the kitchens, where Jeanna and Ula were busy cleaning soiled dishes.

"Tove? Why have you brought our lady here? The kitchen is no place for her royal highness," Ula exclaimed, dabbing her damp hands dry on a severely stained rag. "Oh Goddess Liv, the poor girl is drunk."

"I wanted to get her some bread," Tove explained, directing Belle to a nearby chair. The old wicker was unstable beneath her, and the aged legs groaned with every subtle movement.

"If she'll eat it," Ula muttered, stacking a plate tall with bread and jam. "This'll soak up all that wine, my dear. Please, eat up. You'll be sick if not."

Belle grumbled and brought the bread to her lips. Her pulse quickened, beads of sweat draped across her brow, and when she went to open her mouth, she immediately snapped it closed, her teeth audibly colliding.

Ula frowned, and Tove shot both her and Jeanne a worried glance.

"My lady, you must eat," Tove pressed, but Ula shushed her, apologizing to a trembling Belle as she directed the new housemaiden to gather more cups of tea and return to the party.

"I think I might be sick," Belle admitted, and she stood to her feet, the slice of bread still pinched between shaking fingers.

"I promise the bread will help," Ula kindly explained, her palm flattening between Belle's shoulder blades. "It's your mind being cruel to you, my lady. Food is good, food nour-ishes your body and your soul. Food will not hurt you."

Belle's eyes filled with tears, her bottom lip quivering as she met Ula's soft stare. She wanted to throw her arms around the middle-aged woman—pull her into a tight hug—but in-stead, her shaking hands stayed at her sides, the bread crum-bling between her pinched fingers.

Ula reminded her of her mother. So kind, so gentle. Her mother was never forceful with her aversions, only patient. She'd shovel porridge into her mouth, a single spoonful once every hour, and never complained once, for she'd rather see her child eat slowly, than not at all.

"Just the soft bits," Ula instructed, taking the bread from Belle's hold. She tore the fluffy white center apart from the hardened crust, and offered it to Belle.

The lady took it, a sob threatening to spill from her aching chest, and she stuck her tongue out just barely, her taste buds singing with glee as she placed the bread on her tongue.

Gradually, she ate—trembling the entire time, silent tears slipping down painted cheeks. Her makeup was ruined, and she refused to attend the party once more, so when the lady finished her bread, Ula took her hand and led her upstairs. They took the rear staircase to avoid any guests, and navigated the candlelit halls in silence, nothing but the muffled sound of laughter, music, and glee filling their ears from down be-low.

When they arrived at Belle's bedroom door, the lady tossed her arms around the housemaiden, pulling her close. Ula chuckled, and snaked her arms around Belle's shoulders, patting her several times on the shoulder in reassurance.

"Do you need help getting out of your gown, my lady?" Ula asked, cradling Belle's face with both of her hands. Belle looked so small—so *innocent*—and it reminded the house-maiden of the niece she helped raise, the one who went off to live in The Shores and drowned barely three months later in the beautiful blue water of The Craik.

"No," Belle sniffed, and she rested her forehead against Ula's. "Thank you, Ula. You've been so kind to me."

Ula wore a grin that stretched from ear to ear, and she placed a peck upon Belle's buttoned nose. "Anything for the lady of the house. Sleep well, Lady Belle. The moon bleeds tonight."

With that, Ula excused herself from Belle's presence, and the lady watched as the housemaiden strode down the hall and turned to the left, disappearing from sight.

The moon bleeds tonight.

Belle fell asleep in her ball gown.

The dense fabric created a comfortable cocoon for the lady, surrounding her lithe frame like a blanket.

The oil lamps had begun to die, a gentle, weak glow illuminating the wallpaper. The window was parted only slightly, a winter chill weaving its way in, etching goosebumps along Belle's fair skin. But still, she slept soundly, up until the lock on the door clicked, and the hinges creaked, alerting her of an intruder.

Belle pulled herself up with a gasp, moderately blurred vision studying the open door. Her pulse calmed the moment she blinked the blindness away, revealing a giggling pair of lovers. A bright yellow dress, a dapper navy-blue suit with silver cuffs.

"Belle," Florence breathed, nudging the straps of her dress from her shoulders. "Did we wake you?"

The low lighting created deep shadows across half of both Lyren and Florence's frames, and Belle watched with wonder as Lyren's ring-riddled fingers crawled up to meet the back of

Florence's dress. He slipped each individual button from its hole, one by one, and Florence let her hair fall from the tight updo, a sigh of relief tumbling from her tongue.

Florence's dress fell from her shoulders, pooling at her feet in a sizable heap that nearly came up to her knees. Their gowns were massive—so thick and intricate—and it was a relief to rid her body of the enormous dress.

Lyren extended an arm in Belle's direction, fingers playfully wiggling as he beckoned her forth.

"Your turn, my dear."

A scarlet blush crept up Belle's cheeks, and she shrugged toward the foot of the bed, whereas Florence crawled atop the mattress beside her, wearing nothing but a pair of white underwear. A chill cascaded down her spine, courtesy of the open window, and her nipples bloomed into firm peaks.

Belle took his hand and stood to her feet—the costly white gown swallowing her small frame once more.

"By Goddess, you are a sight to behold." Lyren breathed, raking his eyes over her body. Most of her makeup had wiped away and her hair was frizzy and knotted, but Lyren didn't seem to mind, for he looked at the woman as if she was the most gorgeous creature to ever exist.

"The most beautiful woman," Florence agreed, tucking herself beneath the blankets.

"Turn 'round, sweet girl," Lyren cooed, his index finger rotating. His plump lips pulled back to reveal a bright, pearly grin, dimples decorating his cheeks as Belle released a playful giggle, rotating on her heel to reveal the back of her gown.

The dress was laced up nice and tight with a smooth, snowy string, threaded neatly into the metal grommets. It resembled a corset, and the gown was nice and snug around her center, a perfect fit.

Lyren's fingers got to work on the laces, delicately untying them one by one. The dress fell from Belle's shoulders, and a rush of cold air sent a tremble through her body. Her arms instinctively rose up to cover her upper half—for warmth, or out of embarrassment, she wasn't sure—and Lyren's balmy lips met her collarbone, licking, nipping, sucking. The soft tendrils of his hair tickled her chin, and she released a weighty exhale.

"Come to bed, you two," Florence pressed, her tone riddled with impatience. "I'm cold."

"Should I close the window?" Lyren wondered, but Belle shook her head.

"No. We'll need to cool down soon enough."

The trio melted into a mass of whimpers, sighs, and breathless kisses—the frozen winter air covering their skin in raised bumps. Fiery red hair between brown thighs, ring-clad fingers encircling beaded nipples. Florence welcomed the worship, let it consume her, and as Lyren peppered hot, open-mouthed kisses along her cheeks and neck and Belle found the perfect place between her legs to lick and nip and *suck,* Florence became completely undone, her fingers knotting within Lyren's locks, pulling slightly.

"Good girl," Lyren cooed, snaking his tongue into Florence's mouth. Belle gently bit the inner part of the woman's thigh, prompting Florence to squeak against Lyren's mouth, her eyes rotating to the back of her skull.

Sleep reared its head, pulling her under, and with lazy blinks, she began to disconnect from reality. Both Belle and Lyren lazily trailed kisses along her cheeks and arms, the flat of her stomach, the curves of her breasts. It didn't take long before her chest evenly rose and fell with sleep, and Belle lightly chuckled at the sight.

"Good Goddess, we fucked her straight to sleep."

Lyren laughed and took hold of Belle's wrist. He maneuvered her over a sleeping Florence, her slender figure collapsing atop his. Their lips met in a rushed kiss, his hands on her face, pulling her close. Their legs entangled, fingers entwining, and with ease, he rotated Belle onto her back.

He was warm and hard and perfect, and Belle just couldn't get enough. She kissed him—*hard*—fingers dancing down the slope of his stomach, skillfully coiling around his throbbing length.

"Such a tease," Lyren mewled, and he went south. Down her neck, a wet, hot stripe left behind by an eager tongue. Down her chest, fingertips teasing hardened nipples. Down her stomach, a bite, a kiss. A nip on each inner thigh, a warm breath kissing her clit.

She gasped, and he dove in—his rings cold against her center, his mouth hot and full of want.

"Goddess, Ly," Belle breathed, grabbing a fistful of his hair. She pulled, and he groaned, quickening his pace. She saw stars, and he pulled away, much to her dismay.

"I was almost-"

His lips met hers, and he wrapped her legs around his hips. He teased at her entrance first—playing with her wetness, her warmth—and with an interwoven sigh, he eased in. Slowly. Tenderly.

Their stares met, and Belle's pulse quickened—those damned three words threatening to spill once more. She tried to bite them back, but with every thrust, her lips parted, and she struggled to hold them back.

"Ly," she moaned, the curve of her thumb grazing along his lower lip. He shuttered, barely blinking, as his stare bore into hers, captivated by her striking, deep caramel gaze.

"So beautiful," he murmured, biting back a groan, and he took her hand in his, entwining their fingers, squeezing.

The clouds beyond the cracked window parted, revealing the fullness of the moon within. The once white exterior had transformed—darkened—and painted along its surface was a gaudy red hue. Thick. *Wet.* As if the Goddesses had dipped a paintbrush into a mound of scarlet oil paint, scribbled over the star, and refused to let it dry before adding another coat.

Belle took Lyren's face in her hands, and he began to throb and twitch, his movements growing sloppy, and as the moon painted a sea of vermilion along the blanket of snow just outside, she finally said it.

"I love you," Belle breathed, and Lyren shuttered, a series of moans and whimpers dripping off his tongue as he painted her walls white. All the while, he continued to weakly thrust, riding out his high, a sincere smile pulling at his lips.

"Goddess Lilen in Eden, I love you, Belle. Fuck."

He buried his face in her neck and rolled his hips, a whine crawling up Belle's throat. Her eyes tipped back into her skull, and Lyren's fingers met the place where they remained conjoined.

"I've loved you since the moment I saw you in the sitting room," Lyren revealed, refusing to withdraw from her. He could feel himself softening, but he didn't care. It felt so good—physically, spiritually—to be connected in such a way with the woman.

He never wanted it to end.

Belle gasped, and he continued to rub circles along her, the spot he knew she liked.

"Since the window. I wanted you that day. I needed you that day."

A kiss, a touch, another moan. She was getting close—he could feel her clenching around him—and he moaned in unison. Softly, so that they wouldn't wake their other lover, who soundly slept against her pillow, her hair sprawled around her skull like a halo.

"I love you, Belle. I love you."

She clenched, and released—and the red blaze of the moon flooded the room, a gory glow.

I love you.

CUT ME WIDE OPEN

The manor was snowed in for sixteen days following Yule.

A blinding blizzard followed the bleeding moon, burying the brick roads in an impassable layer of thick, white ice. Henry had a considerable amount of trouble tending to the horses, as the barn was almost completely concealed beneath the snow, and he'd wrapped three blankets around each of

Bramwell's horses, ensuring that the animals stayed as warm as possible.

The latest groundskeeper was used to rotten weather, for he'd grown up in the tiny town called Szo Landing at the uppermost tip of Elantry, just above Castle North. It was winter nearly the entire year there, and although it was on the coast, the ocean was continuously complemented with weighty blocks of ice, and an occasional iceberg would wander into view, just close enough for one to squint their eyes into focus.

The housemaidens had no choice but to stay in the manor, for their separate quarters were inoperative. Several windows had cracked due to the pressure of the blizzard, others had blown out entirely, coating their beds and the floor with sharp shards of glass.

On the eighteenth day—when the sun was warm enough to melt most of the ice and the temperature finally wavered above freezing—Lyren was due back to work.

Henry was busy readying the carriage, his ungloved fingers slipping through the mane of the largest of Bramwell's stallions. It was evident that the young man was particularly fond of his new role as groundskeeper, and although his cottage had been snowed in, he'd worked diligently every day to shovel himself out, creating a perfect path for him to navigate the grounds.

"Let me come with you," Belle begged, already slipping into her overcoat. The inside was lined with a thick layer of fur, a color as beautiful and white as the melting snow beyond her bedroom window.

"You'll be rather bored," Lyren lightly argued, his palm cradling the handle of her bedroom door. As always, he was running a bit behind, all thanks to a needy Belle and her warm, wet mouth.

"I want to see what you do," she argued, stepping into a pair of pure, pricey leather boots that made her feet ache. "Plus, I can explore Valen more. I won't wander off far. I've been wanting to try lunch from one of those food carts you told me about. There's nothing like that in Immorium, or Minnehel. I could even spend time at that little bookstore that you said shares a wall with your practice."

He gave up a half smile and tore open the door.

"Don't go too far if you do decide to wander. Bram'll have my dick if I lose you."

Belle's palms collided with glee; a broad smile snaked across her lips as she followed close on Lyren's heel.

It was difficult for her not to claim his hand in hers whilst they navigated the manor. The housemaidens never left the haunted walls due to the damage in the servant quarters, and even in the late hours of the evening when they'd usually retire to their own private home, the trio had to be careful what they did outside of Belle's bedroom.

Tove, one of the manor's most recent housemaidens, nearly caught them all on several occasions, the closest encounter being when she saw the silver-haired lad and the royal lady slip from the bathroom together. They'd just finished up a bath together, and if she'd opened the door only moments prior, she would've seen Belle on her hands and knees along the tile, the sturdy surface painting her pale skin an angry red.

"Lady Belle, I wasn't expecting your company as well," Henry acknowledged, smiling softly when the pair approached the carriage. The wind was cold and bitter, slicing through Belle's exposed flesh like white hot knives. She looked the groundskeeper up and down, appalled by his choice of clothing—a thin, long-sleeved tunic, a pair of ragged slacks, no hat, no gloves.

"You really are from the arctic, aren't you?" Belle teased. She'd never been above Valen before—especially not to Szo Landing, nearly five hundred miles north—but she'd heard plenty of stories. The never-ending winters, the freezing summers. Icebergs sinking enemy ships in the night, the great stone wall of Elantry stood tall along Szo's coast.

"They baptize freshly born babies in the sea in the Goddesses name," Henry explained, pulling open the carriage door. "I was born in the dead of winter and my father had me submerged when the moon stood tall in the sky. There were icicles in my hair and eyelashes for days. There's no amount of cold that could ever bother me, now. The Goddesses have blessed me with immunity to it, as they have to all of those baptized in the Szo Sea."

Lyren and Belle clambered into the carriage, a sigh of relief tickling each of their tongues as a pleasurable warmth consumed them. Henry had filled a metal box full of steaming hot coals, which took the edge off of the cold quite considerably.

"Goddess, it feels great in here," Lyren commented, not used to such a gesture. Henry had been the first to heat the stagecoach since Belle's arrival to Valen.

"You make a wonderful groundskeeper after all, not that I had any doubts," Belle said, bundling up beneath the thickest of the blankets.

Henry smiled wide, thanking her profusely before latching the door shut. Lyren yanked the curtains closed, and collapsed on the bench beside Belle, a wandering hand creeping up to meet her cheek. His gloved fingers tickled her chin, and without skipping a beat, he latched his lips to hers.

Belle breathed a sigh of content against his mouth, eyelids easing shut as the carriage rocked forward, the start of a short journey down the mountain and into town.

"I love you," Lyren said, barely tearing his lips from hers. She could nearly taste the words that tumbled from his tongue, and the tip of hers wandered out, colliding with smooth, white teeth.

Lyren chuckled, and their tongues began to dance. He tore the gloves from his hands, the need to touch—to *feel*—becoming borderline overbearing. His warm, bare palms met her blushing cheeks, painted pink from the cold, and his thumbs mindlessly traced circles along the skin.

Belle followed suit, removing the thick gloves from her hands, discarding them without a care. Her hands found his hair, and she softly pulled.

A moan.

A sigh.

A giggle.

"And I love you," Belle finally replied, her arms encircling his neck. She pulled him close, their noses flush against one another, and if there was a way for the two to mold completely into one—one body, one *entity*—they surely would have in that moment.

The ride to town was regrettably brief, and when Henry tore the door open, both Lyren and Belle were properly dressed once more. The only evidence of their escapade was that of the raging red blush stamped along their cheeks, as well as irritated, swollen lips.

Henry took no notice, for he kissed another once and only once just before he left Szo Landing to work for Bramwell, on the eve of his sixteenth birthday. It was a girl two years his senior, one he'd grown up with, and she'd proclaimed her adoration for him as he loaded up his belongings for the lengthiest carriage ride of his life, spending the rest of the bronze coins he had to his name on the ride.

It was quick—barely a peck—but he'd tasted her lips for an hour thereafter, his fingers brushing against the surface of his mouth.

"I'll be back close to sundown to collect you both for supper," the groundskeeper said, nodding as the pair clambered from the carriage.

"Many thanks, Henry," Lyren smiled, patting the younger man square between the shoulders. He offered an arm to Belle, and she took it, her cheeks still hot with a lustful blush.

Although the weather was less than satisfactory, the townscenter was as alive as ever—the people of Valen scurrying about each and every way as they went about their day.

It took only moments for the Lady of Valen to be noticed.

Mummy, it's the lady!

Lady Belle!

Her highness!

"Make room for our lady, please," Lyren instructed, tightening his grip on her arm.

The pebbled path was slick with ice, and Lyren caught Belle both times when she'd nearly fallen, a tiny yelp easing off of her lips. The people of Valen had difficulty avoiding her, and the number of eyes glued to her struggling frame made her rather uncomfortable, but nevertheless, she followed Lyren to his practice.

Lyren had claimed that his practice was *nothing special,* but the building was some of the finest architecture Belle had ever seen, just like the rest of Valen. It was evident that the builders took their time crafting the city, creating such a stunning, unique appearance that Belle couldn't quite get enough of.

"On the left is a shoemaker run by Elleen Woodsall, she's seventy and is the same lady who made the shoes on your feet," Lyren explained, pointing out the shop directly beside his practice.

There were six businesses all crammed within the same building, side by side, each with their own separate entrance. Elleen Woodsall's shop was hard to miss, a plethora of neatly stacked shoes on display in the broad, wide window. Her surname was painted in large, loopy letters along the windowpane, and Belle knew that she'd smell the sweet scent of fresh leather as soon as she'd opened the shop door.

"On the right is a bookseller. I'm not entirely certain who works it, the staff rotates more than a windmill. I've always loved the smell of that shop, that aged smell of the books. I think you'd like it there." Lyren said, nodding toward the bookshop.

Navy blue curtains claimed windows identical to both the shoemaker and Lyren's practice, half-drawn and lined with gold. A slightly torn sign was in the center of the glass, sloppy penmanship scrawled along the page, something about a certain author from Westcastle and their newest novel.

Lyren led Belle through the entrance of his practice, unable to stifle the smile that crept across his lips. He was proud of his business, and he'd never brought a lover within *Singlebells* lively walls. Typically, work and pleasure were kept separate, but with Belle, everything in his life appeared to intermix.

"It's cold as ice in here. I'll get a fire started."

Belle shivered within her coat, and took a seat, silently watching as Lyren haphazardly stacked uneven blocks of wood within the fireplace. There was a bottle of half-drank whiskey on the table, and Belle watched with unblinking eyes as Lyren snatched it, drizzling the wood with a light layer. He took a generous step back, lit a match, and tossed it in—an angry, orange flame erupting immediately.

"I suppose that's one way to do it," Belle lightly teased, admiring the office. "I would've never expected to see stained glass windows in a place that carves open the dead."

"All of the color reminds me that I'm alive," Lyren explained, slipping his arms out of his coat. "It's easy to feel as if I'm dead when I'm surrounded by rot."

"Where are they?" Belle wondered, tossing her unwanted coat beside Lyren's. "The dead?"

Lyren nodded toward an additional door near the rear of the room. "Right in there. There's two of them right now, both laid on ice. I don't have much time, the dead rot quick, so I'll be rather busy today, I'm afraid."

"Did they die during the Blood Moon?" Belle wondered, her voice barely above a whisper. Bramwell had told her that people would die when the moon bled, and although she hadn't heard of any death, she knew deep within her chest that something awful *must* have happened that night, just as her husband promised.

Lyren's brows raised, his plump lower lip drawn between gnawing teeth.

"People always die when the moon bleeds," he said. "But those who did are too far gone for me to examine, now. I was stuck up on the mountain just as you were, and even if I wanted to come down, I couldn't. I couldn't even send a letter to my worker to come in, either."

Belle frowned. "I'm sure their families are disappointed."

"One thing I've learned in my nearly thirty years is that you cannot please everyone, Belle. You'll nearly ruin yourself by trying."

Lyren placed a firm kiss upon Belle's lips, tied a fresh white apron around his body, and then disappeared beyond the weighty door. He told her that she was welcome on the other side if she felt comfortable, and that if she wanted to wander, not to go much further than the businesses right next door.

She sat before the fire for nearly half the hour, anxiously picking at the skin surrounding her nails, before finally deciding to peek beyond the door.

She found Lyren planted before a wooden table, a pen pinched between soiled, slender fingers. The rings were absent, replaced now by blood and rot, the evidence of his occupation saturated within his skin.

His back was to Belle, and she'd slipped open the door so gently that he hadn't even noticed her presence. He dipped the steel tip of his pen into a bottle of jet-black ink, scribbling something nearly illegible along a sheet of paper.

The table was occupied by a body—seemingly male and middle aged, Belle thought—their chest cavity carved completely open, exposing what lay within. There was a weeping organ planted atop a metal scale, and Lyren's head rotated to view the reading, returning his attention to the sheet of parchment as the pen scratched along the surface.

Belle's stomach churned, and she contemplated closing the door once more. She'd only ever seen one dead body—Topher Hardt's—and it wasn't quite like this. The room reeked, a scent that reminded her of a wicker basket full of fish that had gone sour due to the summer sun, and she couldn't tear her stare from the man's open chest.

"Ly?"

Lyren twisted on his heel, a gentle grin claiming his features as he set down his pen.

"Sweet Belle," the man cheered, achingly aware of Belle's visible discomfort. "It's a frightening first sight, I do admit."

His gown was caked in blood, smeared and soiled, and it almost appeared as if Lyren had murdered the man himself.

"I'm weighing his heart," Lyren said, filling the silent void. Belle still hadn't spoken, hadn't moved.

"I'll remove all of his vital organs, weigh them, measure them, and then record the results."

When Belle still hadn't spoken, Lyren released a small sigh, soiled fingers lacing around his back, fiddling with the ties on his apron. He tore it from his frame, revealing the clean clothes beneath, and tossed it aside.

"Let me wash up and I'll take you next door to the bookseller. I've heard there's a new publication from a well-known author up in Westcastle."

"I can find it myself," Belle murmured, unable to tear her gaze away from Lyren's blood-soaked hands. She knew what he did for work before she got into the carriage, but to be there—to see it, to *smell* it—she wasn't entirely certain how someone as seemingly sane as Lyren Deth could find joy in such a demented task.

His lips formed into a thin frown.

"It's peculiar, I know. It stinks, I know. To an outsider, this entire scene probably looks absolutely absurd. I'd warned you–"

"You told me that I'd be rather bored, not traumatized," Belle lightly teased, resisting the urge to look at the dead man on the table. Her skin crawled when she was reminded of how his chest cavity was spread wide open, everything that lay within on full display. It almost felt like an invasion of a stranger's privacy.

"Do they know the form of death?"

"Just a suspicion," Lyren said, grabbing his apron once more. "A possible allergy to medication he took."

Belle kept stealing glances at the carved corpse, and Lyren weakly smiled.

"My love."

"I'm all right," Belle assured, swallowing thickly. "You're right, it is an absurd sight. An *intense* sight. I think I will stop by that bookseller just next door."

"Don't wander," Lyren said, tying the apron back around his front. "Stay alert, stay smart. If someone doesn't recognize you, don't say your name. Best to be anonymous, sometimes."

"Right," Belle breathed, clamming palm cradling the cool knob of the door. "I'll be back. I love you."

Lyren blushed. "And I love you."

THE HOST

The bookseller that shared a wall with Lyren's practice was even lovelier inside than it was on the out.

It was considerably cramped, but darling nevertheless, for the scent of leather and paper and dust made Belle's head dizzy with desire.

She wasn't sure which way to go first. There was a table front and center littered with a plethora of newspapers. Valen's biweekly paper was front and center, and to Belle's surprise, she was greeted by a grainy photograph of both her and Bramwell, arm in arm, small smiles etched along their lips. It was from their visit to the townscenter some short time ago, and to see herself on the very front page of the paper made her skin slightly crawl.

It wasn't something she was entirely used to—photographs of her. The first one she'd ever been in was from her wedding, and it was a peculiar thing, to see herself—her *face*—printed on paper. Eight days following the ceremony, the newspaper arrived at the manor, and she'd snuck it up to her bedroom to look at it in private, staring at the dark ink for hours in wonder. Observing the way she appeared to others, how her cheeks look sunken in and sickly, cheekbones pointed and prominent. Eyes wide, round, bulging. Lips full and pronounced.

There were papers from other towns as well, from the southernmost city of Gylsea to the northeast community of Swords Edge. It intrigued her, and she ran her fingers along the frayed edges of the haphazard stack of the newspapers that were shipped in from Gylsea. She'd heard stories of the pirates that frequently raided the border, the thieves that originated from a little lick of land barely off the southern coast of Elantry dubbed The Brother. It was unclaimed and littered with thieves, pirates, prostitutes, and runaways. Most seeking an escape from the law would row themselves out to sea, landing on the land of The Brother where they'd be safe from the Capitol's wrath.

It was the only unclaimed territory near Elantry's mainland beside Wylib up north, a nearly frozen-over spot that barely held a consistent population. If one wished to escape the country, the icy surface of Wylib's limited land was the very last place they'd go. Most would take their risk with the thieves and pirates and criminals of The Brother before ever sailing north.

Belle had been shuffling through a small stack of papers from Westcastle when she was made aware of an additional presence in the bookshop. She'd nearly jumped out of her skin when she noticed her, the colorless hair on her arms standing tall between patches of prickly goosebumps.

"I didn't mean to frighten you," the stranger said, blinking slowly. She was frail—*old*—with weathered limbs that barely moved. Her eyes were sunken and clouded, a pleasant blue hue, and she wore multihued rags for clothes, ones that weighed her aging frame down further to the ground.

"It's quite all right," Belle weakly assured, a small smile stretched along her lips. "I thought I was alone, but then again, that wouldn't make much sense, would it? Are you the shopkeeper?"

"For now," the woman replied with a smile, her teeth stained with age. "Come sit by the window with me, I've just brewed some tea. I have scones, but they're a day too old, I'm afraid."

The woman wobbled toward the wide window, her wrinkled digits claiming the thick, dusty curtains as she struggled to pry them open. Belle stepped forward to assist the elderly woman with her task, and the lady nodded in thanks, offering Belle a seat opposite her.

The chairs were worn and weathered, clearly loved and used. Belle wondered just how many people had sat in that very seat, eyes glued to the pages of a book, a single copper coin burning a hole in their pocket, too little to pay for the book in their hands.

"It's a gorgeous place," Belle complimented, eyes scanning over the endless shelves of disorganized books.

"You're the lady, aren't you?" the woman asked, sighing when she collapsed against the cushion of her seat. Her bones audibly creaked with every miniscule movement, and Belle wondered just how old the woman really was, and why she bothered getting out of bed in the morning to wander into the cold.

"I am," Belle said, her brows furrowed in frustration. She hoped that maybe just this once, she wouldn't be recognized. It seemed impossible at this point for her to go anywhere without being noticed.

"Bramwell's woman," the old lady laughed. "My sweet Bramwell."

Belle's blood shifted to ice within her veins. It was evident that the woman knew Bramwell on a level more personal than most.

"Forgive me, but I thought Bramwell was the only living Hellthorne? Are you related?"

Her weak eyes sparkled, and the old woman couldn't help but grin, her hands trembling as she reached forward to grab her lukewarm cup of tea. Belle leaned forward to assist the woman, gently placing the mug within wrinkled palms.

"I'm his mother," she revealed, taking a generous sip from her cup. Belle's lips parted in protest—*his mother is dead*—but the woman wouldn't let her finish.

"His *true* mother. The bitch that birthed him rots where she stands, as she should. Did you know that the late Lady Sorrel and Lord Ayer II kept Bramwell locked up in the tallest tower of Hellthorne Manor? There was a hole in the ceiling, where flurries would fall in and create a blanket of snow on his floor. He'd go to bed hungry, cold, and alone."

Belle blinked, stunned silent by what the elderly woman spewed. She'd known of the secrecy surrounding Bramwell's existence, but she'd never known much of his childhood. It wasn't a topic in which he frequently spoke of.

"He called upon me one night, the eve of his tenth year, when he went to bed starving and forgotten," the woman added, pausing once more to sip her tea.

"He spoke the words. *Exsurge ab inferis et suscipe me sicut tua.* He needed me. He *wanted* me."

Belle shifted uncomfortably in her seat, her heart thumping thickly within her throat. There was something odd about the elderly woman across from her—*terrifying,* almost—and familiar. It was as if she'd been in her presence before, but she couldn't quite pinpoint when or where.

"What's your name?" Belle kindly wondered, weakly masking the fear in her voice.

The woman took note of her discomfort, and she reached outward, a palm meeting Belle's knee, as if to comfort her.

"He called me Mumma, but you can call me Vel, my sweet."

Her touch wavered, and suddenly, her eyes widened, fixated on Belle's heavily clothed midsection.

"You're with seed," she said. "Oh, the Capitol will be pleased. Very pleased, indeed."

Belle's mouth snapped shut, a sour taste filling her mouth as her hand found her unchanged stomach.

"You're mistaken," Belle calmly stated, shaking her head from side to side. She hadn't bled in six or more weeks, but that was not uncommon for the woman, for her malnourishment often interrupted her cycle, and she'd go several months without having bled.

The elderly woman by the name of Vel only chuckled.

"If you say, my lady. Open your eyes, Lady Belle. If you keep them closed, you'll never see." She sipped her tea. "Your boy toy is here."

The front door opened wide, and a windswept Lyren shuffled into the warmth of the store, a shiver enveloping his spine as his eyes scanned the area. They settled upon a stiff Belle sitting opposite an ancient woman who he had never met, and with a crooked smile, he greeted the pair.

"Ready to eat, my lady?" Lyren wondered, failing to introduce himself to Belle's new acquaintance.

"Yes," Belle nodded, standing to her feet. She bid the strange woman goodbye with very few words, and the pair fled the bookshop. Belle glanced over her shoulder only once before leaving, and when she did, she was met by the black stare of the woman named Vel, whose eyes were once blue but were now as dark as coal.

Belle slipped her hand into Lyren's gloved grasp, and as soon as they were back into the cold, she began to sniffle.

"Who was that?" Lyren wondered, dropping her hand almost as quickly as he'd felt it. There were wanderers around, and if the wrong eyes locked on them, rumors would flood Valen before supper.

"It was Bram's mother," Belle said, and her lover only laughed.

"My love, Bramwell's mother died in his eighteenth year."

"No, not *that* mother." Belle whined, her stomach doing somersaults. "It was his true mother. It was a woman named Vel."

"Vel?" Lyren mocked, his wild eyes meeting Belle's terrified stare. His chest ached at the sight, and suddenly, he felt awful about laughing. "Vel sounds an awful lot like a short name for–"

"For *Velveteen.*" Belle finished, trembling slightly, but not from the cold. The feeling was back—the terror, the *fear*—and she suddenly remembered where she'd encountered that presence before.

Evelin Byron's empty white stare.

The portrait of a dead girl.

The fingers in her hair, the wheezing breaths.

The dead stand below.

Belle began to shake.

If you keep them closed, you'll never see.

Open them wide, or you too will stand below.

Belle fell to her knees, the choppy ice along the pebbled path tearing open the fabric of her gown, and she audibly screamed.

Lady Hell will ring deaths bell.

Lady Hell will be a shell.

SEED

B elle stayed in bed for four days following her encounter with the Queen of the Netherworld.

Before her marriage to Bramwell, she didn't believe in anything of the sort. The Goddesses, the angels, the demons, it was all just fiction to her. A way of controlling the masses. A way to terrify people into behaving.

Only now, she knew that wasn't entirely the case.

Belle wasn't sure what to believe, but she knew what she'd seen—how she *felt*—and with penmanship sloppier than it's ever been before, she wrote her insane sister another letter.

I met her.

The woman who possessed you.

The woman who evidently possessed my husband.

She never possessed him, Evelin. He'd conjured her. Called for her. Brought her into this world. Given her the role of mother.

She raised him, Evelin.

My husband is the son of the Fallen Goddess.

She could hardly read her own writing, for her hand was shaking so violently that she could hardly hold the pen. The silver tip unintentionally struck the side of the ink bottle, and a river of black blinded half of the page, erasing the evidence.

Belle gasped, and then defeatedly sobbed, scrapping the letter as if it never existed at all. As if her sister could even read it at all. Belle knew better. Velveteen's possession had ruined Evelin. *Destroyed* her.

Lady Hell will be a shell.

Just as her sister was, now.

Three weeks later, when the lady was thumbing through an old novel about werebeings and bloodsuckers and the fae, she felt the shift.

Her palm hastily met the flat of her stomach, and she gagged, pulse instantly quickening in panic. Florence was sitting beside her, reading a book of her own, and she took notice of Belle's episode, her features shifting to that of immense worry.

"Belle, what is it?"

Belle shook her head, eyes watering as she stood to her feet. The book toppled from her lap, and she lurched forward, tripping slightly over the wooden leg of the loveseat, and suddenly, the nearby washroom felt a million miles away from the sitting room.

"Good Goddess, I bet one of the housemaidens let the cheese sit out for too long–" Florence cursed, rushing to Belle's side. They barely made it out of the double doors before Belle collapsed along the carpet, her knees weak and wobbly. The room began to spin, and Florence's fingers were in her hair, swiftly peeling the fiery locks out of Belle's face as that afternoon's lunch resurfaced.

"Flo," Belle cried, collapsing within the woman's arms. Tove, one of the newest housemaidens, had stumbled upon the scene, a worrisome gasp tickling her tongue as she went to fetch the proper supplies to clean up Belle's mess.

"Let's get you to your room, Belle," Florence cooed, helping a weak Belle to her feet.

When dusk fell and Lyren was still in the carriage on his way back up the hill, Bramwell made an appearance in Belle's bedroom.

It had been only the fourth time she'd seen him since Yule. There'd been a vibe between them—a stiffness—and Bramwell respected her unspoken wishes and was mostly absent. If he'd turn a corner and see her, he'd walk the opposite way. If the door to the sitting room was parted, he'd find a stuffy old room to shut himself up in, the drapes pulled, dust filling his lungs.

There were whispers within the manor that day, and when he'd heard that the lady of the house had thrown up her lunch whilst collapsing, he couldn't help but feel slightly on edge.

Belle was alone when Bramwell found her, buried beneath a blanket, her oily hair pulled back into neat braids. There was a book in her hands—something about were-beings and bloodsuckers—and a fresh fire was roaring in the hearth, the orange warmth dancing along the walls.

She greeted him with nothing but a thin-lipped grin, and Bramwell took his spot beside her bed, hands stuffed within the pockets of his trousers, his awkward gaze wandering.

"You heard."

"I did," Bramwell said, desperate to meet her gaze. Only, she didn't give it to him. Instead, she emptily studied the same page of her book, eyes unseeing. Her stomach turned, and although she was starving, the thought of food made her want to retch all over Bramwell's shoes.

"Should I send for the physician?" Bramwell kindly wondered, settling his stare on Belle's hair. He could tell that she'd been tampering with it all day, the oil from her fingers left behind in the bright red strands.

"No," Belle muttered, snapping the book closed. Her chest heaved, and she admitted aloud the thing she'd known since her meeting with Velveteen.

"You're going to have an heir."

Bramwell paled. "Are you certain?"

Velveteen's recent host—the poor old shopkeeper that ran the bookseller beside Lyren's practice—consumed Belle's memory. Every time she blinked, she could visualize those sunken eyes, the way they effortlessly shifted from a lovely winter blue to a haunting, deep black. If she'd stayed a second longer, she was almost certain that the elderly woman would have claimed a fistful of her hair, her long, sharp fingernails sinking into the supple skin of Belle's scalp, applying just enough pressure to sever the surface.

She wanted to spill it all before Bramwell—to confess just how much she knew—but instead, her eyes filled with angry tears, and she choked back a stiff sob.

"Does he know?" Bramwell wondered, oblivious to the thoughts that plagued Belle's mind. With each passing day—with every new thing she learned—she'd grown to nearly despise the man, *hate* him, even. He'd always acted so lovely, so *innocent,* but the veil had been lifted. *Torn away.*

He was the son of the Fallen Goddess, cursed by her presence, given the gift of death. He was a murderer, a liar. There was much, much more to Bramwell's story, and Belle was determined to dig it all up, even if she had to use the shovel herself.

"Not yet," Belle whispered, refusing to look her husband in the face. "I'd much appreciate it if you'd allow me to break the news. He deserves to hear it from me."

"Of course," Bramwell replied, as kindly as he could. He adored Belle, and he was blissfully unaware of the tainted image of him that plagued his wife's mind. He fell to his knees beside the bed, arms settled along the mattress, balancing his weight.

It was then that she finally looked at him.

His features were soft—*kind*—and for a brief moment, Belle almost felt herself slip under his spell once more. He was effortlessly charming, and although she'd discovered the haunting truth behind his identity, she could still recognize that he'd never once wronged her, never hurt her. He'd been nothing but good to her, and even still, as she met his deep brown stare, she felt nothing but disgust.

She bit her tongue and turned away.

"You can go, now."

Bramwell's lips parted in protest, but Belle was firm on her statement. With a dismissive wave of her hand, she ushered him out, returning her attention to the book she'd stolen from the sitting room.

Defeated, Bramwell hovered the entryway, a somber stare settling upon his wife. Although they were in the very same room, he felt as if they were miles and miles apart, and admittedly, the fact made his heart ache within his chest.

He didn't mind that she was pregnant with a child that was not his. He didn't mind that two people who were not him laid in her bed from dusk until dawn, one of them being someone he considered a close friend. He didn't mind at all, not even in the slightest.

But Belle's blatant disgust for him, now that he *did* mind. He was nothing but good to her, nothing but sweet. Kind. He fed her, clothed her, pampered her. Anything she wanted—anything she *needed*—was and would always be hers. And yet, it was apparent that she despised him, was *repulsed* by him. He wasn't quite sure what prompted the change, but it made his blood boil.

"The child will take my name," Bramwell said through gritted teeth.

When Belle's stare met his, he knew for certain that there was nothing but hatred behind her eyes. Cold, dark, bitter detestation.

"The *child* is not yours," she countered, her tone as cold as ice. She'd tightened her grip on the novel, knuckles flushed a gaunt white.

He'd never seen her angry.

"And I am not the son of Lord Ayer II," Bramwell revealed, a fact that he'd never once audibly announced. "But I will not allow Valen to label a child within these halls a bastard. Whether it be a son or a daughter, they shall carry the Hellthorne name, and it will be written in history that they are *our* child, not just yours, not just Lyren's. If Lyren chooses to produce another with Florence, or with anyone who is not you, he may have a claim to said child. But this one is *mine.*"

Belle's pulse quickened, her shy brown gaze narrowing into tight slits as she shot her husband the most wicked glare she could possibly produce. She'd never spoken the words aloud—*I hate you, I ruddy fucking hate you*—but she knew that he could tell. From her stare alone, he *knew.*

His posture went rigid, and his jaw locked into place, a sea of fire dancing behind dark eyes as the pair remained in stark silence for far too long. She wanted to throw the book at him. Bash the hard, rigid spine against the softest part of his skull. Make him bleed. Watch him weep.

He could kill her right in that very moment.

It would be simple. He wouldn't have to lift a single finger. Just a part of the lips, an incantation dancing along his tongue, a steady stream of eye contact. He could do it, and she *knew* it.

She refused to tear away her stare, as if to challenge him.

Do it.

He was the first to break the spell.

His stare studied the weeping wallpaper, and with flushed features, he spoke.

"I'll send for a physician to confirm your pregnancy. When you begin to swell, we will go to town to announce the news of my heir. The Capitol will receive word shortly after. The first name will be yours and Lyren's to choose. The family name will be Hellthorne. There will be no further discussion on the matter. No one will know that the heir is a bastard, unless you wish for your child to endure a lifetime of judgment, and possible exile to Minnehel, under The Capitol's decision."

Belle said nothing.

"Lyren's late because he was waiting for Lyudmilla. Did he tell you that?" Bramwell added.

Once again, his wife remained silent. Clutched within her grasp was her book, the pages withered and old.

No, he did not.

When Belle failed to respond, Bramwell continued. He was still staring at the wallpaper, the way it wrinkled near the baseboard, the glue gone bad.

"She's a character, his sister. You'll hate her, I'm sure of it."

Then, he left—slamming the door on his heel, the collision turning the paintings crooked on their nails.

Belle sat for several moments in silence, her hand gravitating down toward her stomach. She laid the book in her lap, the pages fanning inward, her page forgotten. A trembling palm cradled the unchanged surface of her belly, and she applied only the faintest amount of pressure to the surface, as if to feel for any sort of movement at all, something she knew was impossible at such an early stage.

"You're not his," she whispered, hot tears flooding her eyes. "You'll *never* be his. They may call you by his name, but you belong to me, and you belong to Lyren. You are of *Lyren,* and of me."

The tears flowed freely, then. Lyren was on his way back up the hill, stuffed up in a carriage alongside his sister Lyudmilla, a woman Belle had yet to meet. Florence was in the kitchens, watching Tove braid a loaf of sourdough, and stealing a taste of the lentil soup whenever Jeanne looked away.

"I will love you until my last breath," Belle promised, choking back a sob.

Admittedly, she was terrified. She was still young, still youthful, still *childish,* or so she felt. A terrified child trapped in the body of an adult woman.

Her parents would be pleased, as would the people of Valen. Overjoyed, even. They'd toss bird seed and shower their feet with yellow and white roses and each and every person near and far would want to get a glimpse of the Lady of Valen and her swollen belly, to see the woman who would help continue the Hellthorne name.

She'd be in history books, like the very ones she'd read in the sitting room. Her name beside Bramwell's, the name of this child, of every other child she and Lyren would likely create, none of them belonging to him in the eyes of an outsider.

It was severely unfair. The father of her child was *Lyren,* not Bramwell, and never would he take the title.

By the time Lyren and Lyudmilla Deth clambered out of the carriage—a chorus of chuckles cascading between them—Belle had tumbled down the hall and into the washroom, emptying what little food sat on her stomach into the basin.

Lady Hell will be a shell.

LYUDMILLA DETH

Her hair was lighter than his.

More silver, less blond, shiny and soft, with gorgeous gold flecks that seemed to shimmer beneath the candlelight.

Her lips were full and painted a stunning red, almost identical to the color dusted along her cheeks, and her brows were dark in contrast to the hair atop her head—black, almost—a look Belle wasn't quite familiar with.

She lived in Havensworth—Elantry's Capitol—and according to Lyren, she styled hair for the elite. Lyudmilla seemingly took offense to her position, and through a mouthful of bread, she'd said, "I don't *just* do hair, little brother. I'm studying to be a jeweler. See these rings I'm wearing? Worth more than sixty gold coins *each*. Most people in places like Minnehel and Immorium and Sarsin have probably never even seen so much gold in a lifetime, and here I am, wearing its worth."

Bramwell was silent for most of supper.

Belle had met his glare briefly once or twice during Lyudmilla's foolish rants, and for a moment, Belle could've sworn she'd seen his lips pull into a sarcastic smile, only to be hidden by the rim of his whiskey glass.

He was right. Belle *loathed* Lyren's sister.

Not only was she incredibly brash, but her entire presence made Belle's stomach roll several times over. It was nearly impossible for her to sip her soup, and when realization dawned upon her that the child within her womb would be related to that ghastly woman, she nearly retched.

"Rumors have been flying around the Capitol like you wouldn't *believe*, brother," Lyudmilla said, a striking sapphire gaze admiring the sparkling jewels that lined her long, dainty fingers. "They say you're *courting* someone, can you believe that? I could hardly believe it myself, my whore brother courting someone, I laugh every time I hear it!"

Florence had met Lyren's sister only once half a decade prior, and she could still recall just how desperately Lyudmilla had clung to Bramwell, how she practically begged for his hand, how she'd made a fool of herself on more occasions than one.

It was no secret that Lyudmilla had always fancied Bramwell Hellthorne.

"Things have gotten rather serious," Lyren admitted, his pale cheeks blushed a somber scarlet. Florence had remained mostly silent, sipping on the very same lentil soup she'd sampled before, her fingers fiddling with a slice of sourdough.

Lyudmilla's lips parted dramatically, forming an o-shape as she let out a boastful laugh. It was as if both Belle and Bramwell were not even present at the dinner table, for the woman had barely acknowledged either of their existence at all.

"She's not double your age now, is she? You always seemed to have a thing for older women, as if you've been trying to find yourself a new mummy to replace our rotten one. Or perhaps it's due to the fact that you whored around with that woman five years over your age when you were just a teenage boy. I couldn't blame you much, I find myself looking for certain qualities in men to replace what our dreadful father lacked. It's my weakest trait."

Just as Florence's arm extended in reach of a bowl of sugar cubes, he'd claimed her hand, a sweet smile easing across his mouth. He brought her cold fingers to his lips, where he pressed a soft, shy kiss to the surface of her knuckles.

The action puzzled Lyudmilla greatly, and before she could question him, Lyren said, "it's her. Florence Smyth. She's stunning, isn't she, sister?"

Silence.

"Gorgeous one, Florence is."

It was Bramwell who had spoken, for the very first time since they'd gathered for supper. Lyudmilla nearly broke her neck trying to catch a glimpse of his expression, her grip on her wine glass loosening considerably, sending the ruby red liquid sloshing from the sides, staining the emerald tablecloth with the mark of blood.

"His *ward?*" Lyudmilla queried, beside herself in shock. "Lyren, you must be joking. Please tell me you're joking."

Lyren's gaze darkened, and he tightened his hold on Florence's hand, lovingly lacing their fingers together. The flat of his thumb traced reassuring circles along hers, and for a moment so brief that Belle barely noticed, his blue stare met hers—longing. *Sorrowful.*

She still hadn't told him the news, nor had she revealed anything to Florence. Lyudmilla Deth's sudden visit prevented her from doing so, and she wished now more than ever that she could reach across the table and pull the pair into her arms, to scream the news from the rooftops.

"That's enough, Milla. Florence is no lesser of a person and a woman than you are due to her status." Lyren said, clearly agitated with his sister. The conversation had grown rather strained, and although Belle was repulsed by Bram, she couldn't help but shoot him an uncomfortable look, as if to beg him for some sort of reprieve.

He seemed to have read her thoughts.

"Lyudmilla," Bramwell began, digging into the pocket of his shirt in search of a fresh cigar.

Seeing Lyudmilla Deth again made him anxious enough to want to chain smoke. He could still feel her grubby fingers on him, how she'd tugged at the waistline of his trousers several years ago, her red-lined lips smearing stains across his jaw. It made him nauseous—*dizzy*—and even sitting at the very same table as her was enough to make him want to gag.

"Brammy," Lyudmilla beamed, pulling her round bottom lip between her teeth. "I almost forgot you were here, my apologies. It's been so long, hasn't it? Five years or more, no?"

"About," Bramwell confirmed, thumbing around his pocket for a match. "You've barely uttered a word toward my new wife. You're a guest in my home, you'll pay the lady of the house your respects, or you'll be asked to leave."

At this, Lyudmilla paled considerably. The pink blush slapped across her cheeks appeared to flush a ghastly white, and with eyes the size of saucers, she finally met Belle's stare.

"My apologies, Lady Hellthorne," she said, clearly embarrassed by her interaction with Bramwell. She wondered for a moment if Lyren's friend had revealed Lyudmilla's previous advances to Belle, and the thought sent a shiver down Lyren's sister's spine.

She'd never admit it aloud, but she envied the redheaded girl—so much so that her blood nearly boiled within her veins. *That should have been her on his arm, taking his last name, warming his bed in the evening.*

"No apology is necessary, Lyudmilla," Belle said, her tone shy and soft. She couldn't believe that the man she loved had come from the very same womb that grew such a rotten woman.

A woman who shares the blood of her unborn child.

"You're a lucky woman, you are," Lyudmilla added, her stare downcast, somber. She seemed genuinely hurt. "I'm sure you've heard the whispers. There are things I won't outwardly deny, but fear not, my lady. There is nothing I would do to shatter the love that is between you two. There are a few gentlemen awaiting my hand back in Havensworth."

When Belle failed to reply, Lyudmilla returned her attention to Lyren and Florence, who were still hand in hand.

"Mummy would be interested to know of your courtship," she began, avoiding Florence's stern glare. "I'd rather appreciate having some alone time with your new woman, little brother. After all, if things continue on such a positive path, you and I will be sisters in marriage. I've never had a sister, but I've always wanted one."

Before Lyren could protest, Florence shockingly agreed to Lyudmilla's proposal.

"I'd be happy to share a cup of lemon tea with you in the sitting room following the completion of supper." A genuine smile eased along Florence's lips, and Belle's stomach burst into a flurry of butterflies at the sight. She wanted nothing more than to curl up beneath the covers with both of her lovers, to pepper open-mouthed kisses along both of their jaws, to whisper sweet nothings into the bones of their collars.

"I would enjoy that," Lyudmilla replied, and although the statement seemed genuine, Belle wasn't quite sure if Lyren's sister was actually looking forward to the meeting at all. It was evident that she believed she could find a better woman for Lyren, and that Florence was not nearly enough.

If only she knew . . .

Just as Florence promised, she led Lyudmilla to the sitting room immediately following the conclusion of dinner. Bramwell retired to his own respective quarters after assisting Tove with gathering the dishes, and Lyren followed Belle back to her bedroom at a fair distance, cautious not to catch any unwanted attention from either his sister or the housemaidens.

When the silver haired man eventually slipped into Belle's bedroom, she was already stripped of most of her clothing, leaving her upper half bare. She'd torn open the window, the consistent bursts of icy wind sending the dense curtains airborne. Goosebumps lined her arms, dipping down her navel, disappearing into the lining of her panties. Her fingers gravitated toward the place where she would soon bulge, and she admired the sleek blackness of the landscape beyond the window, the way the trees bended and curved, forming indistinguishable shapes that often reminded her of fables her mother once told, the creatures that lived and thrived within the woods.

Lyren fingered the buttons of his lemon-yellow top, the ruffles of the fabric shifting with every burst of wind. His lips found the curve of her shoulder.

"I'm sorry for my sister," he whispered against her frigid flesh, the pale surface like ice against his warm mouth. He shrugged out of his shirt, letting it fall to their feet, before pressing his front up against her back, gentle palms wandering, gliding down the bump-riddled surface of her skin. He was at her neck—nipping, sucking—and when his hand found hers atop the center of her belly, he froze. He could feel her stiffness—her *anxiety*—and with brows knit tightly together in both wonder and worry, his forefinger claimed her chin, urging her head sideways so that their stares could meet.

"My love," he cooed, scanning her features for an inkling of an answer. "What is it? Is it Lyudmilla?"

"Goddess, no," Belle dismissed, blinking back stinging tears. She felt so emotional as of late, and even the idea of tripping over her own two feet was enough to send her into a fit of sobs. "Well, don't be angry, but your sister is rather rotten."

Lyren forced a laugh, his forehead meeting hers with a gentle *thump.*

"Spending years upon years living in the Capitol would turn any maiden sour. We're from Abler Black, did you know that? The farmland right on the coast, directly mirroring The Shores."

She did not know that.

Abler Black was the soonest town just north of her hometown of Immorium, and it was considerably kinder than the land in which she was raised. The inlet separating the island of The Shores and Abler Black, commonly called The Craik, supplied a surplus of high-quality meats, water, and items to the land. It was often spoken of around Immorium that one single swim within The Craik would bring one's family a plentitude of luck, and to be baptized in the waters of The Craik would ensure a pleasant life from the very beginning to the end.

"Immorium speaks highly of Abler Black," Belle muttered, threading her fingers through Lyren's light locks. Their lips met briefly—a whisper of a kiss—and she felt his lips upturn into a grin.

"It's rather lovely there," he admitted, his palm meeting hers. It was then that he'd noticed her peculiar stance—the way she'd been clutching her stomach, as if out of discomfort. "Are you in pain?"

His palm cradled hers, hovering the very place where his child had just begun to blossom.

"No," Belle whispered, choking on the statement. She couldn't help it, then. The dam broke, and the tears flowed, coating her cheeks in a salty wetness that tickled Lyren's tongue as he promptly kissed them away.

"Talk to me," he urged, entwining their fingers.

Silently, she collected both of his hands in hers, directing them downward to meet the bareness of her belly. She arranged his hands in a way that amused her, his fingers pointed downward, the tips of his thumbs barely touching, forming a weak, triangular shape.

"It's of us both," she murmured, resting her forehead against his. Realization dawned upon him, and his knees nearly crumbled.

"Are you certain?" he breathed, large, doe-like eyes glancing down to meet her exposed stomach. There was just barely a swell—a poor excuse for a bump—it almost was as if she'd just consumed a large meal. Nothing but bloat.

"Positively."

He didn't have to ask twice, for in his heart—in his *soul*—he knew. He knew exactly when it had happened, too. It was almost as if he'd known at that very moment what they'd done, what they'd *created*.

When the moon bled in the sky and the clouds wept with tears of gore, Belle had whispered the words he'd been aching to hear since the moment their eyes met. She'd told him that she loved him that night, and whilst the statement slipped from her rosy, red lips, he'd planted a seed—one which would grow, one that would thrive. Physical evidence of their love, blooming within the sweet belly of one of his lovers.

Tears clouded his vision, and their lips met in a rushed, frenzied kiss. Where words failed, passion spoke.

He told her that he loved her more times than he could count, and before succumbing to a peaceful, dreamless snooze, he peppered loving smooches along the flat of her stomach, where beyond the smoothness of her flesh and the meat of her muscle, their child gradually grew.

BURIED BELOW

S he was alone when she woke.

Florence had gone for a trip to town alongside Lyudmilla Deth, who was on the third day of her visit, and hopefully her last. She'd never said just how long she planned to stay at the manor, but as the days droned on, Belle grew tired of her presence.

Florence, on the other hand, had taken a liking to Lyren's sister. The fact almost enraged Belle—*don't you see just how awful that woman is*—but she refused to let any of her worries slip, for Florence was her own, individual person, and if she liked Lyudmilla, then Belle simply had no say in the matter.

With the pair off scampering about town, Lyren back at his practice dissecting another dead body, and Bramwell on a carriage ride to the Capitol for unspoken business, Belle Hellthorne found herself alone.

Well, mostly alone.

The housemaidens busied themselves with meaningless tasks. Some cleaned, others cooked. Jeanne ruined another pot of lentil soup, and Tove took it out to Henry's cottage at the cusp of the mountain, offering him the soiled supper. Henry wasn't picky when it came to food, and if it wasn't sour or spoiled, he'd gulp it down in half the time it would take any ordinary human to consume it.

After thumbing through several boring books and pacing the downstairs wing of the mansion, Belle grew bored. Although she couldn't quite stand Lyudmilla Deth, a part of her wished that she'd accompanied her and Florence into town, for anything would have surely been better than mindlessly wandering the halls.

According to the position of the blinding sun, it was just barely midday, and Belle let out an exasperated groan. Not even the housemaidens could cure the lady's boredom, even with their mundane chatter about nothingness. She'd already heard most of their life stories already, and the days spent within the black walls of Hellthorne Manor began to bleed together.

It was then that she began to wander in places that she knew she shouldn't.

Bramwell had never specifically said that any part of the manor was unattainable, but there were certain areas that Belle typically avoided.

For starters, the attic.

It took one winding staircase to access, and the room was locked at all times, so she'd never even attempted to venture up there. According to Velveteen, Bramwell had spent a majority of his youth in that very room, freezing beneath his bundle of blankets, snow flurries fluttering through the hole in the roof.

There were only a few miscellaneous rooms spread throughout that she'd never expressed interest in see-ing. Most of them were just guest rooms. Boring old four-poster beds, dusty dressers, unlit lamps.

Then, the basement.

The idea of a dark, dungeon-like room buried beneath the floor made Belle's skin crawl. She wasn't even entirely sure of what laid beneath the floorboards, and admittedly, she was too anxious to ask. Bramwell had only mentioned it once, something about being *dangerous* and *unfinished* and *riddled with rats and dust.* Everything he'd said made the basement sound highly unappealing, and never once had Belle felt the desire to locate it.

That was, until the portrait of a dead girl came alive, possessed by the Queen of the Netherworld herself, Velveteen, the very same demon that clambered into Evelin Byron's innocent little frame and ruined her from the inside out.

Every time she closed her eyes, she swore that she could still feel the demons touch—fingers as cold as ice—skin slick with the stench of rot. Her stomach rolled, and she could still hear the words Velveteen spoke, as if she stood before her in that very moment, the poison slipping off of her tongue once more.

The dead stand below.

There was a staircase.

It was stuffed beyond a crooked shelf, filled to the brim with an assortment of trinkets aged nearly a century, it appeared. A layer of dust so thick and dense that it nearly made Belle's eyes water coated a majority of the surface, concealing the artifacts beneath a gray, bleak blanket.

The door to the hidden stairs was propped open—only barely, as if by accident. It was a rickety old oak door, one with a broken brass handle, and when she pried it open, it squealed on its hinges, as if to cry out in protest.

Her eyes flew open in fear, and she glanced over each shoulder, peering down the endless hallway in search of an intruder. Only, no one ventured that far back into the manor.

There were no paintings on the walls within this hall. The rug was frayed and neglected, as if forgotten.

She'd stolen a weeping candle from a nearby hallway, one that wept wax all over her fingers, a stinging hiss. It barely illuminated the area, hardly several centimeters, but nevertheless, she swung the door open, revealing the dingy staircase within.

The stairs were in a dreadful state, the wood rotten and worn, and with every small step, the staircase squeaked and groaned, giving her location away. If anyone dared to venture down the dark hallway, they'd surely hear her creeping down the stairs. They'd see the door to the basement swung wide open, a bright red arrow pointing downward, giving her location away.

"Good Goddess," Belle cursed, steadying her palms against the worn wooden walls. The staircase was cramped and enclosed, a wall on either side, and dipped down into a pitch-black eternal abyss, an ending that she couldn't quite see beyond the poor lighting of her single candle.

"What in Goddess Liv are you *doing,* Bells," she murmured, shaking slightly. She took each step one by one, anxious that one would crumble beneath her weight and send her tumbling into an eternal pit.

It was fair to assume that whatever laid beyond the staircase was something that did not want to be found.

There was no reason for her to go there. There was no reason for *anyone* to go there. According to Bramwell, there was nothing but dust and rats and mold and *rot* beneath the floorboards. It was simply an ancient room beneath the mansion that just—*existed.*

But nothing was so simple at Hellthorne Manor.

Perhaps she was sauntering down to her death. A trap set by Velveteen's demon self, the very one who encouraged her to explore it in the first place.

The dead stand below.

Thus, she pressed on.

Eighty-seven steps. The seventy-fifth stair cracked and crumbled, sending her left foot through. She bit back a scream, and nearly dropped her candle, a plethora of wet wax coating her knuckles.

She cursed, and with a noisy exhale, she planted both feet on the floor.

So far, nothing.

Nothing but blackness. Emptiness. *Dust.*

It was thick—*heavy.* She could feel the dust settling in her lungs with every deep breath. Within her line of sight, there was nothing but an empty room. Puddled pockmarks in the floor, the concrete mushy and wet beneath her feet. The smell of soil, the stench of dirt. There was surely a dead animal or three decaying somewhere—she could nearly taste it—and when she'd come to the conclusion that Bramwell was right about the anticlimactic basement, she heard a sound.

A *human* sound.

It was barely audible, but she'd *heard* it. A moan, or perhaps, more of a groan. It was low, deep. Masculine in nature. Pained, perhaps. Bitter.

With slitted eyes, she scanned the darkness, the candle held high above her head. She couldn't see worth a shit, and she *knew* what she'd heard. There was someone else down here, someone like her.

Another person.

Did someone live down there?

She wanted to call out for them—*hello, is anyone there*—but she nearly choked on the words as they crawled up her throat. Something deep within her convinced her not to, for announcing her presence could possibly put her in danger.

It was brief—she'd almost missed it—but she saw an orange flicker of a flame. A lit oil lamp, hidden beyond another door. It was just barely cracked, similar to the basement entrance, and her breaths thinned. Whoever was down there with her, was surely beyond that door. The oil in the lamp had been fresh, a flame so bright that it was nearly white. Someone had lit it within the last day, that, she was sure.

Either this idea of hers would be the best one she's had, or it would end in her ashen, gray, and dead, bleeding out on the withered floor, never to be found.

Her curled knuckles grazed the splintered wood of the parted door—a breath hitching in her throat, bile coating the rear of her tongue—and she filed in, fully committed.

She could *smell* before she could *see.*

A sweet, wet rot. The stench of decomposition. Coppery, metallic blood, so thick that she could taste it on the tip of her tongue.

Two pairs of eyes met hers—an opaque white, stormy gray—pupils masked, clouded over. *Blurred.* The irises nonexistent, nothing but an empty bleak hue, void of color, void of life.

She sucked in a gasp, and the candlestick fell to her feet.

HIS AND HERS

They weren't violent.

They weren't threatening.

They didn't tear at their chains. They didn't attempt to harm her.

They didn't do much of anything, really. Just stare. Empty, soulless pits of gray. Eyelids that never curtained closed, just remained open indefinitely, a peeled, exposed rotten fruit.

There were two of them. One man, one woman.

He was seated, whereas she stood. Both wrists clad in rusted metal chains, stiff and secure. The chair which held the unchanged man resembled that of an aged throne, navy blue, the fabric warped and wrecked. Taut around his bare wrists were dense iron cuffs, securing him to the decorative wooden arms of the throne.

Buried within weeping white curls was a crown built of thorns, permanently placed atop a bleeding skull. The blood from the barbs had blackened with age—*spoiled*—leaving behind a clumpy and thick texture that haphazardly painted his pale, nearly colorless forehead.

He was easily middle-aged—*if he even still aged at all*—and was dressed in gorgeous green robes, perfectly fit for a king.

Or a lord.

Belle's lips parted in realization, and she nearly lost her breakfast when reality came crashing down on her.

She could hardly bear to face the woman who was directly beside her legal husband, who perhaps had never been a true lover at all.

She was in considerably worse shape than he.

Whereas he was fully dressed, she was somewhat disrobed. A blatant wardrobe malfunction. *Malicious.*

Her skin was moderately covered by a royal blue day dress, a floral pattern stamped into the surface. The chest area was ripped—*torn*—clawed away, revealing both of her breasts. Across each nipple was a gaudy *x*, carved into the skin with a curved blade, crossing them out. *Erasing them.*

Only it appeared as if the attack hadn't occurred once, but multiple times. A *plethora* of times. The mauled flesh had been beaten and abused so many times that it almost resembled ground meat. Where nipples once sat, only gore remained. Carved. Chopped. *Ruined.*

Whether it be for shame, she wasn't certain, but there was a clear motive for such a peculiar action. There was pain. *Torment.* Her attacker had wanted her to pay for something, and the destruction of her breasts had been a bold, slippery statement.

They may as well have scribbled the word *whore* across her forehead. Anything would've been less shameful than what had been done to her.

The chains held her arms down directly by her sides, the shackles clamped down so tight across her flesh that the skin had torn and folded, molding around the metal over time. With every subtle shift, the tissue tore even more, muscles massacred, ligaments snapped and torn. White bone peeked through mutilated skin, desperate to claw its way through.

"Great Goddess in Eden," Belle breathed, blinking back tears. She was beside herself—an abundance of emotion flooding through her core. She couldn't quite distinguish what *kind* of emotion she felt.

Horror.

Disgust.

She didn't even need to ask who had been responsible for such a thing. She hardly had to even wonder.

Bramwell.

Standing before her were the late lord and lady of Valen, Ayer II and Sorrel, respectively. She'd never once seen them—never knew their faces—but right then and there, she just *knew.* As if the wind had whispered the revelation along the shell of her ear.

His parents.

They weren't dead, and yet, they weren't entirely alive. It was as if they just—*were.* Existing. *Being.*

Rotting, still. Decomposing day by day. Their flesh fell from bone, slipping away, exposing the skeletal remains beneath. Eyes still watched—still *moved*—but if they actually could see—could *watch*—she wasn't so certain. The empty orbs would follow her, stiff necks would creak and crack with the slightest shift as what remained of Lord Ayer II and Lady Sorrel kept their stares fixated on the strange visitor.

"Can you speak?" Belle croaked, keeping her distance. She knew that they were shackled—*imprisoned*—but their still demeanor was discomforting. She was just waiting for them to rush forward, to sink their chipping, blackened teeth into her neck, to tear her apart ligament by ligament.

Only they didn't.

They just *watched*.

It was then that she recalled Bramwell's admission of his true identity, how he was not the true son of Lord Ayer II, but a bastard child, born to Sorrel and an unnamed father. Thus, his mother's wounds made perfect sense. Or, *somewhat* made sense. Why he'd chosen to mutilate such a specific part of her body was still yet to be understood, but it made sense for him to harbor a sense of resentment toward the woman who cheated on his legal father.

Belle wasn't any better.

She'd slept with others that were not her spouse. The baby that grew within her womb was *also* a bastard child—not a drop of Hellthorne blood within its veins—and her cheeks blanched, and she nearly heaved when visuals of her in Sorrel's place raided her mind. Of a middle-aged Belle buried beneath the floorboards, eyes empty of emotion, clouded over with death. Day dress torn—*shredded*—her breasts mauled; nipples torn and beaten.

She blinked thrice, hoping that this was a dream. A *nightmare.* But when she rubbed her eyes with balled-up fists and her bottom lip began to tremble, she knew that it wasn't. It was *real.*

The previous lord and lady of Valen had been killed—*murdered*—by their *own son.* He was only in his eighteenth year when reports flooded Elantry—*Lord Ayer Tan-*

nisty Hellthorne II and Lady Sorrel dead—he was practically a child.

A child who killed his own parents.

She took a step closer.

"Lady Sorrel?" Belle whispered, studying the woman's frozen frame. She was—*or had been*—a stunning woman. It was clear beyond the rot that she was once a gorgeous individual, someone who could light up a room just by walking into it.

She'd read the tales of Lady Sorrel, how in comparison to her unsavory life partner, she was rather lovely. He was always angry; she was often kind. She visited town often, shopped at local markets, purchased bundles of fresh flowers from Valen's oldest florist, a woman who was now five years past her ninetieth, and still spoke as if Lady Sorrel still roamed the streets.

Perhaps, the elderly florist could simply feel Sorrel's lingering presence—the undead woman who still stood below Hellthorne Manor, her bloodied bosoms on display, her handmade gown ripped and ruined, her image tarnished.

If only the florist could lay eyes on Lady Sorrel, now. Decaying beneath the floorboards of her very own home. Mauled by the son she nurtured in her very own womb.

It took Belle a considerably long time to realize that the room was scarcely empty. It was difficult to notice her surroundings whilst confronted by the rotting dead, but now that she knew that they were of no immediate threat to her, she opened her eyes fully.

It was crowded. *Cramped.*

The walls were lined with varying papers—news from the Szo Landing tip of Elantry all the way down to the southernmost town of Gylsea. Everyone knew of Valen's most royal, and she felt as if she were reading a story of their lives from the pages plastered along the walls, tacked against the cement like wet wallpaper.

Some stories had faded immensely, the photographs and text nearly illegible. Others were ruined with red ink, hasty phrases strewn along the surface, sloppy penmanship. The worst of them all being the papers covering the news of Lady Sorrel's apparent stillbirth. He'd scribbled a series of statements along the surface, the boldest and brightest being that of a simple word.

LIARS

Belle hadn't asked Bramwell of his true father's identity. She wasn't even sure if he'd known such information. It was curious how his parents had decided to stage his death—to lie so easily about it. Cover it up, like it never even happened. Perhaps Lady Sorrel had feared that Bramwell would look nothing of his father—bear little to no semblance of a true Hellthorne—and thus, she kept him hidden.

Besides the abundance of misled tales glued along the walls, there was a worktable, littered with ancient books with dusty, torn jackets, bottles of half-used ink, empty pens, half-burnt soy candles, a few vials occupied by a mysterious lily-white liquid. Upon further inspection, Belle discovered that they weren't just any ordinary books, but a series of dissimilar grimoires.

Spell books.

The air felt dense. Her ears rang, an electrical current dancing between the invisible atoms above her skull. She wasn't sure how she hadn't noticed it before, for the sensation was blatantly obvious, then. A spell so powerful—so *thick*—that she could open her mouth and taste it. A syrupy sweetness on her tongue. A salted river of honey dribbling down her chin.

The room had been charmed.

Using one of the six or so grimoires scattered along the table, a late teenage Bramwell had managed to cast an enchantment so powerful that not even the dead could truly die.

Belle gulped, and a prickly patch of goosebumps crawled up her neck, a tickle of eight legs, and she anxiously glanced over her shoulder to view the undead people behind her.

She almost screamed when she met their empty eyes.

Lady Sorrel's neck had turned at an abhorrent angle, curious and desperate all at the same time. Wherever Belle wandered within the room, her soulless gaze followed.

Lord Ayer II's stance frightened her further. Most of his body had been concealed by the tall chair that stood as his permanent throne, but he refused to let her wander from his sight. All that was visible of the late lord was the bloodied spikes of his thorn-riddled crown, his unnaturally white hair soiled—*ruined*. His eyes bleak. *Dead*. Not a blink, nor a flinch. Just a steady stare, the remainder of his features concealed by his chair.

"I'm sorry," Belle blurted, a terrified tremble consuming her core. She knew that the pair posed very little threat, but she was cramped in a charmed room with her husband's *dead parents*. The dead parents that he'd killed, enchanted, and tortured. The parents that he evidently visited often, clear by the fresh oil in the flickering lamp.

They served as his playthings. His *toys*.

There was a certain power in keeping the dead alive. A never-ending imprisonment.

She wasn't sure of the logistics of it all. Could they feel each and every sensation? Could they hear? Did they have a conscience?

For their own sake, she hoped that the two were nothing but empty shells of their former selves. Rotting bodies, soulless and hollow.

Lady Sorrel probably resided within Eden, made friends with a Goddess or two. Lord Ayer II was probably less lucky. The stories of his character made Belle wonder if he'd been turned away at the silver gates, shunned to the south, forced to face the demon who was summoned by his own illegitimate son.

The demon Goddess who gifted Bramwell his magick.

Everything began to click into place—a shifting puzzle within Belle's brain—and she wished more than anything that the walls of the manor could speak.

Perhaps they'd been trying all along.

Belle audibly apologized once more, blinking back hot, salty tears. The scene before her would torment her for an eternity, and yet, she wasn't entirely sure if she was ready to look away. She felt considerably guilty leaving the pair where she'd found them, but she was no witch, she harbored no magick. What had been done to Lady Sorrel and Lord Ayer II could not be undone by anyone but the spellcaster who crafted the charm in the first place—Bramwell Hellthorne himself.

Before she left, she hovered the doorway, her sorrowful glare settling upon the husband and wife. They hadn't once diverted their stare from her.

"He won't get away with this," Belle said, unsure if they could even hear or comprehend what she'd said. "That, I swear. To the Goddesses above, I will be sure of it."

She'd located her forgotten candlestick, relit it within the lamp, and left. What she didn't know was that the lady and the lord had both watched the doorway for days following. Waiting. Wondering.

Hoping that the kind redheaded stranger would soon return, a measly candlestick in tow.

DOWN WITH THE CAPITOL

B elle had hardly made it up the basement steps when she heard a shout.

Girlish in nature—*distraught*. There was a frenzy of voices originating from the foyer, and Belle almost tripped over her own two feet as she burst into a sprint.

When she stumbled upon the scene, her eyes nearly rolled upward into their sockets, a shiver enveloping her spine, bile creeping up her throat.

Her love—*her darling*—her sweet Florence laid at the feet of four housemaidens, a red-faced and teary eyed Lyudmilla Deth planted directly beside her. Blood bloomed beneath the shoulder of the periwinkle fabric of Florence's day dress, a thick bead of sweat tickling her brow.

"What in the ruddy *fuck* happened?" Belle shouted, shoving her candlestick into Ula's hands. The housemaiden eyed the object with wonder, brows pulled together in confusion as the lady of the house fell to her knees, immediately claiming Florence's hand within her hold.

"Flo," Belle stuttered, suddenly aware of their audience. "Florence, talk to me. Are you all right?"

"There was a riot," Lyudmilla said, a manicured hand in Florence's hair. "There's talk of burnings in the Capitol. The revolt has turned violent. People want to see the country fall."

"But this isn't the Capitol–"

"Valen's growing antsy, also. There are revolutionists here, too. Many more than I could even fathom. Most of the city wants to secede from Elantry entirely. Fights broke out in the square, there were blades, there was blood–"

"–you let her get *stabbed*–"

"–it was an *accident*–"

"–she could ruddy *die,* Lyudmilla! Do you even fucking realize–"

"Of *course* I do!" Lyudmilla screamed, the color drained from her cheeks. "Do you really believe that I want my brother's betrothed to die?"

Possibly.

Belle's fingernails pried at the soiled section of Florence's dress, desperately tearing the fabric apart to reveal the wound beneath. She'd been stuck with a blade, just as Lyudmilla had weakly described. The frayed flesh was angry, red, *hot.* Belle began to shake.

"We need a physician," the lady whimpered, pale fingers stained with the mark of death. She lightly caressed Florence's wound, watched the way it began to weep, and she nearly fell apart.

"I'll notify the groundskeeper," the housemaiden called Nephele announced, their eyes red-rimmed and wet. Their voice began to tremble. "They're goin' to kill us, ain't they? March right up to the manor and slaughter us all in our nightgowns while we rest in our quarters."

"Don't be absurd, Nephele," Ula snapped, extinguishing the flame on Belle's forgotten candlestick. "The revolutionists are after the *government,* not Valen royalty. Lord Bramwell is well liked. We have nothing to worry about. Now, *go.* Fetch Henry. And Tove, grab Jeanne from the kitchen.

Get a warm bowl of water, some rags, some healing salve. A cup of lemon tea and some bread, too."

"I want you gone," Belle said, and the others fell silent. No one needed to confirm who she meant—they all knew.

"Surely you aren't referring to *me*," Lyudmilla gasped, ring-riddled fingers brushing a pesky piece of silver hair from her eyes.

"I am," Belle confirmed, gaze darkening. "Keahi will help you pack. I want you on the road to Havensworth by dusk."

"My home is at *war*," Lyudmilla exclaimed, beside herself. "You can't expect me to ride back there whilst people are being injured—*getting killed*—in the name of the three Goddesses! You'll be sending me to my grave!"

"Then stay at an inn down in town, I don't ruddy care," Belle snipped, unable to tear her stare from Florence's festering wound. Her lover was brimming the edge of consciousness, eyes bloodshot and wet, cheeks flushed of its natural warmth.

"The cheapest inn will run me easily fifteen silver per week–"

"Bramwell and I will provide payment, then. Or perhaps you could pawn off those expensive jewels wrapped around your fingers? Either way, I want you *out*. I don't want to see you within these walls come dark. I don't want to hear your voice, smell your perfume, see the silver of your hair. I want you gone from my sight." Belle was firm on her decision, and the housemaidens had fallen silent. None of them had ever seen the lady react in such a way—immense hatred oozing off of her every limb—and when Lyudmilla opened her lips to speak once more, Belle nearly exploded.

"Because of you, Lyren's lover may *die*. Because of you, Bramwell's ward—one of my *friends*—may die. To me, you are now *dead*, Lyudmilla Deth. I want you out of my home, out of my life, and out of my sight. If you so much as speak another ruddy word, I'll set that silver hair of yours ablaze, and hand you over to the revolutionists myself."

No one spoke. No one breathed.

The air was still—*stale*—and the housemaiden called Keahi offered Lyudmilla a hand.

Reluctantly, Lyren's sister took it, darkened gaze rimming with hatred as she shot Belle a wicked stare. There was so much she wanted to say to the fiery lady, to insult her looks, her personality, her life. To call her a penniless whore, unworthy of her title. To summon her back to where she came from, back to the cottage in which she was raised, stuffed up in a bedroom with half of her siblings, to eat nothing but leftover food from the sea for an eternity.

Her mouth salivated, and she bit back the urge to spit at Belle's feet. With a glare full of pure venom, Lyudmilla stood to her feet and rounded the corner, disappearing from sight.

After that, no one spoke.

Tove did as she was told and fetched everything Ula had requested. Florence dipped between sleep and a weak conscious state, and by the time Henry arrived with the physician and Lyudmilla had already been taken to town, Lyren returned home, his palms stained pink.

By then, Florence had been moved from the foyer floor to her own bedroom. She was buried beneath two blankets, a flickering fire roaring within the fireplace, a warming pan down below her feet keeping her frigid frame within a comfortable temperature.

The physician was a middle-aged man with a curled mustache, bifocals, and a hearty gap between two front teeth. With Ula's assistance, they'd crafted a salve to apply to Florence's wound, which had been stitched and closed by the physician's steady hands. He was incredibly kind and drank three cups of lemon tea before retiring to the carriage, claiming he'd be back by sunrise to check on his patient.

Bramwell still hadn't returned from his trip to the Capitol, and by what Lyudmilla revealed, Belle hoped that perhaps he'd been caught in the crossfire of a particularly nasty riot. When she closed her eyes, she envisioned his carriage crumbling beneath angry blue flames, the wood warped and soft. Eyeballs melting within their sockets, charred flesh sliding from muscle, bright bones buried beneath seared meat. He'd be another mindless casualty within a war, just another royal death, and Belle would be free of her legal shackles—an unmarried woman.

Only, none of that happened. The riots continued well into the night and even through the early morning, but no one dared to lay a hand on Lord Bramwell Hellthorne. As others had said, he was simply *too well liked.* No one harmed him, and he'd returned to the manor when the sun was at the highest point in the sky, blissfully unaware of a gravely injured Florence within the walls. His only remaining family.

He didn't ask about Lyudmilla's absence. He didn't seem to care. He was, however, intrigued by Florence's state, whether out of worry or sheer curiosity, Belle could not tell.

"How long has she been asleep?" Bramwell wondered, fingering the pocket of his coat. A half-smoked cigar was buried deep within, a singular match lining the bottom of the cozy cove.

"Sixteen hours," Lyren revealed, blinking sleep from his eyes. He was still dressed in the clothing from the previous day, his top wrinkled and worn, long locks knotted and frizzed.

In the bed beside an injured Florence was a snoozing Belle, an off-white nightgown suctioned to the clammy surface of her skin, slick with anxious sweat. She'd woken nearly every hour, her heart racing within her throat, widened eyes scanning Florence for a source of life. When she watched the woman's chest rise and fall with staggered breaths, she'd slip back into a dreamless sleep.

"Havensworth is in flames," Bramwell revealed, wedging the cigar between chapped lips. He seemed relatively unphased by the situation at hand. "Ithabell Throne—you remember her, that terribly annoying woman who nearly pissed herself at Topher's death—was strung up at the statehouse. Awful sight, really. Nothing like I've ever seen with my own two eyes. They'd stripped her bare, lashed her across the front what seemed like twenty times, bloodied her up good. Hanged her by her wrists, let her die good and slow. She poured blood all over the white steps below. Looked like a ruddy massacre."

Lyren's gaze widened considerably. "Good Goddess, Bram. That sounds horrific. You witnessed this?"

"Most of it, yes," Bramwell confirmed, his speech muffled by the presence of his newly lit cigar. The stench of smoke filled the room, and tickled Belle's nostrils, prying her from an unsatisfying sleep.

"Ithabell was acting Head following Topher's death, but now with *her* dead, the Capitol is scrambling. They're trying to find a temporary Head until another can be elected, but everyone is terrified. Government officials have fled from their homes, their families slaughtered, wives assaulted, children sold to thieves and menaces down at The Brother. We're watching the country fall in real time, my dear friend."

"What do we do?" Lyren croaked, unable to stifle the fearful trembles that claimed his spine.

"We stay here," Bramwell said, indifferent glare connecting with Belle's. She'd woken fully now; the whites of her eyes stained a tearful pink. "The manor is safest. Valen royalty is not a threat. They won't come after me. By Goddess, I had rioters insisting that I *join* them. They'd all parted to let my carriage through when I left, and I watched through the windows as they lit the base of the statehouse ablaze."

"You seem confident that they won't turn on you, too," Belle suddenly spoke, a thin sheet of glistening sweat coating her skin. She shivered, and her empty stomach audibly rolled, begging for food.

"You need to eat," Bramwell said, a cloud of toxic smoke circling his head. "You're growing my heir, and if the country shall fall, Valen royalty will be reinstated. It won't just be a title; it'll be a *profession*. The babe within your belly will be a ruler. A leader."

Lyren shifted uncomfortably upon his chair, a trembling hand buried deep within his hair. He knew that his child would be considered Bramwell's, that he would never have a *true* claim to his own offspring. It was difficult to hear Bramwell label the child as his own, and as much as he wanted to stand to his feet—to curl his fingers inward and land a punch directly to the center of his longest friend's nose—he remained silent. *Frozen.*

"Bring me food, then," Belle snipped. She could hardly look him in the face, for every time their eyes met, all she could visualize was the man and woman buried beneath the floorboards, shackled and imprisoned, empty eyes staring into nothingness.

She'd wondered if he'd been down to the basement, yet. If he'd refilled the oil in the lamp. If he'd unsheathed a curved blade, wedged it between the folded flesh of his late mother's bosom, torn the rotting skin open once more, a fresh, weeping wound.

"I'll have Tove draw you a bath," Bramwell replied, finally breaking their stagnant eye contact. He'd platonically loved Belle Byron from the moment they'd joined in union, but as the days droned on and her hatred for him budded and bloomed, his love gradually faltered. *Disappeared.*

She was becoming a nuisance.

"Clare will bring you chicken broth and bread whilst you bathe. If I got any closer, I'm sure I could smell the sweat on your skin."

"Bramwell," Lyren bitterly began, increasingly aware of the tension building between the married pair. "You shouldn't speak to Belle in such a manner."

If looks could kill—*and for Bramwell, they certainly could*—Lyren would've dropped dead in that very moment. The lord's gaze blackened, a bitterness overcoming his features, and instead of muttering the simple enchantment that tickled the tip of his tongue, he simply said, "I will speak to *my wife* in whatever manner I please. Your bastard may be within her womb, but the child will be written in history books as *mine,* not yours. Remember your place, Lyren. You are a guest in this manor, a guest who can be cast out as easily as your sister was."

Lyren didn't dare reply. His teeth snapped shut, anger bubbling within his belly as his fingers encircled Florence's damp wrist. The physician was due to return within the hour, and when he did, Lyren hoped that Bramwell would be nowhere to be found.

Begrudgingly, Belle took her bath. Tove threaded her fingers through the lady's sleek red locks, massaging the soap into her skull, and neither lady spoke for the entirety of the event. Clare spooned broth into Belle's mouth, handed her bits of bread to nibble on, and right before Tove drained the tub and Clare was busy toweling the water from the lady, Belle prematurely revealed her current condition.

Both Tove and Clare's stares widened considerably, jaws agape in shock. It was still too early to tell—Belle's stomach was merely the same—and Clare blinked back joyful tears.

"A baby born during the war," she beamed, palms clamped over her trembling lips. "This'll be such a wonderful thing, Lady Belle. The people of Valen will have hope for the future. The babe in your womb is going to lead the future of our city—of our *country*. When Elantry finally falls, Valen will stand on its own. A country *all* of its own."

A country all of its own.

IN FLAMES

By the fourth month, Belle's tiny frame had greatly changed.

With a gradually swelling belly and swollen ankles, Belle finally filled out most of her day dresses, most of which before had completely consumed her small self.

Lyren's workload doubled. The dead were multiplying—courtesy of the war—and he'd spent several nights sleeping barely a total of two hours on the stiff sofa within his practice, blood and guts still smeared along his soiled white apron, fingers reeking of rot.

On the nights he did return up the hill to the manor, he'd succumb to a deep sleep within Belle's bed, his cheek suctioned to the bare skin of her belly, a palm cradling her hip. A thankfully healthy and healed Florence would either suction herself to his back or tangle her legs within Belle's, a pink scar parallel to the bone of her collar.

Often, Belle would admire the faded scars that lined Lyren's upper arms like a ladder, tracing her forefinger along the raised flesh, closing her eyes in order to memorize the sensation. She had yet to ask him of their origins, and although she knew in her heart that they must have been self-inflicted, she couldn't bring herself to believe it.

After three weeks of bedridden night sweats, nothing but bone broth and bread and small sips of lemon tea, Florence finally healed. She wrote letters to Lyudmilla often, much to Belle's dismay, and would hand them directly to Lyren as he fled the manor on his way to work, certain that he would deliver the envelope.

Staying true to her word, Belle sent Lyren with a velvet mahogany pouch heavy with silver coins every week, more than enough to pay for the inn where his sister currently stayed. It was a stuffy old building filled with dust and mold, and as the days dragged on, a sleepy Lyudmilla felt her lungs slightly weaken and her head persistently pound, but anywhere was better than the Capitol, a place that was hardly a place at all, anymore.

Those who remained of the government ruled from undisclosed locations across Elantry. Rumors hinted at the possibility of the newest Head—a man well into his sixtieth year by the name of Olag Hynne—shacking up with the farmers of Westcastle, but when revolutionaries flooded the farmland, Olag Hynne was nowhere to be found.

Bramwell visited town daily.

He was eager to show his support—to show his people just how much he cared. The people of Valen ate it up like candy, overjoyed by his presence, eager to finally secede from Elantry once and for all. To place a crown of thorn atop Bramwell's brown hair, careful not to let the spikes slice open his skin.

They built him a throne, and in the twentieth week of Belle's pregnancy, only days before they were due to announce the news, a crowd of twenty or so Valen individuals trekked up the hill by foot, carrying the sleek black chair on their backs.

Bramwell pampered them for two days and two nights, feeding them hearty meals, slipping glasses of flaming whiskey into their hands. They placed the throne in the center of the ballroom, tore the sealed shutters on the windows open, the yellow light of the sun pouring into the room. The seat sparkled and almost appeared to glow, and they lined it with fresh purple poppies.

Belle had been vomiting for nearly three hours on the morning of their announcement, and Lyren had to carry his lover down the stairs and into the carriage.

She was dressed in a stunning ruby red gown, one that was pulled tight around her midsection, courtesy of Jeanne's sewing skills. It highlighted her swollen bump perfectly, and although her cheeks were void of color and pale with sickness, she appeared to sparkle beneath the afternoon sun.

Spring had melted the snow, but a bitter breeze still graced the mountainside, sending shivers down Belle's spine. A milky white fur coat covered her arms, but her cheeks felt frozen and numb, watering eyes smearing the light makeup painted along her lids.

"Do I really have to wear this ruddy stuff?" she cursed, black flecks raiding her vision. She'd worn makeup only one other time, and she'd hated every moment of it.

"It looks lovely," Lyren sweetly said, planting a small kiss atop her nose. "Most of the women in the Capitol would wear it."

"Most of the women in the Capitol are ash," Belle countered, tugging Lyren into the carriage. Bramwell was already buried within his seat, his focus fixated on the book balanced atop his lap.

He and Belle hardly spoke. It was best that way. Every time her hateful gaze settled upon him, his vision flushed an angry red, and although he'd promised never to harm her—never to *charm* her—the woman was making it incredibly difficult not to.

What he didn't know was that with every individual trip of his to town, Belle had wandered back down the eighty steps to the basement. Back into the bewitched room, a spell so powerful that it tasted of cherry candy.

She'd spoken to them. Told them stories.

They never replied. Only watched. Listened. *Existed.*

By the fifth visit down below, she reached a hand out. It shook violently, her stomach churning with fear as she barely brushed against the busted knuckles of Lady Sorrel's right hand.

She wasn't sure what she expected the undead woman to do, but when Belle looped her index finger around Lady Sorrel's thumb, she did—*nothing.* Not a single movement. Not a twitch.

"I'm sorry this happened to you," Belle whispered, holding Lady Sorrel's hand fully. The oil lamps were full again, and Lord Ayer II had new wounds on his scalp, as if the thorns on his crown had been intentionally pressed against his skin.

"I hope more than anything that your soul is not still in there."

The townscenter was alive with wonder.

The entirety of Valen's population was in attendance. There was a pleasant roar within the crowd, a buzz of excitement, and the brick road was lined with sword-clad soldiers, weapons at the ready, prepared for any sign of a riot.

Revolutionists had shifted northeast, spotting ships sailing from the ports of Swords Edge, filling the waters of the Barrow. Esteemed members of Elantry's government were on those very ships, headed for safety wherever they could find it. Whether it be the frozen land of Wylib—the nearby unclaimed territory—or perhaps somewhere further, even they weren't sure. Anywhere beyond Elantry's borders was safest, and as soon as the very last government official stepped off of Elantry's land, the country had been officially abandoned.

Free.

When the royal carriage arrived, the crowd exploded with glee. Although not yet official in the eyes of law, a majority of the people considered Lord Bramwell and Lady Belle their rightful leaders. Their government. Their *people.*

When the duo clambered from the safe warmth of the carriage and were met by a fierce frozen burst of wind, those nearby erupted into shocked screams.

The lady of Valen was with child.

Those lining the brick walkway immediately fell to their knees, prayers to the Goddesses above tumbling off of their lips, tears tickling their sight. It had been over thirty years since the last announcement of a Hellthorne child, one that they were told had died. Only now, that dead child stood before them, a bright white smile snaked along his lips, a palm glued to Belle's belly, as if to claim the child within.

Lyren and Florence followed suit, slipping from the carriage hand in hand. It was Florence's first public outing since her attack, and she couldn't help but shake with fear as she scanned the expansive crowd, wondering if and when one onlooker would drive through, blade in tow, ready to blow.

To the people of Valen, it was common knowledge that Lyren was courting Florence. There was no official date for a wedding—with the war going on, it was easier to dismiss such questions—and big, burly men reached their arms out, taking Lyren's hand in theirs, shaking it firmly, congratulating him on his betrothed.

When the foursome took their spots along the marbled steps of the townscenter, the crowd clapped and cheered, calling out to them.

"My family and friends," Bramwell greeted, boasting with confidence. "The war continues in the north. Government officials have fled by ship into the Barrow, abandoning their land. Now, we can officially secede from the union. Create a country all of our own."

He paused briefly, allowing his people to holler and cheer. Elderly women within the front openly wept, grandchildren held within their arms. Belle couldn't tell if they were crying out of fear, or out of joy.

Her stomach rolled.

"Your lady is with child. A babe blooms within her womb, the future of Valen. The future of *you*."

Bramwell's hand slipped into Belle's, squeezing tight. She swallowed a mouthful of bile, a forced smile strung along chapped lips.

It was then that Belle spotted a silver-haired Lyudmilla, front and center, smashed between two women wearing stained, worn rags for dresses. She looked dreadful, her features absent of any paint or makeup, her hair a knotted, tangled mess. She looked worse for wear—ill, even—her nose ruby red and swollen with snot.

A wicked smirk slid along Belle's lips as she met Lyudmilla's stiff stare, and for a split second, she felt a fit of laughter tickle her throat.

"What will you name her, my lady?" the woman directly beside Lyudmilla called, her voice strained and weak.

Before Belle could speak, Bramwell interrupted her.

"It's bad luck to reveal the name of a child before they are born, my fine friend. Surely you know that, yes?"

The woman's cheeks went hot, a bashful blush, and she fell to her knees.

"Forgive me, my lord. I'm nothing but a tavern girl, uneducated."

Belle snatched her hand from Bramwell's, fingers curling into a tight fist.

"Don't speak so lowly of yourself, friend," Belle called, earning a stare from her husband, one which she swiftly ignored. "I have dresses that I've grown out of that may fit you, something nice to wear besides those old rags of yours. I'll send our groundskeeper back down to town to deliver them to you this evening."

"Oh, my lady," the woman wept, shaking in her shoes. Lyudmilla seemed unphased beside her, brows knit together in detest. "How can I ever repay you?"

"By living," Belle said. "By surviving, my friend. Survive, live, fight. Be a part of this world for as long as you possibly can, and that is payment enough."

When Belle removed herself from the steps, Bramwell nearly saw red.

With a stomach swollen full of Lyren's child and a chill cascading up her spine, Belle ventured down and into the crowd, meeting the fallen woman face to face. Lyudmilla's lips had parted, forming an o-shape, sleepy eyes widened to the size of saucers, and she, along with everyone else, watched as the lady of Valen fell to her knees, claiming the stranger's hands in hers.

A nearby serviceman readied his weapon, hovering over Belle's shoulder, and with a glare as sharp as daggers, she dismissed him.

"That won't be necessary," she said, eyeing the weapon. "These are my people. There is no danger here."

Reluctantly, the serviceman fell back into line, not entirely convinced. Nevertheless, Belle redirected her attention, a genuine grin slapped along sweet features as she asked the woman for her name.

"They call me Seela," the stranger said, tone barely above a whisper. Her voice had been damaged over the years—whether from neglect, tobacco abuse, or an illness, Belle did not know—and the lady placed a hand to Seela's face, a gentle cup of her cheek.

"When have you eaten last, Seela?"

The woman struggled to recall, and as if on cue, her stomach noisily turned, alerting Belle of its stark emptiness.

"That simply won't do, Seela." Belle said and stood once more. "Is there a lady by the name of Xylia somewhere in the crowd?"

A hush fell over the people of Valen, and a familiar face emerged, stumbling into the empty walkway of the brick path, as if shoved. It was the same girl who had held onto Belle's arm at the Yule ball, and the lady could hardly contain her glee when she laid eyes on her.

"My friend," Belle beamed, widening her arms. She offered the townsgirl a hug, noticing how violently Xylia was shaking from head to toe, and she whispered a series of reassuring statements against her hair.

Don't be nervous, my friend.

"I told you I'd visit your bakery," Belle began, taking Xylia's hands in hers. Florence stiffened atop the townscenter steps, squeezing Lyren's hand so tightly that he nearly yelped. "Show me to it and let me treat my new friend Seela to some baked goods."

Xylia's expression reddened, and she took both Belle and Seela's hands, steering them down the brick path toward the bakery. It was barely a half a block from the townscenter, but when Belle glanced over her shoulder to view a wide-eyed Lyren, a stiff Florence, and a red-faced Bramwell, she couldn't help but grin.

Bramwell's patience with her was running thin, and once her womb was emptied, she was certain that she'd join the lord and lady beneath the floorboards, her wrists bound by chains, her day dress torn and bloodied, her eyes glossed over for an eternity.

SWEET LIKE SYRUP

H er lips tasted of honey—such a sweet, delicate taste—and Belle needed more.

More more more.

Her fingernails clawed at the tangled tresses of Florence's thick curls—a yank, a *tug*—and her lover mewled against berry red lips, desperate for release.

"A housemaiden is bound to walk by, Bells," Florence muttered, her voice moderately muffled by the presence of Belle's needy mouth.

"Let's give them a show, then," Belle dismissed, her hand slipping up the length of Florence's leg, pressing past nude-hued stockings. She wedged her nail into the fabric, slashing a gaudy slit up the inner thigh, and Florence groaned in protest.

"These aren't cheap, you know."

Belle's glare narrowed, a surge of unfamiliar emotions flooding her core as she tore her touch away from a clearly disinterested Florence.

"If you don't want me, just say so." Belle frowned, lower lip pouted, trembling. "If my condition has made me undesirable–"

"Oh, *enough*," Florence interrupted, claiming Belle's hands in hers. She pressed a quick kiss to each of Belle's knuckles, the tip of her nose caressing the surface. "Your condition hardly bothered me when my head was between your legs last night."

When Belle failed to reply—a singular, salty tear sliding down the reddened curve of her cheek—Florence merely melted. She took the smaller woman into her arms, chin resting atop a tamed mess of wild red locks, fingers dancing down the slope of Belle's clothed spine.

"I love you, Bells," Florence whispered, placing a kiss atop her lover's scalp.

When Belle did nothing but silently weep against Florence's touch, the woman simply sighed, somewhat tickled by her sudden shift in emotion. Belle wasn't one to cry so easily, but as the time ticked by and her stomach swelled twice its size, her emotions transformed.

"Lyren's not due down to town today, you know."

At this revelation, Belle's uncontrollable tears dried up within their ducts. She had been so used to their new or-dinary—how Lyren spent most of his time at his practice, elbows deep in rapidly decaying guts—that she'd assumed that the current day would be identical to the previous forty. Nothing but a short-lived kiss, the tip of a tongue teasing her locked lips, a wandering hand, a palm placed against the bump of her belly.

"Spend the day with him," Florence added, tucking a stray strand of hair behind Belle's ear. "It's been long overdue; you and I both know that much. I'm sure he'd love spending the day wrapped up with you instead of digging through some dead man's innards."

The two women shared a giggle, a kiss, and then Flo-rence departed, abandoning Belle in the washroom, the fragrant bubbles within the porcelain tub still tickling her nose, the water gone cold.

She drained the basin, and fled back to her bedroom, where she was met by a beautiful Lyren Deth, still sound asleep, a mess of overgrown locks draped across sealed eyelids. Yesterday's workwear was still in a dismissive heap at the foot of the bed—exactly where it had been shed—lanky limbs entwined within vermilion silken sheets.

The sweetness of spring bloomed beyond the clear pane of the window, and Belle took several silent steps toward the area, desperate to breathe in the warmth of the outside air. Winter was beyond them now—the ice, snow, and sleet a forgotten memory—and she slid her fingers between loose brass bolts and unlatched the window, easing it open as wide as it would go.

Cozy, warm wind drifted into the room, the curtains dancing between each individual gust, and Belle breathed in deeply, the sweetness of early summer filling her lungs.

She hadn't even noticed Lyren's sudden stirs—the way his arms swayed above his head in a series of stretches—a sleepy groan easing between parted lips. His cock stiffened slightly with wake, courtesy of the dream that stuck to his eyelids, and with a needful touch, he cradled himself in his wake.

"G'mornin'," he mewled, fingers taut around his aching length.

His blurred vision settled on a trim Belle, dressed plainly in a soft-white day dress that tickled the tips of her knees. She cradled the rounded curve of her stomach with both palms, a hum of an unknown tune tickling her lower lip as she admired the mountainside, the way the town of Valen looked so stunning—so *simple*—buried beyond the horizon.

"Good morning to you too," Belle blushed. "Lovely dreams?"

"Not nearly as lovely as the present," Lyren beamed, admiring the scene. He pulled himself into a sitting position, wavy hair fluttering past his shoulders, dipping down past pretty pink nipples. The sheets fell from his limbs, revealing smooth, pasty skin.

"Gorgeous day out," Belle commented, unable to tear her stare from a blushing Lyren.

"Gorgeous indeed," Lyren agreed, tossing the blankets from the bed. His lengthy legs swung sideways, and with only a few short strides, he was by Belle's side, eager lips painting portraits along the exposed flesh of her neck.

"I'm not due in today," he said, peppering hot, open-mouthed smooches along the sharp curve of her jaw. "I suppose the dead have decided to wait."

Not all of them.

Belle swallowed thickly, her stare settling upon a shirtless Henry planted smack dab in the center of a wild patch of purple poppies, his tanned skin slick with sweat, unruly hair a dreadful mess. A steady stream of smoke erupted from the pebbled chimney of his cottage, a fire brewing within, warming the walls.

The cottage that Bramwell's true father once owned, a fact Belle had yet to know.

"What do you think of magick and witchcraft?" Belle asked, dismissing Lyren's lewd touch.

She felt his swollen red lips curl into a toothy grin along her skin.

"Fun fables Father used to tell Lyudmilla and me, especially during baths. He'd bathe us together longer than he should've—lazy, loony bat—but when he'd get real drunk, he'd go on and on about werebeings and bloodsuckers and faes and ondodes–"

Belle's brows crinkled, then raised. That was a word she'd never heard before.

"Ondodes?"

Lyren placed a kiss atop her nose.

"Yeah," he breathed, tangling his fingers within her hair, prying several wispy strands from her eyes. The wind within the window had been unkind to the mane, sending untamed pieces amiss, blinding her sight.

"What are ondodes? I've read plenty of the bloodsuckers and the werebeings and only slightly of the fae, but I've never heard of an ondode."

"They're my favorite," Lyren gloated, a blush creeping up his neck. "Not spoken of as strongly, but nevertheless, a fable that I've always loved. I'd beg Father to tell more stories of them, but even he barely had any. They've hardly been written about, but they're fascinating things. Human from the start, ordinary from birth to death, but after death, something shifts. The body lives on—sees, *moves*—but never truly ages. Frozen in time. The skin rots with time, a slower pace than the true dead. Eyes gloss over, losing their color. A still heart between empty lungs."

Belle's mouth dried considerably, hot tears teasing the corners of her eyes as she silently studied Henry beyond the window, a shovel pinched between reddened palms, sweat pouring over thick brows.

"And their souls?"

It was such a soft statement—barely above a whisper—but Lyren had heard it. He latched his arms around her belly, cradling her stomach as gently as he could, and he whispered the revelation into her ear.

"Trapped within. A slowly rotting prison. They can't speak true words, but they can see. Feel. *Hear.* A physical purgatory."

Belle's knees wobbled, and her palm met her gaping mouth, a horrified gasp spilling over her tongue. The worst she'd feared had been true—the undead couple buried beneath the floorboards were aware.

They heard her. They saw her. They *felt.*

Lady Sorrel could feel the lashes against her raw breasts, the open, festering wounds. The hungry flies that nipped at the rotting mounds. She watched her own son—her *child*—inflict fresh wounds upon her frequently. She'd look him in the eye—unable to utter a word—unable to sob.

Lord Ayer II, as rotten as he may have been, had spent over a decade watching his illegitimate son abuse the woman he married, the woman he at one point loved. All he could do was sit in his chair, wear his bloodied crown of thorns, and stare as Bramwell ruined Sorrel's chest, and then redirected his attention to that of a stiff Ayer, where he'd press the razor-sharp sticks into the decomposing flesh of his face, inflict new wounds over old, unhealed injuries.

"Belle, by Goddess," Lyren cursed, holding her weight. She'd collapsed within his arms, weighty tears coating the apples of her cheeks as she openly sobbed. "They're just fables, my love. *Stories.* Tales we tell children to entertain them. There's no ondodes out there, my dear. No one is trapped in a fleshy prison."

"You're *wrong*," Belle wept, unable to catch her breath. "They aren't just fables, Ly. Just as everything we've seen within these wicked walls. The dead girl in the painting, the possession of my sister. The Holy Man said it himself. The demon Goddess Velveteen is *real*. She overtook my Evelin, *ruined* her."

"That's different–"

"Lyren. *Please.*" Belle slurred, eyes rolling up into her skull. She knew that he had to believe her—the things he'd seen himself were of fables before—but there were no such things as fables. It was all *true.*

"If the Goddesses and the demon Goddess Velveteen exist—if my own sister, my flesh and blood, could be possessed by the demon woman herself, why is it so difficult to believe that other oddities out there are true? Please, Ly, you *have* to believe me."

At this point, Belle had fallen to her knees in the form of a beg. Her palms encircled Lyren's legs, her cheeks flushed with distress.

"Belle, I want to, but I'm just–" Lyren began, shaking his head. He couldn't seem to spit the words out. "I'm *scared,* Belle. The things I've seen in this house have frightened me to my core. I simply don't *want* to believe that those other things exist, because *I don't want them to.*"

"But they *do,*" Belle countered, tightening her hold on his skin. "I can prove it to you, Ly. I can. I can show you how I know this."

With Lyren finally dressed and only trembling minimally from anticipation, Belle led him through the rear of the manor, careful not to cross any stray housemaiden that may be wandering about. There were cobwebbed staircases that lined the back of the mansion, with eight-legged, palm-sized spiders creeping beneath the dust riddled wood, eagerly awaiting their prey. Lyren had never seen that particular part of the house before, and he nearly dropped the oil lamp within his clutch once or twice, his grip slick with sweat.

"Not much further, now," Belle assured him, her pulse quickening when they rounded the pitch-black hallway leading to the basement.

The door was closed that day. Initially, the handle wouldn't turn. It was stiff—*stuck*—and a girlish gasp filled the void, Belle's wild, frantic gaze glued to the door.

"Belle, I don't think we should be down here–" Lyren began, continuously peering over his shoulder, bile creeping up his throat.

"Correct. We shouldn't be." Belle confirmed, and the knob turned with a sharp *click*.

Eighty-seven steps down.

Lyren nearly dropped his lamp two additional times—a curse slipping off of his lips in the form of a hiss as he tightened his hold on Belle's hand, squeezing the life from her limb. Her fingers were numb, but she was pumped so full of adrenaline that she could hardly notice.

He kept begging to turn back. To scurry back up the softened stairs—wood so aged and mistreated that it threatened to spill out beneath their feet. Belle ignored his every request, gripping his fingers so hard that the skin flushed a ghostly white.

By the time they reached the lower landing, Lyren's expression paled. There was a stiffness to the air, a thickness so sweet that he could taste it on his tongue.

It made him want to run.

"Just through this door," Belle said, a grin stretched from ear to ear. She was finally sharing the secret she'd kept for weeks.

It was real.

They were real.

She was married to a monster.

In order not to scream, Lyren had to bite his tongue. Hard. Bulbous beads of blood coated his taste buds, showering his throat in a thick, metallic taste, and just as Belle had done the very first time she saw them, he dropped his light.

"Good Goddess Liv in Eden," Lyren breathed, refusing to budge from the parted doorway.

They were intrigued.

Vast, vacant eyes, void of life. The color had long gone, the identity erased, but nevertheless, Lyren Deth knew exactly who they were. He'd seen them only a handful of times before—when he was a child, no less—but still, he'd recognize each of them even if he were mostly blind.

When Belle dropped his hand and took a step closer, he nearly screamed.

"Belle, *careful!*"

"Settle down, Ly," Belle purred, smiling sweetly. "They know me. They won't hurt me."

Reluctantly, Lyren let go. He watched as his pregnant lover approached the ondodes—mythical beings that he hadn't even fully believed in just that very morning—and his shaking palm met his mouth when she reached out to claim Lady Sorrel's dead, decaying hand.

What remained of Lady Sorrel hardly reacted. A fleshy prison, a tortured existence. He couldn't look away from the wounds on her chest—they were *fresh*—and the confirmation of his truest friend's real identity nearly crushed him entirely.

"He's a Goddess damned monster, Bells," Lyren breathed, biting back tears. Lady Sorrel had shifted her unwavering stare to meet Belle's, and if the ondode could smile, Lyren was certain that she would have in that moment.

No one truly knew how Bramwell's parents had died. When it happened, things were so chaotic that nothing quite made sense. Questions arose, inquiries left unanswered, and barely twenty-four hours following both Lady Sorrel and Lord Ayer II's sudden deaths, an unknown son had traveled down to town, clambering from the royal carriage, dressed in his formal best. He was barely a boy—only in his eighteenth year—and when he'd announced that his wretched father had kept his existence a secret, the entire town melted within his presence.

He'd been abundantly loved since the moment he graced Valen's townscenter, but the scene laid out before Lyren had him questioning everything he'd ever known about Bramwell Hellthorne. A man who he truly thought was the best mate he'd ever had.

A man he never actually knew.

"He's a bastard," Belle revealed, studying Lady Sorrel's mutilated breasts with sad eyes. "Explains why he was kept a secret. I suppose Lord Ayer II was repulsed by the idea of an untrue heir being born, and my best guess is that he forced Sorrel to lie about losing the baby. They must've kept him hidden in the manor until he wandered down into town after their deaths."

"He killed them," Lyren breathed, refusing to break eye contact between him and Lord Ayer II. It was the kindest and calmest he'd ever seen the man—the stories were true, for the former lord was widely disliked, and for decent reasons—but admittedly, he felt awful for him. Whether he was bound for the glory gates of Eden or the wicked walls of the Netherworld, either place would've been a kinder pick than this. Instead, the pair were forced to spend countless years buried within the basement of Hellthorne Manor, their souls imprisoned within rotting bodies, chained and beaten, abused and battered.

Bile crept up Lyren's throat, and he resisted the urge to vomit all over his shoes.

"I never really knew Bram at all," Lyren said, approaching a rigid Lord Ayer II seated upon his throne. "I would've never guessed he'd be capable of such crimes against humanity. Against *life*. He's evil. Treacherous. If he's capable of harming the woman who gave him life, what would he do to me? To *you?*"

Lyren's features blanched. "What would he do to our *child?*"

Belle's blood shifted to ice, and she dropped Sorrel's hand. Her darkened stare met Lyren's—a hatred so blinding, so *blatant*—etched across her features that it made his toes curl within the pricey leather of his shoes.

"He'll never touch our baby," Belle began, fury radiating up her spine, her limbs trembling. "He'll never *meet* our baby. He'll never have any claim to our unborn child, or to me, or to you, or to *anyone*."

Lyren swallowed thickly. "What are you suggesting we do?"

Belle's lips peeled back, exposing her teeth, a wide, wicked grin. It was a terrifying sight—one that made Lyren's knees weak with fright—and as the mother of his child caressed her belly, she spoke a statement that nearly made him faint.

"We kill him."

SURVIVOR SOUP

Florence refused to listen.

It was all just fables to her, just as they had once been to Lyren. Werebeings, bloodsuckers, fae, ondodes. Just stories that parents told their children at the cusp of dark to color their dreams.

The woman hardly believed in Plirity, either. The idea of three Goddesses dictating one's every move was just too silly for her to comprehend. Belle, too, had once felt the very same, until she looked wickedness square in the face, felt the faux flesh of the skin the fallen Goddess would wear besides her own, the whiteness of her sister Evelin's eyes when her soul was buried deep within her being, overridden by the demon called Velveteen.

When Lyren confirmed Belle's claims of the undead bodies of Lady Sorrel and Lord Ayer II existing beneath the floorboards of the manor, Florence merely chuckled.

"It isn't a joke, Flo," Belle bit, her features scrunched up with dissatisfaction. Florence had been stubborn many times before, but this was an incredibly serious topic, and the woman refused to believe either of their claims.

"You must've both been dreaming," Florence simply dismissed with the wave of her hand.

They were in the sitting room, a plethora of books surrounding a seated Florence. She had trouble deciding which novel to indulge in next, and she was busy thumbing through the pages of a dated love story that would surely bring tears to her eyes upon completion.

"Quit being so far up Bram's ass, Flo. You think you know him, how do you think I feel? I befriended him shortly after he emerged for the first time in the townscenter, both of us angsty teen boys, and I was certain I knew everything I could about him. I was *wrong*."

"You're letting her into your *head*, Lyren." Florence said, her expression hardening.

At this, Belle visibly flinched.

"What the ruddy good Goddess are you going on about, Florence?"

Florence lowered her book, a soft sigh tickling her tongue as she met Belle's pained expression. A surplus of sunlight poured in through the windows of the sitting room, dust dancing along the sweet yellow rays as Belle's warm, welcoming orbs shifted to a bitter, dark hue.

"Look, Bells, you know that I love you–"

"Do you, though?" Belle interrupted, arms pulling over her chest. "If you actually loved me, you wouldn't constantly deny everything I say. You always have some kind of explanation—an *easy answer*—it makes me feel as if you hardly even care!"

"Oh, quit that, will you?" Florence countered, returning her attention to the stack of books.

Lyren's fingers curled into fists at his sides, and Belle threw her arms airborne, a series of curses filling the void as she disappeared from sight, fury burrowing deep within her bones.

When it was just Florence and Lyren, the man finally spoke his peace.

"I've learned lately that my longest friend was not at all who I thought he was," he began, his expression as cold as ice. Florence halted her actions, her stare downcast, avoiding Lyren's clearly disappointed expression.

When he finally said the words she'd hoped she would never hear, her heart tumbled down to the deepest depths of her being.

"Maybe, you're not at all who I thought you were, either."

Lyren refused to ride to town following his discovery of the ondodes in the basement.

His friend and fellow worker—Darce Dego—was overjoyed to assist Lyren with the business. He arrived at the practice early and would stay late into the night, reporting back to Lyren with detailed letters about bodies he'd dug through, about a thirteen-year-old girl who had a partially grown fetus in her womb and fingerprints around her neck.

He did everything he could to help Lyren, while Lyren stayed within the manor, refusing to let the mother of his child wander too far from his gaze. The idea of Belle crossing paths with Bramwell was enough to make Lyren's stomach churn well into the night, and when Bramwell walked into the dining room for the first time in months at the start of supper, Lyren nearly fell from his chair.

"Evening," Bramwell plainly greeted, his eyes downcast toward the floor. He hardly looked up to meet both Belle and Lyren's stunned stares, and when he settled into his seat, he smiled at the sight of a mixed vegetable soup.

"Looks lovely," he complimented, nodding curtly at an unphased Florence, who had already drunk half of her bowl.

When nobody spoke for several aching moments, Bramwell's voice filled the room once more.

"How's business been, Lyren?"

"Fine," Lyren shortly replied, shoveling soup into his mouth. His stare shifted to meet Belle's rigid frame opposite him, her food untouched, soup going cold.

Bramwell took notice of her neglect, and with a slice of bread between gnawing teeth, he ordered her to eat.

"You're growing my heir," Bramwell said, his stare void of emotion. "Nourish it, or it will die. If Valen loses another royal child, the regime will collapse. Valen is on the verge of seceding. We're on the cusp of becoming an independent country. The Capitol's been abandoned, the government infiltrated. By next week, Elantry will be no more."

The child within Belle's womb shifted—her fingertips tickling the very spot where what felt like a tiny foot pushed and pressed—and without hesitation, she picked up her spoon and forced the broth down her throat.

"There's word that you haven't left the manor in over a fortnight," Bramwell said, catching Lyren in his lie. The lord still appeared relatively unphased by the revelation, whereas the color promptly drained from Lyren's once pink cheeks.

"I've put Darce up to the task of completing my duties," Lyren dryly explained. "I want to be with Belle until she gives birth, in case something was to go south."

Bramwell took another bite of his bread, the tough, toasted texture crunching between nibbling teeth.

"Not much you could do even then. You work on the dead, not the living." Bramwell replied, and he focused on Belle's shaking frame. "You're shaking. Is it from a lack of nutrients? Can I trust that Lyren will keep my child within your stomach well and fed, or do I have to be sure of it myself?"

Between a spoonful of soup, Florence finally spoke. "That won't be necessary. I've been sure to properly nourish Belle day by day with everything she needs to carry a healthy pregnancy."

Lyren bit back a scoff, and Belle shoveled a shaking spoon full of vegetables into her mouth, chewing slowly, careful not to regurgitate it back up like she wanted. Just the sheer presence of Bramwell was enough to make her anxiety skyrocket, and she wanted to run—to *flee*—to get as far away as possible from the cruel man who held the title of her husband.

She wished more than anything that she could tell him just how much she knew, and just how much she hated him for everything she'd learned.

For the first time that evening, Bramwell smiled.

"You're the best there is, Florence. I can only hope you'll assist the midwife in delivering my child when the moment comes. I know you'll be good to them in their very first moments."

Resentment boiled within Lyren's belly; the mere mention of his child being referred to as Bramwell's was nearly enough for him to lose his head. Only, he knew better, now. Bramwell was dangerous—*relentless*. He was of Velveteen, the demon Goddess of the Netherworld. Magick flooded his veins, consumed his entire being. Clung to his skin like sweat, a sugary sweetness that Lyren could taste on his tongue every time he was near him.

He knew then too just how often Bramwell had charmed him. Made him forget things almost as quickly as they had occurred. Ripped away memories, conversations, ideas. Stripped them from Lyren's brain as if they'd never existed at all.

Taken advantage of his kindness. His *weakness.*
We kill him.

He wished he could do it then. Right at that very moment. Snatch the blunt blade of the butter knife, toss himself along the length of the table, spill the scalding soup down Bramwell's front. Plunge the pointy end into his face, through the spongy surface of his round eyeball. Tear it out, blink the string of blood from his eyes, and swipe it along the clammy front of Bramwell's throat. Sever the skin, tear the tendons. Spill his blood over supper.

End it all.

"The townspeople will be expecting a statement from us soon," Bramwell said, shifting the subject. It came easy to him—faux kindness.

It made Lyren sick.

"A statement for what?" Belle asked, setting down her silverware. If she even attempted to eat another bite, she'd empty the contents of her stomach all over the tablecloth.

Bramwell sighed. "When Elantry falls and Valen becomes an independent country by default, you and I are their leaders. Royalty becomes government. We need the people to know that they are safe with us as their commanders."

Are they, though?

When Belle did not reply, Bramwell shook his head, finishing his supper without another word. Tove and Keahi weaved themselves between the chairs, refilling Lyren's tea and topping off Belle's water, and when Bramwell shuffled his empty dishes into their hands, they met him with a polite curtsy.

"You're about to see what it's like to *really* matter, Belle Byron," Bramwell concluded, stuffing his fingers into the pocket of his vest, retrieving a fresh cigar. He lit it with ease, and a trail of smoke lingered in the air when he left, a collective sigh tumbling from both Lyren and Belle's tongues as the lord finally disappeared from sight.

Bramwell hadn't referred to Belle by her maiden name since before their union. She had always been Hellthorne—always been *his*—but as her revulsion for him grew day by day, he distanced himself further, well aware of her blatant animosity.

He'd told her several times before that he loved her, but she knew with complete certainty that that was no longer a fact.

He'd promised that he would never charm her—never *harm* her—but once the heir of Valen exited her womb, she wasn't entirely sure if he would hold true to his word.

Once the heir of Valen was able to breathe on their own—able to *exist* outside of her body—she wasn't sure if she would even exist any longer,

It's not like Bramwell needed her, anyway. He'd never touched her, kissed her, *fucked* her. He didn't use her, didn't crave her. When her duty was done and she produced a child, and the government that ordered their marriage finally fell, she would no longer be protected. No longer be safe.

There would be nothing to hold Bramwell back from the inevitable.

While Florence softly snored later that night, Belle silently sobbed against Lyren's neck, his fingertips tracing circles along the clothed surface of her spine. He whispered a series of reassuring nothings into the air, all of which seemed useless in the grand scheme of things.

"Soon," Belle breathed, and Lyren craned his neck, glancing down to view the shaking, sobbing woman within his grasp. "We have to do it soon."

With words unspoken, their lips met, and the pair would stay awake come dawn, a mixture of anxious energy and pure fear preventing their minds from slipping into a peaceful sleep.

A SIGN FROM HOME

B elle's trips to the townscenter became more frequent as she grew rounder in the middle.

It was a Tuesday, just at midday—judging by the position of the round, blistering sun in the sky—and it was considerably warm for a spring day.

Sweat tickled her brows, coating the curved flesh of her knuckles as Belle waited for her food at the lunch wagon. She'd bought both herself and the six people around her ham sandwiches and raspberry pie, and the people of Valen couldn't quite keep their eyes (and palms) off of her swollen stomach.

"Not too much longer then, my lady?" one middle-aged woman asked, her cheeks red with blush, sapphire eyes pink with tears. When Belle had offered to pay for her food, she'd burst into sobs—falling to her knees before the woman in a series of thanks.

"I suspect not," Belle replied, forcing herself to smile. She enjoyed visiting the townscenter—entertaining the people of Valen—but admittedly, she was tired of being poked, prodded, and touched constantly without her consent.

The kind man within the lunch wagon handed Belle her sandwich, and she thanked him with a helping of gold, more than he made in an entire year. His eyes had grown to the size of saucers, and immediately after, he packed up his wagon early and went home to his wife.

Bramwell was busy with a nearby crowd—some talks of *government* and *ruling* and *secession*—a bunch of things Belle barely cared to contribute to, and as she took tiny bites of her soft sandwich, Mio the Postman met her side, his thin lips pulled into a tight, toothy grin.

She'd met Mio only a handful of times before when he ventured up the hill to deliver letters and packages. There'd been times where he'd taken Belle's hand in his large, beefy palms, politely placing respectful kisses along her knuckles, a sign of adoration and appreciation.

"My lady, pleasure seeing you down the hill," Mio acknowledged, clearing his throat with an obnoxious cough. Strung along his center was a leather sack, torn and bruised, and his rounded knuckles brushed through its contents, thick brows knit together in confusion.

"Do you have something for me?" Belle asked, finishing off her lunch. The baby within her belly began to shift—as it usually did after she ate something—and her fingers danced along the curve of her dress, eagerly chasing the small foot that protruded.

"'Nother letter from your momma. Sixth one this month. Haven't gotten any outgoing ones from ya, though, m'lady. Not my place to judge—everyone got a different relationship with their parents than I do—but she seems desperate to reach ya. A-*ha!* Here it is. Hefty one. Think she sent some pages of the Good Book or somethin' with it, it's a damn big envelope, it is."

Belle's gaze widened considerably; lips formed into an o-shape as she studied the blond envelope pinched between calloused fingers.

It was the first she'd heard of any letters from home.

"Thank you, Mio," Belle whispered, placing the envelope flush against her chest. Tears teased the innermost corners of her eyes, and the postman dipped his hat, and wobbled away.

Rarely, she would receive mail from one of the house-maidens. Most times, it was Tove, for she'd taken a liking to the round, red-faced Mio—evidently, he reminded her greatly of her late, dead daddy—but recently, Bramwell intercepted the post. He'd barely have to utter a word, a thin grin snaked along sealed lips as Tove would fork over the envelopes, oblivious to what happened to them after they left her grasp.

Bramwell would shuffle through, raise a brow or two at the return addresses he came across, and when he'd land on an envelope from Gladys Byron—a piece of mail that she'd spent three bronzes on—he'd stuff it into the inner pocket of his vest, never to be seen again.

So, when Belle stared blankly at the dated, cheap enve-lope–*one that her mother had surely paid too-many bronze coins for*—balanced within wide, open palms, she saw red.

Deep, dark, *blood* red.

Bramwell had been withholding letters from her. Letters from her own *family*. Letters that could reveal important information that Belle's mother had spent some good bronze on. Letters that Gladys Byron paid for instead of the essentials. Food, medicine, clothing, firewood.

She resisted the urge to crumple the envelope between furious fists, slitted eyes settling across the courtyard to meet a chipper Bramwell, dressed in his very best, a sleek silver chain looped down his right arm. He was sharing a ham sandwich with a filthy townsboy—barely in his tenth year—and Belle shook with rage as she watched the seemingly kind man place pieces of soft, white bread into tiny, dirt-riddled hands.

She wanted to run up to him. To shove the envelope against his chest with a balled-up fist. To knock the air from his lungs, the wind from his throat. To see the way his eyes would widen and then wane. How his brows would pull together, perplexed, and then soften with understanding.

Instead, she remained still. Frozen. *Paralyzed.*

She wasn't sure that it had been possible, but her distaste for Bramwell Hellthorne multiplied greatly, so much so that even his presence ignited a vexed flame within the deepest parts of her belly, the very same one that slowly grew Lyren's child.

She wedged a nail beneath the glued flap of the envelope, and tore it open, revealing the plethora of contents within. Just as Mio the Postman had said, her mother had stuffed several torn and tattered pages of the Good Book in along with her handwritten note. There were inscriptions along the sides, sloppy stars dotted between passages, loopy rings encircling certain statements.

Belle disregarded the religious text, instead shifting her focus to her mother's horrid handwriting, a penmanship nearly impossible to decipher. Nevertheless, she managed, and the sight alone of her mother's wonky script brought fresh, torturous tears to Belle's eyes.

She didn't realize until that very moment just how much she missed her home.

Dearest Belle,

News of your gestation has tickled my heart. Your father and I have been waiting since your nuptials for such an announcement.

I hope Valen is treating you kindly. As you suspect, I have never been. Only your father, when he travels for his trades, and often, like he did with you as a small pup, he'll bring along one of the girls when he makes a sale. Most recently, he took both Lila and Loen to Sarsin. It was his biggest sale of the year. Sold nearly forty pounds of product. You'd be proud of him, Belle. He's such a hard worker.

Lord Bramwell would send quite some coin, as promised, but with the war ongoing, I believe it may have slipped his mind as of late. It's been since Yule that we've received anything. You know that your father and I would never expect such kindness, but it does make us wonder if things are well on the home front. Although, it could very well be possible that he's been focusing his funds on providing for Evelin's care.

Without you both here, the house feels smaller. Imagine that. An already tiny home, even tinier.

Fayne finally learned to use the toilet. She had trouble after you left, anxious attachment, I believe. She's the kindest little soul.

Ema's been talking of visiting you the second she rings in her seventeenth year, Goddess allowing. Only two years from now, but time seems to tick on by like never before, and soon I'll be stuffing her on a carriage just as I had Evelin, packing her a trunk, lending her some old clothes to keep her warm in the Valen winter.

We miss you in Immorium, Belle. I've been watching the post for your notes, but I know things have been busy. When the war is done and Elantry falls, Valen will secede, and you and Lord Bramwell will be true royalty.

If the funds allow, your father and I may very well pack up the girls and our things and move to Valen. I'm not entirely sure I want to see what will become of Immorium when the country falls.

Read the passages I sent you, please. They'll be good for your heart. The Goddesses have their hands in your womb, creating the most perfect little soul.

Your father, sisters, and I all look forward to the arrival of the newest lord or lady.

Please don't make me wait much longer for your letter. I miss you in abundance.

Goddess Be.

Mumma

As she suspected, Gladys attached passages from the Good Book all about pregnancy, newfound life, and the trials and tribulations of a magical gestation.

It was no secret that her mother always dreamt of becoming a grandmother, and Belle couldn't quite contain the cries that consumed her chest. The dam broke, and the tears freely flowed, decorating her mother's letter in a variance of dissimilar shapes.

When her least favorite voice emerged from over a shaking shoulder, Belle dropped the contents within her clutch, a plethora of papers fluttering to her feet in a dreadful mess. The wind threatened to snatch the words away, and the lady fell to her knees with a sob, desperately grabbing each and every last piece of paper between shaking fingers.

"What has you in such hysterics?" Bramwell queried, his tone firm and low.

Several passersby had noticed Belle's meltdown, and one townsgirl in particular had scurried to the lady's side, assisting her in collecting the fallen papers.

"Your lady thanks you for your kindness," Bramwell announced, his lips stretching into a faux, tooth-filled smile.

Clearly, his false friendliness had convinced the teenage girl, and she bowed before him, uttering a short prayer, before returning to her walk, a wicker basket packed with fruit pinched between an elbow.

"I'm fine, Bram," Belle weakly dismissed, unable to stop the storm that burned beyond her blinding vision. She cried hard, attempting to conceal the letter from Bramwell's sight, but he took one single look at Gladys' handwriting and his stomach violently rolled.

"Henry is waiting for us at the carriage," he said, clearing his throat. His fingertips smoothed against the clammy surface of his throat, his pulse quickening beneath flattened fingers as Belle avoided his stern stare.

"Send him back for me when you return," she whispered.

Several townsfolk had noticed her somber state, now, and an elderly woman with worn pink robes and dry, cracked wrinkles slowly approached her, arms outstretched in preparation for a shy embrace.

"Nonsense," Bramwell hissed, and he thrust an arm in the old woman's way, offering her a handshake instead of a hug. Her aged, amber eyes widened with worry.

"My kind woman," Bramwell began, effortlessly shifting his tone. He took the woman's hand within both of his, cradling it kindly, yet firmly. "My wife is not well. I would appreciate your distance while I direct her to the royal carriage."

"Many apologies, my lord," the woman croaked, her voice destroyed by a recent illness. "The lady is such a lovely, gorgeous soul. I have many brews and elixirs that may be of excellent assistance."

She took her hands from his and redirected her attention to the weighty bag draped along a pointed shoulder.

"We have the finest physicians who come up the hill to tend to the lady and her unborn babe," Bramwell began, his expression pinched. "The offer of your services is sweet, but unneeded."

The woman merely ignored Bramwell's speech, and produced several objects, all of which piqued Belle's curiosity.

The first, a crystal phial filled with an unrecognizable golden liquid, a hue that glimmered and shone beneath the heat of the sun, and Bramwell visibly stiffened, knuckles turned inward, fingernails digging deeply into pale palms.

"Mugwort, lavender, and something I like to call *jujin*," the wrinkled woman spoke, placing the vial into Belle's open hands. "Comes from a plant that only grows on the cusp of The Craik. Take it when the babe begins to burst, it'll ease the pain. Make it feel like it's nothin' at all."

"Thank you, my kind woman, but we really must be going," Bramwell interjected, but once again, the woman acted as if the lord was not even there.

It amused Belle greatly, and she bit back a grin, her sorrowful tears drying up.

By the time Bramwell had finally tugged his wife away from the elderly lady, Belle's arms were filled to the brim with an array of items—vials, herb bags, sleek black candlesticks, and a satchel of glimmering, multi-hued crystals.

When Belle glanced over her shoulder to bid the woman goodbye, a stunning scarlet Cardinal landed on the woman's shoulder, blinking twice in Belle's direction, head cocked in recognition.

The ride back up the hill felt impossibly long, and Bramwell refused to tear his rigid stare from Belle's direction. She'd placed her new gifts upon the tip of her belly—treating the surface like a tiny table—and below the items was the bundle of papers from Immorium, the letter her mother had sent her.

"Where did you get that letter?" Bramwell asked, fiddling with the silver chain draped along his arm. His blackened stare felt like a thousand icy daggers, and Belle barely laughed—a forced burst of air emerging from each nostril—and she twirled a pearl white rock between curious fingers.

"Have you thrown the others away? Or burned them in the fireplace, perhaps? If not, I'd appreciate it if you could give them to me. I would like to see what my mother has been trying to tell me."

Bramwell paled, his worries confirmed, and he clapped a palm over his mouth, a stressful sigh dancing along his tongue as he ruffled his hair.

She'd never seen him so jittery, so *anxious*. She'd caught him in a lie—acknowledged his deception—and she met his wild gaze, as if to test him.

The corners of her lips pulled into a taunting smile, and with words unspoken, she teased him. *Tortured* him.

Do it.

"I told you I wouldn't use it on you," he dryly defended, knowing exactly what she was referring to.

They'd grown to despise one another—that much was true—but Bramwell had remained true to his word. He'd never once charmed Belle, never reached inside her head and scrambled her thoughts. Never torn her memories from her brain, ripped them up like he'd ripped up the letters from her mother. Tossed them into the flickering flame, watched silently as the roaring fire ate away at the pages, erasing the evidence.

Belle broke their stare, and she studied the white rock pinched between her forefinger and her thumb, a small sigh filling the carriage.

"As you wish," she said, placing the rock back onto the top of her belly. "But you may come to regret not using your little spells on me, Bramwell. One day soon, you'll wish you'd been charming me all along."

Bramwell bit his tongue, and when the carriage graced the top of the hill and his severely pregnant wife wobbled up the stone steps to the mansion—her arms overfilled with a series of newly found objects—he came completely undone.

The redheaded girl disappeared beyond the double doors of the manor's entryway, and Bramwell exploded with rage, the toe of his boot colliding sharply with the wooden wheel of the carriage. The splintered surface split and cracked, and he redirected his attention to the glass window, a balled-up fist flying directly through.

Mirrored shards peppered the seats and the floor—a horrid mess—and thick, scarlet beads of blood bloomed along reddened knuckles, broken skin raw and oozing.

The horses shifted and sighed, fear filling their loins. Bramwell released a plethora of curses toward the bright blue sky, and he retired toward the mansion, his blooded hand weeping all over his clothes, staining the surface a lurid crimson.

Henry watched with wide eyes as the lord stomped along the steps, resembling that of a child instead of a fully-grown man, and he tended lightly to the animals, attempting to rid them of their worries.

It was the first time he'd ever seen the Lord of Valen in such a state, and he couldn't help but feel an inkling of fear for the sweet, redheaded woman who called herself his wife.

Henry only hoped that Bramwell's blooded, busted knuckles would steer far away from the pale smoothness of Belle's face.

WEEPING WOUNDS

Bramwell's injuries were dressed come breakfast the following morning.

Much to both Lyren and Belle's dismay, the lord continuously joined them both for most meals. As Belle's due date drew nearer and her likeness for the lord dwindled further, he stuck around more.

Following the lord's brief stint with the ruined carriage window, Bramwell disappeared beneath the floorboards of the mansion, hatred heating his core as he skillfully scaled the basement steps. He was still dressed in his best, the pricey clothing soiled and tainted, and when two pairs of undead eyes met his trembling frame, the weight within the room shifted.

It always did when he was around. A certain heaviness consumed the chamber, one that made the rear of his neck sweat, and his mother shifted her weight from either foot as she slightly pulled at her binds, desperate to flee.

"She's ruddy fucking figured me *out*," Bramwell had seethed, resisting the urge to put his already mangled fist through the bleak, brick lined wall.

"Innocent, fickle little seaside girl, thinks she's so fuck-ing invincible. Got a storm coming, she does. Thinks just because I haven't charmed her means she's safe."

Bramwell's rants had been met by silence.

His faux father had watched in wonder and sorrow as the dark-haired lord paced the premises—such an opposite appearance from the late lord—solid, unyielding proof of his wife's blatant infidelity.

"She couldn't just be *good*," Bramwell continued to vent, knowing quite well that neither person within the room would—or even could—respond. "Couldn't be a good little wife. I let her do what she wants. I gave the woman her own room, in her own *wing*. I let her fuck my ward, I let her fuck my best *friend*. I let him put a ruddy fucking *child* inside of her. All for what?"

He'd tossed his arms upward in angst, head shaking from side to side as his prisoners meekly watched.

"I gave this woman everything, and it still isn't enough. She still hates me. She's a miserable little rotten wench and as soon as my heir comes out of her cunt, I'm dragging her down those fucking steps, strapping these chains around her bony little wrists, and I'm going to watch her *rot*."

Bramwell could've sworn that he saw Sorrel's features flinch, but when he steadied his sight on his undead mother, she remained unchanged.

She had stared at him with cold, empty eyes, and if tears could bloom between the rotting lids of her vision, they surely would the moment she saw Bramwell snatch up a bird's beak knife, one with the slightest curve and the sharpest blade.

Her glossy sight remained suctioned to his every move, and as Bramwell wedged the serrated tip into the pockmarked patch of her ruined flesh, he snickered. *Laughed.*

"Fucking whores always get what they deserve," he said, and he reveled in the sight of the bulbous, black beads of blood that emerged from his mother's decomposing breast.

"You'll just love her to pieces," the lord slurred, tearing open decaying flesh.

The inky gore that leaked from Sorrel's skin and dripped down his fingers fascinated him. He paused, rubbing his fingertips together, reveling in the feel. Unlike the blood that spilled from a living, breathing human, the blood that lingered within the veins of an ondode was bleak, black, and cold.

Magnificent.

An unblinking Sorrel stared into Bramwell's soul, watching his every move, the only thing that she could even do. If the woman could react, she would pull her lips from her teeth, expose the yellowed bones within, the blackened tongue, and she'd scream.

Her torpid, jet-black blood covered his fingers, and then, his lips. His mouth. His tongue.

He'd slipped a digit within the cavern of his mouth, then a second, wrapping his tongue around the surface, savoring the flavor. It was unlike anything he'd ever tasted before, and it was wonderful. Riveting. *Delicious.*

Bramwell slipped his fingers from his lips—an audible pop sound—and with stained teeth, he spoke.

"Oh, Mama. You'll just *love* her. My gorgeous, wonderful, soon-to-be-dead wife."

By the time Bramwell's knuckles had scabbed over, Belle began to experience false labor.

The first time it happened, she was forcing spoons full of tomato broth into her mouth, for she hadn't eaten in nearly a day and a half. Anxiety had wormed its way into the very marrow of her bones, and the sheer scent of boiling vegetables, roasting meat, or, quite frankly, any kind of meal with a particularly potent scent made her outwardly gag. She'd tremble with each and every gulp of soup, and Florence etched dizzying circles in between the redheaded woman's shoulder blades with a fingertip.

A sharp spasm consumed her core, and the silver slipped from her fingers, a mess of soupy scarlet staining her dutch-white day dress. A smear of gore directly across her bulbous center, a faux wound.

At the time, Lyren's pointed nose had been stuffed in the dusted pages of a novel he'd read twice before, nails wedged between mindlessly gnawing teeth, apprehension swallowing him whole.

Both he and Belle had been particularly on edge since their visit to the basement. They knew what they had to do—*kill him, kill the awful man*—but as the days droned on, it nearly seemed like a fever dream.

Impossible.

They tried to convince Florence of the ondodes, but just as she'd done originally, she dismissed their tales. Just as she'd dismissed Belle's previous visions. The blood raining down the walls, the portrait of a dead girl, Evelin's possession by the demon Goddess Velveteen.

It's not real.

None of it is real.

Her dismissal formed a wedge. When she slept on her side—cold and alone on the edge of Belle's bed—Lyren would take Belle into his arms. Shower her in love, pepper the exposed flesh in a series of smooches. He'd lift her nightgown, reveal the rounded belly beneath, admire the way her skin warped and pulled. Run a forefinger along the parallel streaks of reddened, angry skin, torn and strained.

Lyren would whisper loving pecks along the skin, admire the way her stomach jutted out, how tiny the rest of her looked in comparison. He'd tell her he loved her until he succumbed to sleep, his eyelids heavy with exhaustion, and Belle would rake her fingers through his hair, the silvery blond locks sweet and soft, pillowy and cozy against her skin.

Eventually, Florence asked Belle if she still loved her. Her eyes were stained red with worry, trembles tickling her spine, fingernails wedged between gnawing teeth.

Belle's expression fell.

She'd been writing another letter for her mother. To Bramwell's utter dismay, she'd insisted on trekking down the hill by carriage, locating Mio whilst he did his rounds, and slipping the envelope into his grasp. The postman never minded much, nor did those around him, for the sight of the Lady of Valen was always a gift to the townspeople. Most had been living in fear and isolation during the war—worried that more of the riots would slip down south—so to see their lady—their *governess*—in the flesh nearly made their knees crumble.

Sleek black ink smeared along the curve of her hand, and she set down her pen. Stunning rays of warm sunlight bled through the parted windows of the sitting room, weighty drapes shifting slightly with each infrequent burst of summer wind, and Lyren craned his neck to view the situation at hand, his bright blue eyes barely visible beyond his chair.

"Flo," Belle muttered, an ache present in her chest. She shifted forward on her chair, the old wicker whining beneath her weight, and she claimed Florence's shaking hands in hers.

"Of course I do. I will always love you. You are the first and only woman I've ever loved, my first real, *true* love. You own a piece of my heart, a fraction of my soul."

Belle paused, blinking back tears, and she rotated her gaze to meet a curious Lyren, wisps of hair dancing within his piercing stare. Florence seemed unbothered by his nosiness, and she squeezed Belle's fingers, as if to urge her onward.

"There's a wall," Florence began, and Lyren's book snapped closed.

"Walls aren't built by mistake," he said, and Belle shot him a stiff glance, as if out of warning. He'd stood to his feet, tossed the novel aside, and extended his arms upward in a full stretch.

"These fables—these *stories*—I just can't entertain them, Bells. You've got Lyren convinced, but I'm not so easily swayed. I thought you didn't believe in Plirity, you insisted you didn't from the start, and now all you speak of is *witchcraft* and *ondodes* and *demons* and if the trio of Goddesses don't exist, how would the fallen Goddess Velveteen? It's just too much for me, my love. I have to see the reality, not the fable. I have to be *sane*."

"So, what do you consider us, then? *Insane*? Worthy of admittance to Azyl? Belle's sister lives out her days within those walls, Florence, all because the wickedness within this manor *ruined* her." Lyren pressed, pacing the room with a palm on each pointed hip.

His patience was thinner than Belle's. Annoyance overcame him easily. Flooded his being, turned his ears hot, a blush slapped across pale cheeks. He hardly paid Florence any mind as of late, and the reality crumbled her. Tore her apart bit by bit, flayed flesh, blood red muscle exposed. Ripped. *Shredded.*

"If you just *listened* to us," Belle breathed, her tone softer. Kinder. "If you let us show you–"

"And disobey Bramwell by wandering where I shouldn't? What if I were to be caught, Belle? I'm not his spouse, like you. I'm not his best friend, like Lyren. There's nothing keeping me here, anymore. He could very easily cast me out on my own."

Florence was in hysterics. Belle had never seen the woman so broken, so *hurt.* Her heart ached, and she shifted forward, pulling the trembling woman into a comforting hug.

"I love you, Florence. I do. I just feel invalidated and hurt by you. I know you're scared—we're *all* ruddy terrified lately—but you need to believe us. You need to *trust* us." Belle ran her thumbs along Florence's cheeks, gathering the warm, wet tears that stained her skin.

"She needs to see them," Lyren said, his tone flat. His arms were crossed, brows tight, jaw clenched.

"Please," Belle whispered, a palm cradling Florence's soaked skin. "Please, let us show you. Bramwell's due down to the townscenter today, you'll have nothing to worry about."

Florence wanted to scream. To shout from the top of her lungs.

She'd seen things, just as Belle and Lyren had. Smelled the blood that dribbled down the walls, how it pooled along the baseboards, stained the rugs. She'd always dismissed it—*it's just another nightmare, another bad fucking dream*—but it wasn't just a bad dream.

It never was.

Six months prior to Belle's arrival, Jeanne nearly put her skull through the foggy, fingerprint riddled pane of a glass window. The housemaiden had just finished pulling a third pan of blueberry scones from the heat, when suddenly, the pastries fell to her feet, a hot metal pan meeting tile, a garish crack. Florence had watched with wide eyes as the mute housemaiden approached the kitchen window, braced either palm against the cool surface, and tossed her neck back.

It wasn't just a bad dream.

Florence squeezed her eyelids shut, terrified tears building against the sealed surface, and she felt Belle's fingers tangle within her fallen braid, tenderly tugging at unkempt knots.

"It's time, Bells," Lyren whispered, looping his arms around the two women. He pulled them close, planted a kiss atop each of their heads, and told them each that he loved them, just in case it would be the very last time he could.

ROT

Belle finished the letter she'd drafted to her mother.

Bulky, fat tears dripped down her nose, decorating the parchment in an array of varying shapes, smudging most of her writing. It was impossible to hide. Her sorrow. Her *grief.* Her mother would open the envelope in less than seven days time, see the dried tears along the surface, and she would just know.

Being away from you, from father, from Evelin and Ema and Lilla and Dorothy and Loen and Fayne . . . It ruins me, Mummy.

It destroys me.

There is a truth that has been hidden behind my teeth. Something I've been trying to spit out. Something I've only told to Evelin in letters, letters I don't even believe reach her.

The tears blinded her vision, and Belle openly gasped, cradling her swollen stomach with a single palm, whereas her opposite hand bitterly brushed the tears away, fingers wet with grief.

When her sight stabilized once more, she continued to read over her note.

My husband is a murderer.

Just as many wondered, and some accused, he was the reason those women died at my wedding.

He's killed more since.

The Holy Man, the one who exorcized Evelin, never left these walls.

Unbeknownst to Belle, Lyren hovered the entryway of the sitting room. His arms were crossed loosely over his chest, a temple rested against the weeping wooden frame of the door, the paint chipped and splintered.

She hadn't noticed his presence yet, and he preferred to keep it as such. She looked so stunning—so *pure*. Tiny form perched atop a hideous olive chair, planted at the desk cradling the window. Yellow rays frolicked along scarlet strands of hair, fresh tears coating her cheeks, glittering gold within the warmth of the sun. Her legs were tucked halfway beneath her bottom, stomach swollen with their young.

She was due any day, and although the thought of meeting his child excited him, it also turned the blood within his veins to thick, icy syrup. If Bramwell wasn't dealt with soon, the moment the baby fled the womb, he would have his hooks in it. Deep. *Piercing.*

Lyren was almost certain that Bramwell would hold his gaze, swallow a snicker, and erase the memories from Lyren's head. He'd reach a hand in, elbow deep, curl his fingers around Lyren's brain. Nails would pierce muscle—*mutilate*—and Lyren would be left with nothing. Oblivious.

Bramwell could make Lyren forget that he'd ever made a child at all. Forget that he'd ever felt the warmth of Belle's mouth, the whisper of her touch, the statement that she loved to trace along his skin.

I love you.

I love you.

I love you.

He watched her finish reading over the letter she'd written for her mother. She sniffled, wiped a few fingers along her cheeks, and then she folded the parchment, tucked it into an envelope, and sealed it with wax. The Hellthorne stamp sat idle on the table, and he watched her eye it, as if debating whether or not to stamp the sigil into the envelope.

She claimed it in her clutch, tossed it beneath the table, and buried it within the depths of the mess. Forgotten. *Unwanted.*

When she finally noticed him, her lips pulled into a small smile.

"Been there long?"

Lyren chuckled. "Long enough to admire the way you look in the sunlight."

His gaze trailed downward, and Belle's womb visibly shifted. A wandering hand, a kicking foot. She winced, and Lyren's pulse fluttered within his throat.

"My gorgeous girl," he mused, filing into the room. He fell to his knees before her, cradling her belly, lips grazing the sunny yellow dress that cloaked her flesh. "Have I told you just how proud I am of you?"

Belle's brows shifted upward, as if in question.

"I know this pregnancy hasn't been easy," Lyren began, lacing his fingers between hers. He brought their conjoined hands to the very spot where their fetus kicked, and Belle giggled at the sensation.

"I think I feel both feet," she said, pressing down hard. "He or she just must really love to hear their father's voice."

A bright blush claimed Lyren's cheeks, and he peppered noisy, playful smooches along the rounded surface, earning a laugh from his lover and an additional kick from his child.

"As I was saying," he continued, his ocean blue stare meeting a glossy pair of auburn eyes. "As if the pregnancy wasn't difficult enough—with your difficulties with eating on top of it all—this house, this ruddy portal to the Netherworld itself, has been testing you. *Taunting* you. You've done a fabulous job of staying sane, my dear."

"Is that what you consider this? *Sane*?" Belle teased, motioning to the dried tears splattered along her cheeks. "I love you, Lyren Deth. It's been a privilege to carry your young."

Lyren smiled—a big, goofy grin—and their mouths met; sloppy, wet, warm. His tongue snaked into her mouth, and a pleasant moan tickled her chest. She could never get close enough. Their flesh would be flush—*suctioned*—and she'd still want more. If only she could pry open the cavity of his chest, crawl right in, nuzzle her head against the steady drum of his heart.

Own it.

Florence peered around the doorway, and with a tone so small that they barely heard her, she announced Bramwell's recent departure. Lyren beckoned her over, and she shyly joined, burying her nose into Belle's neck, painting polite portraits along the flesh with needy lips.

It had been far too long, and Florence was starved.

"Get out of those clothes," Lyren ordered, though neither woman was certain of who he had been referring to. That was, until he took it upon himself to tear open the ties on Florence's floral dress.

"This is my favorite day dress," Florence droned, her expression falling, but Lyren hushed her with a kiss. A peck, initially, and then a smooch. A sigh. A *whine*.

He hadn't told Florence of their risky plans yet, and he wondered if it was even worth it to reveal them at all. In that moment, everything seemed wonderful. Lovely. *Blissful.*

Nothing could stop them.

Lyren's fingers wandered and pried, pulling the fabric of Florence's brasserie away from her breasts. His mouth found a nipple, a flick of a tongue, and Florence let out a mewl, eyes rotating upwards into her skull.

"The door is open," Belle acknowledged, running her fingers through Lyren's hair. She watched the way his mouth worked Florence's breast, how his lips reddened from the friction.

They'd never be so open about their affection anywhere other than Belle's personal bedroom or washroom. The housemaidens seldom wandered into either of those areas, out of respect for the lady's privacy, but any one of Bramwell's employees could stumble upon the trio at any moment. Anyone could hear them—*see* them—and although the idea frightened Belle, it somewhat excited her.

The thought of rumors flying, of townspeople whispering of an affair. Of Lyren fathering Belle's child. Of Bramwell's ward occupying the Lady of Valen's bed.

Belle's cunt throbbed, and she hoped that someone would walk by.

Florence had fallen to her back, her skirt pulled up, exposing her underwear. She was a ripe, red apple, juicy and sweet, and Lyren was famished. *Starved.*

"I've missed you," he purred, and Florence blushed; cheeks pink and flushed. Lyren claimed Belle's hand, interlacing their fingers, and said, "I've missed having you both. All laid out before me, pretty with want."

Florence fought back tears—she'd missed it, too—and she beckoned Belle to the floor, a chuckle bouncing between the trio as Belle struggled to lower herself.

"Give me a moment," she teased, and Lyren traded between the two, planting sweet kisses on each of their mouths.

He told each of them that he loved them between hushed, frantic smooches, and he crawled between Florence's legs, hooked a forefinger within the damp fabric of her underwear and pried it aside. His mouth met her center before she could comprehend the absence of his kisses, and Belle silenced Florence's whines with the presence of her mouth, the tip of her tongue teasing her teeth.

Silver tresses tickled Florence's inner thighs—the contrast between tones striking, *artsy*—and Belle swallowed the woman's whines as Lyren's tongue traced circles against her clit.

Belle steered south, focusing her attention on Florence's breasts—a palm on one, her mouth on the other—and Lyren freed himself from the constraints of his trousers, popping open a trio of buttons, loosening the laced ties. Florence weaved her legs around his waist, drawing him close—*in in in*—and he obeyed, working her open with three fingers before easing himself in.

The three melted into one another's embrace—a steady rhythm, a gentle rock of the hips—and Florence clawed at Lyren's clothed back, wrinkling the fabric of his silken blouse.

Florence wasn't sure of whose mouth was on hers—it was all such a blur. Belle's warm, gentle touch had traveled toward Florence's clit, a burning ember, and she kneaded wide circles against the surface. She massaged the place where Lyren and Florence lay intertwined, rubbing—*massaging*—and then, there were two mouths on Florence's, too impatient to take turns.

There was a whisper—a gasp—but the three were too preoccupied, too self-absorbed to even care.

Nothing mattered, anymore. Not then, not ever.

Never again.

TO THE END

S he helped her into her dress.

Black, just like the manor. The pitch-dark paint that coated the walls. Hellthorne's staple.

Darkness.

Death.

Despair.

When she was done with the lace, the ties nice and tight, she stepped into her own gown, identical in hue, dissimilar in style. What remained of her ruined day dress remained in the sitting room, draped over the sofa.

"According to Ula, he shouldn't be back until dusk. The townspeople are officially electing him to leadership today, or so they say." Lyren said, struggling to latch the buttons on his milky white top.

Whereas the women were clad in nothing but black, Lyren wore all white. Unpigmented. *Colorless.*

"We mustn't dawdle," Florence pressed, assisting Lyren in sealing the binds on his shirt. She brushed his trembling hands aside, planted a kiss atop his nose, and told him that she loved him.

"I love you," Lyren muttered, his stare downcast, studying the way Florence's fingers skillfully buttoned him up.

The sun still hung high within the sky, bruising the horizon with a modest orange glow. It was a stunning summer day, and the man wished that he could crawl into the bed beside them, to pull both women into his arms, slip his eyes closed, and sleep. *Dream.*

Only, he couldn't. *They* couldn't. Florence had finally crumbled—the walls had been torn away—and if he and Belle didn't pull her down the basement stairs and show her what existed within the bowels of the manor, they may never get their chance.

As the trio navigated the halls—cautious not to catch any unwanted attention—they were blissfully unaware of the hushed murmurs that consumed the kitchen. Fingers kneading fresh dough, flour flying airborne, dusting the atmosphere, staining their clothes.

I always knew something was going on.

Filthy fucking whore.

And with the lady, too!

Bramwell's best pal!

The deceit!

Belle shuffled a burning candlestick into Florence's clutch, curling the woman's fingers inward, tightening her hold.

"You'll need this," she said. "It gets dark down there."

Florence audibly gulped, panic settling within her bones, and Lyren ran a reassuring hand along the small of her back, lips placing a kiss along her temple.

"I'll keep you safe," he whispered, his features dully illuminated by his own candle. "I'll keep you *both* safe. Until my very last breath."

Belle directed them toward the basement door, the lock routinely unlatched, the hinges noisy, needing oil. Florence craned her neck, a shiver of fear cascading up her spine as the sound prompted her to glance down the hall to see if anyone had heard.

Only, there was no one. None of the housemaidens ventured this far back into the manor. Even she had never gone so deep beyond the unknown. She never even knew that these halls even existed, a darkness so bleak, so *black* that it hurt her eyes.

Belle guided her two lovers down the steep staircase—eighty-seven agonizing steps—and Florence kept looking over her shoulder, watching the open doorway, wondering when the portal would seal itself for good. Trap them.

It was only Lyren's second time down to the depths of the basement, but it felt no different than the first. He, too, felt anxious. Weak. *Frightened.* He knew what stood below, but to see them again—to *smell* them again—his stomach did somersaults at the thought.

"I feel as if I'm dreaming," Florence admitted, tightening her hold on Belle's hand. She squeezed tight, and Belle winced, audibly requesting that she let up on her hold.

"Now you'll know the horrors and hells I've been facing since I arrived at the manor," Belle replied, reminding Lyren of the broken step near the end of the staircase. "The man you call family—the man I *married*—is a wicked, cruel, *evil* man. Capable of terrible things, Flo."

"It can't be possible," Florence dismissed, wanting to sob for what seemed like the millionth time that day.

Bramwell had always been good to her—*kind* to her—and to wander within an area that was so strictly off-limits seemed like such a blatant betrayal to the person who had done such good for her. He never had to take her in after her mother's death. He could have left her to rot down in Mylop. To live on the streets, to scavenge for food.

"I didn't believe it myself until I saw it with my own two eyes," Lyren admitted, and he followed close on Belle's heel as she led them through the blackened abyss that was the basement, dragging them to the room that held two very real ondodes. Beings that Florence didn't even believe existed.

The rotting, living corpses of the late lord and lady of Valen.

"Just through this door," Belle breathed, anticipation bubbling within her belly. The child within her womb delivered a series of kicks along the wall of her uterus, as if they, too, could absorb her energy.

Perhaps they could.

The closer they got to the room, Florence grew antsy. *Fidgety.* Her palms slick with sweat, damp fingers threatening to drop the candlestick. She tried to drop Belle's hand, but Lyren only grabbed her other one, leading her to their destination.

The air grew thick, and she found herself nearly gasping, unable to inhale deeply. There was a heaviness to the atmosphere, a strange shift. It was unlike anything Florence had ever felt, and with her mouth still closed, she swore that she could taste it, as if it were a tangible, edible thing.

A saccharine sweetness, like molasses. Candied and profuse, so thick she nearly choked on it.

Her lips parted—*what in Goddess Liv is that*—but Belle's knuckles had already graced the wood of the door, brushed it open, revealed the contents within.

As promised, the fabled pair of ondodes stood silently within, wrists shackled in chains, ashen eyes rotating toward the source of the noise.

Only, they weren't alone.

There was someone else inside. Buried within the cove of their chair, a burning cigar pinched between gore-smeared fingers.

Two out of three dropped their candlesticks, the glimmering flames extinguishing upon impact, and the lord merely laughed, the sound moderately muffled by the presence of his cigar.

He took a long pull, exhaled a cloud of sickly smoke, and then, finally spoke.

"I started to think that you wouldn't show."

BLOODY POPPIES

She wanted to run.

To tear her hand from both Belle and Lyren's. To trip over the obstacles hidden within the dark, to cascade up the staircase, tripping halfway up, crawling on all fours to the top. To slam the door, latch the lock, breathe a sigh of relief.

To leave it all behind.

She knew then exactly what her lovers had meant. The Bramwell Hellthorne perched before her was a fraction of the man she'd come to know. It was almost as if he'd trans-formed—*shifted*—turned into someone entirely divergent.

She could smell the wickedness—the *sinfulness*—radiat-ing off of his flesh like a cheap bottle of cologne. It gagged her, made her want to retch, and her palm clamped over her gaping mouth, stifling a sob.

Florence had noticed them almost immediately. The on-dodes. *The undead.* She knew of their identities instantly. She'd know who they were from a mile away.

She'd never once met her Aunt Sorrel, but the similarities between her own mother and the undead lady was dreadfully uncanny. She could see her own mother in the features of Lady Sorrel's face. The shape of her cheeks, the curve of her lips. Strikingly similar, and undoubtedly siblings. She was, without a doubt, Bramwell's true family.

With words unspoken, she knew. She *understood.* The man she'd trusted, the man she'd lived with for an entire decade—shared a *wife* with—had murdered his own parents. Murdered her mother's *sister.* He'd enchanted them and kept them unalive in the basement of his home. She'd known of his abilities, of his charms—*such silly, simple spells*—but it was much more than that. Much more *sinister* than that.

He wasn't an ordinary kitchen witch. No, he was malev-olent. Demonic. *Evil.*

"Is anyone going to speak, or should I start?" Bramwell wondered, twirling the cigar between his fingers. The situation clearly amused him, and when none of the three guests replied, he only laughed, extinguishing the flame on the rusted orange cloth of his chair.

He climbed to his feet, and looked the trio up and down, extending an arm sideways to show off his prized possessions.

"I'm sure you know who these fine individuals are," the lord began, a sinister smirk snaking along thin lips. Both Lady Sorrel and Lord Ayer II, with heads turned, looked the guests square in the face. "Such a pity you have to meet the sister of your dead mother this way, Florence. They seldom spoke after your mother shacked up with that father of yours, or so I was told."

He rounded the shackled pair, his gaze settling upon the bulbous mounds of meat that once made up his mother's breasts, the very same ones that supplied him with necessary nutrients for the first ten years of his life.

"The fine Lady Sorrel Evaniene Alesek, Hellthorne by marriage, an *unfaithful* marriage. Went out and whored herself, got pregnant by another, pretended the child was of her husband," Bramwell began, dipping his fingers into the depths of his pants pocket. He extracted a curved blade, ran his scarlet stained fingers along the silver surface, and brought it to the blackened flesh of his mother's chest.

"Whores deserve to be punished," Bramwell said, hooking the tip of the steel into a fatty flap of meat. Before he tore into the skin, his stare met Belle's, rotating between her dark gaze and the swollen surface of her stomach.

"*All* whores deserve to be punished."

Bramwell tore the fatty flesh open—the already cavernous crater enlarging—and Florence screamed, falling to her knees as the rotten stench of dead blood permeated the room.

Lady Sorrel—or, rather, what *remained* of Lady Sorrel—barely flinched. She didn't even do so much as blink. The spoiled skin flayed away, the gray muscle beneath blotchy and necrose.

"You sick fuck," Lyren seethed, bile rising up his throat. "You sick fucking *bastard*. I never really knew you at all."

Bramwell cackled—a sardonic, sour sound—and he tore the patch of flesh from his mother's bosom, held it above his head, and balanced it before the light of a nearby oil lamp, intrigued by the sight.

"No, my dear friend. You never really knew me at all."

"Why did you bring me here?" Belle asked, appearing unphased by Bramwell's deranged deeds.

She'd loathed him for months, then, and to see his cruelness on display was something she'd dreamt of for countless nights before that very one. From the moment she'd uncovered his true self, the night terrors began. Visions of him—blade in tow—carving patterns into her skin, peeling flesh from muscle, muscle from bone. She should've known from the start—saw past his façade—but admittedly, to an outsider, he wore a particularly pleasant face.

"I had to," Bramwell shrugged, tossing the meat from his mother's breast to the floor, stomping it with the sole of his boot. "Well, with Elantry fallen, I suppose I don't *have* to keep you around, now. Once you squeeze the heir to Valen out of that tight little cunt of yours, I'll have no true use for you."

Lyren's patience broke. *Snapped.*

His jaw flexed, and he nearly screamed—charging forward, his arm extended back, elbow curved, fingers curling into a taut fist. Bramwell barely reacted, and his longest friend delivered a thick punch square to the center of his face, shattering the cartilage of his nose, blood bursting from each nostril.

The skinning knife toppled from his clutch, clattering to the floor. Bramwell toppled backward, unsteady on his feet, a gory palm cradling a sopping, broken nose. He nearly tripped over the leg of his illegitimate father's chair, threatening to topple directly into the lap of the man he murdered, charmed, and kept as a trophy in his own basement.

Bramwell's gaze darkened, his expression pinched, and he dismissively wiped the blood from his nostrils with curled fingers, a sour mixture of fluids blemishing his skin. The crowned lord seated below him craned his head, the declining bones shifting within his neck.

For a moment, Belle noticed a variation. *A shift.*

Lord Ayer II's fingers had twitched—*moved*—and if the binds containing his thin wrists hadn't been present, Belle was almost certain that the ondode would've looped its arms around Bramwell's shoulders, forced the man onto his lap, unlocked its jaw, dug its broken, yellowed teeth into a shy skin of Bramwell's neck, and rip. Tear. *Shred.* Go back in for seconds. *Thirds.*

Only, the undead lord merely winced. The smallest movement, barely a whisper, unnoticed by anyone but her.

A flame flickered behind her eyes. A thought. An idea.

Bramwell had burst into boasting, taunting laughter—*don't you know who I am, you ruddy fucking fool*—and Florence took a step forward when the lord took ahold of the collar of Lyren's top, fisting the fabric, pulling him close.

I'm the son of Velveteen, the fallen Goddess, the Queen of the Netherworld.

Bramwell's fist found purchase against Lyren's face—a short clip across a pink cheek—and Florence brushed past a frozen Belle, her arms encircling her cousin's neck, legs thrown airborne, her full weight balanced along the curved surface of his back. She swatted loose, flimsy fists against a dark-haired scalp, tears blinding her sight, sobs tickling her tongue.

Belle took that moment to act.

Whilst her lovers quarreled with the man she vowed herself to for an eternity, she fell to her knees, careful to cradle her protruding bump, and claimed the blade Bramwell had dropped. It was shiny, silver, and slick with blood, the metal curved and sharp.

Florence took a fistful of Bramwell's hair between her fingers—tugging, *pulling*—whereas Lyren steadied a palm on the man's shoulder before delivering a calculated blow to his sternum.

The lord laughed—teeth smeared with shining scarlet—and he caught a glimpse of his wife on the floor, her rounded, bulbous belly cradled within a single hand, the other holding a weapon.

At the sight, he roared with laughter, blood trickling down the length of his chin. He looped his fingers around Florence's arms, penetrating her flesh with the edges of his nails.

She yelped, and tumbled from his back, her bottom colliding flat with Lord Ayer II's lap. The rear of her skull met the honed barbs of his thorny crown, probing her the surface.

As Belle climbed to her feet, her knobby knees wobbling with a mixture of anxiety and fear—Bramwell took hold of Lyren's lengthy locks, pinching the long, soft hair between raw fingers.

"Such a sharp toy for such a weak woman," Bramwell called, looking Belle up and down.

She looked so small—so *delicate*—standing there opposite them. With a severely swollen midsection, quivering legs, and palms slick with sweat, she looked just as he'd described. *Weak.* Spineless.

Afraid.

"Don't hurt yourself, little thing," Bramwell drawled, clearly amused by his banter, and whilst he remained momentarily distracted, Lyren slipped from his hold.

Florence was still seated upon the ondodes lap, her shivering touch gravitating to the weeping wound on her scalp. The rusted bonds fastened around the undead lord's wrists shifted slightly, and the woman's pulse quickened when realization finally struck. *She was on the lap of an undead lord.*

She craned her neck, and wide, warm eyes met the vacant glare of death. A hazy, overcast exterior—a dense, cloudy day—and for a split second, she swore that she could see a flicker of life beyond the snowy shadowed surface.

Their noses scarcely struck—for the ondode had shifted in his seat, slithering further, as if to lean in for a kiss.

A scream crawled up Florence's throat just as Bramwell's clenched hand met Lyren's jaw, sending him to the floor with a *thump.* The curve of Lyren's scalp met the pebbled earth, blinding stars cluttering his vision as the lord clambered atop his hips.

"Should've just minded your fucking business, Lyren Deth," Bramwell seethed, features flushed a vexed crimson.

He'd seemingly forgotten about Belle's blade—how she held the knife between tight white fingers—and as the two men continued to throw fists at one another, she began her mission.

Everything seemingly happened all at once.

Florence fell from the lord's ghostly lap, crawling along the grimy ground with shaking palms. A plenitude of dirt coated her skin, soiling her dress, and the sharp gravel bruised her touch, leaving behind considerable impressions of varying shapes and sizes.

Belle had taken her place before the seated lord, her unblinking stare settling upon milky orbs. The mutilated lady planted directly beside them parted her lips—an airy gasp—and Belle wondered if she may have tried to speak.

If she could, the woman was certain that the ondode would've told her to run.

"Don't fail me, my lord," Belle murmured, latching her warm fingers around the crisp, sickly skin of Lord Ayer II's left wrist. She brought the blade to the putrid surface, and with a throat full of bile, she began to carve.

First, through the thin skin that remained. It wasn't much—most had whittled away over the years, courtesy of the iron binds—but once the tarnished tissue flayed away, it revealed a mass of muscle.

Then, bone.

Lyren yelped—coughed up a burst of blood—rotated to his side, knees drawn up to his chest. Florence, still bleeding from the rear of her scalp, slithered between the raging men, a weak attempt to pry them apart.

"*Go,* Flo," Lyren weakly begged, and Bramwell laughed, a twine of spittle and blood slipping between parted lips, coating the cotton of Florence's gown.

"You're fucking *weak,* all of you!" Bramwell spat, standing to his feet.

He swayed once to the side, and before he could glance over his shoulder to view a frantic Belle before his father—swiftly sawing away at the bitter white bones of a wrist—Lyren's leg jutted outward, catching Bramwell's lower limbs. The dark-haired man stumbled—nearly falling flat faced onto a sore Lyren laid upon the floor—and as his stare met Florence's, he grinned.

Wide. *Wild.* Lips pulled back, exposing smeared, gory teeth. He spat a clot to the ground, barely missing Lyren's writhing frame, and he held Florence's gaze.

"Good girl," Bramwell breathed, panting slightly. His palms steadied against his knees, and without as much as a single blink, his vision bore into hers.

"Always the best girl, Florence. Always my best girl," he continued, and just as Belle got to work on the right wrist—her fingers sore and wet with blood—recognition flooded Lyren's features, and he fisted the middle of Florence's dress, attempting to claim her chin, to tear her stare from Bramwell's.

"Florence—*no!*"

"Piss off, Lyren," Bramwell dismissed, shoving the man aside with a bitter palm.

After all, the deed had already been done.

It took mere moments—a fraction of a second—for the lord to dip his fingers into the chasmic depths of Florence's mind. To mangle her memories, tear the pieces apart as if they were wilting pages of an old book. He shuffled through with ease—he'd done it a million times before, it was nothing new—and Florence shrieked as he withdrew, leaving her stripped. Vacant.

Irrecoverable.

There was a thud. The clatter of corroded chains.

A grunt, a sigh, a gasp.

And then, mayhem.

Fangs met flesh.

Wet. Hot. *Gushing.*

Blood engulfed the cavern of a covetous mouth, tickling what remained of the taste buds smeared along a rotting tongue.

There was a slurp, a shout, and rows of teeth tore away smooth, tanned skin like butter.

The kiss of death.

Belle stood fixed within her place, the back of her knees brushing the throne where the ondode once sat. Two maimed hands occupied the immediate area surrounding her—shredded muscle, mangled bone.

The stumpy mounds where hands once sat remained stationary against the ondodes sides, all the while, his teeth ravaging the surface of Bramwell's neck. Tendons snapped, blood vessels burst, and Bramwell weakly attempted to flee from his attacker, salted tears coating the apples of his cheeks, terror carved along flushed features.

Both Lyren and Florence watched in horror as the ondode attacked their old friend. The way its stumpy arms remained at each side, a consistent stream of inky blood leaking from the amputated limbs, blemishing the floor beneath their feet with the cancerous stench of rot.

All the while, what remained of Lord Ayer II kept its eyes wide open—white, milky marbles—and as the creature shredded Bramwell's neck, it didn't once blink. Like a starved shark delighting in a fresh kill, it feasted. *Fed.*

Belle and Lyren's stares swiftly met, and with words unspoken—as Bramwell's cries of pain filled the sweet, syrupy air—the silver-haired man awkwardly crawled on all fours toward the bundle of tarnished chains forgotten on the floor. Belle knelt to claim them, shivers enveloping her spine at Bramwell's pained shouts, and she shuffled the mess of metal into Lyren's open clutch, his palms trembling and slick with blood and dirt.

A shaken sea of blue met a warm caramel stare, and Lyren mouthed those three words she always loved to hear before pulling himself to his feet.

Everything blended into a disorderly blur.

Just as Lyren elbowed the ondode aside—the undead creature toppling to the floor in a rigid heap—Belle's undergarments flooded. There was a pop—a gush—and amniotic fluid swamped her thighs, dripped down into her shoes, and produced a puddle along the cobblestone floor.

The iron bonds coiled around Bramwell's maimed throat, and Lyren pulled. *Squeezed.* A grunt emerging from gritted teeth, two crimson paths—one from each nostril—soiling the determined man's lips and chin.

A sequence of curses spilled over Lyren's tongue as he pulled the chains tighter, the iron imprinting along his blushed fingers. Bramwell floated between alertness—the fork of life and death—and Lyren pulled him backward, shoving him down into the chair where Lord Ayer II's ondode once sat.

Belle stumbled sideways—making room for the flailing men—and she fell to her knees before a doe-eyed Florence, who was still seated upon the floor, shock riddling her features.

"Lady Belle," Florence breathed, reaching out to claim Belle's shaking hands, and the redheaded lady shot her a disoriented glance—*what did you just call me*—and her uterus excruciatingly contracted.

"You'll never lead the new nation," Lyren exclaimed, spittle coating his chin, intermixing with the mass of blood from his broken nose. Bramwell teetered on the edge of existence, eyelids struggling to stay open, his throat shredded, bruised, and bloodied.

"You'll never claim my child as your own," Lyren added, scooping the shackles up from the ground, tightening them around Bramwell's limp wrists. He secured them as tightly as they would go—constricting his circulation—and he spat in Bramwell's face.

"You'll never charm another. Never *kill* another," Lyren wedged the curve of his knee against Bramwell's groin, earning an agonizing grunt from the dying man. "And most importantly, you'll *never* lay another fucking finger on either of my ladies. You'll sit down in this room, beneath the floorboards of the manor, and you'll rot. Death would be too kind for you. You don't deserve to die, Bramwell."

Bramwell's lips separated, and with a weakened, dying breath, he said, "Mummy will have your head."

Lyren snickered—a wicked, wild grin stretched along scarlet lips—and he applied the full pressure of his body weight against Bramwell's crotch. The expiring lord wept, limbs too weak to move, and Lyren trailed his fingertips along Bramwell's jaw.

"Your demon *mummy* will be giving *me* head come dawn," Lyren taunted, a flare of fury dancing behind Bramwell's ebbing eyes.

"Where's your *mummy* now?" Lyren removed his knee from Bramwell's groin, and with a mocking laugh, he tossed his arms airborne on either side. "Where is she, Bram? Your little demon Goddess mother. *Velveteen the great.* Where is she now, when her son is dying?"

Both of the ondodes stood silently watching. *Studying.* Lady Sorrel was still bound by her chains, while her husband stood motionless, his absent limbs held by his sides.

When Belle suddenly groaned—unable to bite back the discomfort any longer—Lady Sorrel's gray glare shifted, her lips forming into an o-shape. Her throat gurgled, and Belle could've sworn that the ondode had attempted to *speak* just then.

Lyren's wicked stare shifted, neck craned at an abnormal angle to view the two women settled along the floor. He took note of the way Belle cradled her stomach, the way her features contorted to that of immense discomfort, and Florence's blank, muddled glare, brows pulled together in confusion.

The woman looked completely lost, and Lyren's heart plummeted to the depths of his bowels. He knew exactly what that look meant.

Bramwell took one final breath, and with half-lidded eyes, he died.

"Ly," Belle breathed, blinking back tears. Her pulse quickened, and she couldn't help but notice that all eyes were on her—including the empty, dead eyes of both of the ondodes, one of which was unchained. *Free.*

They knew what the creature could do. They'd all seen it—witnessed the way teeth tore at skin—and whether it had hands or not, it was more than capable of shredding each of them limb from limb.

And yet, it didn't.

Instead, it just stood. Statuette. *Frozen.* Not a single movement besides the slight shift of its eyes, rotating between the newly dead man seated in its original seat, and the living woman in active labor.

"The baby," Belle stammered, breathing her way through an additional contraction. "Ly, our *baby.* It's coming."

A sharp inhale—a twinge within his chest—and then, he acted. Fingers coiling around Belle's wrists, rushed statements urging a senile Florence from the floor. She couldn't tear her stare away from a dead Bramwell Hellthorne within his throne. Wrists securely bound, half of his throat shredded, a work of art.

Champagne tinted eyes began to shift—*morph*. The hue dwindled and drained, a luxuriant rain cloud masking the surface.

"He's dead," Florence squeaked, her mouth dry. She sounded so small—so *innocent*—and Belle attempted to take her hand in hers, only to have it snatched away.

"Flo, what's your deal?" Belle snipped, unaware of what Bramwell had done. "Our baby is coming—*your* baby, too. Get me the ruddy hell out of this room before Bram begins to shift!"

"No!" Florence cried, stomping her foot. She shook her head from side to side, and as Lyren cradled a pain-stricken Belle, he softly sighed.

"Forgive me—*Goddess allowing*—but the lord is *dead!* Lyren Deth just murdered your husband right before your eyes! His *friend,* his trusted companion, he *killed* him!"

The woman was shivering, palms cupping her elbows, and her cheeks were slick with tears. She wasn't even sure how to bring up the presence of the ondodes—creatures that she'd never thought existed until that very moment, but nevertheless, there they were—and her breakfast suddenly felt very, *very* heavy on her stomach.

Belle paused, eyes narrowing, and she tightened her hold on Lyren's hand.

"Florence, look at me."

Her lower lip trembled, and she met Belle's firm stare. Florence's lips parted, and she uttered the words Belle wished she'd never heard.

"Yes, my lady?"

CRADLE OF ICHOR

By the time Belle had been lowered onto her bed, she was screaming, begging for one of the housemaidens to fetch her the vial that she'd received from the mystery woman down in town, one that would lessen the pain.

Four housemaidens—Clare, Ula, Tove, and Jeanne—were by her side, as well as a discombobulated Florence and a panicked Lyren.

The Lord of Valen was dead beneath the floor—along with the lord and lady before him. His mother and father.

Florence hovered the doorway, lips sealed in silence, and she watched as Lyren laced his fingers between Lady Belle's.

There was a flicker of recognition—a tease of a forgotten memory—and then, it was gone. Time had been lost to her. Every memory including both Belle and Lyren deliberately destroyed. The last solid memory she could clearly picture was the sweet, stolen glances she and Belle had shared barely a week following her arrival at the manor.

Only that had been well over a year prior, and Florence couldn't quite puzzle together what had happened since then. Whatever events had transpired had somehow led to that very moment: a severely pregnant Lady Belle, and a very dead Lord Bramwell.

Who had been murdered by his longest, truest friend.

The friend whose hand was currently pinched between the whitened knuckles of the Lady of Valen. The friend who looked lovingly into said woman's eyes as if she was the most wonderful thing he'd ever seen.

The surrounding housemaidens took notice, their stares shifting between one another as they gathered the necessary supplies to assist with a birth. There wasn't enough time to send Henry down the hill by carriage to alert the physician to gather a midwife, and thus, the responsibility fell upon them.

Florence wanted to tell them what she'd seen. What had transpired beneath their very feet. About the ondodes—Lord Ayer II and Lady Sorrel themselves—how Bramwell was surely destined to become one of them as well.

Nothing seemed real, and Florence's head pulsated in pain as she desperately attempted to piece together the missing parts of her memory.

"Should we fetch Lord Bramwell? Alert him of your labor?" Tove asked, a warm, damp cloth pinched between manicured fingers. She dotted the rag along the clammy surface of Belle's forehead, ridding the skin of a profusion of sweat, and the lady shook her head from side to side, blinking back tears.

"No, please. I don't want him here." Belle emphasized, holding Tove's stare. The young housemaiden only frowned, her vision fixated on the way Lyren Deth held the woman's hand, how he threaded his fingers through her knotted hair.

How his face and fingers were caked with grime and blood.

"My lady," Tove pleaded, lowering the cloth. "I'm certain that the lord would like to be present for the birth of his child."

"I said fucking *no*, Tove!" Belle cursed, and another contraction consumed her core.

When it finally passed and she could breathe once again, the lady's eyes scanned the room, eventually settling upon a still Florence in the entryway, her hands folded over one another, lips formed into a thin line.

"Florence," Belle called, a simple directness present in her shy tone. "Come to my side, please. And Tove, *fuck off* with that damned rag and put it to use on something good, like cleaning up Lyren's face, will you?"

Tove's cheeks flushed a soft scarlet, and she nodded curtly. "Yes'm, Lady Belle. Right away."

The housemaiden beckoned Lyren forth, and with trembling hands, she wiped the gore from his face, careful to avoid his injured nose. Bruises bloomed beneath the thin skin of Lyren's eyes, deep purple patches of ecchymosis, and Tove bit her tongue, refusing to ask where he'd received such injuries.

When Florence didn't move, Belle called her name once more. This time, it emerged as an angry rasp, and she tossed her head back with a shout.

"Part your legs, my lady," Ula instructed, hovering at the foot of the bed. She was on her knees before the mattress, the sleeves of her uniform shirt rolled up past her elbows, an abundance of clean rags piled up beside her legs.

Florence eventually obeyed, joining Lyren by Belle's side, and her heart achingly raced. She'd always found the lady effortlessly stunning, and even more so now in her condition. The way beads of sweat peppered her forehead, how her pale cheeks were now a light pink. Her hair was a matted, oily mess, and Florence watched in wonder as Lyren's thumb traced motley little shapes along her skin.

"She's crowning," Ula announced, and Lyren's hand found Florence's.

The woman stiffened, widened stare gravitating toward the place where the pair lay entwined, and her heart danced within her chest like a caged bird, frenzied wings thrashing against her ribs.

"My lady, I really think that we should fetch Lord–" Tove began once more, but Belle wouldn't let her finish.

The woman thrust an arm sideways, forefinger pointed directly at the doorway of her bedroom, and she ordered both her and a silent Clare from the room.

"Get the *fuck* out! Both of you!"

Clare's expression twisted, and with a slight stutter, she'd demanded to know what she'd done. Ula informed Belle that it was time for her to push—*the babe is coming, my lady*—and as a string of obscenities crawled up Belle's throat, she answered Clare's question.

"I'll do you one better, Clare. Go to your quarters, gather your things, and get the fuck out of my house."

With tear-stained eyes, Clare fled the room, followed closely by a stunned Tove, her bouncing stroll disappearing beyond the wall.

"You need to push now, Belle," Ula ordered, her honey gaze fixated on the scene at hand, and a mute Jeanne claimed

Belle's opposite hand, fingertips reassuringly stroking along her flesh.

"I love you," Lyren blurted, and the air within the bedroom thickened.

Florence attempted to drop Lyren's hand—for she still couldn't quite believe that the man she'd lusted after for more years than she could count was actually *holding her hand*—but when her hold loosened, he only tightened his. His winter blue eyes met hers, and with a shy smile, he told her the very same statement that he'd spoken to Belle only moments prior, one that she'd never dream she'd hear from anyone, nevertheless *Lyren Deth*.

Belle wailed, and before Ula could process what she'd just witnessed—*good Goddess Lilen, the three of them are romantically involved*—there was an infant in her arms. Swollen. Red. *Warm*.

A lipid-rich, waxy vernix coating varnished the sweet little child— a wonderful, protective layer—and tears tickled the innermost corners of Ula's eyes as she admired the fine-haired newborn cradled within her arms.

From that very first look, the housemaiden knew that the child was of Lyren. Hair so blond that it was nearly a shade of silver claimed the child's small scalp, and its tiny, button-like nose was identical in both shape and appearance to the mans.

Queries raided her mind—*how could this be, does the lord know?*—but none of them mattered, for the baby she'd just help deliver was the most marvelous, decidedly *delightful* thing she'd ever seen.

The child cried its first true breath, and Ula gleamed.

"The littlest Lady of Valen."

Lyren openly wept, joyful tears spilling over blemished lids, and cheered, "our little girl."

Belle's lips met his—hurried, rushed—and she opened her arms wide, eager to accept the little lady she'd birthed.

When Ula placed the child into her hold, Belle bit back a sob, her clouded vision struggling to focus on the tiny red baby within her clutch.

"I want to call her Flowen," Belle breathed, and she met Florence's vast, doe-like stare. The woman's lips parted in protest—*why would you ever name your child after me*—and Lyren squeezed her hand, bringing her knuckles to his lips, dusting a kiss along the surface.

"You don't remember right now," he began, meeting Florence's befuddled stare. "But you will. There's so much he's stolen from you, Flo. From *us*. We'll make sure you get it all back."

Jeanne and Ula exchanged perplexed glances, and just as Belle's lips grazed the surface of little Flowen's face, her uterus contracted once more.

She gasped, and Ula fell back to her knees, prying the lady's legs apart as wide as they would go. With boggled, bug-like eyes, she met Belle's mystified glare, and revealed the impossible.

"My lady, there's another."

Another infant.

Belle's vision waned, her sight clouded with fuzzy, black spots, and she nearly slipped into the comfort of unconsciousness.

Lyren's lips feathered along the sharp curve of Belle's jaw, and for a final time, she began to push.

LOVE LIKE HONEY

Word spread around Valen like wildfire.

There had been not just one, but *two* heirs born from Belle's womb.

A girl, and a boy.

Mere hours before the birth of the twins, Valen had officially seceded from what remained of the country of Elantry. The nation cracked and crumbled, the government dissolving, and the territories were quick to withdraw.

Just as they'd dreamed of doing for centuries, Valen became an independent nation, replacing the idea of a government with the power of royalty.

Only, when a week went by following the birth of Belle's children, and neither she—nor Bramwell—had shown their faces, people began to wonder.

Worry.

Housemaiden Clare had been dismissed from her duties, and the woman's mouth ran. She'd ventured down the hill, shacked up in the very same inn where Lyren's sister Lyudmilla had been staying, and she spilled the innermost secrets of Hellthorne Manor.

Most didn't believe it. Many refused to even listen. After all, she was merely a disgruntled housemaiden who had been axed from her position. Rumors were frowned upon to the townspeople of Valen, and most refused to trust the words that toppled off of Clare's tongue.

After all, the idea of Valen's heirs being bastard children was—admittedly—quite devastating.

If only they'd known of Bramwell's true status.

The bastard boy born of a lady and a groundskeeper, who spent his days in the attic, suckled at his mother's teat for far too long, and summoned the demon Goddess Velveteen herself.

The bastard boy who was dead and rotting beneath Hellthorne Manor. A creature of the fables they'd told their children. Trapped in an undead, fleshy prison, with milky, clouded eyes, shackled wrists, and a mangled throat.

Perhaps, an unrestrained Lord Ayer II would suction his mouth to Bramwell's skin once more and consume him entirely until there was nothing left.

Perhaps, just perhaps.

"We need you to tell us where the lord is," Ula gently pressed, placing a tray full of fresh fruit and scones beside Belle's bed.

The lady cradled a snoozing Elordi across her bare chest—her sweet little son—dreams dancing along the innards of his eyelids as he soundly slept, a stomach full of his mother's milk.

Laid up directly beside her was a partially dressed Lyren, silken loungewear clung loosely to his bony hips. Shy snores slipped through parted lips; a mess of silver blond hair draped over sealed lids. The bruises beneath his eyes and along his busted nose were mostly concealed by his hair, and laid within the crook of his arm was a sleepy Flowen, drunken from the taste of Belle's milk.

Who wasn't present—much to both Belle and Lyren's dismay—was their darling Florence.

She'd spent the last six nights buried beneath the covers of her own bed. Most evenings, she'd lie awake, frantically attempting to shuffle the disarray of memories within her brain back together, but to no avail. There were too many cavities. Vacant spaces. Black holes.

It frustrated her—*angered* her—and typically by witching hour, she'd stumble to the washroom and sob into the echoic basin of the toilet, emptying what little sat on her stomach.

Whenever she would sleep, her dreams would shift to nightmares, and the mangled, unsightly surface of Bramwell's neck raided her vision. The milky white orbs that claimed the skulls of the ondodes would shake her from her sleep, the way they'd pierce into her soul.

By day four, she nearly wandered back down the steps. Disappeared into the blackness of the basement, crept through the maze, and located the enchanted room.

She wondered if Bramwell's eyes had hazed over, too.

"Belle," Ula nagged, picking at the dry, flaky skin between her fingers. "You *have* to tell me. Bramwell has been missing for a week now. The townspeople are growing antsy. *You* are their new leader."

"Ula," Belle murmured, admiring Elordi's tiny toes. "I need you to listen good, and listen close. Bramwell threatened to kill me as soon as I gave birth."

Ula's brows tightened, a peculiar ache present within her chest as she feared in inevitable.

"We didn't have a choice, Ula. I hope you understand."

The housemaiden went rigid, and she wanted to wrap her fingers around the new mother's throat. To berate her with an influx of questions—*how did you do it, why did you do it, where did you do it*—but instead, with a mouth drier than bone, she stood silent and still beside Belle's bed.

There'd been suspicions of Belle's infidelity. Housemaidens would notice the way the lady would steal glances at Florence every chance she got, how the ward would often be found in Belle's bedroom instead of her own.

When Keahi and Nephele had rushed to the kitchen to spill what they'd witnessed the morning of Belle's delivery, Ula had waved them away with a bitter hand. Shamed them for fibbing in the face of the Goddesses.

Only, the young housemaidens had been persistent. They knew what they'd seen. A whining, whimpering Florence, legs spread wide, looped around the hips of the one and only Lyren Deth, who had been calculated and cautious with his thrusts, eager to please. How the lady of the house, a significantly pregnant Belle Hellthorne, had brushed her fingers along Florence's clit, teasing the place where she and Lyren lay conjoined.

Ula stared at them now—the way Lyren laid in Belle's bed as if he'd been there a million times before—and she knew then that it was because he had been.

As if Belle could read the housemaidens thoughts, she said, "he knew, Ula. Bram knew, and he approved of the arrangement. He never once touched me, never once kissed me. He married me to appease the Capitol. I think you always knew that, though. How many women had you seen on his arm over the years before I came around?"

Words failed Ula, and although she wanted to deny it, she knew that it was true.

"Where's the body?"

Elordi stirred within Belle's hold, eyelids scrunched in distaste as he teetered the edge of consciousness. The outside world was so cold compared to the warm safety of his mother's womb, and a fickle cry crawled up his throat.

"Gone," Belle shortly dismissed, and the housemaiden pried no further.

Instead, she bid a good day to the drowsy new mother, and she glanced once more at a dozing Lyren, his hair still shielding his eyes, his secure, protective hold tight around his dreaming daughter.

Ula took one final glance at the pair snuggled within the bed and abandoned the room.

Come nightfall, she would gather her garments, fold her bed linens up nice and neat, and rap her knuckles against the door of Henry's cottage, requesting a carriage ride down the hill.

By the following afternoon, when the sun was at the highest point in the sky, Ula would step into a second carriage, one bound for Abler Black.

She'd never step foot in Valen again.

A storm brewed behind his eyes.

Pallid. Gray. *Deceased.*

Like weeping rain clouds, the tint took over his once lively orbs, the winsome shade engulfed by quietus.

He stared vacantly at the redheaded woman, her limbs clad in a satin sage nightdress, one that stroked the bend of her knees.

Bramwell was exactly where they'd left him, sat upon the throne where his father had remained for an entire decade.

He'd shifted, too. Transformed.

The dormant heart buried within an unmoving chest refused to beat, a pair of lungs empty of air, and yet, the man still existed. Trapped within a fleshy, spoiling prison.

Microscopic insects feasted on the open wound along his neck, a lethal injury courtesy of Lord Ayer II's limbless ondode, a fabled creature that had been freed from its binds but refused to flee.

Instead, the ondode remained reticent. *Still.* Standing tall beside the seat in which its illegitimate son sat. Even with an unreadable expression, the being looked proud—*pleased.*

Belle stepped forward, nodding curtly in Lord Ayer II's direction. She audibly assured him that she meant no harm, and with steady hands, she reached up to meet the crown coiled around his scalp.

She was careful not to nick herself on the serrated spikes, and as she peeled the demented diadem away, patches of dead flesh flayed away.

Belle winced, and openly apologized, finally ridding the ondode of its brand.

"You saved my life," Belle rasped, blinking back the sobs that threatened to spew. Lord Ayer II's ondodes blankly stared, refusing to break eye contact, and if the man could speak, Belle was certain that he'd shower her with an abundance of love.

What was once a callous man in life had transformed into an altruistic being in death.

Belle studied the stumps where the ondodes hands had once been, and with a tight-knit frown, she said, "I'm dreadfully sorry for taking away your hands."

The woman stepped aside, meeting the empty stare of what remained of Bramwell Hellthorne once more. Similar to his parents, the man did nothing but stare.

"There is where you belong," Belle began, steadying her weight against Bramwell's knees. "Down here, in the prison of your creation. Charmed for an eternity by your own magick."

She propped the crown of thorns atop a head of dark hair, and Lady Sorrel's ondode shifted beside her, a clatter of tarnished chains, a somber stare.

"*Oh,*" Belle chirped, her attention fixated on the undead lady. "I have something for you, my lady."

If Lady Sorrel's ondode could smile, Belle was certain that its lips would peel apart, big and wide, revealing the rotten teeth within. In Belle's clutch was a smooth, silken scarf, an inky black, and the ondode watched in wonder as Belle threaded the fabric along her bosom, concealing the mangled mounds from sight.

"There," Belle cooed, admiring the sight. "You have your dignity and your privacy back, my lady."

Before Belle abandoned the basement, she located a hammer draped along the cluttered desk, the wood smooth beneath her fingertips. She admired the weapon, and approached what remained of her husband once more, her posture rigid, her gaze narrowed.

"A crown fit for a lord," she said, and she pounded the thorns into the fine flesh of his forehead, drawing beads of blood to the surface.

When she left, the only ondode that remained within chains was that of Bramwell Hellthorne, himself.

THE LAST ACT

They gathered by the hundreds, crammed back to front within an eager crowd.

Eventide bruised the skyline—such a bewitching, orange glow—and each and every ordinary townsperson wished to catch only a single, simple glance of the royal twins.

When the carriage creaked along the pebbled path, the horde erupted with glee—such an ebullient, happy sound—and when the woman cloaked in nothing but black emerged from the cozy cabin, the entirety of Valen fell to their knees.

A quartet of armed servicemen and a chipper Henry escorted the woman with hair as red as a rose, and each and every ordinary townsperson craned their necks, desperate to catch a glimpse of the two children bundled within the Lady of Valen's arms.

Following close on her heel was a delicately dressed Lyren Deth, a variety of dissimilar jewels claiming his fingers, wrists, and ears.

Florence Smyth hovered the carriage, her hands folded before her, her features void of emotion. She still slept in her own room on the opposite end of the manor, though on several occasions, she'd woken to Belle's palms on her shoulders, shaking her awake. The lady's eyes were often wet with tears, red-rimmed and swollen, and she'd beg for Florence to venture across the manor, to slip beneath the silken sheets of Belle's bed and fall asleep on her chest.

The memories had yet to return.

There was an inkling—an overwhelming desire of lust—but the sensations often terrified Florence, for it was evident that there was a history between not only her and Lyren Deth, but her and Belle Hellthorne, as well.

A history that she couldn't quite puzzle together, regardless of how hard she tried.

Lyren spotted a tidily dressed Lyudmilla near the front of the crowd, an assortment of accessories claiming her arms and neck, and the silver-haired man thrust his arms around his sister's neck, drawing her close, breathing her in.

"Sister," he marveled, delighted by her presence. "Thank the Goddesses you're safe here in Valen."

"When it's safe, I'll venture back to Abler Black. Back to home, and back to Mumma." Lyudmilla replied, a sadness behind her eyes, for she mourned the life she once lived within the now defunct Capitol, the place that was nothing but rubble and ruin.

Lady Belle took her place upon the monument, taking each step with caution as she held a sleeping child in each of her arms. When she rotated on her heels to face the crowd, the townsfolk exploded into a fit of cheers.

It was her first formal appearance since Valen's secession.

Her first formal appearance as actual, *true* royalty.

The very same curly-headed man with a wispy mustache announced her presence, just as he always had plenty of times before. He seemed eager to do so, hands held behind his back, thin lips pulled into a beaming grin.

"Introducing her elegancy, Lady Belle Diantha Byron Hellthorne, the daughter of Hemlock Ere Byron and his darling Gladys Janeen Byron, daughter of the sea, girl of Immorium, the lady of Valen, and the leader of the Val."

The leader of the Val.

Belle's lips upturned; a bold grin slapped along her features as her eyes scanned the crowd. Everyone had been eager to catch even the smallest glimpse of the children within her arms, and she stole a stare at each of them, admiring the way they both laid within her arms, so innocent and small.

"Before we begin, I'd like to introduce two very special people." Belle announced, enunciating her voice so that every individual far and wide could hear her speak.

The crowd drew closer, curiosity piqued, and Lyren took his place at the foot of the steps, stealing a wink at the woman who now governed all of Valen.

"In my left arm, my son. Lord Elordi Onyx, house of Hellthorne, son of Valen." She paused, allowing the people to cheer, and then continued. "In my right arm, my daughter. Lady Flowen Orvyena, house of Hellthorne, daughter of Valen."

Flowen stirred within her bundle of blankets, and Belle smoothed the flat of her thumb along the little lady's cheek, soothing her back to sleep.

"It is with a heavy heart that I announce the passing of my husband, Lord Bramwell Hellthorne, who succumbed to a brief illness seven days ago. Though he would want you all to grieve, you must know that he would want for you all to move forward into this new era with determination."

It was then that the people went silent. The once lively crowd had gone taciturn and numb. Tears flooded widened eyes, palms shielded gaping mouths. There was neither a whisper, nary a gasp, and her people patiently awaited some kind of explanation—one they'd never fully receive. It felt like just yesterday when the unknown lord had traveled down the hill, eighteen years of age and orphaned by choice (a fact that townspeople had not known). They could still remember his youthful expression, the way his honey eyes glistened and gleamed, and now, just like the parents who kept him hidden away—*locked up*—he was dead.

A flicker of silence, and then, there was chaos.

Fury. *Fear.*

Elantry was gone. *Disbanded.* A smoldering shell of what it once was. A country crumbled to nothing but ruin, and just as Valen had seceded—become its own entity, its own *country*—their leader, their *lord*, was dead.

Many pressed forward, fingers curled into fists, a scarlet flush budding at their cheeks, and the armed servicemen formed a wall—weapons drawn, arms at the ready.

There was a plethora of statements that filled the air. Most were difficult for Belle to make out, but she was almost certain that she'd heard some of the townsfolk accuse her of Bramwell's demise.

If only they truly knew.

Belle's gaze widened, terror trickling down her spine as she watched the people whine and roar, and she met Lyren's equally frightened stare.

"My people," she purred, the children within her arms anxiously stirring, off-put by the bitter roar of the crowd. "I know you feel anger. I know you feel *fear*. But I can promise you this. It will be my greatest honor to lead with utmost efficiency, love, and care. As an independent nation, we will strive to improve upon every area in which the fallen country of Elantry has failed."

She paused, and Lyren glanced over his shoulder, a small smile snaking across his lips, his black eyes and broken nose masked by a thick layer of powder. His petrified gaze had softened significantly, and a calmness consumed the crowd. Servicemen lowered their weapons, townspeople blinked back furious tears.

"It is a frightening time, this much I know." Belle continued, swallowing the lump of bile wedged within her throat. She stole a single glance at Lyudmilla, watched the way the silver-haired woman's brown brows pull together in detest, and she continued on with her speech. "This is our world, now. By my side will be Bramwell's longest friend, Lyren Deth, who will assume the duties of fatherhood in place of my late spouse, as well as take on the roles in which your late lord would have filled."

Belle's chest ached with uncertainty, and she met Lyren's soft, sweet stare. His lips peeled into a lively smirk, a gorgeous grin on display, pointed canine teeth nice and white. Belle blushed at the sight, her skin a sweet scarlet, and as she parted her lips in preparation to satisfy the people even more, most of the townsfolk rejoiced, repeating her name over and over, pleased grins claiming most of their expressions.

There were, however, a considerable number of individuals who appeared vastly unpleased. No doubt, they'd heard the tales from Clare's loose tongue. Listened to the whispers of infidelity, of the distaste that had been present between the lord and his lady, the hostile environment in which they'd lived. And now, the Lord of Valen was dead. *Gone.* No body, no funeral, no celebrations of life. As if he'd never existed at all, the way his illegitimate father had intended for it to be.

A majority of Valen's population was easily pleased, and those who were desperate for someone to lead had begun to cheer, chanting Lady Belle's name over and over until they were short of breath.

Among the unconvinced was none other than Lyudmilla Deth herself, whose arms were crossed along her chest, a sour scowl slapped along features that considerably resembled Lyren's. Belle met her stare with a smirk—*remember who pays for your lodging fees*—and the two infants within her hold began to whine and stir in search of their next meal.

A series of servicemen delivered a sleek shadowy throne, hand-crafted and stamped with the Hellthorne sigil, and Belle took a seat upon the royal chair, unable to stifle the smile that slithered along her lips. Her cheeks grew sore from the persistent grin, but nevertheless, she basked in her new-found glory.

When the infants began to snivel, she let the fabric of her gown fall from each shoulder, revealing her breasts. The twins nursed in tandem, one on each side, and the Lady of Valen radiated with merriment as the townsfolk commended her every move.

To the Lady of Valen, long may she reign.

It was half past witching hour when she woke with a sweat.

The silken sheets clung to the slick skin of her bare limbs like a needy lover, and she could barely catch her breath before she saw what had woken her.

The oil had run out in the lamps, cloaking the bedroom in an ominous darkness that covered her arms and legs with patches of gooseflesh. The drapes had been pulled shut—*sealed*—enveloping the space in a blackness that nearly blinded her.

Even in the night, she saw it.

Two eyes, white as snow. Each pupil a perfect sphere smacked in the center of unpigmented orbs. There was a body attached to them—surely—but the blackness of the room shielded everything but the glowing globes.

At first, there was nothing but eyes. Suspended. *Floating*. Planted beyond the foot of her bed. Watching her. Watching *them*.

With a tremble, Belle craned her neck, a dozing Lyren slipping into view. She could hardly make out his features—the shape of his being—within the dark, but surely, he was there.

Florence, once again, was absent. *Away*. Stuffed up in the confines of her own bedroom, a fresh fire roaring behind the metal grate, the curtains drawn, revealing the moon. A stack of books claimed her bedside, and the woman studied the spines of each, exhausted eyes desperate to sleep, a racing mind preventing it.

The children, Elordi and Flowen, were in the neighboring bedroom, packed into individual cribs, aged furniture Lyren spotted in forgotten bedrooms within what was once Bramwell's wing.

When she returned her attention to the figure, she gulped. Hard. *Heavy*. The wickedness within Hellthorne Manor's halls hadn't stopped due to Bramwell's death—*no*—she was convinced that nothing would truly terminate the fiends that crawled between the walls.

She didn't have to see a body to know who was in her room. The unidentifiable eyes had been enough of a clue.

"Your son is in the basement."

The shadow figure snickered—*chuckled*—and then, there were teeth, too. A wide, white grin, bright and blinding, an unnatural number of bones. Layers upon layers, stacked and warped.

"That was no son of mine," the figure said, and Velveteen finally formed, taking on a form so twisted that Belle bit back a gasp.

"I'm not afraid of you anymore, Velveteen," Belle said, her tone riddled with doubt.

"It's not me you should fear, Lady Hell," Velveteen began, her voice smooth like butter. It turned Belle's blood to sludge. "What you should fear is *yourself*."

Before Belle could blink, Velveteen's form had met the mattress, knees bent inward, bones within bandy limbs crackling with every miniscule movement. She crawled atop a sleeping Lyren—soft snores tickling his parted lips, eyelids fluttering with sleep—and a black, rancid tongue snaked from her mouth, abnormally long, dipping down to meet bare, white flesh.

"Don't ruddy *fucking* touch him!" Belle seethed, a burst of bravery consuming her core. Before that moment, Velveteen had incredibly frightened her—a terror so mighty that her limbs would lock up—but things had shifted. *Changed*.

If Bramwell could be killed, perhaps his demon mother could be, too.

Velveteen only laughed—an awful, sour sound—and she peeled the sheet from Lyren's midsection with clawed fingers, revealing the naked flesh beneath. Her expression brightened, a seductive sneer, and she flattened her tongue against his softened length.

Belle exploded with rage, and she flung herself forward on shaking knees, palms flattening against bony, demonic shoulders. The demon Goddess grew unsteady on her weight, and when she attempted to violate an unconscious Lyren once more, Belle took the entity's stringy, inanimate hair between her fingers and pulled.

Slimy strands of dead hair abandoned their home, vacating Velveteen's scalp, intertwining with Belle's fingers. Her pulse raced, gaze widening to the size of saucers as the fallen Goddess burst into joyous laughter, the tip of her forefinger trailing down Lyren's chest, dipping down his navel, slipping into the curve of his bellybutton.

"He's *mine*," Velveteen sneered, "he belongs to *me* now."

A vexed shriek crawled up Belle's throat, and when she reached out to wrap her fingers around Velveteen's throat, she was blinded by a sudden blackness.

Sealed eyelids, scrunched with worry, whimpers tickling her tongue. An uneasy Lyren shook her from her sleep, her skin slick with sweat.

When Belle finally surfaced—pupils dilated to the size of saucers—Lyren breathed a sigh of relief, pecked lips dotting along her clammy chest.

"Good *Goddess*, Bells, I didn't think you'd wake."

"W-What?" Belle stammered, disoriented and muddled; her vision spotted with black. She felt dizzy and sick, her bare skin drenched with a layer of sticky, salted sweat.

"You were having a nightmare," Lyren revealed, kind blue eyes riddled with worry. "I've been trying to wake you for what seems like five minutes or more. You wouldn't resurface."

Belle shot up in the bed, the soft tawny dance of the weak flame within the oil lamp hardly illuminating the room. She frantically glanced around for any sight of the demon Goddess Velveteen, but the creature had vanished, as if she'd never existed at all. As if she hadn't been atop their bed, straddling Lyren, violating him—*assaulting* him—whilst he soundly slept.

"She was here," Belle mumbled, tossing her legs over the side of the mattress. The soles of her bare feet met the rug, goosebumps coating her exposed flesh as she rounded the room.

"Who, Bells?" Lyren shifted beneath the sheets, bottom lip pulled between his teeth. "You're scaring me, my love."

"Velveteen," Belle hissed, and then it dawned upon her. A ball of light within her head. A realization.

She shuffled her arms into the sleeves of her robe, frantic thoughts flooding her head. Through the wall, she could hear a flicker of a whine—one of her children waking from sleep—and she located the tray of half-eaten sourdough scones, a mound of blackberry jam, partially sipped teacups, and wilting lemon wedges beside the bed.

There was a glimmer of silver—a knife for the jam—and she claimed the weapon, pinching it between frigid fingers.

"Bells, what in the ruddy Nether–" Lyren began, the rest of his statement silenced into a series of mumbles as he shuffled from the mattress and dipped his legs into a pair of sleep pants.

Belle had already abandoned the room, frantic stare scanning the dimly lit hall that housed the painting.

The portrait of a dead girl.

Velveteen's portrait.

Velveteen's *portal.*

The demon Goddess had been using the portrait to shuffle between the Netherworld and the manor—arriving and departing as she pleased—disappearing from existence whenever warranted, only to reappear when necessary.

Lyren tumbled into the hall behind her, and the pair locked eyes on a gaunt figure—all bones and sharp corners—crawling on all fours toward the empty painting down the hall.

Velveteen's neck inhumanly snapped sideways—a hideous crack—bug-like eyes widening, a grin hidden within. She openly mocked them with a laugh, rolled her head across her shoulders, and then scaled the wall, peeling open the portal within her portrait, climbing inside.

The portrait sealed, taking on its original form, and Belle froze before the painting, chest inordinately heaving.

"It's a portal," Belle spoke, studying the dead woman within the painting. The eyes were identical to the hue the ondodes below the floorboards had—milky, clouded, *dead.*

There was a hint of a grin painted along Velveteen's lips, as if she was particularly pleased with herself, and a bitter shout bubbled within Belle's chest. Vengeful. *Angry.*

Lyren's sight settled on the portrait, and he outwardly gasped—knees buckling, legs trembling. He hadn't seen the painting since the very first encounter a year prior, and he forcefully swallowed the bile that crept up his esophagus.

"It's real," Lyren sobbed, steadying his weight against the wall with a slick palm. "I knew it was real. I *knew* it was."

"She's been using it as a tether between the Netherworld and here," Belle explained, and she tightened her hold on the blade. "But no longer. Just like we killed her son, we'll kill her, too."

Before Lyren could question her—*how could we possibly kill the fallen Goddess*—Belle raised the jam knife above her head. She released a single shout, and she struck the portrait.

Once.

Twice.

Three times.

A rip, a tear. Shredding the linen rag paper with ease. She drew asymmetrical lines along the surface, slicing into Velveteen's features, mangling them, destroying them. The clouded orbs disappeared, along with the crooked smirk, and when Belle was finished, the portrait was nothing but a mangled, brutalized mess. If the painting could bleed, she was certain that her feet would be flooded with gore.

Lyren claimed Belle's wrist, a spate of hushed, gentle coos tickling the shell of her ear as he flattened himself against her.

The lady sobbed, and Lyren gently wriggled the knife from her clutch. His lips found purchase against her cheek, and he peppered soft kisses along the surface, a whisper of sweet nothings dancing along her skin, one statement in particular sending shivers down her spine.

It's over.

He led her back to the bedroom, tucked her beneath the warmth of the sheets, and disappeared one last time to fetch the twins. When he returned—one on each arm—the tears finally slipped from Belle's eyes, flooding her cheeks, a salty sweetness coating her lips.

Lyren slid back into bed alongside his lover, shuffling one of the infants into her open arms, whereas he kept the other.

"I love you, Belle," he whispered, placing a short, sealed-lip kiss against her nose before peppering identical kisses along both Elordi and Flowen's features.

She repeated the phrase back to him, and as she fed her children and the man that she loved succumbed to sleep once more beside her, her thoughts were plagued with an array of visuals.

Of Florence Smyth, her first true love, stuffed up in her own wing, buried beneath cold sheets, presumably wide awake, as she always seemed to be. Head void of valuable memories, a severe sense of longingness consuming her core.

Of Bramwell Hellthorne, her husband by arranged marriage, undead beneath the floorboards, shackled to throne that once belonged to his father. Blank stare glossed over with a thick layer of storm clouds. Heart refusing to beat, lungs empty of air. A festering, rotten wound splayed along the skin of his neck.

Of the townspeople of Valen—*her people*—busying themselves at the bottom of the hill, anticipating the future they would live now that Valen was an independent country. Now that Belle was their *leader*.

And of Velveteen, the fallen Goddess, the fourth sister, the demon who possessed Evelin, ruining the teenage girl from the inside out. The Queen of the Netherworld. How she crawled atop a sleeping Lyren, claimed him as her own, but not before speaking a statement to Belle that haunted her to the very bone.

It's not me you should fear, Lady Hell.

What you should fear is yourself.

Hours later, when Belle Hellthorne eventually surrendered to sleep—her legs entwined with Lyren's, both infants fast asleep between the pair—the air shifted.

Thick. Syrupy. *Sweet.*

The oil lamps promptly extinguished within the hall, as if by a sharp wind, and the mangled portrait of a dead girl along the wall transformed.

There was a shift of iron chains down below, and the torn paper mended itself, slipping back into its proper place as if it had never been altered at all.

Even, precise brush strokes with oil-based paint created a haunting image. A dead, empty-eyed teenage girl sat upon a brown chair. Wrists crossed, hands folded, back straightened.

Perfectly posed.

A small smile slithered along her lips, drafting an image that would plague both Belle and Lyren's dreams for hours to come.

Beyond the windows, the clouds wept bright, bulbous tears of blood.

ACKNOWLEDGEMENTS

This one was a long time coming.

I started *Lady Hell* during my obsession with the film *Crimson Peak*. I'd always had a soft spot for gothic themes, and the idea of exploring my own gothic Victorian time-piece excited me.

I created the document in August of 2021, and this story took me *entirely* too long to write. Due to drastic changes in my own personal life, I'd stepped away from writing and Belle's world for a long period of time.

Finally, when all seemed right in my life again, I returned to Hellthorne Manor, and the result was beyond my wildest dreams.

I'd like to start off with a massive thank you to all of the artists that worked with me to bring this story to life:

To Zoe Violett, the artist behind Belle's portrait on the front cover. She not only created the most gorgeous portrait of a character that I've ever seen, but she *painted it by hand.* Yes, that's right! The cover of *Lady Hell* is the digital scan of a real-life oil painting, a painting that is currently hanging in my living room.

To Darcy Kelly-Laviolette, the artist behind the chapter art. She took my descriptions of Velveteen and she turned her into something both beautiful and absolutely terrifying. It was such an honor to work with!

To Edward Ortego, the artist behind the title art. He created such a gorgeous take on Hellthorne Manor, and I'm absolutely obsessed. It was a perfect addition to the novel, and it was such a pleasure to include!

To Christine, my wonderful, stunning mother. She stepped into the role of editor after I lost Lauren. It was a big role to fill, but she handled it wonderfully, and her input and edits helped shape Belle's story into what it is. She's always been my biggest fan, my loudest supporter, and my best friend.

To Lauren, my late editor, who we tragically lost last year. I was looking forward to working together on this story, and I know you were, too. I dedicate this tale to you, and every story hereafter, because every book I publish without your name on it just will never feel quite right. I miss you dearly.

To Cassidy, my childhood best friend, the person I've always dedicated my stories to, and will continue to. You've been a part of my writing journey from the very start, from the days of our youth, when everything I wrote made hardly any sense, yet you read it anyway. I know you'd be proud of me, and in that thought, I find comfort. I find it difficult to believe that the world has been without you for so long already. I miss you every single day.

To my beta readers, those who were there from the first, sloppy draft. Those who have read multiple versions of Belle's story, and still loved every single one.

To you, my reader. The one who gave my story a chance. I am forever thankful for your support.

tales from the

PORTRAIT OF A DEAD GIRL

Lady HELL

FIRST INSTALLMENT

Lord DEATH

SECOND INSTALLMENT

www.ingramcontent.com/pod-product-compliance
Lightning Source LLC
Chambersburg PA
CBHW051306190726
48290CB00001B/23